ADVANCE PRAISE

Fourteen Stones may be Kris Faatz' first full-length fantasy, but the novel unfolds with astonishing depth and symbolism. I am in awe at the smooth and carefully rendered characters that remind the reader of many Indigenous people's wisdom, their ever-ongoing struggle to make the world hear and the rare beauty of human emotion drawn with profound artistry. *Fourteen Stones* is a rare gem, meant for fantasy readers but meaty enough to satisfy the most astute reader of fine fiction.

— LINDA S. CLARE, AWARD WINNING
AUTHOR OF *THE FENCE MY FATHER BUILT*

In *Fourteen Stones*, author Kris Faatz takes us on a captivating journey through a rich, imaginative world with its own special kind of magic. Young Khari, forced to leave her ancestral home, must lead her tribe of refugees out into a hostile world with only her visions and her inner courage as guideposts. Set in an intricate and immersive realm with deeply developed characters and cultures, *Fourteen Stones* is full of plot twists you won't see coming. It's unlike any fantasy you've read before!

— JOHN W. MALY,
AUTHOR OF *JURIS EX MACHINA*

Fourteen Stones. This book. My words can't do it justice. It creates a whole world and brings you right into it, following along with the different characters, getting to know and love them...you find yourself cheering them on and hoping for their success. It is beautifully written and allows your imagination to see everything the author has so carefully constructed...I was truly blown away. It is everything our society needs right now. knew as soon as I finished reading it, I would be sad it was over. Hallmark of a most amazing story!

— JENNIFER GESSLER

Beautifully written, imaginative, original.

— DIANE DORMAN

This book is incredible! A fantastic read for sure. If you love reading, I highly recommend it!

— PHYLLIS BRYN-JULSON SUTHERLAND

The four narrators are compelling characters, and each knows or meets other characters who are so interesting. They all became real to me. In addition, I love the description of setting and am amazed at how the story is plotted. Suspense kept me reading

— CARLA OTTENHEIMER

FOURTEEN STONES

ALSO BY KRIS FAATZ

To Love a Stranger

FOURTEEN STONES

KRIS FAATZ

HIGHLANDER
PRESS

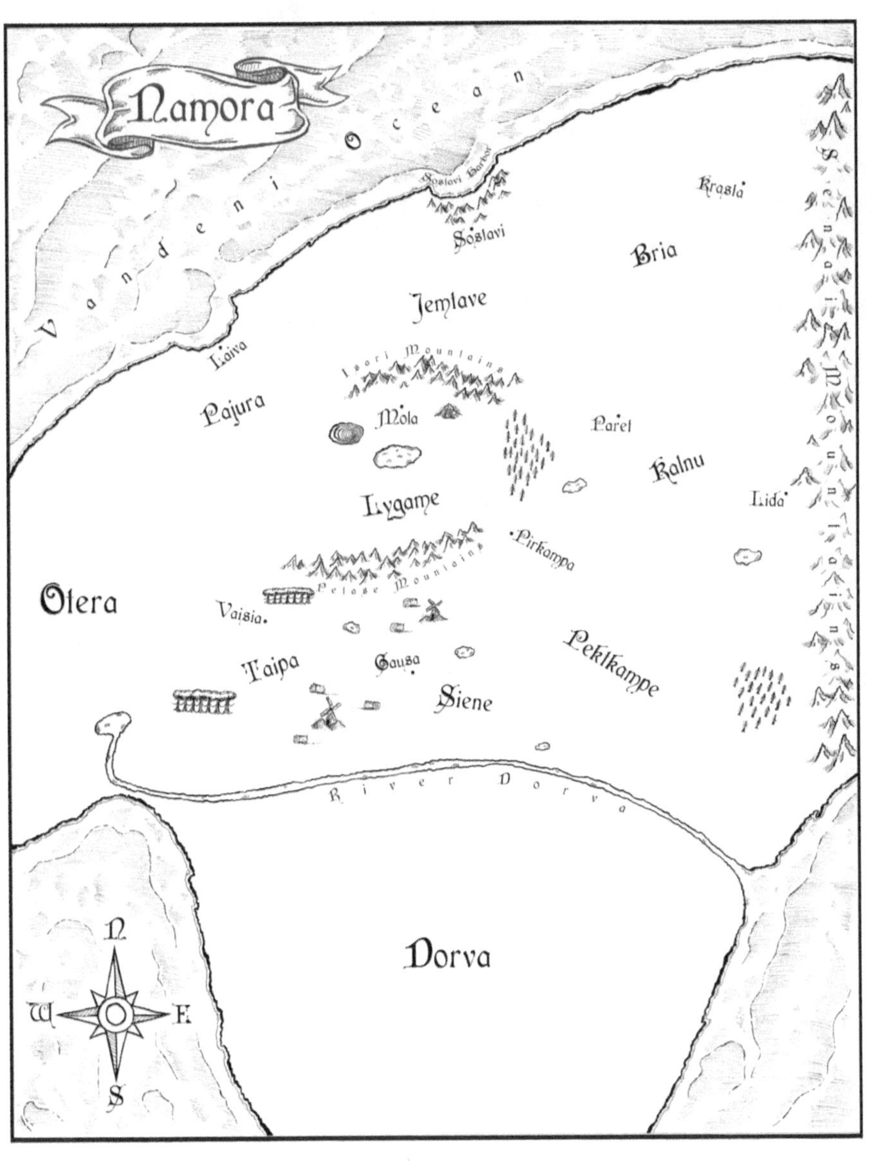

Namora
Vandeni Ocean
Sostavi Harbor
Sostavi
Krasla
Bria
Jemlave
Laiva
Isari Mountains
Pajura
Mola
Parel
Kalnu
Lida
Lygame
Pirkampa
Pelose Mountains
Otera
Vaisia
Peklkampe
Taipa
Gausa
Siene
River Dorva
Dorva
N
W
E
S

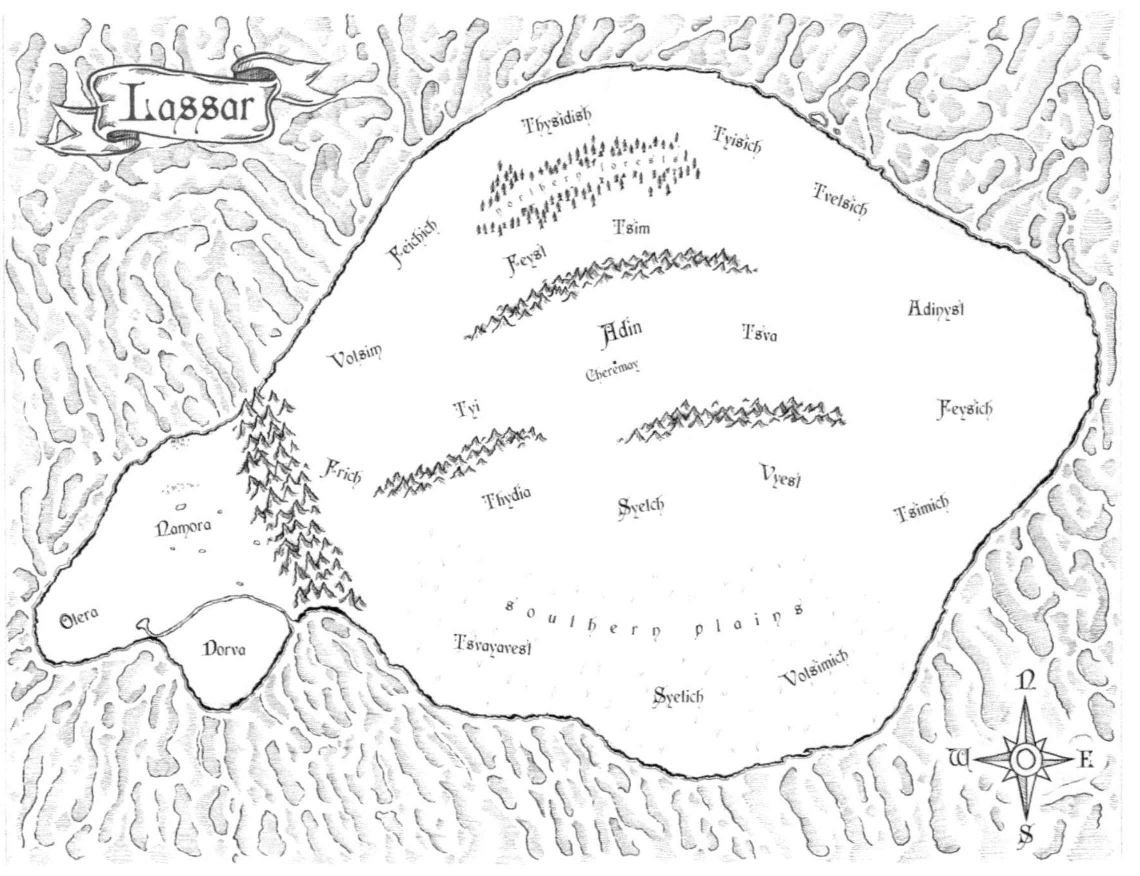

Lassar
Thysidish
Tyisich
Tvetsich
northern forests
Feichich
Tsim
Feysl
Adinyst
Volsim
Adin
Tsva
Cheremav
Tyi
Feysich
Frich
Vyest
Thydia
Syelch
Tsimich
southern plains
Namora
Tsvayavest
Volsimich
Otera
Dorva
Syelich
N
W
E
S

CONTENTS

Characters — xv
Explanatory notes — xvii
Namoran calendar — xix
Acknowledgments — xxi

Prologue — 1

Book 1: The Lamp Carrier — 5

1. In Lassar, Year 1665 SM — 7
2. The Zhinin — 21
3. The Tavo Balsa — 37
4. The Lasska soldier — 55
5. Khari — 75
6. Ribas — 85
7. Valdena — 115
8. Bereg — 137
9. Khari — 151
10. Ribas — 167
11. Valdena — 191
12. Bereg — 207
13. Khari — 219

Book 2: The Zhinin — 233

14. Ribas — 235
15. Valdena — 265
16. Bereg — 289
17. Khari — 309
18. Ribas — 331
19. Valdena — 355
20. Bereg — 365
21. Khari — 399
22. Ribas — 417

23. Valdena   453
24. Bereg   465
25. Khari   479
26. Ribas   491

About the Author   511
About the Publisher   513

CHARACTERS

1. The Pala Vaia

Khari: young Lamp-Carrier
Vatiri: older Lamp-Carrier
Pradesh: Lodestone (tribal leader)
Radavan: brother of Pradesh
Handan: nephew of Pradesh; hunter
Mandhani: brother of Handan; hunter
Rahul: young member of the tribe, esteemed for intelligence
Dahila: wife of Radavan; Khari's sister
Bakar: tribal elder

2. The Namorans

Ribas Silvaikas: *zhinin*, priest of the lowest rank in the
Namoran hierarchy
Maryut Ribenis: Ribas's wife
Gedrin Silvaikas: Ribas's brother
Virta Gedrenis: Gedrin's wife

Raulin and Asira: Gedrin's children
Pelayut Silvenis: Ribas and Gedrin's mother
Silvas Jadraikas (dec'd): Ribas and Gedrin's father
Danayut (Danya) and Jano: Ribas's apprentices (*mosevine*)
Tayo Nevas: healer in Lida village
Valdena (Valda) Filtraikas: second-in-command to
Namora's ruler
Tavin Ardinas: Namora's ruler
Galvo Dendraikas: *sventin* (high-ranking priest); member
of Namora's ruling council
Lesvin Berenaikas: *sventin* (high-ranking priest);
member of Namora's ruling council
Tayo Bodin: healer in the Namoran capital Sostavi

3. The Lasska

Bereg Orlon: high-ranking Lasska soldier
Nela Orlon: Bereg's wife
Ania Orlon: Bereg's daughter
Fisa Vasem: high-ranking Lasska soldier
Shurik: ruler of Lassar (*Impera*)
Mangevar (dec'd): Shurik's father; previous ruler of
Lassar

EXPLANATORY NOTES
NAMORAN AND LASSKA LANGUAGES

Namoran:

- Vowels are pronounced as follows: A = ah, E = eh, I = ee, O = oh, U = oo
- "J" is pronounced as "Y" (Example: Jano = Yah-noh)
- All syllables, including final "e"s, are pronounced (Example: zhinine = zhee-nee-neh)
- In two-syllable names, the stress belongs on the first syllable (Example: Ribas = *Ree*-bahs); *except* as noted in nicknames with a marked accent on the second syllable (Example: Gedrí = geh-*dree*)
- Namoran "last names" are patronymics, with –aikas (lit. "child of") added to the first syllable of the father's name. Accent belongs on the second syllable of the patronymic. [Examples: Silvaikas (derived from Silvas) = seel-*vye*-kahs; Jadraikas (derived from Jadras) = yahd-*rye*-kahs]
- Married Namoran women's "last names" are derivatives of their husband's first names. Accent belongs on the

second syllable. [Example: Maryut Ribenis (Maryut, wife of Ribas) = *mahr*-yoot ree-*beh*-nees]

Lasska:

- Lasska vowels are not as standardized as Namoran. Many are pronounced long, but vowels in final syllables, particularly, can be short:
- Bereg = *Behr*-egg
- Shurik = *Shoo*-rick
- The country is Las-*sar* (accent on the second syllable), but the language is *Lass*-ka (accent on the first syllable)
- "TH" is pronounced as in "with"
- "CH" is pronounced as in "church"
- "Y" is pronounced "ee"
- "S" is often voiced (pronounced similar to "z") before the letter "I"
- Example of the above four notes: Thysidich = *Thee*-zih-ditch
- Final vowels are pronounced (Example: Silde = *Seel*-deh)

NAMORAN CALENDAR

Years are numbered "SM," lit. *saska metai,* "count of years." Year 1 SM is marked as the year in which formal worship of the Goddess Kenavi began.

Each of the twelve months has four weeks, made up of eight days each.

Days of the week:

- Pirdina (First Day)
- Antdina (Second Day)
- Tretdina (Third Day)
- Ketdina (Fourth Day)
- Pektdina (Fifth Day)
- Sesdina (Sixth Day)
- Setdina (Seventh Day)
- Ashdina (Eighth Day)

Months of the year:

- Akena: Sacrifice (commemorating the death of the woman who became the Goddess Kenavi)
- Algima: Rebirth (commemorating Kenavi's ascension as the Goddess)
- Ivesta: Planting (first month of spring; planting season)
- Ketva: Fourth
- Pekta: Fifth
- Jeska: Fish (height of fishing season for coastal communities)
- Vasara: Midsummer
- Ashta: Eighth
- Rudua: Autumn
- Derla: Harvest
- Vienela: Eleventh
- Tyla: Quiet (contemplative time before Akena observances)

ACKNOWLEDGMENTS

Writing this book, my first full-length fantasy, was one of the most joyful things I've ever done. Thank you for exploring these pages!

For readers who might be curious about how a writer came up with a fictional world, a little explanation. The geography of Namora is based on northwestern Spain, which my husband and I visited in 2015. Our trip gave me the first seeds of this story. Namora's language is drawn from Lithuanian, which is part of my cultural heritage. Lassar, especially in its history as a superpower, was inspired by Imperial Russia; its first Impera, Curin, is loosely based on Peter the Great. The story of the nomadic Pala Vaia has its roots in the experiences of Romani people, particularly in Renaissance Europe.

Fourteen Stones's two volumes are each dedicated to a friend who helped shape the story and its people: in the case of *The Lamp-Carrier*, through active example, and in the case of *The Zhinin*, through honored memory. This book would never have come to be without the help and support of many others as well.

I'd particularly like to thank my friends Susan Ingram, Louise Marburg, and Tom Andes, whose support during the first-draft process was invaluable, and my writing students, who have made me a better teacher and a much better storyteller. A special shoutout to my friend Jen Geissler, who cheered for this book at every stage and encouraged me through all the ups and downs of sending it out into the world.

Many thanks to The Patchwork Raven, the New Zealand

publisher who released the first edition of *Fourteen Stones*, and the Raven's editor Jax Goss, who believed at once in this long and intricate project of my heart. And many thanks to my longtime friend and fellow writing-adventurer Deborah Kevin, and her wonderful team at Highlander Press, who championed the story and gave it its new incarnation here in the States.

And finally, always, all thanks and love to my husband Paul, who is my anchor, and who has made it possible for me to figure out this writer I've turned out to be.

Welcome to Namora and Lassar!

PROLOGUE

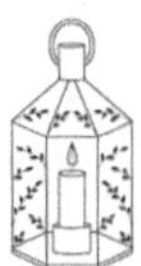

"Fourteen Stones," a Namoran folk tale dating to the earliest
years of worship of the Goddess Kenavi (first century SM)

Once there was a woman who wished to build a house. Not a house
for her husband and children: she had no husband yet, was too young
to have children, and in any case she meant to live alone a while
longer. She loved the scent of the wind, the warmth of the sun, and
the sound of the sea as it rushed and broke against the rocky shore of
her land. While she could, she wanted to have those things all to
herself.

She was a strange woman, or at least, so her people thought. She
had strange eyes, the color of the sky on a cloudless autumn day, and
she had a strange will, all edges and corners, without any softness.
And she did not seem to understand that people must find their
safety in each other. The world was an uncertain place. Enemy tribes
roamed the land. Wild creatures fed on the tame goats that meant

food and certainty. In such a world, people must live together behind high stone walls, with spears to guard themselves.

This woman loved to walk beyond those safe walls, fearing no strange man or creature. Her people called her Klaya, which means wanderer. She walked under the sun that browned her skin and let the wind brush her hair, let the sea lick her fingers. At those times, delight softened the proud blue of her stare, but none of her people were there to see it.

When her people built houses, they made them of stone. Stone houses clustered like eggs in a nest behind the stone guarding wall where spear-wielding men paced back and forth. The village stood on a long green hill at the end of a peninsula. To build a new house, people dug rock out of the hill or carried it from the shore. You must build your home out of the home land.

But Klaya loved the wider land. The peninsula and the village rested in her heart, but the broad mainland fanned itself out before her eyes. She walked there at will, greeting the woods, learning the feel of the grass of the plains under her bare feet. She knew she would build her house on the green hill, but she would build it separate, touching no other walls, sharing no other air. And she would build it not only out of the stone of home, but out of pieces of the world beyond.

Houses needed many heavy rocks, carried and shaped and laid into place by scarred and callused hands. Klaya's hands were strong, toughened by years of weaving rope and working skins, of digging and planting in the earth. But her body was slender, a tall young tree. Her muscles were not hard but supple, her chest and shoulders fine and narrow.

One day, her people watched her leave behind the safety of the guarding wall and walk out to the mainland. They muttered and whispered about her strangeness, the house she meant to build and live in all alone. They asked themselves why she could not be a woman such as any other. And they watched, later, as she limped back, dragging behind her a rough-made sledge of branches that carried a single large stone.

The next day they watched her go out again. And they whispered about how she could dig stone here on the green hill, or carry it up from the shore. She wished to punish herself, surely. She wished to show how wayward she was. They said they would leave her to it.

But on the third day, as she left again, one man went with her. She did not ask for his help; she lifted her head proudly and walked alone, with him following behind. When they came back, the sledge held two stones.

That night, over his cooking fire, the man told others that, during their day of searching, Klaya had explained herself to him. That alone surprised those who heard. The explanation surprised them more: that Klaya wished to bring stone from each part of the mainland she knew – the forests, the coast, the grassy plains – and have pieces of each place she loved in her home.

What difference did it make, the people asked. One stone looked like another. Surely no one could see the difference between a stone dug from the hillside and one carried from the mainland forest. But the next day, two men left the village with Klaya. When they came back, the sledge held three stones.

On it went. Another day, and another, and now the women of the village joined, and then the children. Always Klaya walked at the head of the group, her head held high. Each day the sledge returned with a bigger load.

On the day they brought back eight stones, they built a bigger sledge. And still they went out again, and again. On the last day, all of the tribe went. The smallest children rode on their parents' backs or in their arms. The elderly leaned on the strength of the young. When they came back to the village as the sun dipped down to the horizon, the sledge carried its biggest load of fourteen great stones.

Klaya declared herself satisfied. She could build her house out of the stones the tribe had helped her carry.

She meant to live alone, but the village did not leave her to build her house alone. The people stayed, helping Klaya cut and shape the rock with chisel and mallet, helping her lift and set each piece into place.

Then the house was finished and the village went about its business. Klaya lived on the green hillside with the freshness of the sea wind and the warmth of the sun around her, and the home her people had helped her build out of the world she loved.

BOOK 1:
THE LAMP CARRIER

for Alison Halsey

1

IN LASSAR, YEAR 1665 SM

On the morning that marked the start of her sixteenth year, Khari sat cross-legged on the floor of the tent she shared with her *amma* Vatiri, trying not to notice how strange the new fabric of her white blouse felt around her body. The tent flap hung open, letting in a ripple of breeze that still tasted of summer and the fragrance of the tall grass that ringed the tribe's camp. Early morning sunlight slanted through the open tent flap and fell across Khari's back and shoulders, so that she thought the white blouse must glow like the Moon Woman herself.

Vatiri, Khari's mother-in-truth, knelt behind her, weaving Khari's long hair into braids. The two of them had done this every morning since Khari was eight years old and began having the dreams that marked her as a future Lamp-Carrier. As of today, the tribe had two Lamp-Carriers. Vatiri had held that place since long before Khari was born, and now, with the start of her sixteenth year, Khari stepped into it too.

Vatiri's quick fingers moved through Khari's hair, smoothing and dividing it. She said, "You should wear white ribbon today."

That made Khari smile. White ribbon braided in her hair, to

match the blouse that showed her rank. At the same time, nervousness curled in her stomach. Tonight, the tribe's Lodestone, Pradesh, would have a council to decide where the tribe should spend the winter. Khari would sit at that council for the first time, in her new role and her new blouse.

"Whatever you think, amma," Khari said.

Vatiri laughed, a quiet sound like birdsong. "I remember when you weren't so cooperative."

Khari remembered it too. At age eight, she hadn't wanted to leave her parents' tent and her three older sisters to live with "the old Lamp-Carrier." She hadn't cared about learning to do the work, or how important the dreams made her, and she had actually fought and kicked when her father bodily picked her up and carried her to Vatiri's tent. For the first couple of days with the older woman, she hadn't opened her mouth even to put food in it. She'd turned her back every time Vatiri spoke to her.

But Vatiri had never given up or lost her temper. Now, as much as Khari still honored her mother-in-body, she loved her mother-in-truth even more.

"I don't think I'll be much help at the council, amma," Khari said. "I didn't dream anything last night."

The tribe's Lodestone, always a man, had to set the course for the tribe's travels and direct its daily life. To do this, he needed the Lamp-Carrier, who was always a woman and always born to the work. Most importantly, she must have and interpret the pathdreams that helped the Lodestone make his decisions.

After eight years of training, Khari knew better than to expect pathdreams every night, or even most nights. Still, on the first day that she wore the white of the Moon Woman, the second-greatest of the three Powers that guarded the tribe, she wished she'd had more to offer.

"Don't worry, child." Khari felt Vatiri finish the second braid, tying it off with the end of the ribbon she had woven into it. "Pradesh will have all the guidance he needs."

Khari thought she heard something strange in the older woman's voice: a thread of something like sadness. When she turned around to see her, though, Vatiri smiled. The autumn sunlight washed over her face, bringing out the deep tracery of lines at the corners of her eyes and around her mouth. She gently tweaked the end of Khari's braid. "Now your turn," she said.

They traded places. Exactly as Vatiri had done for her, Khari brushed out the older woman's hair. She wove it into a single long braid with a strand of white ribbon, to match her own, running through it. Vatiri's hair had once been as dark as Khari's, but now it was such a pale silver that the ribbon barely stood out against it.

For eight years, Vatiri had taught Khari how to dream with her "hidden eye" always open, watching the pictures that moved across her mind, constantly sifting them for what mattered. The Lamp-Carrier's dreams were a gift from the Moon Woman, but it took skill to hold onto them in daylight and know what they meant. Vatiri said that Khari would soon be at least as good at that work as she was herself.

Khari had always felt proud of that. She'd liked to imagine Pradesh trusting her as absolutely as he, and the two Lodestones before him, trusted her amma. Now, though, she didn't want to see Vatiri's age, or think about the day when the tribe would only have a single Lamp-Carrier again.

"Amma," she said, as her fingers worked quickly, "did you have a dream last night?"

They usually talked about their pathdreams, if one of them had one. Now Vatiri didn't answer right away. Khari had worked her way down to the end of the braid before the older woman said, "We don't need to think about it now."

That same sadness. Khari tied off the braid. "But what was it?" she asked. She didn't like the idea that she might have missed something in her own dreams. Today especially, she didn't want to fail.

"Not now," Vatiri said. When she looked over her shoulder, for a moment Khari saw the firmness she remembered from eight years ago, when Vatiri had finally set a clay plate of flatbread and roast venison in front of her and said that was enough nonsense, Khari wouldn't leave the tent again until she had eaten every bite. Eight-year-old Khari had felt her stubborn anger shrivel up under those dark eyes. Besides, after two days, she'd been hungry.

For as long as Vatiri lived, Khari was supposed to obey her. "All right, amma," she said. She held the questions in, but they still nudged at her.

That night, while the rest of the tribe went about its usual evening work, Khari and Vatiri joined Pradesh's council around a fire at the edge of the camp.

The tribe was only one of the many groups of Pala Vaia people who lived in Lassar. Khari knew the story: how the Pala Vaia, the "First and Lost Ones," as her people called themselves, had crossed the great mountains in the west and arrived in this land, more genera-tions ago than anyone could count. Other people, with paler skin and a different language, had come later. The newcomers had claimed the place as theirs, because they built houses, then villages, towns, and cities. The Vaia didn't leave marks on the land. They went where the seasons took them.

In summer, they looked for cooler weather, fertile land, and good hunting. In winter, when snow came to the Lasska woods and moun-tains, they went south to the friendlier plains. Khari's tribe had spent the summer in northeastern Lassar. Now, the year was fading into autumn, so the tribe must furl its tents, load its carts and horses, and move again.

Khari sat next to Vatiri by the fire, close enough for the warmth to hold off the chilly night breeze. With them were Pradesh's younger brother Radavan, and the old man Bakar who had marked seventy-eight years, and Pradesh's nephews Handan and Mandhani, the tribe's two strongest and, Khari thought, most arrogant men. There was also young Rahul, who had only marked eighteen years and had no ties to the Lodestone's family, but he was already known as one of the most intelligent men in the tribe.

When everyone else had settled around the fire, Pradesh came up to take his place. Khari wasn't surprised to see the Lodestone carrying the heavy chair of machia wood he had bought years ago in a Lasska village. As he set it down, the chair gleamed in the firelight, its grain a pattern of spiderweb-thin dark swirls against a gleaming silvery background.

Khari sighed. Pradesh was a decent enough Lodestone, everyone thought so, but too proud. If he had to have the chair at all – such a heavy thing to drag along every time the tribe traveled – he should have offered it to old Bakar, whose bones probably didn't appreciate the hard ground tonight.

Pradesh settled into his chair and folded his hands against the spread of his yellow shirt. Only Lodestones wore yellow, the color of the Sun God. Khari couldn't help thinking that Pradesh seemed to want to look like the Sun God in girth, too, but she arranged her face into its most respectful expression when his eyes passed over her.

He turned to Vatiri first. "Lamp-Carrier. What do you have to tell us?"

Khari bit her lip. She had never sat at a council before, but she thought even a Lodestone ought to sound more respectful. Vatiri had marked sixty years, enough to be Pradesh's mother, but Khari knew the older woman respected the Lodestone as second only to the Sun God and the other Powers themselves. She had tried to teach Khari the same lesson. Khari had never been as good at it.

Vatiri answered with no hint of annoyance. "Last night I had a pathdream."

Again Khari felt the curl of worry in her stomach. Why hadn't she had one too? And why hadn't Vatiri wanted to talk about hers?

Then Vatiri turned to look at her. The sadness Khari had heard in the older woman's voice this morning was out in the open now, as plain on her face as the marks of her years. Khari's worry melded into a solid stone of fear.

Amma, she wanted to say. *What is it? Please.*

As if the two of them had been alone, Vatiri said, "I'm afraid of what's going to happen to us. Our tribe, and all the Vaia people."

All of the Vaia? What could this be? Khari had no chance to speak. Pradesh said, "Explain."

The older woman turned away from Khari to face the Lodestone and the rest of the circle. "Lassar's new ruler," she said. "Shurik."

All of them knew the name. The Vaia never settled in Lasska towns or villages, and had as little to do with the people as they could. They all knew, though, that Shurik had become Lassar's new ruler – the *impera,* he was called – at the end of the summer, after his father Mangevar died. Mangevar had been an old man and Shurik was a young one. Khari didn't know anything more.

Now Vatiri said, "He doesn't want the Vaia here."

Again Khari felt the edges of that stone of fear, deep in her gut. Bakar spoke up. "No Lasska ruler has wanted us here."

Khari looked across the circle at the old man, who sat at Pradesh's left. The tribe's younger men cut their hair short, but Bakar wore his long, the old way, in a single white braid down his back. His skin stood out dark against the bright blue fabric of his shirt. Khari thought he looked as strong as old wood, the kind that weathered so tough that if you took an axe to it, it would bite back.

Bakar said, "The Lasska have wanted us gone from the beginning, but we have more right to this place than they do."

Khari understood that. Her people had lived here since time beyond memory. But Vatiri said, "Shurik is different."

Pradesh asked, "How?"

Vatiri closed her eyes briefly. To Khari, her face looked shrunken, her white blouse too much like the cloths the tribe used in burying the dead. Then she opened her eyes again, and her words fell on the circle like the endless snow that fell on Lassar's northern forests.

"In the great city, Cheremay," Vatiri said, "Shurik is calling his fighting men to him."

Khari had never seen Cheremay, the "eye of Lassar" where the rulers lived. She had only heard about the throngs of people, the shoulder-to-shoulder houses and buildings, the sky-clawing temples the Lasska built to their bear-shaped god. It all sounded brutal and strange. Vatiri said, "He is giving the men weapons. Swords, knives, and the powder that burns and explodes and throws balls of lead."

Khari had heard about this too. She had never understood how a powder, apparently not much different to look at than earth, could explode. Vatiri finished, her voice still calm and quiet, "Shurik is sending his men out, with their weapons, to hunt us."

Hunt people, the way you would hunt deer and rabbits to cook over the fire? Did Shurik's men eat human flesh? Khari knew why Vatiri had kept this terrible, shadowy secret to herself. Mother-love, like the ritual of the braids and the matching ribbon that said that she and Khari belonged to each other. But what kind of dream could have shown Vatiri all this? And even while fear left tracks all over her skin, Khari wondered why she herself had seen nothing.

Across the circle, Bakar shook his head, whether in disgust or disbelief Khari couldn't tell. Neither he nor Pradesh spoke.

Pradesh's younger brother Radavan did. "Where are these fighting men now?"

Khari liked Radavan. He might be the Lodestone's brother, but he didn't have Pradesh's arrogance. He knew how to listen. Six years ago, he'd taken Khari's oldest sister, Dahila, as his wife, and they had twin girls and a boy, with another child on the way.

Vatiri said, "The soldiers are in Cheremay and other great cities. Shurik is gathering them together and telling them what to do. He will send them out soon."

Handan, Pradesh's older nephew, spoke up loudly. "So they'll come and we'll fight them. Lasska men are soft and flabby. They sit on cushions all day and nag their wives for honey cakes."

Through her fear, Khari glared at Handan. The hunter, and his brother Mandhani, might be able to run and wrestle, but as far as she could tell, they had nothing between their ears except muscle. Everyone knew about the fierce, hard-trained Lasska soldiers. Mandhani agreed with his brother now: "We're stronger than any of them. Let them come."

Vatiri's voice cut through their pride. "They're well-armed. Their weapons are more dangerous than anything we have." Khari knew this was true. The Vaia had no exploding powder, and while her people were strong-bodied and adapted to hunting and journeying, they were all smaller-built than the big pale-skinned Lasska. Vatiri added quietly, "They will kill us if they can."

Handan jumped to his feet. "Let them try!" Mandhani scrambled up too, as if ready to face off against Lasska soldiers then and there. Rahul said something to Bakar that Khari couldn't hear. Radavan held his hand out as if trying to quiet the chaos.

Pradesh said, "Enough."

The word fell into the circle like a stone into water. The talk died and the Lodestone's nephews sat back down. Pradesh said to Vatiri, "What did the dream say we should do?"

Vatiri turned to Khari again. Khari knew that somehow, whatever she was about to say would be worse than anything they had heard yet.

"The dream," Vatiri said gently, as if to Khari alone, "said we can't do anything."

Handan and Mandhani started shouting again. Khari heard them from what felt like a long way away. She understood: Vatiri's dream had meant the end of the tribe.

Khari read endless grief in the older woman's eyes. She couldn't take it in. She had only marked sixteen years. She had barely become a woman, had never served as a real Lamp-Carrier or offered the Lodestone a single pathdream. How could such a thing happen to them now? But Vatiri's dreams never lied.

"Enough!"

This time the word was a shout. Pradesh had gotten to his feet.

Anger burned in his face. For the first time, Khari understood how his authority could stand second only to the Powers.

"Vatiri," he said. His voice was quiet now, but deep and full of fire. "I want to hear exactly what you saw."

Asking a Lamp-Carrier to describe her dream amounted to challenging her truth. Vatiri didn't question or argue. "I saw a great bear," she said. "Too big to live in the world. And I saw a stone house that stood taller than any trees. Its roof was so high it disappeared into the sky."

Khari had trained in reading dreams long enough to know that the bear was the Lasska god Mesha. For some reason, the Lasska believed in a god they couldn't see, instead of the Sun God, Moon Woman and Mouth of Winds, Powers that actually moved in the world. The stone house, Khari knew, must be the place in Cheremay where the impera lived. Together, the house and the bear meant Shurik.

Vatiri went on, "I saw a river. Many streams came together to make it: streams out of the forests in the north, and the plains in the south, and the coast in the east, and the mountains in the west." She had closed her eyes again, and spoke as if she was drawing one word at a time out of a deep place in herself. Khari knew how hard it was for Lamp-Carriers to talk about their dreams. How much harder would it be to do it now, in front of the men, with the awful shadow hanging over them all?

Vatiri said, "The river ran fast and steady, straight into the stone house."

Handan said, "A river doesn't go into a…"

Khari spun around to snap at him, not caring that he was the Lodestone's nephew, but Pradesh got there first. "Quiet, boy."

Boy was an insult to a grown man and a skilled hunter. Khari was glad to see Handan's face redden in the firelight. Vatiri went on as if no one had interrupted. "The water ran through the house and came out the other side. When it came out, it formed a pool. A lake. It was burning."

Pradesh spoke quietly. "The water was burning?"

Vatiri nodded without opening her eyes. "Yes. It shone like metal, and the fire rose up from it. The bear stood waiting outside the house. It watched the pool form and spread. Then, when all the water had gathered there, burning, the bear reared into the air and pawed at the sky."

Khari could see it: the huge bear, its massive claws raking the air, its mouth open and snarling. She shivered.

Pradesh asked, "And what happened then?"

Again Vatiri paused. Then, head down, as if speaking to her hands folded in her lap, she said, "The water began to flow again, in streams, back toward the places it came from. It burned as it went."

Khari saw it all. The skills Vatiri had taught her told her the older woman was right: Shurik had armed his men with fire and danger, and now he would send them out, streams of them moving like living weapons through the world, destroying what they touched. Vatiri said, so quietly Khari held her breath to hear, "The last thing I saw was a field, a patch of sunlight on the grass. One of the streams came to it and burned it away. Not just the grass, but the light too. The light was gone."

Khari knew no one could mistake the meaning of that. The sun meant the Vaia, their God. Shurik's river had taken it. Vatiri had stopped speaking and sat very still. She looked exhausted. Khari wanted to reach out, touch her shoulder or take her hand, but the fear had frozen her.

Pradesh said, "Khari."

Khari managed to look up. The Lodestone had taken his seat again. In the firelight, with the anger gone from his face, he suddenly looked much older than his thirty-nine years. He said, "Did you see this too?"

Khari felt sick. She didn't wish she could say she had seen it – how could she wish for that? – but she hated having to admit her failure. It couldn't matter now, in the face of this, but she was supposed to be a Lamp-Carrier too.

She made herself open her mouth. "No, Lodestone." Her voice sounded strained and thin, not like her voice at all. "I didn't see anything."

For a moment they all took this in. Then Mandhani said, "If she didn't see it..."

Khari hated to hear the hope in his voice. *If she didn't see it, maybe it's not real.* But no one should trust her over Vatiri.

Handan seemed to hear her thought. "She's still only a girl. She's not a real Lamp-Carrier."

Khari couldn't make herself argue. Never mind the white blouse or the fact that yes, today, she was both of those things.

The men started clamoring again. Handan first, insisting they could fight the Lasska, they could train and... Radavan reminding the hunter that the tribe didn't have the right weapons. Rahul trying to make himself heard over Mandhani, who once again tried to support his brother. The noise swirled around Khari. Beside her, she heard Vatiri sigh, a sound of pure exhaustion. Her eyes still closed, the lines etched deep on her face in the firelight, she looked older and frailer than Khari had ever seen her.

Khari's arms felt stiff as she reached out to put them around her mother-in-truth. "Amma," she said. "Are you all right?"

The older woman's eyes opened. In spite of everything, she smiled. "I'm fine, child. Only tired."

Somehow Radavan made himself heard. "Khari, you and Vatiri go back to your tent. Don't speak about this to anyone else yet."

Khari was only too glad to get away from the circle, as if none of this would be true if only she could go somewhere else. She helped Vatiri to her feet. The two of them made their way slowly away from the fire, while behind them, Pradesh called the men to order for a debate that, Khari felt sure, would go on through the night.

She wanted to ask Vatiri why she, Khari, hadn't had the same terrible dream. She wanted to beg the older woman for answers, for some kind of hope, but what hope could anyone find tonight? Khari held up Vatiri's weight as the older woman leaned on her like a crutch. They walked back to their tent, through the camp that had settled into nighttime stillness. Khari was glad to see no one. If anyone had spoken to her, she might have let the impossible secret fly out of her mouth, so it would stop choking her.

In the tent, Vatiri lay down on her pallet without stopping to get undressed. Khari bent over her. "Do you need anything, amma?"

Vatiri smiled again, without opening her eyes. She pressed Khari's hand. "Don't worry about me. Let's both get some rest."

Khari doubted she could rest, but she closed the tent's cloth flap. She hadn't carried a lantern or lit one inside the tent, but she knew the space too well to need light.

Eight years she and Vatiri had shared this tent. Many years before that, Vatiri herself had woven the fabric for it, strong undyed wool, and oiled it with sheep fat against the weather. Most Vaia kept only what they could carry, so the tent only held a few things: two cooking pots, clay plates and mugs, a few extra clothes, the sleeping pallets. Vatiri had hung bunches of sweet herbs from the center pole. Their light clean fragrance filled the space.

Khari took off her blouse and leather breeches and folded them before she laid them on the floor next to her pallet. She unbraided and brushed out her hair, carefully unwinding the white ribbon, and pulled her light wool shift over her head.

How could she think of herself as a Lamp-Carrier after tonight? What good was she to the tribe? Khari lay back on her pallet and pulled the blanket up over her against the fall chill. She didn't think she could sleep, but her eyes ached with tiredness and her body felt like a wrung-out cloth.

After a long silent while, in spite of the worry that lay heavy on her chest, her eyes closed and shut out the empty dark. Dreams rose and lapped around her.

You must keep your hidden eye open. That tiny corner of herself stayed awake, watching. Probably she wouldn't see anything. Probably she would find no hope or help, none of the direction a Lamp-Carrier should find...

...but as sleep took her, she saw something.

A man's face: no one she had ever seen before. Light-skinned. Hair the brown of autumn leaves, but heavily streaked with silver. Not a young face, but not an old one. A plain face, except...

...the eyes. Blue eyes. Deep lines at their corners, but the blue of a cloudless sky.

Khari slept. Her hidden eye stayed open, watching.

2

———

THE ZHININ

Huge Lassar, newly under the rule of Impera Shurik, had three neighbors to the west, on the far side of the chain of mountains that ran between Lassar's northern and southern coasts. Those three neighbors – Namora, Dorva, and Otera – together made up less than half of Lassar's size. Only the biggest of them, Namora, shared a border with Lassar. The little country's eastern edge crouched in the shadow of the Senai Mountains.

The three small countries together were called the Fisheries, because all of them relied heavily on the rich waters of the Vandeni Ocean. Namora had farms and vineyards along with its fishing boats. Derla, Namora's Harvest Month, was the third month before the end of the year, when life sped up to a feverish pace. Everyone pulled together at harvest time to deal with the relentless work, especially in the little villages where the center of town gave way quickly to spreading fields and orchards.

One such village, Lida, sat just to the west of the Senai's foothills, almost exactly halfway between Namora's ocean coast to the north and the bay coast to the south. Lida's craftspeople and tavern-keepers had their businesses clustered around the village square. Five roads, lined with wooden houses roofed with tiles of gray-blue Namoran clay, came out from the square like the spokes of a wheel. Banks of mint took over the sides of the road beyond the village, and the gravel gave way to dirt track through open fields.

Back in the square, one building made of gray stone stood out in the cluster of white-painted shops and houses. Its shape made it unusual too: it was perfectly round, with a conical wooden roof whose point reached higher into the sky than any of the peaked tiled roofs around it.

This was Lida's Circle House. Here on Pirdina, the First Day of every week, all the villagers came together to worship the goddess Kenavi. No one able to leave their house would miss that tribute. Throughout the week, the House's doors stood open from morning to night. Anyone in need of the Goddess's guidance, or quiet time alone in the cool circle of the stone walls, might go in and set down, for a while, whatever burdens they had brought with them.

The priest in Lida was a *zhinin,* the lowest of the four ranks of the Namoran *dagira.* His name was Ribas Silvaikas. He had grown up in Lida and served in its Circle House since he came of age at eighteen.

He was unusual in more ways than one. A childhood fever had left him with both a chronic weakness and an exceptional kind of strength. Now, almost fifteen years after he'd become a zhinin, he knew every man, woman, and child in Lida and the nearby villages. The life of his home felt to him like one great heartbeat: the people and the land they tended, the grasses and trees, the fields and water and mountains. Every day, the gift left by his illness let him stand guard over that heartbeat as no other priest could.

Today was Antdina, a Second Day in the middle of Derla, the harvest month. The sun had just cleared the horizon. Swatches of butter-yellow light lay across Lida's cobbled streets when Ribas and his wife Maryut left the zhinin's house just behind the Circle House.

As they did every Derla, they were going up to his mother's farm on the northern edge of the village to help with the harvest for a few days. Ribas's nemesis, the heart weakness and chest pain left over from the worst time of his childhood, had kept him awake most of the night before. Maryut put her arm through his and said, "I suppose you still won't let me talk you into riding up there."

"You're right. I won't. The walk will do me good."

Maryut's mouth quirked. He knew that look and heard the word that went with it even before she said it. "Stubborn."

"Always," he agreed.

She laughed. A dozen years of marriage and more, and her laugh always wrapped around him like sunlight. Sometimes he still wondered how she could have chosen him, the plain, half-crippled farmer's-boy-turned-zhinin.

They went across the square to the road that headed most directly north out of the village. The scent of the late-growing mint blended with the dry earthiness of fallen leaves and the cool clear taste you only found in the mountains. Past the outskirts of the village, birds sang and rustled in the tall grass, late insects chattered, and to the east, the gray peaks of the Senai reached up toward the cloudless sky.

The north-running road went past three farms before it got out into the open land between Lida and Paret, the closest real town. The farthest of the three farms belonged to Ribas's mother Pelayut. He and his brother Gedrin had grown up there, in the house their great-grandfather had built almost a hundred years ago.

Gedrin. Normally Ribas looked forward to seeing his younger brother, who still seemed like a boy in spite of marriage, two children, and years of running the farm. Today, though, uneasiness stirred in the back of Ribas's mind. He hadn't admitted it to anyone yet, even Maryut, but he was starting to worry about Gedrin.

As they passed the second of the farmsteads, Maryut pressed his arm. "Will you listen if I tell you not to work too hard today?"

Her voice teased him, but he knew she meant it. She had married him knowing he would never have perfect health again, and she spent their shared life taking care of him and trying to protect him from the people who, she sometimes argued, needed him too much. He already looked older than he was, with his brown hair fading to silver, but he promised himself every day that he would make it into old age.

Now he smiled down at her. "I'll be careful."

"You'd better."

A clean, new split-rail fence marked the edge of Pelayut's land. The lower fields had a good crop of squash, potatoes, and tall grass for hay, but the main work of the day would happen up in the proud apple orchard that stretched from the northwest to the southeast edge of the property.

Pelayut Silvenis's apples, and everything she made from them, were famous in Lida. Ribas's younger brother Gedrin had taken over the orchard and its harvest when he turned eighteen, but everyone still talked about Pelya's apples and Pelya's cider as if she, rather than her father and grandfather, had set out the trees and tended and refined the crop until you couldn't find a better apple anywhere in Namora. The fruit had firm pinkish-gold skin and pink-veined flesh that combined just the right amounts of tartness and sugar. When pressed, it yielded a cider so richly gold it looked like sunlight distilled into a bottle. Whether you drank it fresh or fermented it to make the hair-curling *abuvisk*, people said a drop on a dead person's tongue would bring him back to life.

Ribas and Maryut walked up to the sprawling old farmhouse. Before they reached the porch, the front door swung open.

"Uncle Ribé!"

Gedrin's four-year-old daughter Asira flew across the porch to them, her dark curls streaming out behind her, her little shoes thumping on the wooden boards. Ribas bent to catch her. She twined her arms around his neck and pressed her face against his shoulder as he scooped her up. Hurt and upset rose off her like steam.

"Sira, child." He put his hand on her tangled hair. "What's the matter?"

Her voice came up, muffled in the fabric of his shirt. "Tell Da, Uncle Ribé. Tell him it's not fair."

What about your da? Ribas didn't like the sound of this. "What's not fair?" he asked.

Asira lifted her head enough to see him. Her green eyes looked huge with tears. "He was mean. I'm big enough to pick apples." She pushed out her lower lip in a pout.

If it had been any other child, Ribas might have wanted to smile, but that word *mean* lodged somewhere in his chest. And it wasn't like his happy, confident little niece to cry. Ribas touched the cloud of hurt around her and felt something worse: a thread of fear.

No doubt Gedrin had decided Asira was still too little to help with the harvest. Fair enough. The orchard had hazards, and during the busiest season, a small child could get underfoot and get hurt. But Asira had never been scared of her father.

"Well," he said gently, brushing her tears away, "I think we have to let your da decide what he wants you to do."

"It's not fair!" Asira insisted. More tears welled up. "I told him I could do it, and he got mad. He was mean, Uncle Ribé."

That word again. Ribas's uneasiness solidified into hard worry. When he glanced at Maryut over the little girl's head, her face told him she had the same thought he did.

Gedrin was brisk and cheerful, full of energy. He had all the health and strength Ribas didn't, but he had something else too. In looks, he was the living image of their father.

He had only been three months old when Silvas Jadraikas died. Ribas would have said his brother was much too young for the shadow of their father's anger and unhappiness to mark him. He had no memory of the fear and hurt that had once filled the old house. Surely he had no reason to become the same kind of man Silvas had been.

If that was true, then what was happening here? Ribas asked Asira, "How was your da mean?"

Before she could answer, the house door opened again and Ribas's mother came out onto the porch. Pelayut Silvenis was no longer young, but she stood tall and moved with an easy grace that denied her age. Her hair, under her widow's kerchief, was silver rather than the wheat-gold Ribas remembered, but her eyes, like Ribas's own, were still the striking blue of a cloudless sky.

Ribas remembered when Mama had been beautiful but fragile, more a girl than a woman in spite of marriage and motherhood. Now, and for a long time, the fragility had gone, replaced by strength that made Ribas think of a proud tree unbent by wind and weather.

Her eyes stopped on Ribas's face. "Ribé. Should you be here?"

The walk in the clear, cool air had eased the tightness in his chest, but Ribas knew his face probably still showed traces of last night. Maryut answered before he did. "I asked him that already, Mama."

Mama sighed. "I'm sure you did."

The two women were very different in height and features, but they looked uncannily similar as they fixed Ribas with identical looks. In spite of his worry over what Asira said, he had to swallow a laugh. "You know I can't miss the harvest," he said.

"I know you won't," Mama said. "That's not the same thing." To the little girl, who still had her arms around Ribas's neck, she said, "Lamb, Grandmama needs to talk to your uncle for a minute. Can you get down now?"

Asira protested, but Ribas gently set her on her feet, promising her he'd be back outside soon, and Maryut held out her hand to the little girl. "How about we go up to the orchard," she said. "We'll see how the work's going."

Asira obeyed reluctantly. Mama held the farmhouse door open and motioned Ribas inside. "Let's talk in here."

The zhinin's house by the village square had been Ribas's home for fifteen years, ever since he had finished his apprenticeship and been installed to serve in the Circle House. As he stepped into the farmhouse, into the front room with its dim light and the taste of the smoke of generations of hearth fires, he felt for a moment, as he always did, as if half a lifetime or so had fallen away from him. He was a boy coming home.

Mama went over to the hearth. "Come sit."

The great open stone hearth was the heart of the house, the oldest part of the original farmhouse and the place where every generation of the family had gathered since Mama's great-grandfather's time. Even the kitchen, down at the end of the narrow hallway that gave off the front room, was a generation younger, not quite as fully a part of the family's life as this room.

Even though this place was home as no other place could be, even though the very texture of the wood and stone here had been woven into his life from birth, Ribas felt an old uneasiness as he took a seat in one of the straight-backed chairs that stood by the hearth. Once, years ago, a terrible thing had happened in this room. That night – the worst time he could remember – still reached out for him across all the time in between.

Mama sat down facing him. Again, her eyes rested on his face. "You're sure you're all right, my dove?"

My dove. If she was that worried, he must look worse than he'd thought. He made it a joke. "Mama, you're not going to tell me off for coming up today, are you?"

Here, alone with her, he could feel the worry wrapped around her as clearly as he'd felt Asira's hurt. *He was mean...*

His mother smiled. "No, I won't scold you. I need to talk to my zhinin."

Ribas held his hand out, palm up: the zhinin's ritual, asking for a confidence. She laid her hand palm-down on his and he closed his fingers gently, sealing the contact. "Tell me," he said. The contact of hand with hand was an ancient promise. The zhinin would tell no one what he or she heard in the next moments.

When he let go, Mama folded her hands in the lap of her brown homespun dress. "I'm worried about Gedri."

Ribas had known that already. Cold tightened around him. "What's going on, Mama?"

"He seems different to me. Angry."

It was happening, then, exactly as he had hoped it never would. Ribas knew he had to listen to everything. No matter how hard this might be for him, it was much worse for his mother, to see these changes happening to her son.

"Tell me," he said again.

Mama looked at him steadily. She had learned so much courage during the worst times long ago. "This morning at breakfast," she said, "Raulí was talking about how many apples he'd pick today." Seven-year-old Raulin, Gedrin's son, had been proudly helping with the harvest for the past three years. "Sira said she would pick more," Mama said. "They were laughing, you know, teasing each other. Then Gedrí told Sira he didn't want her in the orchard."

Her face changed. In it, Ribas saw the echo of his father's anger. The shadow his brother couldn't remember, but that he and Mama had never forgotten.

Mama said, "She started to argue, the way she does. Talking back, you know." Ribas did know. "Usually Gedrí laughs when she does that. This time, he didn't."

Ribas pictured his brother's face. He'd been almost seven years old when Gedrin was born. He'd watched his brother grow up, watched him look more like their father with each passing year. Still, he had hoped, tried to believe, that he would never hear what he was hearing now.

Mama said, "He was cold, Ribé. Cold enough to scare her."

Ribas knew the kind of cold she meant. Again, that long-ago night, and what had happened by this hearth, woke up in his memory. The chill that moved through his body now felt like an echo of the fever that had taken him when he was a child, that same summer when his father died. The fever that had left him with his damaged heart and almost taken him away for good.

His father's anger had filled this old house with a chill that hadn't lifted for hours. That had been Silvas's mildest anger, the kind that didn't leave Mama in tears, or split skin open, or leave bruises that ached bone-deep.

Mama said, "I want to ask you to look at him, Ribé. Into his mind."

There it was. The other legacy from his illness.

When it first happened, he had thought it was because of the fever-dreams. He'd thought he was still imagining things that weren't really there, but then the fever left and the things he saw stayed. Around people, animals, anything with a mind, he saw lines and patterns of light. Their colors and brightness told him what the owner of that mind felt, in every detail.

He didn't know how he understood the patterns, but somehow he had, right from the beginning. As if he knew a language without having to learn the words. That alone would have been strange enough, but then he learned he could change the patterns too. He could cut pain. Ease fear. Help grief to heal.

With such a qualification, he'd had to become a zhinin. As a boy, he'd only ever wanted to work this farm, but his body wasn't up to it and the world seemed to have other plans for him. After fifteen years of using his strange gift to help everyone he could reach, he had gotten used to carrying it, but he always used it carefully. It claimed a price for what it gave.

Now he said, "I'll look, Mama. But if something's wrong, I can't promise to fix it."

"I know."

Some people thought the gift was magic, or should be. When Ribas first became Lida's zhinin, Namora's powers-that-be, in the capital in Sostavi, had wanted to bring him there and put him to work. They'd thought it was a waste for him to stay a zhinin in a back-water village. Ribas had needed every drop of his stubbornness to weather that storm.

Mama said, "I only want you to look. If something's happening..." Her hands tightened briefly around each other, and then relaxed again. "It's best if we know."

Maybe it's nothing. Ribas thought the words, but didn't say them.

The two of them went outside. Mama went to the barn to check on the work going on around the farm's big cider press. Ribas went to the southeast corner of the orchard, where the picking was well underway.

High up in one of the nearest trees, Maryut's brother Darin picked apples from the upper branches and loaded them into a wicker basket tied to a rope looped over another branch. Darin and his two tall sons helped with every year's harvest. Maryut herself stood at the base of Darin's tree, holding the other end of the rope taut, ready to lower the filled basket to the ground. Seven-year-old Raulin, with a basket of his own, worked on the lower branches of the same tree. Ribas's friend Seldo, who owned Lida's Sheaf and Barrel Inn, and Seldo's wife Milya made a team at another tree. Seldo and Milya bought a lot of Mama's cider. Beyond them, Ribas saw Gedrin and Gedrin's wife Virta at a third tree.

Apparently Gedrin hadn't noticed yet that Asira, instead of staying out of the way, was scurrying around, picking up apples that had fallen on the ground and adding them to her brother's basket. Raulin made no protest. In fact, when the little boy saw Ribas, he snuck over to whisper, "Sira and I are going to get the most baskets. You watch."

In spite of his uneasiness, Ribas nodded gravely. "I believe you."

Raulin, small and serious-faced, with tousled brown hair, reminded Ribas of himself as a child. The boy said, "You won't tell Da she's picking, will you?"

Ribas watched Asira for a few seconds. She was being careful, glancing up to keep an eye on the activity in the trees above her. She checked the apples she picked up for soft spots and put the bad ones in the pile at the edge of the orchard. She knew what to do.

Ribas winked at his nephew. "I won't say a word." If there was any trouble, he decided, Gedrin could blame him.

Raulin grinned. "Thanks, Uncle Ribé." As he went back to work, Ribas walked over to the base of his brother's tree.

Virta, Gedrin's wife, saw him coming and waved. Eight years ago, before she'd married Gedrin, she had been a town girl from Paret. Paret, a day's journey northwest of Lida, was the closest thing to a city in Namora's east-central Kalnu region. It couldn't begin to compete with mighty Sostavi on the northern coast, but its *viduris,* the priests' school, had trained generations of dagira, Ribas included.

Virta still didn't dress like a farmer's wife. Any time she could spare, she embroidered complicated designs on her simple homespun dresses because she loved pretty things. Ribas knew some of the villagers, especially farm women, looked down their noses at that, but he sympathized. His brother's wife was delicate and lovely, with soft curling hair and big green eyes. The embroidery she loved suited her better than the hard, unending farm work, but she did the best she could.

"Morning, Ribé!" she called to him.

He didn't see any signs of trouble in her face. That was hopeful, at least. "Morning, sister," he said. "How are things?"

She pointed up toward the basket hanging from a high branch. "Almost full already. Gedrí!" she called up. "Your brother's here!"

Ribas heard rustling up above. Gedrin's face appeared through a gap in the branches. "Took you long enough!"

Ribas felt a wave of relief. His brother sounded the same as ever. "I do the best I can," he retorted. "These old bones don't move too fast, you know."

"You *are* old. It's a fact. Wait a minute, I'm coming down."

Gedrin shinned down the tree as easily as a boy. From a low branch, he jumped down to the ground.

Ribas knew that no one seeing the two of them together for the first time would take them for brothers. He had gotten Mama's height and lighter coloring, while Gedrin had Silvas's strong stocky build, and hair and eyes the color of freshly turned earth. Both their parents had been handsome. Ribas thought that, except for the blue eyes he'd inherited from Mama, he himself must have taken after some nondescript cousin or uncle lost to the past.

Gedrin grinned at him. "Glad you're here." Then he seemed to see something else. "Are you up for this?"

Ribas kept his voice light, not to show his brother either his worry or his relief. "Marya and Mama already asked me that. Don't you start."

Gedrin laughed. He put a hand on Ribas's shoulder. "You know you don't have to work."

"I don't know that at all."

Gedrin, always barreling through life on overflowing energy, had never been able to imagine how it felt not to trust your own body. Ribas remembered, when they were boys, how upset Gedrin had gotten when Ribas gave up his claim to their mother's farm so he could join the dagira. Ten-year-old Gedrin had insisted to the point of tears that Ribas shouldn't do it. He had to stay on the farm, Gedrin had said: the two of them had to work the land together. He'd refused to listen when Ribas explained that he couldn't keep up with the work. Gedrin had firmly believed that Ribas could be a farmer, if only he tried hard enough.

Now Gedrin understood Ribas's nemesis better, but he didn't know how it felt to live with such a thing. Ribas was glad for that. He said, "Seems to me you won't get all this work done by yourself."

Gedrin waved a hand at the busy workers at the other trees. "Do I look like I'm by myself?"

"You need somebody responsible here."

Virta overheard that and laughed. If Ribas was old, at least according to family rules, Gedrin was permanently young and reckless. Ribas kept a straight face, but he knew he had to look into Gedrin's mind, and soon. The gift only worked when he could look directly at the mind's owner. He said, "Where do you want me?"

"How about here? Get a basket and take the low branches." Then Gedrin looked past Ribas at something else. "Goddess hear me! I told that girl to stay back!"

He had spotted Asira. Ribas saw the change in his brother's face. Even without using the gift, he knew the truth. He had hoped for years that whatever had hurt their father, whatever had been wrong in Silvas's mind to make him the way he was, wouldn't come for Gedrin too. Now that hope was gone.

No, Da! A child's voice, his own, echoed in his mind. Standing up for Mama when he was far too small to help her. *No, Da! Don't you hurt her!*

The zhinin couldn't be afraid. Ribas put his hand on his brother's arm. "Gedri."

His brother looked back at him. Anger, out of place but far too familiar, twisted the face Ribas knew so well. In the moment of eye contact, Ribas reached for the gift. It unspooled the patterns for him and gave him proof of what he already knew.

Anger made a net around his brother. Too-thick, too-bright red lines wove around Gedrin's mind, trapping and gripping it tight.

Ribas had never looked into his father's mind. Silvas had died before Ribas had the gift. But if he could have, Ribas knew, he would have seen exactly this kind of anger, that could tear up anything it touched.

Gedrin's face clouded with suspicion. "Brother, I didn't ask you to do that trick of yours."

He couldn't know Ribas was looking, but he knew, as everyone did, that Ribas made it a rule never to use the gift without permission. Ribas said, "If I'm giving you a funny look, it's because I don't think you should scold your daughter for working. You want her to grow up lazy?"

He had learned to control his own feelings a long time ago, and he had offered thanks to the Goddess, many times, that no one could read him the way he read others. Gedrin seemed to believe him now. "Is it better for her to grow up disobedient? I told her not to work today."

The immediate anger was fading. Ribas knew the net was still there, but at least Gedrin's face had lost that ugly cast. Ribas said, "She's stubborn. She comes by it honestly, in this family."

Gedrin smiled reluctantly. Ribas knew he had won, for now. "Fine," his brother said. "But if she starts whining because she's tired, or if an apple falls and knocks her on the head, you're dealing with it."

"Fair enough."

They got to work. Gedrin climbed the tree again as easily as he'd come down it. Ribas got a basket and started on the lower branches.

Up above, Gedrin launched into a tune about the merry spring-time. He had a good voice, rich and warm, and he belted unapologetically about digging furrows and sowing seeds until Virta reminded him that this month was Derla, not Ivesta, and maybe Gedrin should think about the little ones who could hear him singing, not to mention his brother the zhinin. Gedrin called back down that everybody here knew the basic facts of life, but all right, he'd change the words if nothing else would do, so he sang about Derla and plump apples ripening on the branches and the delights of sweet juicy fruit until Virta shouted at him to stop, that was worse than ever. Laughter and scolding flew back and forth between them.

Ribas worked steadily, filling his own basket with the rhythm of picking that came back to him every year. Sometimes, when he came up here, he felt as if he'd slipped into the life he had imagined for himself when he was a boy. A life where he had stayed healthy, the gift had never come to him, and instead, he and Gedrin had shared the farm and worked out how to divide it between their families.

Today, though, those imaginings didn't come. The weight of the gift on him, and the zhinin's responsibility, were solid and real. The harvesting group would take a break for the midday meal. He would have to get Mama alone then and tell her what he'd seen. He knew what the news would mean to her, and how her face would change as she heard it.

She had told him, many times over the years since his father's death, that Silvas had once been different. That when he and Mama had first gotten married, Silvas had been happy. Never mind the fact that, by then, Silvas's life hadn't gone the way he'd wanted.

If anyone turned out like him, Ribas thought, *it should have been me.* From all he could gather, Gedrin might have their father's looks, but Ribas – as much as he hated the idea – must have had a lot in common with Silvas's mind. Silvas had studied to be a zhinin too. He had gone all the way to Sostavi, to the Great Circle House there, but something had happened that he never told his family about. He had abandoned that world and whatever success he'd found in it to come back to Lida.

Ribas had gone to the same priests' school his father had attended. All the time he'd been there, he'd pushed away the knowledge that he was sitting in the same classrooms his father had known, reading the same texts, listening to the same lessons. He'd done all he could to ignore the fact that the head teacher, Kunin Dergo, had actually been in Silvas's class. Ribas had convinced himself it couldn't matter. His own career would be different, because he would never go to Sostavi. He would only serve in Lida.

And now he was here. And what was he going to do for his brother?

Sometime between his marriage and Ribas's earliest memories of him, Silvas had changed. Now Gedrin was changing. Gedrin, who had never carried bruises left by his father's fists, who had never listened to Mama cry at night, or crept out to the dark silent hearth to climb into her lap and hug her and wish, uselessly, that he was big and fierce enough to protect her. Gedrin, who had never tried to use his own small body as a barrier between his parents, and who had no memory of the crystallized horror of the night when Silvas died.

The sun climbed slowly higher in the sky. Ribas stayed in the rhythm of bending, reaching, picking, as the air slowly warmed around him even in the shade of the trees and Gedrin, above him, whistled another tune.

Could he help his brother? The red lines of the web burned in Ribas's mind as he worked. He knew that the gift would, at least, let him reach in and try to cut one line of the web at a time, until it loosed its hold on Gedrin. He also knew the price the gift would take. It had no strength of its own, so it would take all that Ribas had and more. And even if he could cut the net, the anger would still be there in Gedrin's mind, the lines of it like branches ready to re-grow after pruning.

Maybe if Ribas hadn't had a bad night. Maybe if he didn't feel so tired now, he would believe he could cut those lines and set his brother free. Right now, with his worn heart aching in his chest, and his muscles pushing against fatigue to carry on the rhythm of the work, he felt helpless.

The work went on in the bright, beautiful morning. Ribas pulled the fruit down and wished, with all the hurt and hopelessness he'd felt as a child, for the strength he didn't have.

3

THE TAVO BALSA

In Namora's capital city, Sostavi, the Great Circle House rose above the clusters of white-walled buildings that clung like crystals to the high hills. Down below, the deep turquoise of the Vandeni Ocean met the shallower, silver-blue water of the harbor. The summer would see fleets of fishing boats leaving the harbor before dawn to come back in the evening riding low in the water, weighed down with their rich burdens.

Now, though, early in the Harvest Month, activity of a different kind filled the city. Tavin Ardinas, Ruler of Namora, was dying.

Ardinas lay in his bedchamber in the House of the Tavin, the tall, slender, elegant house which adjoined the Great Circle House in Sostavi's central square. The old priest had served as Namora's Tavin for over thirty years. Few people could remember him now as the young man who had arrived in Sostavi from Lygame, Namora's hardscrabble clay quarry region, a lifetime ago.

The woman who spent every hour she could spare with him certainly couldn't remember that young dark-haired priest. She was Valdena Filtraikas, the Tavo Balsa: Voice of the Tavin.

Valda, as her fellow Great House priests called her, was thirty-four, more than young enough to be Tavin Ardinas's daughter. She had come to Sostavi some fifteen years earlier, a new zhinin anxious to climb the dagira ladder, but the clawings of ambition she'd felt in those days had faded a long time ago. Now she filled her role, stepping in for the services that Ardinas could no longer perform, and listened to her colleagues murmuring and whispering about the election of the next Tavin, which couldn't take place until after Ardinas died. None of it interested her much. She went through the days behind a quiet mask that only lifted when she came into Ardinas's bedchamber, where a low fire always crackled on the stone hearth, and sat in the gentle light beside the old priest's bed.

One night near the end of Derla, she arrived at the bedchamber just as Tayo Bodin, the Tavin's personal healer, was ushering the last of Ardinas's visitors out for the day. Valda knew that the Great House dagira – the zhinine, kunine, and sventine who served directly under Ardinas – liked to be seen in this room, trooping in and out in twos and threes, then huddling in the sitting room outside in flocks to look mournful and whisper officiously to one another. No doubt some of the sventine, the members of the Senior Council and the highest-ranking priests below Ardinas, thought showing their devotion to the Tavin now would improve their chances of winning the upcoming election.

Valda had no time for any of them. Neither did Tayo Bodin, who was older than the Tavin himself, bent-backed and white-haired. The tayo's dark eyes still snapped under his bushy eyebrows and his sharp tongue could send even the most stubborn sventin scuttling for the door. Tonight he let Valda in with the courtly flourish he always gave her, a gesture from an older time. Then he ordered the last visiting kunin out in the voice of a father scolding a troublesome child. He clapped the door shut behind the offended swirl of gray robes and set the latch firmly.

Valda, still in her brown robes of office from the evening service she had just performed, went to her usual chair by the bed. Ardinas lay still, his pale eyelids closed, his age-spotted hands resting on the fine linen sheets that covered him. Valda was sure he was asleep. He spent most of his days sleeping, and she had often prayed that when death came for him, he would feel it as only the gentlest of changes.

When she sat down, though, his eyes opened. "Well," he said. "That was a fine fuss."

His voice sounded thin and weak, but she heard laughter in it. His bright hazel eyes looked straight into hers. Sometimes, even now, his eyes let her imagine the young man he must have been.

"Valda," he said, holding out a hand. She took it. His skin felt cool, as soft as if dusted with flour. He said, "Bodin here protects me very well, don't you think?"

So he'd heard the healer scolding the kunin. "Yes, Tavin," Valda said. "He does."

Tayo Bodin snorted. He stood over the low table by the hearth, his pale green healer's robes stained with the orange firelight. "You know, my lord, you could save me a lot of trouble." *My lord,* like his salute to Valda, was another of the tayo's old-fashioned formalities. Bodin set two glass vials inside the wooden case he carried. It was pain medicine, Valda knew, and probably a sleeping draught; she had never seen Ardinas take either one, but the healer would offer what he could. Bodin said, "You could sit up now and then and tell those boys off yourself."

Boys. Valda knew exactly what the members of the Senior Council of Sventine would say if they could hear that. She wished they could, and that she could see their faces when they did.

Ardinas smiled. Lines crossed his face in every direction, as if his skin were a piece of paper that had been crumpled and then smoothed out. He had little hair left on his head, but his beard was still a mass of tight white curls. He said, "But you do it so well, tayo. Sometimes I think you're enjoying it."

Bodin folded his arms. "How long were you really asleep today, my lord? I'm starting to think you're lying there having a good rest and laughing at us all."

For a moment, Valda let herself believe it. Ardinas was playing a joke on them and would get out of bed tomorrow, healthy and strong as ever. Longing wrapped around her so tightly it hurt.

The Tavin said, "That's for me to know, tayo. You go and rest now."

"Do you need anything before I leave?"

"Not unless you have an elixir of youth, my friend."

He was teasing, but Bodin shook his head. "If I did," he said quietly, "you'd have had it a long time ago." He put his hand over his heart and bowed. "Raimaté, Tavin."

Peace be with you, the salute between priests and from a non-priest to a member of the dagira. Ardinas rested one worn hand on his beard and nodded as much as the angle of the pillow would let him. "Raimaté, tayo." Then Bodin went out, leaving Valda and Ardinas together.

Ardinas pressed Valda's hand and let it go. His eyes looked bright and alert now. "You know what I'm going to tell you."

He would tell her that she should rest too. She would ignore it. Ardinas had no wife, no children to stay with him during his ending time. Valda had no ties either, but she had never wished for them except once, long ago...but those memories didn't belong here.

She would stand in for Ardinas's family at this bedside, as she stood in for the priest himself in the Great House. "Yes," she said, "I know what you'll say. And you know what I'll answer, Tavin."

"That I do."

He smiled, the kind of smile she had never seen on her own father's face. "So," he said, "since you're determined to stay, tell me how the world is getting along."

When she had arrived in Sostavi, she had never dreamed of wearing the brown robes of the Tavo Balsa and standing on the great dais, performing the water and salt rituals in the sumptuous Great House where, some of the stories said, the Goddess Herself had lived as a mortal woman. Now, the robes and the rituals were so familiar that she couldn't imagine any other life. She told Ardinas about the services she had performed that day and the throngs of people who had lined up at the Great House doors afterward to ask about the Tavin's health. "They miss you," she said. "I'm not much of a substitute."

Neither she nor Ardinas avoided the fact that he would never officiate in the Great House again. The Namoran faith taught that the death of the body released the *sela*, soul, to be part of the wholeness of the world. Ardinas had told Valda that he was looking forward to finding out what that felt like.

Now he waved a hand, brushing off her words. "You're a fine substitute. Anyone who doesn't think so has terrible taste."

Everyone who came to the Great House would have to listen to her until after the election and the installation of a new Tavin. No one could be sure when the election would happen, but the new candidate wouldn't be installed until spring, in Ketva, the Fourth Month, because the long-held traditions of the faith stated that a High Installation could conflict neither with the high holy months of Akena and Algima, which commemorated the sacrifice and rebirth of the Goddess, nor with the month of Ivesta, planting season. A High Installation required the country's full focus.

Valda would have to officiate in the Great House until spring. She was glad that her rank as Tavo Balsa, which meant she had to oversee the election, meant that she couldn't put herself forward as a candidate for Tavin. For the same reason, she wouldn't cast a vote.

As if he'd heard the train of her thoughts, Ardinas gave her a sidelong look. "And how are your colleagues in the Council?"

How, indeed. Valda couldn't quite keep the curl of disdain out of her voice. "They aren't saying much, Tavin."

Ardinas laughed. Like his eyes, his laugh still seemed much younger than he was. "I'm sure they aren't. They aren't, for instance, discussing those sixteen votes the Council will cast, or who's likeliest to get the nine they need to win."

Again Valda was grateful to be the Council's seventeenth member. She didn't want to be Tavin, or have any reason to count votes in her head while she sat here with Ardinas. "No," she said, "they aren't talking about that at all."

"And I suspect I can guess who isn't saying the most."

Now it was Valda's turn to laugh, in spite of the scorn she felt. "I'm sure you can. Sventin Galvo and Sventin Lesvin."

Galvo Dendraikas and Lesvin Berenaikas, both members of the Council of Sventine, certainly did sit at the heart of the discussions the Council wasn't having out loud. Galvo had served in the Council since shortly after Ardinas became Tavin. No one knew more than Galvo about the intricacies of dagira politics, and no one carried himself more confidently in meetings or spoke his views with more finely tuned diplomacy. Lesvin, meanwhile, had become a sventin only five years earlier, moving up from the ranks of Great House kunine after the death of one of the oldest Council members. Most of his colleagues still considered him young and green, but his fervent devotion to the Goddess had won him support as a possible Tavin-to-be.

Ardinas nodded. "Galvo and Lesvin. The obvious candidates. So tell me, Tavo Balsa, if you could vote for one of them, which would it be?"

"You know I shouldn't have an opinion." Valda knew perfectly well that her fellow Council members would hope for her "influence" in the election, once it was under way, but as an impartial referee, she wasn't supposed to have any.

Ardinas waved that away too. "You can tell me. I can't interfere from where I'm going."

Valda's breath caught in her throat. She tried not to think about how much she would miss this old man. "Truthfully, then," she said, "I don't much like either of them."

She knew that wasn't necessarily fair. Galvo, for instance, with his long experience, would certainly be the reliable choice. She had never met anyone smarter, though she didn't entirely trust either his flair for political intrigue or his oily diplomacy. Lesvin, younger than Valda herself, had energy and drive, but Valda wasn't sure how far she trusted him either. His fervent prayers sometimes made him seem less faithful than under the grip of an obsession.

She knew Ardinas already knew most of this. The Tavin had worked with both of those men every day for years. She said, "Both of them are too interested in themselves."

That disgusted her more than anything else. The two of them weighing their chances and grubbing for votes, as if Ardinas's death was only a temporary inconvenience before they could get on with what really mattered.

But the old priest said, "It's only natural. Back in the old days, you know, three of us on Tavin Matas's Council thought we might get the vote when he died. The poor man was down to his last breaths, trapped in bed, getting hauled out every time he had to use the chamberpot." Ardinas motioned toward his own body under the sheet. "Sounds familiar, doesn't it? There he was, and there we were, each of us acting like the Goddess Herself had laid Her hand on us and promised us the Tavinate. Whispering and backstabbing. Promises and insults flying all over the place."

Valda couldn't hide her expression. The bright hazel eyes rested on her. Ardinas said, "Fact of life, Tavo Balsa. You wouldn't be here in Sostavi if you weren't ambitious."

That was true. Valda had plenty of reason to know it, but she still couldn't picture Ardinas grubbing for votes. "I'm glad you won."

"So am I." He smiled. "Maybe I used the best insults, or maybe I was the best candidate after all, and the Goddess guided the vote, as we must believe she does." His fingers, still strong despite the blue veins that showed under the skin, twisted the edge of the finely embroidered sheet that covered him. "Between the two of us, Valda, I agree with you about Galvo and Lesvin. They're both decent enough, but..."

His voice trailed off. Valda saw his eyes move past her, toward the hearth and the tapestry on the wall above it. In this richly appointed chamber, the tapestry was the richest piece of all: an expanse of pure color, swirls of green and blue and purple that made no specific shape but called up the shifting colors of the ocean. Valda knew how much Ardinas loved it. He wouldn't see the ocean again in life, but these colors linked him to it.

His eyes came back to her face. "The next Tavin will have a difficult job," he said. "Lassar's new impera, young Shurik. I see trouble there."

Valda wanted to lift his worry away. He shouldn't have to spend the handfuls of time he had left thinking of what might happen when he was gone. At the same time, she had been thinking about Lassar too.

No one in Namora knew much about the huge country east of the Senai Mountains. Lasska rulers since time out of mind had kept the place shut in on itself. Almost nothing from the outside world got in, and no Lasska – or so few they had been forgotten – seemed to travel outside it. Valda knew one particularly strange thing about the empire: even though it had a sea coast on three sides, it had no sailors or shipbuilders. Apparently the first Lasska impera, Curin, had hated and feared the sea. He had put his capital, Cheremay, in the middle of the country, with ranges of mountains between him and the faraway coasts, and he had ordered his people to stay off the water. He had said it was the will of Mesha, the bear-shaped god they worshipped. For generations, the Lasska had obeyed.

Lassar had no navy, but Valda knew that if rumors held any hint of the truth, their army could overmatch any military force in the world. Curin had brought scattered tribes, tiny countries, and thatch-roofed kingdoms under his heel to create the empire. He had needed a massive military to do it. These days, Valda couldn't imagine that shut-in Lassar needed such a huge force, but every impera since Curin had maintained and trained it. They probably believed their god had ordered that too.

Valda knew almost nothing about Lassar's new ruler. The Tavin had maintained a respectful, distant relationship with Shurik's father Mangevar. Perhaps once every year, Ardinas had sent Mangevar a carefully-worded salutation from one leader to another, offering the impera his respects and assuring him of Namora's well-wishes for the Lasska country and people. The messages were always in Namoran; not even Ardinas knew much about the Lasska language. He had gotten perfunctory but reasonably polite replies, also in Namoran, and there the relationship had ended. After Mangevar's death, Ardinas had extended condolences to Shurik.

Valda said, "We haven't had trouble with Lassar before, Tavin. Why now?"

Because, of course, their relationship with Impera Mangevar had been stable, and a new ruler might be different. Valda wanted to believe that was all. Ardinas's face, though, looked gaunter than ever in the firelight, his skin almost as colorless as his beard.

"Shurik makes me uneasy," he said. His fingers worked the edge of the sheet again. "He replied to my letter, only a few lines, but they were full of *the Great God Mesha,* and *the God's directives* and *the God's will.* He sounded less like a ruler than a priest."

Valda hadn't seen Shurik's reply. She said gently, "Priests can be good rulers, Tavin. We ought to know that."

Ardinas laughed again, but it sounded tired and fitful. "We're trained for it, Tavo Balsa. Lasska rulers have always been warlords, or something like it. They rule the country while the priests fill the temples and collect the offerings to the God. Do you see what I mean? Now suppose one impera is different. Thinks he can hear the voice of Mesha in his head."

In spite of the fire and her heavy robes, Valda felt cold creep over her. "Does he think that?"

"I believe so. And now consider their God. What kinds of things do you think Mesha will tell this young impera to do?"

Valda thought of the few pictures she had seen of the Lasska bear-god. A snarling face, sharp teeth, hot angry eyes.

Ardinas was watching her. "Yes." He sounded more tired than ever. "Mesha is far different from our own Kenavi. Shurik is young and deciding what kind of ruler to be. I think we can guess how his God might shape him."

And tiny Namora, with no standing army, sat in Lassar's shadow. Valda tried not to shiver. Ardinas was right about what the next Tavin might have to face.

Ardinas reached for her hand again. Valda gave it to him and swallowed past the dryness in her throat. "The Goddess will guide us." She wished she sounded more certain.

The old priest pressed her fingers. For a few moments, the only sound in the room was the faint pop and crackle of the dying hearth fire. Then Ardinas seemed to leave their talk of Shurik and Lassar behind. "Do you know," he said, "lately, I've been thinking very much about someone I've never met."

Worry pooled in Valda's chest. Were his thoughts wandering? He'd seemed lucid all evening, but...

As if she had spoken aloud, he said, "I promise you, my wits are as good as they've ever been."

She shifted guiltily in her chair. He pressed her hand again and let it go. "I realize," he said, "that must sound strange. I'm thinking of someone who caused a great fuss here in Sostavi, oh, something like fifteen years ago."

Fifteen years. That was around the same time Valda herself had come to Sostavi, leaving the security of a Circle House in Paret willing to keep her on as a new zhinin. Ambition had driven her far. Ardinas said, "He was a young zhinin, just installed in a Circle House in a mountain village. He never came to Sostavi, but he certainly stirred a bee's nest here."

Valda felt the blood rising into her face. But, surely, she couldn't be so silly after all this time.

Ardinas could only mean one person. Valda knew exactly who it was, even before Ardinas went on, "He was a farmer's son, I think, but he had an extraordinary gift. The *dovne kenavnis*. Gift of Kenavi."

Oh yes. Only one person matched that description. A farmer's son, a mountain village, and that astonishing gift. Valda braced herself. Tonight was no time to give into old weakness.

"Ribas Silvaikas, Tavin?"

Her voice sounded steadier than she'd expected. It ought to be steady enough. Fifteen years ago, she had done all she could to put that part of her life away forever.

Light came back into Ardinas's face. "That's exactly the name. You know him?"

"I knew him well, a long time ago." She tried to sound as if she was talking about any colleague. "We studied at the same viduris. He was a dear friend."

The viduris in Paret. The classrooms, the dusty benches and old desks, the slow movement of sunlight down the white walls. Gray-haired Kunin Dergo, the head teacher, whose chilly presence could silence a chattering room in less time than it took to blink. Valda had put the memories away, but now they bloomed out as fresh and strong as scent from an unstoppered bottle. The village boy with the startlingly blue eyes and the kindest smile she had ever seen.

"I do wish I could have met him." Ardinas sighed. "For some reason I found myself thinking about him recently. I'd have liked to know more about his gift. What it might be able to do."

Valda heard the words Ardinas didn't say. If trouble was coming, could the dovne kenavnis help? She couldn't blame him for thinking it. But Ribas...the thought of seeing Ribas again, for any reason, shouldn't make her feel so young and fragile. Not now, when so much might happen in the days and weeks to come; although, she had to admit, maybe that was why it did.

Ardinas said, "Maybe I should have listened to Galvo years ago."

Valda started. "Galvo?"

"Oh yes. He wanted Zhinin Ribas to come to Sostavi and serve in the Great House."

Valda had never known that. Ardinas said, "He wasn't the only one, to be sure. The dovne kenavnis here in Sostavi...well, you can understand how the Council felt." Yes, Valda understood. She also knew what she herself would have felt, in those days, if she had known that the Council was trying to bring Ribas here. The rack of hope and fear that would have stretched her; the misery that would have drowned her when he didn't come. Ardinas went on, "Galvo took it on himself to write to him, several times I believe, until finally Zhinin Ribas wrote directly to me. I told Galvo to stop bothering the man and let him do his work in his village."

Valda had never known that Ribas had written to the Tavin. The kind of courage it must have taken for a young zhinin, just starting out, to stand up to a sventin in the Council, to write to the Tavin himself...Valda cut that line of thought short, but not before she saw those blue eyes again. *Stubborn.* Her own voice from more than fifteen years ago echoed in her ears, carrying the laughter only he had been able to coax from her. *Always so stubborn, Ribé.*

Throughout their talk, Ardinas had looked increasingly tired. Now he closed his eyes. "Go and rest," he said. "You've given an old man enough company for one evening."

Valda didn't like to leave him alone, but she knew she should sleep for at least a few hours. "I'll come back in the morning," she said. "Raimaté, Tavin."

Ardinas smiled without opening his eyes. His hands lay quiet on the sheet. "Raimaté, Tavo Balsa."

Valda slipped out of the bedchamber. In the sitting room, she made sure one of Ardinas's two attendants was on duty. Then she left the house and went out into the dark evening.

The dagira who served in the Great House also had houses of their own: the House of the Zhinine, House of the Kunine, and House of the Sventine. The three residences flanked the Great Circle House on Sostavi's main square.

During the day, crowds of people came to this square. Even the fountain at its center, graceful stone curves inset with a rainbow of colored glass, was one of the jewels of Sostavi. The faithful flocked here to worship and petition the dagira for prayers and help.

Countless other visitors only came to admire the beauty around them.

On this clear, still night, Valda had the square to herself. Her talk with Ardinas had left her feeling wrung out, but the solitude let her breathe. She stopped by the fountain to look up at the Great House.

Heart of Sostavi, heart of Namora. After fifteen years of service here, Valda knew every inch of it, inside and out. It was built of gray stone, like all Circle Houses, with a conical wooden roof. Unlike all the others, though, the Great House had windows made of colored glass, showing images of the ocean, the mountains, and Namora's golden flatlands. In daylight, the glass glowed with all the colors of the rainbow and splashed the floor with reflected radiance. Valda felt sure that if ever the Goddess heard Her people at prayer, it happened here in the place that offered Her so much beauty.

A cool breeze, smelling of salt, drifted through the square from the harbor. Tonight the moon was only a sliver, hanging in the west. The stars seemed huge and much nearer, close enough to touch.

Valda knew that soon, the real chill would settle on Namora, as the cold northern winds came in from the ocean. By Tyla, the Quiet month, snow would hold the country still. Valda had spent every Tyla for the past six years helping Ardinas prepare for the four weeks of Akena, the high holy month that commemorated the Goddess's great Sacrifice. Then, together, she and the Tavin had gone through the monthlong celebration of Algima, honoring the fact that after her death as a mortal woman, Kenavi was reborn as the Goddess.

This year, Ardinas would take no part in those preparations. By Tyla, most likely, his soul would have become one again with the world. Valda would go through service after service alone, until the installation of the next Tavin. The Tavin who would have to deal with whatever trouble came out of Lassar and the young ruler who thought his God spoke to him.

Someone touched her arm. Valda jerked out of her thoughts. A polite voice said, "Raimaté, Tavo Balsa. I'm sorry to disturb you."

Sventin Galvo. Valda recognized his voice first, and then made out his white robes, gleaming in the dark. "Raimaté, sventin," she said.

He smiled as naturally as if they were exchanging greetings in the Council chambers, rather than standing alone in the deserted square late at night. He was well past fifty, Valda knew, but age had been kind to him. He was small but strong-built, his back as straight as a young man's, his movements graceful with no hint of stiffness. His thick silver hair swept back from a smooth, high forehead, and his fine features looked as aristocratic as they must have when he was young.

Valda had often considered him handsome, but something in his smile had never sat entirely right with her. It seemed to float on the surface to hide whatever lay underneath.

"You've been visiting the Tavin?" he said.

He knew she had been. "Yes."

Galvo's smile disappeared, a candle blown out at precisely the right moment, leaving his face sober and sympathetic. "It's a difficult duty. You're very kind, Valda, to spend so much time with him."

She kept her voice polite. "I'm glad to do it."

"Of course." Galvo put his hand on her arm again. "You must be tired. I won't keep you long, but I hoped I might have a quick word with you in private."

Valda tried not to let her face show what she felt. She owed Galvo a great deal. When she had first arrived in Sostavi, taking the wild and terrible chance of coming to the capital with no real hope of finding a place at a Circle House, the sventin had taken an immediate interest in her. Valda had gone to a morning Pirdina service in the Great House. For some reason, out of all the people in the House that day, Galvo's quick eyes had fixed on her. She had been wearing her sea-blue zhinin's robes, but she was hardly the only one. She had undoubtedly looked bashful and countrified among the wealthy city congregants and elegantly-robed dagira.

After the service, though, Galvo had made a point of finding and speaking to her. She had been young and confused, overwhelmed by the great city after small Paret in the east, but hungry to find a place here in the capital. Galvo had been remarkably kind, asking about her training and evidently interested in news from the little town she had left. Valda hadn't understood, at the time, why Galvo had recommended her for a place among the Great House's zhinine, or why he had kept his interest in her ever since, shepherding and encouraging her rise through the ranks.

Now, though, she understood better. Galvo didn't perform favors without hope of return.

"Of course," she said. "I'm happy to talk with you."

He took her arm and began to walk slowly around the fountain, as if they were out for a stroll together. "I wanted to tell you," he said, keeping his voice low, "that if the Council chooses to elect me, I will of course ask you to continue to serve as Tavo Balsa."

That didn't surprise her. Like everyone else, he knew that Valda should neither have nor express opinions about the candidates for the Tavinate. He also knew that in reality, she could have a quiet word with her fellow Council members. As the one who had worked so closely with Ardinas for the past six years, her opinions carried weight.

He went on, "Naturally, I couldn't mention this to you where others might hear. No doubt it would concern some of our colleagues, to think I was over-eager to step into a role that isn't mine."

No doubt, indeed, it would "concern" them to hear Galvo offering her a bribe. Valda swallowed her distaste. She tried to remember what Ardinas had said about *promises and insults*: this was simply the way the game was played. "That's very kind, Galvo."

"Everyone knows how well you've filled the role. Frankly, I can't imagine any Tavin could want a better Voice."

And, she thought, it would keep her out of the running in the next election too. She would very likely outlive Galvo, given that she was much younger. Maybe he intended to groom a successor. More likely, Valda decided, he simply thought of her as useful, and he wanted her to be useful to him. And maybe she, and the other Council members, ought to feel thankful that someone with Galvo's long experience should be so eager to step into a role that now held unknown risks.

As she murmured thanks for his compliment, another suspicion darted through her mind. Fifteen years ago, Galvo had pressed Ribas to come to Sostavi, and Ribas had refused. Around the same time, Valda had arrived in Sostavi from Paret. She thought of that conversation with Galvo again, on that long-ago Pirdina. He had asked about her training...and she had talked about the town, and the viduris, and Kunin Dergo, the head of the school.

Beyond question, Galvo had known where Ribas had trained. Valda could believe that he had known, or suspected, that she had known Ribas at the viduris, perhaps been in his class. So suppose that by the time Valda came to Sostavi, Tavin Ardinas had already put a stop to Galvo's "invitations" to Ribas. Had the sventin decided that Valda might be another way to get what he wanted?

Galvo was talking now, saying something about his concern that the election might be a difficult process, that Sventin Lesvin was of course also a worthy candidate with many excellent points. Valda didn't pay much attention.

If Galvo had thought she would be a link to the zhinin in Lida, he had been wrong. Valda hadn't been in touch with Ribas since her arrival here. Galvo had certainly never asked her about him that she could remember. And none of it explained why Galvo had taken notice of her at that one Pirdina service, when he hadn't even known who she was.

Even so, as they finished another slow circuit around the fountain and Galvo wrapped up whatever he had been saying, Valda said, "You know, sventin, Tavin Ardinas told me something interesting tonight. He said that at one time, you were in touch with an old friend of mine."

"Really?"

His face showed nothing but polite interest, but Valda felt certain, to the soles of her feet, that he knew exactly who she meant.

She played along. "A zhinin in Lida village, near the mountains. Ribas Silvaikas. We were in school together."

Carefully measured recognition lit Galvo's face. "Oh, yes, Zhinin Ribas. Certainly. That was quite a while ago."

"Tavin Ardinas said you hoped he would serve here in Sostavi."

"To be sure. I thought Sostavi was by far the best place for someone of his abilities. I must admit I also thought he would be eager for the chance." Another disarming smile, gleaming in the dark. "As it turned out, I was wrong."

Nothing to see or hear there. Somehow, though, Valda couldn't shake the feeling that Galvo had never given up on his idea. Why had he held onto it for so long?

They had arrived in front of the House of the Sventine now. Galvo moved toward the front entrance. "I should let you rest. Thank you for hearing me out, Valda."

"My pleasure."

They parted at the door with a polite goodnight. Galvo went up the stairs to his chambers, on the second floor. One of the House's many quiet-footed attendants met Valda as she went down the first-floor hallway to her own. "Raimaté, Sventin Valdena," he said. "Will you need anything this evening?"

She kept walking. "No, thank you." At her chambers, she let herself in and shut the door securely behind her. Absurd though it was, she felt as if she was running from something.

Galvo wanted to be certain of her help in making him the next Tavin. That came as no surprise. But, beyond a doubt, Galvo also still had something in mind for Ribas. Valda couldn't imagine what, or why, but the certainty was lodged in her now, hard as rock.

She changed into a linen shift and woolen wrap and unwove the red-gold braids she wore neatly coiled at the back of her head. Her hair was her one beauty, as her father hadn't hesitated to tell her when she was a child. His only daughter had never interested him much. He'd been glad to send her to the viduris and have her off his hands.

Unbound, Valda's hair fell to her waist. Individual strands caught the light of the low-burning fire on the hearth and gleamed: polished copper with no trace of silver in it. As she brushed it out, she couldn't help remembering the voice she had tried to forget. *It's beautiful, Valda.* The touch of his fingers as he drew a strand of her hair gently between them. *You know that, don't you?*

She had tried to put all of that away. Now the longing rushed back in, as sharp as if no time had passed at all.

4

THE LASSKA SOLDIER

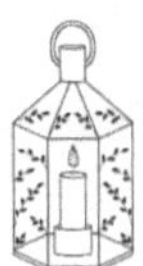

After thirty years of service with Lassar's Imperial Commission of Roads, lifelong soldier Bereg Orlon asked for nothing more than the right to retire. That, and to be allowed to go home.

Bereg came from northern Lassar, the heavily forested Kovik Thysidich region. In Thysidich, the fourteenth of the twenty Kovkya, the Claws of the Bear that made up the Lasska empire, Bereg had grown up with the spicy scent of machia sap and the chill of long winters in his blood. As a boy, he'd helped his father, a master wood-cutter, harvest machia trees to ship to Kovik Tyi, the Third Claw. Tyi's skilled carpenters had turned the silvery, dark-grained planks and rounds into beautiful furniture that Bereg's family could never have afforded to buy, but Bereg had been proud to have a small part in making it. Most of all, he had loved the hours he spent outside with his father, the two of them working in silent rhythm, running the great double-handled saw back and forth along rich cuts of wood.

Bereg would have been happy to spend his life as a woodcutter, but everyone knew that the army offered the best living. Most of the wealth of Lassar's forests and farms, its granaries and stockyards, went to the capital city Cheremay, to feed the impera's forces. The army oversaw everything, from the security of Lassar's coasts and the border with the western countries, to the roads and the postal service, to the empire's schools, to the personal safety of the impera himself. Lassar couldn't function without the great regiments of graycoats. Serving in the army, in any capacity, was the proudest career for any young Lasska. So although Bereg didn't want to leave the forests of Thysidich, he listened when his father told him to make a better life for himself.

When he joined the army, he reported to Cheremay, as all new soldiers did. Since then, he had spent most of his career in the middle-south regions: Kovik Adin, the First Claw, and Kovkya Tsva and Syetch, the Second and Ninth. Those regions had few trees, and the temperature never went below middling-cool, but they offered plenty of work building and maintaining the great system of well-paved, well-designed roads that linked the twenty Claws together. If Cheremay, where the impera sat on the bear-headed throne, was the heart of Lassar, the roads were its lifeblood.

Bereg knew he was lucky to serve on the Road Commission. He got good pay, and he got to work outdoors the way he liked. In fact, he'd turned down more than one offer of promotion, which at best, would have taken him off the road crew and sat him on a horse as an overseer, and at worst, would have stuck him in an office drawing maps. He had no reason to complain about any aspect of his job. Still, when a man had grandchildren, and when his hair had been gray for so long that most people had forgotten its original color, surely he could think about putting his feet up and slowing the pace of the time that moved past him.

Bereg thought he'd earned the right to go back to his forests for good, instead of catch-as-catch-can visits of a few weeks or a month. Also, though he didn't admit this out loud to anyone, when it got to be a choice between retiring and serving under an impera more than young enough to be your son, you might be better off deciding your working days were over.

So he planned to retire. But this got upended during the summer when his third grandchild was born, after Impera Mangevar had gone to his sickbed and the country braced itself to hear that the old ruler's eldest son, Shurik, was going to take up the mantle.

~

The rest of the country's eyes were on Cheremay, their prayers going up for the impera who was dying and the new impera who would take his father's place. Meanwhile, in Thysidich, another life slipped away.

Bereg's son-in-law, Torvar, died of fever at the end of the summer. Torvar and Ania, Bereg's daughter, had three children. The youngest was only a month old.

Bereg couldn't be with his daughter at either her child's birth or her husband's death. The Road Commission had sent him to Adin, the First Claw, to repair the roads in and around Cheremay. Only the best Road Commission soldiers, including Bereg, were worthy to do that work. He appreciated the honor, but his wife's and daughter's letters from home made red-hot lines across his heart.

From Ania: *Mother says I must move home, Father, but I cannot put such a burden on you.* Her precise words and clear schoolroom-taught handwriting papered over what Bereg knew was a bottomless pit of pain. She and Torvar had loved each other since they were children building dolls' houses out of twigs. *You have earned your retirement. I will find work. The children and I will be all right.*

From Bereg's wife Nela: *She can't care for those young ones alone.* Nela's handwriting was less steady, showing more of what she had gone through as she nursed her son-in-law, trying and failing to save him. *Her little ones need her and she's not strong enough to work. Tell her that, Bereg. She'll listen to you.*

Bereg wanted to tell Ania not to worry, that her old father was still more than strong enough to work and care for her and her children. He wanted to tell her that he didn't care about retirement; he only wanted her to come back to the house she had made bright during her own childhood, so she could look after her young ones, cook with her mother, and learn to laugh again.

Faced with pen and paper, the words always dried up inside him. How could lines and dots of ink on a page tell his girl how much he loved her and hurt for her grief? Helpless, he wrote, *Daughter, you will do as your mother tells you. I will continue to work.* She would listen, as Nela said, because he was her father.

He did at least put in for a transfer back to Thysidich. Those roads needed attention too. The high commander in Cheremay approved his application. In mid-autumn, once the main work in Adin was finished, Bereg would join a lesser team working near his own village. He would be able to live at home with his family.

Autumn came. Bereg counted the time until he would leave Adin. Three weeks. Two weeks. One.

The transfer was five days away, and Bereg had begun packing his bags to prepare for the long journey north, trying not to let his workmates see how he could already taste the air of the machia forests, when he got a notice at his team's work camp in Adin. It came directly from the palace, carrying young Impera Shurik's own seal. Bereg and a handful of the other most senior and experienced soldiers on the team had to report to the palace in two days' time.

No one knew what the orders were about. Two days barely gave enough time to make the journey from the southern border of Adin, where the team was camped, to Cheremay. Bereg and the others made it in all haste and arrived in the great city on the morning of the third day.

There they met up with a similar contingent from the border of Kovkya Adin and Tyi, and another from the border with Tsva. All of them had gotten the same orders, to report at once to the palace. All of them, like Bereg, were career soldiers who had served for decades in various branches of the military. The youngest, a woman from Tyi, was over forty years old. One of the officers, a man from northern Adin, joked, "What does the impera want with us fogeys?"

Bereg didn't know. He tried not to show how uneasy the orders made him. As the impera's servant, he shouldn't worry about how this business, whatever it was, might affect his transfer, but he couldn't help it. For too long now, he'd let himself believe that he would soon put his arms around his daughter and help her carry her grief.

At the palace, one of Impera Shurik's personal guard met the contingent outside. "The Impera wishes you to breakfast in the barracks," the young woman told them. "Then join him in the Hall of the Bear when you have rested and eaten."

Bereg had never seen the inside of the palace. The Hall of the Bear was the throne room where the impera held audiences. In spite of everything, Bereg felt a thrill of pride that he was actually going to see the legendary throne where every impera since Curin had sat. He told himself that in a couple of weeks, as soon as he made the journey home, he would be able to tell Nela and Ania all about it.

In the great barracks near the palace, any soldier wearing the gray coat and army insignia was welcome to take a meal. You only had to find a seat at one of the long tables that filled each of five mess halls. Breakfast was thick fresh bread with butter and honey, fruit brought all the way from the rich plains of Kovkya Tsvavyest and Votsimich, and even cuts of broiled pork. Civilian Lasska only ate meat a couple of times a week and never for breakfast.

Younger soldiers were trained to give place to older ones and officers. Several foot soldiers who looked barely out of puberty quickly picked up their plates and cleared the end of a table for Bereg and the other "fogeys." While they ate, the woman from Tyi said, "If this is our last meal, it's a good one."

Her strong-featured face didn't relax into a smile, but Bereg and a couple of others laughed. A man even older than Bereg, who served on the School Commission in Adin, said, "You may not be wrong. Impera Shurik may want to clear out the dead wood to let the younger trees in."

"Come on now," another man said. He was a few years younger than Bereg and had told them he worked with the Central Office of the Post. "I've never heard of an impera executing officers for being old."

The school commissioner said, "Who knows what this new one will do?"

"Careful," the woman from Tyi said. "How do you know any of us aren't Eyes?"

The group called the Eyes of the Impera was rumored to be the most elite force in the army. It was so secret that neither Bereg, nor anyone he had ever worked with, seemed to know for certain whether it existed at all.

The post officer leaned past the school commissioner to look the woman from Tyi in the face. "Are you one of them?"

Bereg couldn't help laughing again, though the Eyes, if they weren't a rumor, certainly weren't a joking matter. Lasska military scuttlebutt said that members of the elite force could be anywhere, at any time. They were trained to watch for anything that carried even the faintest whiff of disloyalty to the impera. In the face of their testimony, rumor said that an honest man's life wasn't worth a dead autumn leaf.

The woman said, "For all you know, I might be one of them. I might have been ordered to join this group to watch you."

Bereg didn't know what branch of the service she worked in. She hadn't volunteered the information, and no Lasska soldier asked unnecessary questions. Even so, Bereg didn't honestly think she was an Eye, but he did wonder where her apparent sourness came from. Older soldiers didn't have the fresh-faced eagerness of new recruits, but they mostly liked the life well enough.

He drank a swallow of the strong smoky tea the army ran on and set his thick ceramic mug down by his plate. "Well," he said, "if Impera Shurik would like to give my job here in Adin to a younger man, he's welcome to it. I'm leaving for Thysidich in a few days." Saying out loud might make it true.

The school commissioner wanted to know why anyone would leave bustling, cosmopolitan Adin for frosty tree-infested Thysidich. Bereg put up a spirited defense that led to talk about the Kovkya each of them came from. All of them joined in except the woman from Tyi, who sat silent, picking at the last of her pork.

After breakfast, they walked back to the palace. Cheremay, Bereg had always thought, was a remarkably gray city, especially here at its center. Wide gray flagstones paved the square. The great barracks were gray stone, likewise the Temple of Mesha whose tower, with its capping ring of huge teeth, scraped the sky. On a gloomy day in winter, or during the endless wet spring when you wondered if the sun would ever come out again, the air itself seemed gray, as if sky and ground and buildings bled together into a haze.

This morning, though, the sky had no clouds in it. Fine autumn sunlight warmed the flagstones and softened the spires on the Temple. Bereg tried to enjoy the warmth. He tried to believe that soon, in a couple of weeks, he would be back home.

Of course, he told himself, he'd have to brace himself for the cold in Thysidich. Even on summer nights, you had to wear a coat, and he would be home just in time for winter, when you didn't dare go outside without wrapping a scarf around your face and hiding your hands in the heaviest gloves you could find. But the air would clear and spicy, without the heaviness of city air that too many people breathed. Sunlight would make the snow glitter and the sky would look like pale blue glass. And inside his warm house, there would be fires, and the rich scents of butter and dried fruit from the *tortye* Nela would make. Bereg would sit by the hearth every evening, when his work was done, with a grandchild in his lap and his daughter across from him. Ania's eyes would smile again. Bereg held onto that picture of his family, so tightly he could almost feel the warm weight of the baby against his chest, as the impera's guard escorted him and the others into the palace.

The Palace of the Impera made no display. Impera Curin had ordered it built conspicuously smaller than both the Temple of the

God and the great barracks nearby, to remind all imperi that they served the God and owed their position to the military. The walls were plain gray stone, set with small square windows. The building's only ornament was the flag that flew above the heavy wooden doors. The brown head of Mesha, sharp-toothed and angry-eyed, snarled against a bright white background.

Inside, no tapestries decorated the entrance hall. No carpet softened the chill of the stone floor. Lasska imperi refused even to keep the palace any warmer than necessary. Fires were lit when the first snow fell; until then, the bare walls soaked up the cold.

The guard led Bereg's group into the long, narrow Hall of the Bear. Here the impera held audiences, listened to petitions, and gave out judgment in those cases that required the personal verdict of the Servant of Mesha. As much of an honor as it was to enter this room, Bereg couldn't help noticing the still deeper chill of it, as if its bare empty length held onto all the cold air of all the winters since Impera Curin's day. As if, Bereg thought, all the nerves of every petitioner who had shivered in front of the impera had soaked into the stone.

This room had no ornaments either, except one. At the center of the raised dais at the far end of the room stood the great luxury of the palace: the peerless Lasska throne.

The small high-set windows above the dais let in bands of sunlight. They fell across the stone and across the gleaming, silvery-pale throne, with its unmistakable rich dark grain.

Machia wood. But no single tree that Bereg had ever seen, or that his father had ever cut, would have been broad enough for Curin's carpenters to carve out this throne in a single piece. The curved back, the wide seat, the massive arms and legs: the throne looked fit to hold a giant. The carpenters must have joined separate cuts of wood together, but as closely as he peered, Bereg could see no sign of the splices. The grain aligned perfectly. Into the back of the throne, directly above the place where the impera's own head would rest as he sat, an artist had carved a life-sized head of a bear.

Bereg wished he knew that artist's name. No Lasska, except of course for the impera, could leave his or her name on history. You gave your work to the God and the empire. Bereg would never question the rightness of that, but here, he felt a twinge of regret that the woodworker who had done this couldn't share its immortality.

The carving had such fine detail that Bereg could make out the texture of the bear's fur. If he could have touched it, he would almost have expected it to feel rough and warm under his fingers. This bear didn't look like the flag of Mesha outside: no gaping, hungry mouth, or narrowed, vengeful eyes. This bear looked quietly out into the room, its expression watchful and, Bereg thought, somehow sad. Jagged crisscrossing lines on its muzzle – the grain of the wood – looked like a pattern of old scars. Bereg found himself imagining a wound: an enemy knife, say, laying the hide open and cutting into the exposed flesh. This was no young, hungry warrior. This was an old survivor who knew about battles and pain.

A door behind the dais opened. A guard's flat voice announced, "The most noble Servant of Mesha, his Highness Impera Shurik."

Bereg's joints protested as he quickly knelt beside the other soldiers and lowered his head. He felt the cold stone through the fabric of his pants.

"Soldiers of Lassar. I greet you in the Name of the God."

The voice sounded oddly distant, as if, Bereg thought, someone had interrupted its owner in the middle of a dream, and he was still pulling his thoughts together out of some other place. That voice didn't match the sharp, authoritative footsteps that came across the dais and stopped in front of the throne.

The formal greeting gave the group permission to look up. Bereg did so, careful not to look the new impera directly in the eye.

Bereg had never met Impera Mangevar, but he had seen him at a distance, when Mangevar had greeted his subjects from the front doors of the palace. The old impera had looked no taller than Bereg himself, but he had been broad in the shoulder, barrel-chested, as if he, too, had spent his youth outside, doing hard work with his hands.

At first glance, Bereg wouldn't have taken Shurik for Mangevar's son. The young impera was tall and slim-built. His hands were slender and smooth, his wrists, laid bare by the rolled-up cuffs of his shirt, delicate-looking. Bereg couldn't help thinking that those hands had never dug earth or laid stone. And Shurik favored fine clothes: his shirt was dark green silk, his pants linen. His leather vest and boots looked expensively tooled. And his face – Bereg glanced quickly at it and away – looked pale, as if the young impera had never spent time outside the palace walls. A shock of dark hair fell into his eyes, which looked pale too, like shallow water.

You could not think things like *He's too young*. You did not, even in the privacy of your own head, wonder how someone who wore silk and linen and boots without so much as a scuff on them could command the greatest army the world had ever seen.

Shurik's thin hand moved, brushing the hair away from his face. "You may stand," he said.

His voice still had that oddly distant sound, but his movements – his footsteps, his hand – were quick and impatient. Bereg scrambled to his feet with the others. His knees and hips protested again.

Shurik said, "I offer you welcome and thank you for your attendance on me."

Correct words. Bereg couldn't imagine what soldier would risk his life by refusing an impera's summons. The young man stood erect, shoulders back, hands at his sides, as if he was pressing his back to a wall. Bereg risked another look at Shurik's face. He'd seen that hectic, too-bright look in the eyes of a man with fever.

A boy. He's a boy whose father is dead.

Shurik said, "I know all of your names, of course, but I haven't the pleasure of knowing which name belongs to which of you. Introduce yourselves." Another quick motion of the hand, this time pointing at Bereg in his place at the end of the line. "You start."

Bereg swallowed. Boy or not, he had never spoken directly to an impera before.

"Bereg Orlon, Impera." He bowed.

"Of course. Silde Orlon." The title gave Bereg his due rank as a senior soldier. "You are the one who applied to transfer to Kovik Thysidich, are you not?"

Shurik's voice sounded sharper now, more alert. Bereg felt cold seeping up from the floor, through the soles of his shoes and up into his body.

"Yes, Impera. I am due to go home in a few days."

"That won't be possible now, Silde. Your new orders will require you to remain here in Adin."

Bereg knew his face must show nothing. Especially, he must not let the impera see how his heart seemed to have dropped to the floor, leaving an empty space in his chest.

"Of course, Impera," he said.

Shurik went on down the line. Bereg barely heard the other officers give their names. He could only picture his daughter's eyes, holding all the hurt in the world.

He came back to himself when Shurik spoke again. The impera said, "I rely on all of you as experienced soldiers and faithful servants of my father." The words sounded crisp and firm. "Your new orders are of a sensitive and particular nature. That is why I wish to give them to you myself."

Bereg knew he should care about his orders. Shurik's voice went on, the words beating against Bereg's ears now like hailstones rattling on a roof. "First, I would like to know which of you have had direct experience of the tribal peoples we call *strenyi*. I believe their name for themselves, in their tongue, is Pala Vaia."

Bereg wondered vaguely why the impera wanted to know about the strenyi: the strangers, as their name meant in Lasska. He had never seen any, but everyone knew they were wanderers, uncivilized heathens who thought the sun and moon were gods. They contributed nothing to the empire.

The woman from Tyi, Fisa Vasem, said, "I once saw some of them, Impera."

Shurik turned to her. Bereg saw an odd look in the young man's face: intent, even hungry. "Tell us what you saw."

The woman kept her eyes on the floor when she answered, as was proper. "A tribe came to my village several years ago." She spoke with no particular expression, reciting facts. "One of their men bought a chair in a carpentry shop. They left after a little while."

"How many were there?"

"Half a dozen or so. I don't know if it was the whole tribe or if only some of them came into the village."

"Did any of them speak to you?"

"No. The man must have talked to the carpenter, but I didn't hear. I was outside in the road. The rest of them stayed outside the shop and kept to themselves."

"Tell us what they looked like, how they were dressed." Shurik's voice sounded sharper still, Bereg thought. Like the blade of a shovel biting into the ground, turning the soil to find something hidden.

"They had dark skin and long hair, men and women both." Fisa Vasem's voice had no more expression in it than before. "They were built small, but they looked strong and wiry. Their clothes..." She paused, gathering the memory. "They wore close-fitting leather breeches and bright-colored shirts. Some of them had bright yarn in their hair. All the ones I saw were grown. No children." She added as an afterthought, "The man who bought the chair wore a yellow shirt."

Bereg saw Shurik's face flush like a boy who'd won a prize. The shovel had turned up what it was hunting for. But why, he wondered, did any of this matter?

Shurik said, "The man in the yellow shirt would have been their leader. Only the leaders can wear yellow. Did you see any of them wearing white?"

"I don't remember, Impera."

Shurik waved that away. "It doesn't matter." The flush in his cheeks seemed to deepen. "All of this confirms what I have read. It will help us. Thank you, Silde Vasem."

She bowed without speaking. Shurik's eyes went up and down

the line of soldiers. When they reached Bereg, he quickly looked away, to avoid that unsettling brightness.

"I will now explain your orders," Shurik said. "As all of you know, my honored father served Lassar well. I revere his memory, but it is not for me to grieve his death." Bereg caught the faintest shiver in the word "death." *You do grieve.* "The Great God Mesha requires a task of me," Shurik said, "and of all of you. He has told me what we must do."

Bereg couldn't help glancing up at that. *Told me.* Did Shurik mean he had heard the voice of the God?

Shurik continued, "The strenyi, the 'First and Lost People' as they call themselves, believe many wrong things. They believe, for instance, that they have more of a right to this land than the Lasska do, because their stories tell them they were here first. And they believe that the sun, the moon, and the winds are gods themselves, rather than mindless forces that answer to Lord Mesha, as all right-minded people know they must."

His voice had a new edge in it now. He said, "It is my firm knowledge that Lord Mesha does not wish to have these strangers, these heretics, here among his faithful people. So it will now be my duty, as your impera, to rid us all of this danger."

Bereg didn't understand. How could the strenyi be a danger to him, when he'd never seen them?

Someone said, "My lord Impera. Forgive my intrusion, but do you mean to say that the God has spoken to you?"

Fisa Vasem, again. Her voice, quiet as it was, hit Bereg like the lash of a whip. How did she dare interrupt when the impera was speaking? And *do you mean to say,* as if she questioned Shurik's intentions.

But Shurik didn't look at all angry. When he smiled, pride lit his face like a lamp in a window.

"Yes. I have been honored to hear the will of the God."

Impera Curin, long ago, had spoken to Lord Mesha, and the God had answered him. Mesha Himself had carried Curin's armies to victory in the battles to unify the empire. Everyone knew that history. Everyone also knew that Mesha had spoken to no other ruler since.

But this young impera believed he had heard the God's voice. Bereg saw that he believed it absolutely. The feverish, brittle look had disappeared from Shurik's face. Conviction made him look stronger, like a leader of armies.

"All of you here today," Shurik said, "along with others of my most experienced soldiers in other Kovkya, will lead your junior soldiers in a particular task. Throughout Lassar, you are to find the places where the strenyi make their winter camps."

During the winter, he went on to explain, the strenyi made semi-permanent camps, living in the same place for weeks at a time. They preferred the southern plains, where the bitterest winter weather did not come, but he wanted an exhaustive search made throughout Lassar.

"Your Thysidich will also be searched, Silde Orlon." The pale blue eyes came back to Bereg. "But I cannot ask you to lead that detachment. I want the best of my officers to go south."

Perhaps the God had spoken to Shurik. Bereg had no right to doubt it. Maybe it was the will of Mesha Himself that Bereg shouldn't go home.

"Of course, Impera," he said. His fingers ached as he let his regret go.

Shurik explained that he had taken all of the leaders of the searching detachments from non-fighting branches of the army. "I want strong, experienced leaders," he said, "who use their minds instead of force. You will have small contingents of fighting soldiers under your commands, but during the initial search, I want no violence."

The initial search would gather information. Each detachment would have a designated area to scout. The soldiers must locate all strenyi camps within a Kovik, map them, and report back to the governor of that Kovik. The reports must also include all possible information on the size of each camp, approximate numbers of adults, children, and the elderly that the camp contained, and anything the scouts might consider relevant about the condition of the people they saw.

"For example," Shurik said, "do they seem healthy? Is there hunger in the camp, or illness?" He also told them to look particularly for the yellow-shirted leaders, and for women wearing white. "These women are of crucial importance to the strenyi," Shurik said. "The tribes believe that they are some kind of witch, that their dreams can tell the future. Tribal leaders base all their decisions on what these women tell them." Bereg heard the curl of disgust in Shurik's voice. "The leaders and the witch-women are the most valuable people in each tribe. It's crucial that we know where and how many they are."

Bereg listened, from a numb place on the far side of pain, as Shurik explained that the search detachments must gather as much information as they could in order to minimize danger to Lasska soldiers and civilians, if any lived near the strenyi camps. "Ideally, I want no Lasska casualties." Once the detachments had gathered all the information they could, the second phase of operations would begin.

Based on what the searchers learned, Shurik and the Kovkya governors would send out fighting forces large enough to deal with each of the camps. Children younger than five years old were to be spared. "At that age, they can be adopted by Lasska families and raised as faithful servants to the God. The strenyi false beliefs and lies will be trained out of them. We should not squander their lives." The fighting forces would have to make their best guesses as to which children were young enough to spare. The search detachments could help by getting rough counts. All other strenyi were to be, as Shurik said, "exterminated," beginning with the yellow-shirted leaders and white-shirted witch-women.

Bereg took all this in without blinking. You didn't question the impera's orders. Especially not if they might have come from the God Himself.

Then another voice reached him. "Forgive me, Impera. May I be certain I understand?"

Fisa Vasem, again. Shurik said, "Of course."

"So we," she said, "your senior servants, are to lead groups of searchers to collect information on the strenyi camps. Your Lordship will then send groups of fighting forces, each assembled according to what we learn about the camps. Those forces will kill all of the people in each camp except the youngest children, who will be taken captive?"

Her voice held no more emotion in it than before, but her words cut through Bereg's numbness like ice touching bare skin. *Kill. Captive.* Shurik hadn't said that.

"That is direct and accurate, Silde Vasem," Shurik said. "We must remember that the strenyi's continued presence in Lassar is an affront to Lord Mesha Himself. The God has instructed me that we must erase what we can't repair, and we cannot hope to change the minds of strenyi men and women who have walked in wrong ways all their lives. But second, and no less important, we must save the children who can learn the right ways and serve Lord Mesha. He wants no less."

Silde Vasem said nothing else. Shurik added, "I also assure you all, your work in this will be finished as soon as your detachments submit their reports. You will have served me and Lord Mesha nobly, and I will reward you well."

Reward you well. Bereg tried to tamp it down, but he couldn't squash the tendril of hope that woke up in him. As if Shurik had sensed it, the impera turned to him.

"For example, Silde Orlon." His smile was full of understanding. "If you serve me well in this, as I am certain you will, it will be my pleasure to send you home in the spring with all the compensation a soldier of your stature deserves. I wish you to enjoy your retirement with your family."

For a moment Bereg thought his knees would buckle. Not only go home, but to be granted his retirement and enough money to be comfortable. He saw his daughter's face as he came through the door, felt his wife's arms around him. He shut his eyes to hold the tears back and bowed so low his back ached.

"You are gracious, my lord Impera."

He barely heard Shurik explain that he and the other soldiers would stay in Cheremay for a few days, while the search detachments were organized, and then begin the southward sweep through Kovkya Tsvavyest and Syetich. As long as Bereg followed his orders, he would go home. He could follow orders. He'd done it all his life.

"May the God in His Power walk with you."

The formal blessing. Bereg repeated the response with the others: "And with you, Impera." Then, somehow, they were out of the palace in the warm daylight. Bereg felt as if he had been underground for hours. The sun dazzled his eyes.

He would go straight to the great barracks, find the quarters assigned to him, and write to Nela and Ania. He would tell them everything Shurik had said about the reward he would have as long as he did this one last task. They'd only have to wait for him until spring. The impera knew exactly what Bereg needed and wanted, as clearly as if he were inside Bereg's head.

For an instant, barely a breath, it made Bereg uneasy. He hadn't even applied for retirement before Ania's husband died. Shurik had known so much about him...

But as young as Shurik was, he was wise enough to guess that a man of Bereg's age might want some rest in his later years. An impera should know such things. Bereg shook off his thoughts and started toward the barracks.

Someone gripped his arm. "Silde Orlon."

Bereg glanced around. It was Silde Vasem.

The rest of the group had gone off in different directions, pairs and threesomes chatting together, moving toward the barracks or the Temple or the streets that went off the square. Bereg realized that he didn't particularly want to be alone with this woman. Her gray eyes were dark and unfriendly, her mouth set in a tight line. Loose strands of her silvery-dark hair straggled across her face in the breeze.

You had to be polite to a fellow soldier. "Yes?" he said.

Her grip on his arm tightened. Her eyes moved over his face as if she was looking for something. She had to be at least ten years his junior, but something about her expression suggested that she carried anger much older than her age. For a heartbeat or two, he wondered if she really was an Eye, if she had asked those questions in front of Shurik to test her fellow soldiers, and if by some impossible chance she had something on Bereg now...though he couldn't imagine what.

Then she said, her voice so low he had to lean forward to hear it, "You seem like a decent man." Her grip was so tight it hurt. "Are you going to do what he said?"

It took him a moment to understand what she meant. His mind refused to accept it. Who would dare to disobey the impera's orders?

She must have read his answer in his face. "Silde Orlon." Her voice made him think of a finger braced on the trigger of a vindula, a Lasska rifle, ready to pull. "He told us to kill men and women who haven't harmed him or us. He told us to kidnap their children."

Bereg swallowed. Her fingers dug into the gray fabric of his coat. It was treason to argue with or challenge any order of the impera's: Bereg knew that, knew he could bring punishment down on this woman here and now, but as he looked into her face, something held him back.

Kill. Captive. Kidnap.

You could not question orders. He said, "We're only leading the search parties."

She laughed, a noise of raw disgust and rage. "You heard what he'll do with the information we give him."

Maybe she was an Eye after all. Maybe she was testing him. Bereg clung to the idea, though his gut told him it wasn't true, because he didn't want – with all his strength, he didn't want – to hear what she was telling him.

He said, "The Lord Mesha..."

"The Lord Mesha has nothing to do with this." Blatant heresy. "This is Shurik's decision. I know he thinks he bought you, but you could make a different choice."

Bought him. Ice slid down into Bereg's stomach. He should not listen to this. He should pull his arm free and walk away.

"Ask your conscience, Silde Orlon, if you still have one. Ask it what happens to children who see their parents murdered."

Her angry stare drilled into him. Then she let go of his arm, turned on her heel, and disappeared into a knot of people moving across the square.

5

KHARI

The day after the tribe's council around the fire, when Khari heard her mother-in-truth's dream that meant the end of the Vaia tribes, she woke up with a light in her mind.

The man in her dream was no one she knew or had ever seen. She was sure about that. His pale skin might mean he was Lasska. He had lines at the corners of his eyes and silver in his hair that suggested age, but he didn't have the shrunken, fragile look many elderly people did. His eyes were the most striking thing about him. Some Lasska had blue eyes, she knew, but they tended to look pale and faded, like dye with too much water in it. This man's eyes had the brilliance of the ocean in summer.

Khari woke up with the man's face as clear in her mind as if she had just spent all night talking to him. The dream showed her a place, too: a perfectly round stone building, not like the square houses Lasska built or the big boxes they put up to their God. Khari woke up buoyed with certainty. The dream meant something important. She would find it.

By the time she got up and dressed, though, and mixed the aniseed-flavored dough for breakfast flatcakes, that certainty had drained out of her. She hadn't seen her mother-in-truth's dream about Shurik and his fighting men, the most important and terrible dream any Lamp-Carrier had ever had. How could Khari think her dreams were worth anything? Her imagination had probably invented some nonsense.

"What is it, child?"

Vatiri was sitting on her pallet, mending a tear in the sleeve of one of her blouses. Khari hadn't even felt the older woman's eyes on her.

She shaped the two flatcakes and laid them on the rack over the small morning fire before she answered. "Nothing, Amma."

She couldn't talk about the dream. Not in daylight, while children ran and shouted outside, and mothers called their families in for breakfast, and horses whickered for their fodder. The tribe was real and alive, and so was the terrible thing Vatiri had seen. Khari's dream felt childish and stupid.

Vatiri said, "Not nothing." Her needle moved steadily through the fabric, in and out. "I know you better than that."

The fresh morning air and sweet scent of the baking cakes filled the tent. How many more mornings like this would they have? Khari still couldn't believe the tribe's days were ending. How could they, when the trees were starting to show their autumn colors, and the air had a taste of frost in it, and soon it would be winter, with the quiet pattern of meat-curing and sewing, stories and songs by evening fires, that she'd loved all her life?

She said, "I had a dream last night."

Vatiri looked up. Khari saw surprise in her face. "I didn't."

The flatcakes had toasted enough on one side. Khari turned them over with a long wooden fork. "I thought it was a pathdream, but now I don't know. I don't see how it could help us."

Vatiri set the blouse down. "Tell me what you dreamed."

Khari made herself describe the man. It sounded even sillier out loud: *a man with blue eyes, no one we know.* Vatiri didn't say a word to question or challenge. By then, the flatcakes were ready, so Khari put them on earthenware plates and gave one to Vatiri. She sat cross-legged on the floor by the older woman's pallet. "I saw a building, too," she said. She might as well tell all of it. "A round stone building with a cone for a roof."

Vatiri took a bite of her bread and chewed thoughtfully. "Interesting," she said. Her face had the intent, searching focus Khari had seen many times when she wove meaning from dreams. As if Khari's absurd dream might actually matter.

Khari pushed down the thin ray of hope that woke up inside her. She made herself swallow a bite of flatcake. "I don't see how it could mean anything."

Vatiri put her empty plate aside. Her eyes rested on the open tent flap, but Khari knew she wasn't looking at it. "The round building," she said. "I think that means Namora."

Namora? Khari knew the other country existed, but she had never heard of anyone who had actually crossed Lassar's western mountains and seen it. "Why?" she said.

"They build round temples to their goddess," Vatiri said. "Or at one time they did. It might only be a story now."

Khari had never heard of this. "How do you know?"

Now Vatiri smiled. "I haven't told you enough old stories, have I? We'll have to see about that. When I was a girl, my amma told me a couple of stories about the people to the west. She said they had a woman they called a goddess. She had died, this woman, but her people built round houses to honor her."

Khari knew the Vaia had stories as old as the Powers themselves. She couldn't help wondering why they had stories about a country they had never seen. And how could an ordinary woman be a goddess, especially if she had died?

Vatiri said, "You had the dream even though you'd never heard of the Namoran temples. It must be a pathdream."

Khari bit down on her hope again. "The man, though. What does he mean?"

Vatiri didn't hesitate. "He must be Namoran."

Khari felt more confused than ever. "I don't understand, Amma. What is the dream telling us to do?"

Vatiri took a swallow of tea. Her calm expression didn't change. "The only answer I can see is that we're supposed to go to Namora and find him."

Shock made Khari's hands shake. She set her plate down before she could drop it. Vatiri went on, "I think your dream is the answer to mine. I think it says that this man can help us."

Khari didn't dare believe it. That hope was so huge, if she let it in, it would crack her open. "We don't know who he is," she said, trying to keep her voice steady. "We don't know how to find him."

Namora. Uncounted miles away on the other side of the mountains. And if Vatiri's dream was right – and she had never been wrong – Shurik's fighting men would be coming after the tribe any day. They were supposed to get across the mountains while they were running from the Lasska army? Khari said, "Amma, it can't be right." She let the hope go before it could hurt. "If the man meant anything, you'd have dreamed about him too." Vatiri's dreams would never miss such a thing.

Her mother-in-truth smiled. Somehow it had no sadness in it. "We all get older, child. You know you'll replace me one day. Maybe your eyes are already better than mine."

A different kind of ache squeezed Khari's chest. "Amma." Today of all days, she wasn't going to think about a time when the tribe wouldn't have Vatiri anymore. "I don't want..."

Vatiri touched her cheek, gently cutting her off. "We need to tell the Lodestone what you saw."

From the outside, Pradesh's tent looked like all the others, the same undyed wool neatly draped and pinned over sturdy hardwood rods. Inside, though, he had covered the bare earth with a fine woven Lasska rug, deep red with a rich brown border. The machia wood chair stood in the rug's exact center. Normally any visitor coming to speak to the Lodestone would find him seated in his chair like a Lasska impera on his throne.

This morning, Khari and Vatiri found the chair empty. The Lodestone sat cross-legged on the floor with Radavan and Rahul. All three of them had mugs of tea in their hands and looked ashy-faced, as if they hadn't slept.

Pradesh's yellow shirt was rumpled and the lines at the corners of his mouth stood out dark, but he greeted the two women courteously. "Lamp-Carriers. What do you have to tell us?"

Khari's estimation of him went up a notch. After last night, he was dealing with a nightmare no other Lodestone had imagined, and he seemed to be bearing it bravely.

Vatiri sat down by the cooking fire and motioned Khari down next to her. "Khari had a pathdream last night," she said. "I believe it's the answer to mine."

Radavan leaned forward. Khari saw the hope in his worn face. She knew he was thinking about Dahila and the children; she'd thought about them all the time too, especially the unborn one in her sister's belly.

Vatiri described the dream. Khari knew her mother-in-truth was protecting her, giving the weight of her belief to what Khari had seen. The three men looked confused. Pradesh quickly turned impatient.

"How could we find this man, even if we knew who he was? One person out of everyone in Namora, a place we've never seen?"

Vatiri said, "I think the dream is telling us that if we go to Namora, we *will* find him. Khari saw what he looks like so that she'll know him."

Rahul said, "And he's going to help us? How?"

All the eyes went to Khari. "I don't know," she admitted. She forced herself not to twist her fingers together in her lap like a child. "I only saw his face."

Pradesh set his empty mug down hard on the rug. Anger etched his broad face. "It's impossible. We can't go chasing across the mountains, even if we could get that far, hoping we'll find one person out of the Powers only know how many thousands. One person who can do what, exactly?"

Vatiri said, "Lodestone, Namora is much smaller than Lassar."

"Meaning that we could comb the whole country? Do you hear how foolish that sounds?"

Khari knew he was right. Even so, a thread of anger ran up her spine. If Vatiri had had the dream, would Pradesh have called it foolish?

Radavan said, "Forgive me, Lodestone, but what choice do we have? If my sister's dream is showing us an answer, we have to trust it." His voice stayed quiet, but he looked older this morning than Khari had ever seen him. In the deep circles under his eyes, she saw his terror for his family. "*I* have to trust it," he said.

Rahul agreed. "We can't see anything else to do, Lodestone." He, too, looked worn-down but calm. If Khari hadn't known he was only two years older than she was, she would have thought he was older than hotheaded Handan. He said, "The only other way is to try to fight Shurik's soldiers. We know we don't have the strength."

Pradesh looked cornered. "I want to believe this dream. But..."

"I'm too young." Khari said it before he could. "Inexperienced." The words burned in her mouth.

Vatiri said, "Lodestone, you know a Lamp-Carrier's age doesn't matter. I trust Khari's eyes."

"But what are we supposed to do?" Pradesh demanded. "Try to get the whole tribe across the mountains? What about the other tribes?"

Radavan answered immediately. "If we can find safety on the other side of the mountains, then yes. We have to get as many people there as we can."

Rahul shook his head. "Khari's dream didn't say that. It said to find this man. I think we should send a smaller group, strong riders who could travel fast, to look for him."

Pradesh turned to Khari. "What do you think, Lamp-Carrier?"

Khari swallowed. He was testing her, forcing her to stand up for her dream when she knew he didn't believe it. How could she know what to do? The Lodestone had to decide how to act on a pathdream.

She glanced at Vatiri. The older woman said nothing, but her fingers moved to the sleeve of her own white blouse and rested there. Khari heard what she didn't say aloud. *Lamp-Carrier.*

She thought as hard and fast as she could. Yes, they had to find the man. Yes, he had to be an answer to Vatiri's dream. But Khari found that she didn't believe the whole tribe should go to Namora. Her dream hadn't shown her anything to say that all her people, the strong ones and the weak, the elderly and the youngest children, had to make such a journey.

She was staking lives on her answer. She could not hesitate, or the fear would swallow her voice.

"I agree with Rahul, Lodestone," she said. "We need to send searchers."

Radavan closed his eyes briefly. Khari ached for his disappointment. Vatiri nodded. Pradesh looked into Khari's face, studying her, and she kept her chin up and held his stare. Her sweat-dampened blouse clung to her shoulderblades.

He sighed. "All right, Lamp-Carrier. That is what we'll do."

That afternoon, Pradesh called all the tribe together. Eighteen families, some fifty people, from the oldest white-haired grandfather to the youngest child at the breast. He had them assemble in the clear ground just north of the camp.

Some had already heard the news. Radavan had told his family, and Dahila rushed to find Khari as the tribe came together in the clearing. "Sister," she said. Her fingers caught hold of Khari's arm. "Is this true?"

Khari could see how much her pregnancy weighed on her. Dahila wasn't young anymore; this newest child was a risk. Her eyes looked sunken in her thin face, but her belly was huge, as if the baby inside her was taking all the food she ate. She was a strong mother and a loyal wife. Khari wished she could promise her that her children would live to grow old.

Before she could say anything, Vatiri came up beside her. "Pradesh will explain," Vatiri said. She put an arm around Dahila. "We need to be patient a little longer."

Dahila let go of Khari's arm and let herself lean on Vatiri. Khari breathed out in relief, even though she could hear the whispering and muttering around her that said the news was already spreading. Then Pradesh appeared in the clearing, pulling his chair.

At the sight of him, the noise died down. He stood up on the chair to speak. The sun caught his yellow shirt, making it glow.

"People of the Sun God." His strong, deep voice carried easily. "Today we must put our trust in the Powers. They have shown us both danger and hope."

Khari couldn't help admiring him. His voice had no fear in it even as he told the tribe about Vatiri's dream and what it meant. As the people took it in, Khari heard gasps and whispers, but Pradesh held up a hand before the panic could catch fire.

"This is one pathdream the Moon Woman has given us today," he said. "Now listen to the other."

He explained Khari's dream as if he had never doubted it. He told the tribe he would assemble the search party that day and they would leave for Namora the next morning. "Our Lamp-Carriers feel certain we'll find help there."

All the rest of the afternoon and well into the night, Khari and Vatiri were at the center of a storm of questions. Khari couldn't decide whether her people's fear or hope was worse. She had convinced Pradesh to believe her, but she was still only sixteen, barely a Lamp-Carrier at all. What if, in the end, her dream didn't mean what she thought?

She would go with the searchers, of course. She resigned herself to the fact that Handan and Mandhani were going too, though she didn't want to think about weeks of dealing with them in close quarters, without Pradesh to make them behave. Because the Lodestone, of course, was staying behind with the rest of the tribe.

Rahul was going. So was Radavan, who had insisted on it. It had taken Pradesh's direct order to make Dahila stay behind with her children. Her pregnancy meant she couldn't travel fast enough.

That night, when the camp had finally quieted, Khari begged Vatiri to go too. The two of them were alone in their tent, each on her pallet in the dark. "We need you, Amma." Khari didn't say *I need you*, but she knew Vatiri understood. "You're strong. You can travel as well as any of us."

When Vatiri answered, Khari couldn't see her face, but she could hear her smiling. "You know better than that, child. The Lodestone needs one of us to stay with him."

Khari had never spent a night away from her since that day her father had carried her to Vatiri's tent. The thought of doing it now, tomorrow, made her feel as if the ground had yawned open underneath her.

"You need to do this," Vatiri said. "Go, find help, and come back to us."

The long hours of darkness crawled past. Khari didn't sleep. At dawn, she and the rest of the search party met up at the western edge of the camp. They had the tribe's fastest horses, bows and knives for hunting, and bedrolls with the little they needed to carry. They would travel as light as they could.

The tribe gathered to see them off. Pradesh called on the Powers to guide the searchers on their way. Before Khari mounted her horse, Vatiri came up and took the girl's hands between her own.

"You'll find him." Her smile made Khari's throat ache. "You'll get help for us."

Khari wanted to throw her arms around the older woman and not let go. She couldn't do that with everyone watching. Vatiri let go of her hands and Khari swung herself up bareback, wiping tears away on her sleeve.

Handan led the search group. Khari was more than happy to let him. They rode away from camp, hard and fast, heading southwest for the warm plains. The rest of the tribe would follow more slowly, moving toward one of the regular winter camps. Pradesh would get them as close to the mountains as he could.

Khari rode at the back of the group. She forced herself not to look behind, but in her mind, she saw Shurik's soldiers, rivers of graycoats riding out with their flame-throwing weapons to find and kill her people. So many of them. So small and slow-moving the tribe she had just left behind.

She wondered if she would ever see Vatiri again.

6

RIBAS

On the first day of the apple harvest, during the midday meal, Ribas took his mother aside in the old farmhouse. He told her that he'd looked into his brother's mind, the way she had wanted him to. He told her about the net of fierce, destructive anger he'd found there: the danger he'd hoped never to see.

Grief and fear shadowed her face, so briefly that anyone else might have missed them, but so clear to him that he wanted to put his arms around her the way he had as a little boy, when his father's violence had left her aching and terrified. Then she lifted her chin and wrapped her hard-won strength around her like a coat against bad weather.

"Can you help him?" she asked.

The two of them had left the kitchen, where the rest of the apple harvesters were eating a quick midday meal. They'd taken their plates of bread, sliced apples, and thick nut butter to the farmhouse's front room. Standing up made eating more awkward, but they didn't sit down by the hearth. Neither of them, Ribas knew, wanted to call up certain memories, in the middle of this new trouble.

"I don't know if I can," he admitted. He hated to say it.

"If you tried, would it hurt you?"

The gift might let him do something, but it would probably need more strength than his weak heart could stand. When it took too much, it left him dizzy and sick. Sometimes it made him so weak he fainted. Mama had made him promise a long time ago not to risk himself more than he had to. Maryut had asked for the same promise again when she married him. He couldn't always keep his word, but he tried.

"Yes," he said. "I think it would."

Put simple words to trouble. Mama had taught him that a long time ago. She'd said she had let Silvas hide his own trouble, the family's trouble, for too long. *Don't let it sit in the dark. Look it in the face, and then you can see what to do.* He said, "But Gedrí's in a trap, Mama. What's happening to him, I'm sure it's the same thing that..."

Even now, so many years after his father's death, he never used the word *Da* to mean Silvas. That word meant things like love and protection and safety. Mama heard the rest of his thought. "Why is it happening to Gedrí?" Her steady eyes searched his face. "With your father, I thought Sostavi might have done something. Whatever happened to him there. But Gedrí's never had a disappointment like that, has he?"

Silvas had been disappointed in his career. *Whatever happened to him in Sostavi:* Ribas had never known what that was, or why his father had abandoned his apparently successful work as a priest to come back to Lida and help Mama grow apples. And he must have been successful, or he'd never have served in the Great Circle House.

"No," Ribas said. "Gedrí's happy with the farm. He loves his family." He would have staked his own life on that.

"That's what I thought."

"His mind is doing something." Had Silvas's mind done the same thing? Had Sostavi pushed him along, or would it have happened anyway? Useless questions Ribas couldn't help asking himself. "Something's changing in him. I think it's happening on its own."

Again a flash of sadness in Mama's face. She hid it, biting into a slice of apple and chewing thoughtfully, but he knew how helpless she must feel. He felt it too.

She swallowed the apple. "I don't want you to risk yourself."

That wasn't right. The gift was all he had to offer. "Mama. If I can do anything, cut the net even a little, it would help him. It…"

"No, Ribé." She put her free hand on his arm. "If you get sick, you can't help anyone. Gedrí would tell you the same."

The look she gave him took him straight back to those first weeks after Silvas's death, after Ribas himself had finally gotten over the worst of his fever. He and Mama had been survivors together, wounded and limping, struggling to shape something like a better life out of the wreckage. Every hour of every day, he'd pushed himself to be the right hand his mother needed. When she knew he was pushing too hard – and she always did, no matter how he tried to hide it – she had given him exactly the look she was giving him now. *Enough, my dove.*

She was right, of course. At its worst, his heart could leave him bedridden for days, no use to anybody. "All right," he said. He didn't have to tell her how much he didn't like it. "But I'll watch him, Mama. If there's any chance to help, I will."

Four days later, on Sesdina, the busiest part of the apple harvest was done. The apples were gathered and sorted: some for eating and selling right away, some for drying, the rest for the new batch of cider that was already putting the big press to work. Ribas would go back to his normal duties at the Circle House the next day. On Sesdina evening, his friend Seldo, who owned the Sheaf and Barrel Inn in Lida and had helped with the harvest, asked everyone down to the Sheaf for the annual post-harvest supper.

Ribas had kept a sharp eye on Gedrin through those four days. His brother seemed to be in good spirits, laughing and talking, but the anger-net around him never faded or dimmed. They rode down to the Sheaf together in the farm's wagon. On the way, Gedrin told Ribas, "I hate to say it, but you were right about Sira. She did a good job."

Gedrin was driving. Ribas sat up front beside him on the seat while Maryut and Virta and the children rode in the back. Mama had gone down to the village ahead of them, with Seldo and his wife Milya, to get the fires lit at the inn and start supper.

"Of course she did," Ribas said. The chilly evening air helped him stay awake, even as the motion of the wagon and the warmth of the heavy coat Maryut had made him bring made him want to close his eyes and drift off. "See? You needed her help after all."

Gedrin laughed. "You don't have to be smug about it."

From the wagon bed, Asira started singing one of her favorite songs, "I will go down to the sea." Raulin joined in. Their light young voices sent the sweet tune up into the dark sky.

I will go down to the sea,
Where the wild waves reach for the sand,
Where the winds cry out loud and free...

It was a "Klaya song," one of the many about one of the favorite characters in Namoran folklore. Ribas had always loved the stories about the free-spirited, fiercely independent girl who had lived in Namora long before the time of the Goddess, although not before the time of the round houses that would later honor Kenavi. Klaya's stories spoke to Ribas in his bones, both her deep-rooted love for her home and her eager curiosity about the world outside.

He loved this song, too. It was funny, he thought: neither Asira nor Raulin had ever seen the ocean, and might never have reason to, but they sang as if they knew exactly how the waves frothed and pounded at the sand, and how the wind, tasting of salt, rushed along the shore. Ribas hadn't seen the coast in years, not since he'd taken a little time to travel before he'd started his duties as Lida's zhinin. He might never have reason to see it again, but he would never forget it.

The wagon wheels crunched over gravel. Smoke from evening hearth fires rose from the village chimneys and hung in the air. As the wagon rolled into the square, Ribas looked up at the sky. There was no moon tonight. The stars gleamed like handfuls of white pebbles, polished to brilliance, scattered on a dark cloth.

The square was quiet and empty. Most people had already settled into their houses for the night. Four lamps, each on a tall wooden post, stood on each side of the square, their wicks lit and gleaming behind their clear glass globes. The Sheaf stood on the south side of the square, directly opposite the Circle House. Its wooden sign, bright in the lamplight, showed a proud sheaf of plump yellow heads of wheat standing in a brown barrel like flowers in a vase.

Gedrin drove the wagon around to the stables behind the inn. Raulin and Sira jumped down as soon as the wagon stopped. They raced around to the front door with their mother behind, calling after them, "You two behave yourselves, now! Don't you get in the way in the kitchen!"

Gedrin stayed back to stable the mare. Maryut put her arm around Ribas as they made their own slower way inside. "Are you sure you want to stay for this?" she asked. "You look like you should go to bed."

It seemed strange to think about trouble tonight, with the tiredness and peace of another finished harvest behind them, and the quiet of the village around them. Home was only a couple of streets away. For a moment Ribas thought longingly about the comfort of bed and the warmth of a quilt pulled up over him.

He wouldn't let Gedrin out of his sight until he had to. He smiled down at Maryut. "I'm all right. I promise."

She raised a skeptical eyebrow, but then they were inside, in the warmth and light of the inn's front room. The fire on the main hearth was lit. Lamps in glass shields hung on the walls. Mouthwatering smells of roasting potatoes and chicken floated out of the kitchen behind the bar.

The Sheaf and Barrel did steady business with travelers and villagers alike. Seldo and Milya kept a handful of plain but clean rooms upstairs and served four good meals a day. The bar, well-stocked with "Pelya's cider," abuvisk, ale, and wine from the vineyards in Taipa and Siene in southwestern Namora, was a constant draw in all seasons. Milya said every year that she looked forward to the few days during the harvest when she and Seldo closed the inn. The long days in the orchard, she claimed, were nothing next to the usual round of cooking and scrubbing and serving.

Seldo had set up one of the big square tables near the hearth for the harvest supper. The inn didn't use tablecloths, but the blue clay plates and mugs were ready and waiting. Asira and Raulin laid out homespun napkins and gleaming wooden forks and spoons.

Seldo himself came out of the kitchen as Ribas and Maryut hung up their coats on hooks by the door. The innkeeper was as tall as Ribas, but barrel-chested and thick-muscled from years of hauling kegs of ale, crates of potatoes, and sacks of flour for the inn. Some years ago he'd gotten tired of his thick curly hair, so with his wife's help, he had shaved it all off and kept it bald ever since. He looked like the kind of person you might cross a street to avoid, but Ribas had also known him to cup flies that strayed into the inn between his hands and let them out the windows.

"Where's that brother of yours?" Seldo demanded. He never bothered with an apron when he was cooking or tending bar, so his rough shirt and pants were always dusted with flour and patterned with splashes of sauce and cooking fat. "My wife says I'm allowed to play Capture till supper's ready."

Capture was the most popular strategy game in Namora. Seldo, who had never left Lida or had any schooling besides the basics of reading, writing, and ciphering that every child learned at home, was one of the smartest people Ribas knew and one of the best Capture players in the village. Ribas would never play against him unless he needed a taste of abject humiliation. Only Gedrin was a match for the innkeeper.

Maryut went back to the kitchen with Asira to help with the food, but Ribas and Raulin stayed in the front room to watch the Capture game. Ribas sat at the table, grateful to lean on the sturdy wood. Seldo set up the board: seven Raiders, three Defenders, and one tiny Master stone for each player. His stones were silver-gray. Gedrin would play green.

"Someday," Seldo told Ribas, positioning the pieces with deft fingers, "I really am going to teach you how to play right."

"You've been trying for years. What makes you think I can learn?"

"You're plenty smart enough." Seldo sat down next to Ribas. The wooden chair creaked under his weight. "You taught me Old Namoran. Tell me I can't teach you a simple game."

When Ribas had gone to the viduris in Paret, Seldo had wanted to hear about everything that went on there. He never wanted to join the dagira himself, but he was curious about the school and it fascinated him when Ribas talked about learning other languages. During Ribas's breaks during the summer and at harvest time, the two friends had sat down at one of these tables at the inn and pored over Ribas's schoolbooks together. Seldo had, in fact, learned quite a bit of Old Namoran, and even a little Pirlevis, the "First Tongue" that had been used to write the oldest stories about the Goddess.

Gedrin came in, rubbing his hands in the chill. As usual, he hadn't bothered to wear a coat. Seldo said, "Let's go, Gedrí."

Gedrin didn't need to be asked twice to play Capture. As the game started, Raulin looked up at Ribas with a shy question in his face.

Ribas understood. When he'd been Raulin's age, trying to take over as much of his father's work on the farm as he could, he'd started to think he'd gotten too big to sit on a lap. Not that he hadn't still needed that comfort. And Raulin didn't have to try to grow up too fast.

He held out a hand to his nephew. "Let's put our heads together," he said. "Maybe you can help me finally figure this game out."

Gedrin laughed. Eyes on the board, he said, "Raulí, you'd better learn Capture faster than your uncle."

Raulin climbed into Ribas's lap and rested his head on his uncle's shoulder. His hair smelled of fresh air and the dry leaves in the orchard. Ribas put an arm around him and watched the game. The goal was to capture your opponent's Master. To do that, you had to get as many of their Raiders and Defenders off the board as you could, without risking too many of your own. Seldo's and Gedrin's hands darted over the board. Their pieces hit the wood with barely a space between them. *Click. Click. Click.*

The two had very different playing styles. Seldo protected his Master and kept his Raiders out of Gedrin's way. Gedrin's Raiders charged all over the board, aiming to clear Seldo's pieces before they could come after him. Different styles but evenly matched. Ribas couldn't follow the moves fast enough to see why each player made his decisions, but the gray and green pieces came off the board in a more or less even trade.

Finally each of them had one Raider plus their Master. Masters couldn't capture each other, so your final Raider was always safe. Ribas had never gotten to that point in any game. If he managed to steal a few of his opponent's Raiders before his own Master went down, it was a triumph.

Raulin had dozed off in his lap, a warm weight against his chest. Ribas watched as the four remaining pieces tracked each other around the board. Both players were fully intent on the game, Gedrin's dark head and Seldo's bald gleaming one bent over the board, both of them oblivious to the sounds and scents from the kitchen. Gedrin had always liked this part of the game best. The more of a fight his opponent put up, the better.

After a few moves, though, something felt wrong. Ribas saw his brother's mouth tighten. His dark eyebrows drew together and his free hand, resting on the table, closed and opened restlessly. Where his moves had been quick and eager before, now they seemed sharp and impatient.

The game needed to end. Ribas didn't need the gift to see his brother's temper winding tighter with every move. Memory came back in a wave: Silvas sitting by the hearth in the farmhouse, following Mama's directions to weave straw to repair holes in the harvest baskets. Fumbling and having trouble. The rough tips of the broken straw poking at his fingertips. Laughter turning into silence, silence turning into anger, and Ribas, not quite four, feeling the cold seeping into him, welling in through the soles of his feet and all the way up into his chest.

He'd already known, at that age, not to say a word or make a sound that would push his father's anger that last tiny distance. He knew he couldn't tip Gedrin's fragile balance now. In his lap, Raulin slept peacefully. Seldo, too, didn't seem to notice anything wrong.

Then it happened. Even Ribas saw his brother make a mistake. Gedrin left his Master wide open to attack when Seldo's last Raider was much too close. As soon as Gedrin let go of his own Raider, which he'd pushed to the other end of the board, Seldo's final attacker swept forward.

The innkeeper caught Gedrin's green Master up in his hand. "Got you!" He laughed. "What happened to you, Gedrí? You should have seen that coming."

Ribas knew Seldo shouldn't have said that. He knew it even before Gedrin's face darkened and twisted, even before it perfectly mirrored the same look Ribas remembered from so many years ago.

No, Gedrí. Not you too.

Gedrin surged to his feet. His heavy chair crashed backward to the floor. Anger contorted his face almost beyond recognition. He looked like a caged beast ready to lunge at his captors.

Seldo stared at him. "Gedrí." He sounded more baffled than worried. "What's wrong with you?"

The crash of the chair falling woke Raulin up with a gasp. He stared at his father, then turned to see Ribas. "Uncle Ribé, what's going on?"

In his eyes, Ribas saw the same fear he had known all too well. He and Mama had worn themselves into shadows trying to tiptoe around Silvas's anger. "It's all right, Raulí," he said, keeping his arm tight around the little boy. "Gedrin," he said. "That's enough."

He didn't know if his brother heard him. Gedrin stepped forward and swept the Capture board off the table. It landed on the floor with a clatter. The playing pieces flew everywhere, rattling as they hit furniture and walls.

Ribas heard the door to the kitchen open, heard Virta's voice asking what that noise was. At the table, Seldo got to his feet, still baffled but ready to defend himself. Ribas couldn't move, between Raulin's weight and his own exhaustion, but he knew what he had to do.

Seldo was more than a match even for strong stocky Gedrin, but Ribas couldn't let it come to that. Someone might get hurt. He reached for the gift, knowing how dangerous it would be to use it when he was this tired. The lines unspooled. There had to be a weak place in the net, somewhere, anywhere...

Seldo said, "Gedrin Silvaikas." Now he sounded annoyed. "What in the Goddess's name do you think you're doing?"

Raulin gripped Ribas's arm. "Uncle Ribé. What's wrong with Da?"

Ribas heard tears in the little boy's voice. "I'm not sure, Raulí." He closed his eyes to see the lines more clearly. "We're going to try to fix it."

For an impossibly long moment, silence, as Ribas held his breath and raced along the hot gleaming lines of the net. He couldn't find any weakness, but there must be something. Anything he could do, that might not be as dangerous as he thought, that might let him help...

Then his brother's voice reached him. "Ribé. Don't."

Two words as flat and blunt as stones hitting the ground. Ribas opened his eyes. Gedrin was looking at him, his face still too flushed, but that ugly brutish cast had faded.

"I know what you're doing." Now Gedrin's voice sounded hoarse and tired. "Don't. You're worn out."

Their eyes met. At the sight of Gedrin's confusion and fear, frustration clawed at Ribas's throat. He had to solve this.

Seldo said, "Gedrin, since when are you such a bad loser?"

Gedrin's laugh sounded forced. "I made a stupid mistake. I guess I got upset." Before anyone could say anything else, he bent down, hunting the Capture pieces on the floor. "I'll clean up my mess," he said. "I'm sorry."

Seldo looked around at Ribas and shrugged. *Who knows? Never mind.* Raulin looked up into his uncle's face again. "Is Da better?"

He was still uneasy. Ribas wished he could promise everything was fine. "I think so."

The little boy climbed down. "I'll help you, Da."

"That'd be good, Raulí. Thank you."

It had all happened so fast. Virta came into the room, puzzled. "What was that?" she asked Ribas. "Did they have a fight?"

Gedrin stood up with the Capture board in his hands. "No, love. I just made a bad play, is all."

Virta seemed to accept it. "Well, supper will be ready in a minute. You all should get washed up."

She went back to the kitchen. Gedrin set the board and a handful of pieces down on the table and put his hand on Ribas's shoulder.

"Ribé." He spoke quietly enough that Seldo and Raulin wouldn't hear. "Don't do that for me."

I couldn't help our father. "You know better than that, Gedrí. I'll do anything I can."

Gedrin looked worn and anxious, his boyishness suddenly gone. "I don't want you hurting yourself. Too many people need you."

The kitchen door opened again. Virta and Maryut brought out platters of food, calling everyone to come and eat. Gedrin squeezed Ribas's shoulder. "Don't talk about it with Mama either. I don't want her worrying."

He went to the kitchen to wash up. Ribas watched him go. The lines of the net burned in his mind.

~

The next day, Setdina, Ribas met the pair of students who would help him with the work of the Circle House through the winter and spring. Students at the viduris in Paret, *mosevine* as they were called, always had a year-long apprenticeship after they finished their three years of school study. The most promising ones would be installed somewhere as full zhinine when their apprenticeships ended. Ribas himself had apprenticed in Lida, with old Zhinin Odilas, since that House was intended for him as soon as he was ready to take it.

He had been Lida's first mosevin apprentice, but the work of the House had grown hugely since he had become zhinin and news of his skill, and the gift, had spread. Ribas had never wanted or asked for promotion, or subordinate priests to serve him. He didn't care about that kind of politicking. But when Kunin Dergo at the Paret viduris first wrote to ask if he would train some of the likeliest mosevine, and incidentally accept some help in his House, Ribas had agreed.

Late on Setdina afternoon, Ribas and Maryut waited at the Circle House together to greet the mosevine. Ribas had just finished the short Setdina prayer service and was still wearing his sea-blue robes of office. It always took a while for the House to clear, because everyone had to stop and talk to him and Maryut. It didn't matter that they saw him more or less every day, or that the zhinin's house stood open whenever he wasn't at the Circle House, for anyone who needed help or advice or simply an ear to listen. If the village was a wheel, the zhinin was its center. Ribas welcomed every handshake and hug, especially after the few days he'd been away for the harvest.

A thin drizzle fell outside. Gray clouds hung over the village and a chilly breeze blew in from the north, carrying a taste of the winter that would come soon. Once the House emptied, Ribas and Maryut stood under the shelter of the narrow wooden awning above its front doors. Tomorrow, the square would be full of farm stands and crafts-people's tables for one of the last weekly markets before winter. No matter what the weather did, the village would turn out to chat and barter and haggle. Today, though, with no reason to linger, people hurried to get out of the chilly damp.

The coach clattered into the square, the horses' hooves ringing on the cobblestones. This was a hired coach from the viduris, sleeker and more comfortable than the bare-bones mail coach that came to Lida from Paret every Tretdina. The driver pulled up in front of the Sheaf and Barrel and went around to get the mosevine's trunks down from the roof.

"He's going to leave them over there?" Maryut said. "He can see where the House is, can't he?"

Provided the driver had working eyes, he could certainly see the Circle House. "He probably wants his cider," Ribas said.

The two students were the coach's only occupants. The boy jumped down quickly and held out his hand to the girl. The two could have been brother and sister, both slim and dark, with narrow faces. Kunin Dergo had sent Ribas their names earlier in the month; the boy was Jano Pavraikas and the girl was Danayut Matvaikas.

Ribas and Maryut started across the square. "Look at them," Maryut said. "Thin as lampposts."

"Three years of viduris cooking," Ribas reminded her.

"You'd think that school could do better, after all this time."

"Oh, but the food's an education in itself."

She laughed. The driver finished hauling the trunks down and wasted no time climbing back onto his seat. The coach clattered off to the Sheaf's stables. The two mosevine stood by their luggage, looking forlorn in the gloomy weather.

"They're not going to drag those trunks over here," Ribas said.

"Neither are you, love."

Unfortunately, that was true. "I bet Seldo will help."

The boy, Jano, saw them coming first. When he said something to Danayut, Ribas saw the girl glance toward them and then duck her head quickly, as if she wanted to hide. He was sorry he hadn't had a chance to change out of the robes. Some mosevine were shy when they first met him, and the extra formality wouldn't help.

Jano, though, hurried to meet them. He put his hand over his heart as soon as he was in earshot and managed a half-bow in mid-walk. "Raimaté, zhinin."

He looked excited, nervous, and incredibly young. Ribas returned the salute gravely enough, but then smiled and held out his hand. "Glad to have you, Jano."

The boy shook hands eagerly. He was shorter than Ribas, only a little taller than Maryut. His long, well-cut woolen coat and polished shoes suggested he came from a comfortable home. "I never thought I'd get this apprenticeship, zhinin," he said. "I hope you never see some of my exams."

Ribas couldn't help laughing. "You didn't have to worry," he said. His mosevine had to want to work. Perfect marks came a distant second. "You should have seen some of mine."

Jano looked round-eyed. The mosevine tended to think Ribas must have been an irreproachable student, but if they'd asked Kunin Dergo, they'd have known otherwise. Even now, Ribas suspected, the kunin wouldn't paint a particularly flattering picture of a student who'd taken assignments in the directions that interested him most, instead of turning in exactly what his teachers expected. Some of Ribas's teachers had loved that. Kunin Dergo hadn't been one of them.

The kunin had, though, backed Ribas up in his most daring flight of stubbornness: learning some basics of the Lasska language. No viduris taught that. Ribas knew how lucky he'd been that Kunin Dergo had been able and more or less willing to help him. His own mosevine would hear about that, along with a lot more of the language than could possibly interest them, during their months in Lida.

Right now, he left Jano to Maryut's motherly greetings – "let's get you out of the cold; you look like you need a good meal" – and went over to Danayut. The girl had sat down on her trunk and was looking blankly toward the Sheaf and Barrel. Very tired, Ribas guessed, or very shy, or both.

As he came up, she scrambled to her feet. "Raimaté, zhinin."

Her voice sounded low and tight. As she spoke, she ducked her head again. She was small, a little shorter than Maryut, and wore a plain dark dress with a shapeless homespun coat over it buttoned up to her throat. Her head was bare. Droplets of rain beaded her dark braid, which she wore coiled and pinned to the back of her head in the style of a matron, or a widow.

"Raimaté, mosevin," Ribas said gently. Face to face, he could feel fear rising off her. "Danya, is it?"

He hoped using the nickname might help her relax. She nodded, keeping her eyes down. "Welcome, Danya," he said, holding his hand out. "I'm glad you're here."

She looked up then. Her eyes were startlingly dark in her pale face. She didn't smile, but shook his hand briefly. Her fingers were cold.

Shyness and fear. Ribas had seen something so similar, years ago. Another girl's face, very different from Danya's in looks, but with the same expression in it.

Valda. Ribas knew she had gone to Sostavi years ago, had risen through the ranks of the dagira and now served as Tavo Balsa, second-in-command to Tavin Ardinas himself. He'd had none of her news from herself, but through Kunin Dergo in Paret and the ever-present dagira grapevine. For a while it had felt wrong not to hear from Valda directly, after they had been so close: the kind of wrongness you felt when someone sang a familiar tune out of key. He understood, though, why she never wrote, and had always respected her wish for distance.

Now he remembered eyes much like Danya's looking up at him from a table in the viduris's dining hall. He had wanted to try to reach the girl who talked to no one and seemed so unhappy. *Good morning, is it all right if I sit with you?* He'd been surprised when she'd said yes, but not nearly as surprised as she had seemed herself.

Maryut came over now and wrapped Danya in maternal bustle. "Welcome, dear. Let's show you and Jano your rooms. Seldo's going to have a couple of his kitchen hands help with the trunks." Her glance at Ribas, as the two Sheaf workers came out to carry the luggage over to the Circle House, told him she felt the girl's discomfort as clearly as he did.

The mosevine had quarters in the building that joined onto the back of the Circle House. A passage behind the House's hearth linked the two buildings. The second building held the big kitchen, where the communal Pirdina meal happened each week, and the library. The two mosevin's quarters, identical small square rooms, had been added to the complex ten years ago, when Kunin Dergo first asked Ribas about sending apprentices to Lida.

Ribas and Maryut gave the mosevine time to settle in and rest and told them where to find the zhinin's house for supper. Over the meal, which involved no robes of office or formality of any kind, Jano talked cheerfully about the trip from Paret, passed along Kunin Dergo's greetings to Ribas, and discussed the studies at the viduris. The language classes had been his favorites, especially Pirlevis, the "First Tongue," and he'd especially liked studying the oldest stories about Kenavi in their original language. He complimented Maryut's cooking and said, yes, the viduris's meals were still as bad as Ribas remembered.

All through supper, Danya stayed quiet. She answered questions, but kept her eyes on her plate and said as little as she could. Afterward, when the mosevine had gone back to the House for the night, Maryut said, "What do you think's the matter with that poor thing?"

She was cleaning up the supper dishes, having refused Ribas's help. "I don't know," Ribas said. Again he thought of Valda. But that had been at the beginning of their time at the viduris, when everyone was still getting used to the strange place and all the new faces. Danya had three years of study behind her. Good years, or Kunin Dergo wouldn't have sent her here.

"She's a little mouse," Maryut said, reaching up into a cabinet to put away the plates. "So shy. I hope she's not going to give you too much trouble."

Ribas got up from the table and went over to put his hands on her waist. "Trouble is my job, love." He kissed the side of her neck.

"Get away," she scolded, but when she twisted around to see him, her eyes were full of laughter. "Let me finish this, zhinin."

"Don't be too long." He bent to kiss her again, this time on the lips.

Two days later, on Pirdina, the Circle House filled for the First Day service and the meal that would follow. More modern Circle Houses had done away with *Rane Atvire,* the old tradition of Open Hands, but Lida held onto the potluck dinner. It honored the Goddess Kenavi's wish that Her people should keep their hands open to one another, to reach out, share, and hold.

Ribas stood on the dais by the hearth, setting up the front table with the salt, glass pitcher and bowl, and basket of prayer stones. It made him smile to look out at the rows of benches steadily filling up. Mama and Maryut were here, of course, in their usual bench near the front with Gedrin and Virta and the children. All of them had arrived early to help set up the kitchen for the meal. Gedrin seemed like himself again this morning, quick to laugh and quick to help. Ribas wished he knew how long that would last.

Every Circle House had a great hearth at the front. In Vienela, the eleventh month, Ribas would have a fire lit, but this autumn had been mild so far. In deep winter, even the fire wouldn't keep the House warm all the time, because the windows had to stay open for the prayer stone ritual. Now Ribas left the dais and began a circuit of the House, making sure each window stood open and had a basket beside it, where people would leave their prayer stones once they had made their offerings to the Goddess.

The circuit of the House always took a while. Even though Ribas wore the robes of office for the service, nobody ever stood on ceremony about stopping him to say good morning and shake hands.

Parents told their children to behave and not bother the zhinin, but plenty of little ones squirmed free of the parental grip and ran up to demand Ribas's attention. He was never too busy to give it. His soul loved the peace of the service, but the real worship of the Goddess, he had always felt, happened when Her people cared for one another.

By the time he got back to the front of the House, Jano and Danya were standing in position on either side of the hearth. In their matching wine-red mosevin's robes, they could have been twins. Jano gave Ribas a quick smile that didn't hide his tension. Danya stood motionless, staring out the window opposite her. Ribas couldn't help noticing how pale she looked. Most mosevine assisting in their first service got nervous, especially on Pirdina in front of all those eyes. Ribas had never forgotten his own first service as an apprentice, in front of so many people who'd known him from birth, and had known his father too.

Ribas stepped to the front of the dais. When he held out his hands, invoking the reminder of *rane atvire*, the talk in the House died out at once.

"Raimaté," he greeted the village.

The answer came back, a collective murmur. "Raimaté, zhinin."

Ribas led the opening prayer, calling the Goddess's people together, and then stepped aside for Jano to give the first reading from the *Book of Kenavi*. The village already knew the mosevine: news didn't even need a day to spread to every house, and most people had made a point of stopping by the Circle House the day before to give the new apprentices their own welcome.

The reading told about the world as it had been when Kenavi was a mortal woman living in the place that would become Namora. Ribas listened to the familiar words, which Jano read clearly and well. The stories said that Kenavi had lived on Namora's northern coast: some of the dagira firmly believed she had lived in a grand dwelling that later became the Great House in Sostavi, but Ribas had never been sure about that. He liked to imagine a village like the one in the most famous Klaya folktale, "Fourteen Stones." Like Klaya,

Kenavi had loved the land. As Jano read, Ribas conjured up his own pictures of the coasts and the forests, the plains rich with yellow and purple flowers, the quarries that yielded Namora's blue clay. Unlike Klaya, though, who'd held herself fiercely apart in her village, Kenavi had been gentle-souled and devoted to her people. The stories said that the two women had lived generations apart, but Ribas sometimes thought they could have been sisters, or even two faces of the same woman. Not that he'd suggest such an idea to any other dagira.

When Jano finished, Danya gave the second reading: a familiar Old Namoran text that told one of the early stories of how Kenavi, as a mortal girl, had won the attention of the Old Gods early on for her generosity and kindness. Ribas had never lost his student fascination with Old Namoran, so similar and yet in some ways so different from the language he spoke every day. He had also always loved the idea of going back to stories written closer to the days when the Goddess was alive.

Danya read the Old Namoran text first, then Ribas's prepared translation. She spoke clearly but tonelessly and kept her eyes down on the text. Ribas thought, once she got over her nerves a little, he would speak to her about looking up now and then and giving the reading more expression. Your listeners had to know that the stories mattered to you.

After the readings came the water and salt rituals, commemorating the sacrifice of the Goddess. The faith told that Kenavi, as a mortal woman, had walked into the ocean, offering herself in surrender to the wind and waves during what later became Akena, the coldest and fiercest month of the year. The Old Gods, Sea and Wind, Sun and Moon, had become angry with Kenavi's people for their careless use of the lands they had been given. Kenavi sacrificed her life in trade for her people. The gods had both accepted the offering and, in return for her courage, allowed her rebirth as the Goddess. To her, they had given the care of the land that would become Namora.

Every Circle House service included the water and salt rituals.

Every Namoran grew up watching and hearing them. Today Ribas turned them over to his mosevine, as one of the most important tests a zhinin had to pass.

Jano performed the water ritual first, pouring water carefully out of the clear glass pitcher on the table and into the glass bowl. They were the same pitcher and bowl Zhinin Odilas, and Zhinin Matevas before him, had used, long before Ribas was born. As Jano poured, he recited the simple words: "In Your name, O Goddess, we invoke the strength of the wind and the water, whose anger You tamed by Your sacrifice."

The so-familiar rituals always had to have power, no matter how often you did them. You had to give the words meaning, as you spoke them, but you couldn't exaggerate them or make them mystical or pompous. Ribas thought Jano did a decent job. The boy's hands shook as he held the pitcher, so that some water splashed onto the white tablecloth, but no doubt he felt the pressure of all the stares. Ribas remembered feeling them himself, that first time Zhinin Odilas had turned the rituals over to him.

Jano finished, set the pitcher on the table, and stepped back with obvious relief. When glanced at Ribas for approval, Ribas gave him the shadow of a wink. Jano looked down quickly to hide a grin.

Now Danya opened the carved wooden box of salt. Its old hinges creaked in the stillness of the room. She scooped grains up between her fingers.

In this ritual, the salt was sprinkled in the glass bowl of water. The officiant then gently stirred the water by passing his or her hands through it. Danya sprinkled the salt carefully, not letting any stray on the tablecloth. Her hands moved toward the bowl. Ribas saw her looking down at the water, drawing a breath to say the words: "In Your name, O Goddess, we invoke the power of the ocean, and remember Your love as You gave Yourself up for us."

For a heartbeat, Ribas was sure she was about to do it. Then her hands stopped in the air.

She had forgotten. Ribas didn't look at her panic, but he felt it, solid as ice around her. *You know what to do,* he thought to her. *"In Your name, O Goddess…"*

She stood there, staring at the water, helpless. For a moment Ribas thought about reaching out with the gift to cut her fear, but it was too late for that, even if he'd had her permission to do it.

He stepped forward and touched her shoulder. She backed away from the table without raising her head or looking at him. Ribas finished the ritual, passing his hands through the water and reciting the words as if nothing had happened.

The prayer stone ritual came just before the closing blessing. Everyone in the House lined up down the center aisle and came forward to the dais to take a prayer stone out of the basket on the table. Many of the stones went back to Zhinin Odilas's time, but Ribas had also bought some in Paret before he was installed here, choosing each one for color, shape, and gloss. All of them fit snugly in the palm of the hand. Each one had something about it that made it satisfying to touch and hold.

The line of people moved forward. Some people picked up stones without looking at them, trusting their fingers to go to the right one. Others took a moment to find one that seemed right. Parents held little children up to choose their own. As each person chose, they moved to one of the eight lines forming at the House's different windows, to send their prayers out into the air.

This was Ribas's favorite part of the service. With everyone together, in the stillness of the silently offered prayers, Ribas felt the Goddess's presence most clearly. In spite of all his training, he always found it easier to think of Her as the woman she had been, the real person who had loved her land and a village, maybe, that hadn't looked so different from Lida. When she died, before she was reborn as the Goddess, her spirit must have gone out to touch the wholeness of everything she had cared about. Ribas could feel that easily. He trusted that the Goddess he served wouldn't fault him for using that mortal picture of her as a crutch.

He and the two mosevine offered their prayers last, at the

windows closest to the hearth. Ribas chose an earth-brown stone and stood by the window to the left of the hearth to send out a prayer for his brother. *Goddess who guides us, show me how to help him.* At the window on the other side of the hearth, Danya stood pale and stiff, her head down. Ribas saw her drop her stone in the basket again and close her hand tight as she backed away. Pain hovered around her.

After the prayers ended, when everyone had gotten back to their seats, Ribas stepped down from the dais to give the closing blessing. With the final "Tebena" – "so be it" – the stillness of the service gave way to talk and bustle.

Danya. Ribas turned back to the dais right away to find her, but her red robes were already disappearing through the House's back door. He tried to hope she was only going back to the kitchen to help with the meal, but when he got there himself a little while later, only Jano stood by the two big tables where everyone had set out their potluck offerings.

Every kitchen in Lida had turned something out for this meal. A confusion of rich scents filled the warm room: roast chicken and lamb, potatoes and root vegetables, lemon and mint and cinnamon, honey and the warm yeast scent of new bread. People had lined up for food and laid coats and hats on benches to claim their seats at the other long tables. There was talk and laughter, the scrape of benches against the flagstone floor, shrieks from children who raced each other around the room while their parents filled the family's plates.

Ribas made it through the press to Jano, who had assigned himself the job of pouring out cider. The mosevin looked up and grinned as he handed a mug to a waiting customer. "That went all right, didn't you think, zhinin?"

"It went very well," Ribas agreed. "Where's Danya?"

Jano's grin faded. "She went to her room. She's pretty upset."

A hand landed on Ribas's shoulder. "Ribé." Seldo. "I want to talk to you about that Old Namoran passage," he said. "Couple things in your translation I wondered about."

Seldo was probably the only person in Lida, apart from Jano and

Danya, who could have followed the Old Namoran enough to have any questions about it. "Good," Ribas said, "but give me a minute. I need to find my other mosevin."

Seldo took the cider jug from Jano. "Let me do that, son. I'm sure your zhinin has other work for you."

"Not really," Ribas said. "Go ahead and eat, Jano."

The boy hurried away to get a plate. Ribas went out into the empty passage, which felt chilly after the warm crowded kitchen. The door to Jano's room stood open, but Danya's door was shut. Ribas knocked lightly.

No answer. He pushed the door open.

The room was small but reasonably comfortable. It had its own small hearth, along with a square window that looked out on the street behind the House, a desk, bookshelf, and bed, and a wardrobe in the corner with a basin and pitcher sitting on top. Danya hadn't left any books or papers scattered around on the desk, or clothes lying on the chair or floor. She hadn't lit a fire either. The grate was cold and empty.

Danya herself was sitting on the bed. Her red robes made a bright splash of color against the gray stone walls and plain homespun blankets. They looked too big on her, as if she had shrunken inside them. She sat motionless with her hands folded in her lap.

She wasn't crying. Everything about her said *stillness*, as if she might disappear if only she could stay quiet enough. Her face looked so fragile it could have been made of glass.

Ribas ached for her. He wished he could use the gift right then, to see the fear and pain that gripped her and cut her free of them if he could. "Danya," he said gently.

Her head jerked up. She actually shrank back on the bed, still gripping her hands tight together.

She mustn't be scared, certainly not of him. "It's all right," Ribas said. "May I come in?"

He would leave her alone if she said no, but she nodded, a small

tight motion. Her eyes stayed on him with a kind of frightened fascination, as if she wanted to look away but couldn't.

"May I sit down?" he asked.

She nodded again. He sat on the end of the mattress, with a little
distance between them. Again he found himself remembering the girl
at the viduris, alone at a table with a book propped in front of her like
a shield. *Good morning.* Her eyes when she looked up at him,
shocked at the intrusion, as if she didn't think she deserved anyone
caring about her. *Is it all right if I sit with you?*

To the girl beside him, he said, "Don't worry about the service.
That little mistake was nothing."

She lowered her head then, staring at the floor. "I'm sorry,
zhinin." The words tumbled out, so low he could barely hear them.
"I'm sorry. I know that ritual. I don't know what happened."

"You were nervous," he said. "It happens." He tried to see her
face, but she kept her head down and turned away from him, so he
could only see her dark hair pinned up in that single coiled braid, too
old for her years. "Come now," he said, as gently as before. "Look
at me."

I hope she doesn't give you too much trouble, Maryut had said.
The mosevine were supposed to help him, true; but this girl's trouble,
whatever it was, was his too.

She obeyed. The look on her face cut at him. "We all forget
things sometimes," he said. He knew this was about more than the
service. "What's bothering you so much?"

Very quietly, with her eyes on the blanket, she said, "I'm never
good enough." A simple statement of fact.

"Why would you say that?"

Her eyes flicked up to his face, then back down to the blanket.
"Back home...my family..." She hesitated. Then, hard and flat, "My
mother."

In those two words, Ribas heard a lifetime of history. Now that
she had started talking, Danya seemed to want to continue. "She...my

mother...she said I shouldn't go to the viduris. She said I'd never make it through. She said..."

She stopped, as if the words had dammed up again behind some a inside her. Ribas had heard family histories like this before. Parents who didn't understand the power they had, or who were too unhappy themselves to see what they were doing to their children. He never let himself show the anger that boiled in his chest every time he heard it.

Now he said, "But you did make it through. And you wouldn't be here in Lida if you weren't good enough."

Her eyes came up to his face again. "I wanted to work with you." This time she didn't look away. The words came out hot and angry. "I wanted to meet you. I never thought I would." A tear slid down her face. "When Kunin Dergo said he was sending me here, I didn't believe it. And then I came and..." She swallowed, fighting for air, her hands twisting together in her lap. "I came here and ruined it the way I always do."

Ribas had to look into her mind. There had to be a way to ease the shame she pointed like a knife at herself. First, though, he moved over on the bed, close enough to put his hand on her shoulder.

"Danya. You haven't ruined anything."

She shook her head. The tears were coming hard and fast now. He didn't need her to tell him what kind of words her mother had thrown at her; he could guess well enough. "Listen to me," he said. "What you've said about yourself, the mistakes you make, it isn't true."

She mopped impatiently at her face with her sleeve. "You don't know me."

He didn't smile. "That's true. I don't know you very well yet, but I know the kunin. I know his standards, and he knows mine."

That got her to look at him again. He said, "He would never send me a mosevin who didn't deserve to be here." Her face said she still didn't believe him. "With your permission, I'd like to take a look at your mind."

She knew what that meant. He saw her swallow. "Why?"

"I might be able to help you. It wouldn't necessarily be permanent." He thought of the net around Gedrin. If Danya's trap was set that firmly, he might not be able to do anything, but he would still try. "It would be like opening a door," he said, "to let in some fresh air."

"Why do you think I need it?"

Some people came to him eager to see what kind of "magic" the gift could give them. Others didn't know what to make of that strange meddling. Danya seemed to be one of the second kind. Ribas said, "I think you need a rest from what you think about yourself."

He saw her take that in. "You could give me that?"

It wasn't much more than a whisper, but it decided him. He must find a way to spring her trap, push that door open, if only for a little while. "I can try," he said.

"Please."

She watched his face as if she hoped to see the gift working. Once it unspooled the patterns, he closed his eyes to see them better.

Fear. Harsh blue lines wove a net around Danya's mind. Ribas had never known how ugly a color blue could be until the first time he'd seen what fear looked like: sullen and dark, like fouled water, with hints of the yellow and purple of a bruise. The net around Danya had anger in it too, hot red lines threading the blue together, pulling them tighter.

But this net wasn't as strong as the one around Gedrin. Ribas knew he could do something here. He still had to be careful; the gift would need to borrow his strength.

He bent his mind on a single blue fear-strand. If he could cut it, the net might unravel and fall away, at least for now. He reached for it.

He could never explain this part, as often as people asked. He didn't only see the lines: he felt them too, against his own mind and even against his body. Fear felt like the touch of ice against bare skin. Reaching in – only with his mind, he didn't have to move a muscle – could hurt. It did now. He'd long since gotten used to that.

With enough strength, and the right intent in his mind, he could call on the gift to cut the strand. He would never forget the first time he had realized he could do that. The surge of excitement as he'd realized, twenty-five years ago now, that he could cut through pain, that day, and stop an animal's suffering.

Now he trained his strength and intent on that single fear-strand and called on the gift again.

Cut.

The shock went through his body. Like a snapped bowstring, the fear-strand lashed against his mind as it gave way. He felt the stinging slice of it, but more, he felt the strength rush out of him.

The gift had taken more than he'd thought. For a moment the room whirled. He kept his eyes shut, bracing himself on the bed, waiting it out.

The first time, twenty-five years ago. The nanny in the barn, her side torn open on a nail, fighting and screaming as Mama tried to get the halter on to hold her still. The moment when Ribas looked into the nanny's mind and saw what he could do...the wave of triumph and exhaustion when he did it...and then the look on Mama's face.

"No, my dove, I'm not scared."

And when he said, yes, you are, and she said, maybe a little..."No, Mama, I know it's not just a little, I can see it," and he had been crying by then, shivering as she put her arms around him.

Twenty-five years ago. Dovne kenavnis.

Now the spinning slowed enough for him to raise his head. At least the effort hadn't made his heart pound and ache, the way it sometimes did. He opened his eyes, carefully.

Danya's face told him it had worked. He knew that stunned, relieved look, when a burden someone had carried too long seemed to sprout wings and fly away.

She stared at him. "How..."

"You know I can't tell you that." His voice sounded steady and normal. "I wish I could."

All the apprentices who came to Lida knew he couldn't teach

them the gift, but that didn't stop some of them from hoping. "I know," she said. "It's just, I've never…"

She had never felt that kind of relief. "I'm glad it worked," he said. "Now, you see how we've opened the door. It's going to need your help to stay open."

He wasn't sure how quickly the net might re-grow. Sometimes they didn't. He suspected Danya's would, but it might be slow enough to control.

"What can I do?" she said.

She looked ready to do anything. This wasn't the same frightened girl he had only met three days ago. Times like this reminded him why he had to give this work everything he had.

"I need you to tell me if you start having trouble again. Any time you feel a change."

She looked doubtful. "I don't want to bother you, zhinin."

"I have a feeling, mosevin, you'll be much more help to me without that extra burden. It's worth the bother."

He had never seen her smile before. It lit up the room like lamp-light, as if a candle inside her, almost extinguished, had caught its breath and begun to glow again.

"Thank you."

Her face was all the thanks he needed. "Of course. Now, let's go and get some dinner before everyone else eats it all." The weak feeling had passed. He'd be able to trust his legs when he stood up.

Maryut met them at the kitchen door. "Sit down and eat, zhinin. I've got a plate ready. Seldo can't wait to argue with you about that Old Namoran translation." One look at Danya, Ribas saw, told her most of what she needed to know about the past few minutes. She put her arm around the girl. "You come along and get some food too, mosevin. You worked hard this morning."

Ribas took a seat at the table with his family, across from Seldo and Milya. He and Seldo were still deep in talk, debating points about the translation of two particular Old Namoran words, by the time both their plates were empty. Then Seldo looked over Ribas's shoulder. "Messenger for you, I think."

Ribas turned around. He didn't recognize the short, thickset boy standing behind him. He had a shock of reddish-brown hair and dusty clothes that said he'd traveled some distance fast.

He held out an envelope. "Zhinin Ribas. Urgent letter from Kunin Dergo."

If the kunin had paid to send a courier, it certainly was urgent. Ribas took the envelope. It had the familiar gray wax seal on the back, stamped with the Circle House design all dagira used. "Thank you," he told the boy. "You're welcome to have some dinner if you'd like."

Seldo leaned across the table. "What's that?"

"Letter from the viduris." Ribas unfolded the single sheet of paper. The kitchen was still full of talk and noise, but silence seemed to settle on him as he read.

Kunin Dergo's handwriting was still strong and clear, though he was old now, his hair entirely white. Many years had gone by since Ribas had pestered him with questions, turned in unexpected assignments, and asked to learn improbable languages.

Now the kunin wrote with the most urgent news any member of the dagira could receive. As Ribas took it in, the stillness settled deep in him and seemed to spread out into the room.

Someone touched his arm. "Ribé? What's going on?"

Ribas looked up at Maryut. The rest of the family was listening too, Gedrin at the far end of the table leaning as far in as he could. Ribas knew he would have to make an announcement. Everyone in this room needed to hear what Kunin Dergo had written, but for now he could say it to just these few.

"Tavin Ardinas is dead."

He saw his own feelings mirrored in their faces. Everyone knew the Tavin had served a long time, that his health had been failing since the summer, but the Tavin was the heart of Namora and his loss brought both grief and strangeness. No one in this room had met him. Only Ribas had had any direct contact with him, and he would never forget the kindness of the priest who had supported a young zhinin in his wish to stay in his village and serve his own people.

Out of the little group at the table, Mama spoke first. "*Sela seraidit.*"

May his soul fly. The closing prayer said at the ceremony of release for someone who had died. "*Sela seraidit,*" Ribas answered. For a moment all of them were quiet. Then Ribas got up from the bench and went to the kitchen hearth, to ask his people to join him in praying for their Tavin who was gone.

7

VALDENA

Valda had her last conversation with Tavin Ardinas on the night when Galvo came to meet her in the square. After that evening, Ardinas slipped into a deep sleep he never fully woke from.

During the last days, Valda sat by his bedside hour after hour. Partly because she hoped the old priest might open his eyes one more time and know her. Partly because someone had to be with him when his soul set out from his body.

She and the Tavin's healer, Tayo Bodin, were there on the last night, toward the middle of Derla. No one else was with them. Together they watched Ardinas's slow, fragile breathing, the rise and fall of his chest. Valda pulled her chair up against the bed and held the old priest's unresponsive hand. The tayo sat opposite her. He had told Valda he thought the end would come that night. When it did, it was so quiet, so gentle, that it felt like nothing more than a cessation of motion they had barely seen before it stopped.

Tavin Ardinas was gone. His soul had gone out into the wholeness of the world again. Valda didn't have time to grieve, and in any case, grief didn't describe the hollow, cold feeling that filled her. As

Tavo Balsa, she had to officiate at the Tavin's ceremonies of memory and release.

The ceremony of memory for Ardinas meant a packed Great Circle House, crowds spreading out into the square and the streets beyond, and the stillness of mourning like an ocean fog filling Sostavi. Valda went through the rites, standing on the Great House dais in her white sventin's robes. Today the Tavo Balsa could not fill the Tavin's empty place.

In her white robes, in front of the eyes of all the dagira and all the people who had come to Sostavi to pay tribute to Namora's leader, Valda felt as cold and exposed as a single tree in a snow-swept field. She knew her voice must hold steady and clear as she recited the prayers and read the countless tributes to Ardinas gathered from those who had served with him. The ceremony of memory did its best to capture all that a life had meant. Valda must not blur that memory with her own sense of loss.

She wove her own voice into a curtain of words, a shield to hold up between herself and all the watching eyes. Behind that shield, in the moments of stillness during the service, she sent herself away from the Great House and down to the harbor and the ocean beyond. She asked the Goddess to guide Ardinas's soul out there, to meet the wind and mingle with the waves he had loved.

That night, when she was finally alone in her chambers in the House of the Sventine, Valda found herself wrapped in different memories. Not of Ardinas, but he had woken them up in her, that last evening when they talked.

Those first days at the viduris. The lonely chill of that time seemed to reach out of the past now and twist around Valda's heart and mind. She'd been a fragile soul, tightly coiled on herself. She still remembered the fear that had kept her from reaching out to anyone, even her roommate, to try to be friends, in case she found that her deepest fears were right. She really didn't belong in this over-whelming place with all these clever people, all these strange faces and voices.

She'd had dreams even then. She had let herself dream about Sostavi from the first time she realized she wanted to go to the viduris. At her first classes, the teachers' words all seemed to blur together. Kunin Dergo's stern look made her want to hide in a corner. She knew she'd never see Sostavi; she could never keep up with this work.

As Valda remembered it now, her chambers seemed to fall away, and all the things that defined her rank, as if those things had been the dream and only the memory was real. She was the lonely girl in the red mosevin's robes again, with no one to talk to, no one to trust.

One morning in the viduris's dining hall, more than a week into Rudua, the first month of the school's year. The teachers enforced a strict code of behavior at meals, so there was no rowdiness, but murmurs of talk and occasional short bursts of laughter filled the room. Outside, it was a chilly gray autumn day. Inside, the hearth warmed the bare stone floor and whitewashed walls, and there were smells of porridge and toast. Breakfast tended to be the viduris's best meal, free from over-boiled vegetables and tough questionable meat.

Valda sat alone at a table in one corner of the room, with her back to one of the tall windows. Most of the other round tables had students clustered around them, first-years through third-years, but already, people seemed to know to leave Valda alone. No one asked to sit with her, but no one bothered her either. She propped her book in front of her, determined to understand the Old Namoran teacher's last lecture on declensions. It was hard to get absorbed, because she felt as if people were looking at her, their stares like pinpricks on her skin. She told herself nobody cared what she did. She told herself she was glad.

She was staring at the chart of noun endings, trying to see the difference between accusative and ablative case, when someone said, "Good morning."

Valda almost dropped the book. She recognized the boy standing in front of her, of course. Everyone seemed to know him already. He was a tall, plain-looking farmer's boy from a little village no one had ever heard of. He wouldn't have stood out, except he was brave enough to ask Kunin Dergo questions, and he made friends so easily that Valda hadn't thought he could be a first-year too. And, she noticed now, he had the most striking blue eyes she had ever seen.

"Good morning." Her voice felt rusty, as if she hadn't used it in too long.

"Is it all right if I sit with you?"

Why did he want to? Valda gulped. "Yes," she said, and then wished she hadn't. How was she going to talk to him?

He set his bowl of porridge and mug of tea down and sat across from her. "I'm Ribas," he said.

"I know who you are."

The words came out before she thought. Valda felt the blush surge into her face. She could have told him her name, or said "Nice to meet you."

He laughed. There was no ridicule in it, only friendliness. "Then we're even," he said. "I know who you are, too. Valdena, right?"

Why would he have noticed her? Valda had no idea, but for the first time since she'd gotten to the viduris, she found herself smiling. "That's right."

A log shifted on the hearth in Valda's chambers, landing with a crunch on the stone and sending up a burst of sparks. The sound and light pulled her back to Sostavi and the House of the Sventine.

Ribé.

It hadn't been hard to talk to him after all. Not even a little. He'd told her about Lida, and his family, and the farm where he'd grown up, and he admitted his homesickness so candidly that she had felt safe telling him how huge and scary the viduris felt to her. They'd talked about Old Namoran declensions, and the kunin's lecture the day before on the *Book of Kenavi,* and he had gotten her laughing about the unguessable stew they'd been served for dinner last night.

She'd forgotten how good it felt to laugh. And he'd said, with the smile Valda would still know anywhere, that the viduris was a strange place sure enough, but they'd figure it out. They'd get through this together.

Looking back, Valda knew that as impressive as the dovne kenavnis was, it wasn't Ribas's real gift. He made people feel safe. You knew you could lean on his kindness.

And now Valda was here, and Ardinas was gone, and Ribas was hundreds of miles away in that little mountain village, and she hadn't been in touch with him in fifteen years. Tomorrow, and the next day, and the day after that, the Tavo Balsa would have to stand in front of the dagira and do the tasks demanded of her. Alone.

Ribé. Goddess hear me, I miss you.

A week after the ceremony of memory for the Tavin, Valda performed the ceremony of release for the same packed House. This second ceremony ended the week of formal mourning and sent the Tavin's soul on its way with the prayers and blessings of all his people. *Sela seraidit.*

The life of the dagira now had to continue. Valda had to take on the Tavo Balsa's next and most important duty: the election.

The day after the ceremony of release, on an otherwise ordinary Tretdina, the Council of Sventine met in its chambers. All sixteen members wore their formal white robes of office to convene in the meeting room. Valda now appeared as Tavo Balsa, in the brown robes that gave her all the authority over this crucial business.

The long meeting room had wood-paneled walls, rich carpeting, and tall windows that looked out over Sostavi Harbor far below. The Council members sat around a single long oval table, made of machia wood, which was exceptionally rare in Namora. The table had seventeen matching chairs around it, with one slightly taller chair at the head. The taller chair rightly belonged to the Tavin. It was Valda's seat now. As she took it, she thought distantly that once upon a time, she would have been amazed to think of herself in this place, the only woman on the Council and one of its youngest members, leading the process that would determine Namora's next ruler.

She called the Council to order and opened the meeting with the traditional prayer. All her male colleagues, dark- and light- and gray-headed, bent their heads obediently as she invoked the Goddess's guidance on this assembly. Then she read through the rules of election laid out in the *Rituals and Duties of the Council of Sventine*, first written over a thousand years ago during the leaderships of the earliest Tavine.

"The Council shall, with the guidance of the Goddess, select the Ruler of Namora over a period of time which shall neither exceed nor fall short of the full measure of one week.

"Day the First: the Council shall accept the nomination of worthy candidates. No sventin shall declare his or her own candidacy, but shall be selected as worthy and so named and presented to the Council by his or her colleagues.

"Day the Second: the Council shall determine, by vote, the two candidates who shall, by their devotion to the Goddess, diligence, and character, best display their worthiness to serve the Goddess and Her people as Tavin.

"Day the Third: Begins a period of deliberation neither to exceed nor fall short of five days, that the Council may consider its vote.

"Day the Eighth: the Council shall reconvene, and shall select, by vote, the candidate best qualified to accept the leadership of Namora, as the servant of the Goddess."

Everyone on the Council knew the process, but Valda read through it in detail. Most sventine would only vote once in their lives to elect a Tavin. She also read the stipulations that Council members might abstain from the final vote if they did not feel either chosen candidate was qualified to serve, and that if neither candidate received the nine-vote majority, the Tavo Balsa, "that the Country shall not lack leadership," would be installed as the next Tavin.

This was another reason why no Tavo Balsa could put him- or herself forward as a candidate or take part in the vote. Valda knew perfectly well that she, like every other Tavo Balsa in Namora's history, stood a slight chance of becoming the next ruler. It had happened a handful of times, but no one wanted that outcome. The sanction of the Council vote meant the certainty of the Goddess's blessing. A Tavo Balsa who became Tavin by default came into the role with hands tied and authority in question.

Valda felt sure her colleagues wouldn't let the vote fail this time. They must not, because she had no wish ever to be Tavin.

When she finished reading the rules, she asked the formal question, "Does any member of the Council wish to raise a query?"

No one did. Valda said, "Then I hereby open the floor to nominations."

Instantly, the room hummed with tension. The election process formally began right now. For at least two of these sventine, and no doubt others, this was their chance to reach out for the fruit they'd tasted for years in their dreams.

Hands went up around the table. Valda had guessed ahead of time who would speak up and who would most likely sit quiet, waiting to be nominated. The Council members had debated and agreed on these maneuvers all the week before, between Ardinas's ceremonies of memory and release. Valda didn't let her face show her distaste.

She chose one of the raised hands. "Sventin Eldin."

Eldin was one of the oldest members of the Council, white-haired and white-bearded. He got to his feet, no easy achievement given his girth. "Tavo Balsa, Sventine," he said, puffing a little on the words. "I wish to nominate my colleague Galvo Dendraikas."

As expected. "Thank you, sventin," Valda said. "Sventin Galvo, do you accept the nomination?"

"I do, Tavo Balsa."

Of course he did. No doubt he and Eldin had settled the nomination beforehand, and no doubt Galvo had specifically wanted his name brought up by one of the oldest, and therefore most experienced, Council members. His face showed no hint of triumph, but she knew he must feel it.

Valda chose another hand. "Sventin Rano."

Rano was one of the younger members. He was already on his feet by the time Eldin had gotten back into his chair, and he spoke up quickly, with no formal greeting. "I wish to nominate Sventin Lesvin Berenaikas."

Also as expected. "Sventin Lesvin," Valda said, "do you accept the nomination?"

Lesvin was much younger than Galvo, thin-faced and pale-haired, with vivid green eyes. He didn't try to hide either his smile or his flush of pleasure. "Yes, Tavo Balsa."

Three other sventine nominated candidates. When everyone had spoken who wished to, Valda called on the five nominees to stand.

"Sventine," she addressed the Council, "you must choose our next Tavin from among these worthy candidates. Tomorrow this Council will reconvene to select the two who will stand for the final vote."

She felt certain she knew who the final two would be. The next morning, Ketdina, the Council gathered again. The vote for the two candidates was done by show of hands. It went exactly as Valda had expected: seven votes for Galvo, four for Lesvin, and the other three nominees dividing five votes between them.

"Council of Sventine," Valda said. "Here are your candidates to serve as Namora's next Tavin: Galvo Dendraikas and Lesvin Berenaikas."

Again, Galvo's face stayed perfectly calm. Lesvin's, on the other hand, had the same excited flush on it, as if he'd gotten a gift he hardly dared to believe. The three rejected nominees did their best to hide their disappointment, but Valda felt sure everyone had more or less expected this outcome.

Now she brought out the materials for the final vote, which would take place in six days. Forty-eight round stones, sixteen pure white, sixteen deep blue, and sixteen slate gray, kept in a beautifully carved box of golden pine.

The Council had used the same stones in every Tavin election since time out of mind. Solemnity tightened in the room as Valda unwrapped the box from its cloth covering and opened it. She explained, as the *Rituals and Duties* dictated, that she would give each member of the Council one stone of each color. In this election, she said, the white stones would be used to vote for Sventin Lesvin, the blue for Sventin Galvo. The gray stones were to be used only if a sventin wished to abstain from the vote.

Each Council member must take all three voting stones with him when this meeting adjourned. He must spend time, between now and the next Tretdina, considering his vote and asking the Goddess's guidance. When the Council reconvened in six days, Valda would again open the box. Each sventin must come forward and place his chosen voting stone in it. When all had voted, Valda would count the stones for everyone to see.

Valda dismissed the Council with a closing prayer. Most of them left quickly, off to duties in the House, or a late breakfast, or to their chambers for study and reflection. Galvo hung back, looking as if he wanted to speak to her, but Valda felt relieved when Lesvin stayed too. She didn't need any reminders from Galvo that he wanted to make her his Tavo Balsa, or that she might help "guide" her colleagues' decisions between today and the vote.

When Galvo saw that Lesvin wasn't leaving, he smiled at Valda, as polite and urbane as usual, and left the meeting room. As soon as he was gone, Lesvin said, "Tavo Balsa, may I speak to you?"

She wrapped the pine box in its cloth again. "Of course, sventin."

She hoped Lesvin wasn't also going to promise that she could keep her position if she supported him now. She didn't know him well at all; he always called her by her full title, not even Valdena, much less the informal Valda, and she certainly couldn't imagine calling him Lesví. His happiness after the morning's vote had disappeared. The intensity of the look he gave her now made her uneasy.

He said, "I'm concerned, Tavo Balsa. Do you think Sventin Galvo will win the election?"

The answer was yes. Galvo had gotten seven votes today. He only needed two more to win, and Valda felt sure he could find those in the next five days, assuming he hadn't already.

She knew better than to tell Lesvin that. "It isn't for me to say," she told him. "The Goddess will decide."

He fidgeted with the belt of his robes. "I'm afraid he may not be the best guide for Namora."

If it comes to that, I don't know that you are, either. She remembered that last talk with Tavin Ardinas and what the old ruler had said about Impera Shurik in Lassar. *He thinks his God speaks to him.* She didn't think Ardinas would want to see Lesvin win now, but he hadn't felt much more enthusiastic about Galvo.

She said, "What would you do differently from Galvo if you were elected?"

"I would ask for the Goddess's guidance in all things." He said it immediately, with total conviction. "I would take no step without being certain of Her will. I'm afraid that Sventin Galvo thinks too much about human wills and desires."

Undoubtedly, Lesvin would make the same case over the next five days to whichever of his colleagues he thought would listen. Valda was glad, again, that she wouldn't cast a vote. She had plenty of reservations about Galvo herself, but the older sventin certainly understood diplomacy, and the reality that people were people. He was probably best equipped to deal with whatever challenges might come from Lassar.

She said, "What would you do, sventin, if you couldn't be sure of the Goddess's will?"

She thought the question might make Lesvin angry. His answer surprised her.

"I would listen, Tavo Balsa. I would listen closely and do the best I could."

Valda picked up the pine box in its wrapper. Lesvin's answer was wiser than his years. It didn't change the fact that he would still probably have to put up with Tavin Galvo, but he might hope to outlive the older sventin and have another chance to be Tavin one day.

As kindly as she could, she said, "Then we must listen for the Goddess's will now. We must trust that She will choose Her Tavin."

Lesvin looked unhappy. "I will pray."

"So will I," Valda said. "Raimaté, sventin."

"Raimaté, Tavo Balsa." He stood where he was as she left the room.

Valda didn't want to involve herself at all in the Council's "deliberations" before the final vote. No doubt Galvo and Lesvin were twisting every arm they could reach.

For two days after the nominations, she kept to herself as much as she could, staying in her chambers when she wasn't in the Great House. On the third morning, before she had even sat down with a cup of tea, a servant knocked at her chamber door. "Tavo Balsa, Sventin Galvo to see you."

Valda didn't let herself sigh out loud. "Very well." What could he have to tell her, aside from the promises he'd already made?

When Galvo came in, Valda thought she saw the faintest tightness in the set of his jaw, but his voice sounded as smooth as ever. "Good morning, Valda. I'm sorry to intrude so early."

"It's no trouble. Would you like tea?"

"No, thank you."

As early as it was, he'd dressed in his robes of office. Valda had on the simple woolen dress she wore to be comfortable. She wore slippers and her hair hung in a single long braid down her back. Next to Galvo, she knew she must look very young.

She motioned him toward the two chairs by her hearth. "Please, sit down."

"I won't trouble you long," he said. He sat straight-backed in the chair, graceful and easy as always. Valda felt younger than she was, cupping her own warm mug between her hands like a little girl with hot milk. He said, "I've heard news I thought you would want to know as well, if you aren't already aware of it."

Again Valda thought she saw that tension in his face, the smallest hairline crack in his usual polish. "I haven't heard any news."

"Then you don't know about Sventin Lesvin's plan?"

The question came out as sharp as a whiplash. The accusation in it snapped Valda fully alert. She might look like a girl, but he should remember who he was talking to.

"What plan, sventin?" She injected every word with ice.

"I beg your pardon," Galvo said, all politeness again. "I should have known you'd keep yourself apart from such things."

Valda was in no mood for intrigue. "I haven't discussed the vote with anyone," she said. "I'm not aware of any plan."

Galvo leaned forward. "It seems Sventin Lesvin's supporters don't expect him to win the election. If they can, they want to keep me from winning too. They're trying to persuade some sventine to abstain in the vote."

Valda tried to take this in. It was still early in the morning, she was tired, and the idea sounded ridiculous. Deadlock the vote because your candidate couldn't win? If anyone but Galvo, with his long experience, had brought this "plan" to her, she would have thought they were spinning stories.

He had seven votes to begin with. Valda felt sure he would keep them. If Lesvin's supporters – four, based on yesterday's vote – wanted to make sure he didn't get the last two he needed, and if they couldn't swing more votes for their own candidate, they would have to talk five Council members into abstaining. Everyone knew how important it was to get a majority. Did enough sventine really dislike Galvo enough to throw their votes away?

Galvo said, "I came to you because you know what happens if they succeed."

Valda's thoughts sped up to a whir. Of course she knew. She saw the passage in the election rules she'd read yesterday: *That the country shall not lack leadership, the Tavo Balsa shall be installed...*

"No."

She didn't realize she'd said it out loud until she saw the satisfaction in Galvo's face. He said, "I hoped you would see it that way."

Valda gripped the warm mug tightly. "You thought I knew about this? You thought I wanted them to deadlock the vote?"

Galvo held up a deprecating hand. "I hoped I knew you better than that, Valda. Forgive me for doubting. This business is..." He smiled, mocking himself. "Difficult."

Valda fought the urge to close her eyes. Out of nowhere, she found herself remembering another face, a much different smile. Someone who wouldn't have had any more patience with this maneuvering than she did. Someone who never, she couldn't help thinking, would have thrown the kind of accusation at her that Galvo just had.

She said, "I would never try to sabotage the vote. I don't want to be Tavin."

Galvo reached over to press her hand. "I know that." His voice sounded fatherly now. "That's also why I thought you should know about this. A word in the right place could be a great help, to make sure we have no difficulties."

Another ugly possibility reared up in Valda's mind. Had Galvo created this "sabotage the vote" story to get her involved, force her to press Council members to vote for him? She fought the urge to pull away.

That didn't make sense, though. He only needed two more votes. Even with his ambition, Valda couldn't believe Galvo would stoop such a lie when he was already so close to what he wanted.

She did say, "How do you know about this?"

He waved a hand. "Sventin Eldin told me he overheard Rano talking to Vadimas." Rano had been the one who nominated Lesvin. Vadimas was an older member of the Council. Valda knew he had no particular fondness for Galvo, but she doubted he would want to support someone as young and untried as Lesvin. Galvo said, "Eldin told me Rano was trying to convince Vadimas to abstain. I did some digging of my own after that."

No doubt he had. Rumors and gossip, *promises and insults,* as Tavin Ardinas had said.

"I don't ask you to tell our colleagues how to vote," Galvo said, as if he'd heard some of her thoughts earlier. "I only though you might remind them, as their Tavo Balsa, how important it is to have a majority here. And you might make clear that you, personally, don't wish the vote to fail."

Tiredness swamped Valda. She couldn't believe that enough of her colleagues disliked both candidates enough to force her into the Tavin's seat. If anyone actually meant to abstain from voting, maybe they weren't thinking about what it would mean. Or maybe they wouldn't actually do it, no matter what Galvo and Eldin thought they'd heard.

Still, it wasn't worth the risk. The vote must not fail.

"I'll speak to them," she said. "Thank you for telling me this."

Galvo pressed her hand again and stood up. "Thank you, Tavo Balsa. I'll see myself out." Before he turned away, Valda felt sure she saw triumph on his face.

Valda didn't want to tell any of her colleagues, in so many words, about Galvo's visit or what he'd said. If anyone thought he was trying to bribe or coerce her into pushing the vote for him, that might backfire and hurt his chances. As carefully as she could, she spoke with each Council member over the next two days. She used vague words about "wanting the vote to go smoothly" and "feeling sure of a majority." As much as she could, she made it clear that she would take no responsibility for a failed vote, though she couldn't say the words she thought every hour.

I will not be your new Tavin.

She couldn't ask anyone directly how they intended to vote.

With a few of the older sventine, she made a point of reminding them how young she was. "Sventin Lesvin is only a year or two older than I am. He's achieved a great deal in a short time." If they didn't like Lesvin's youth, she felt sure they wouldn't want any chance of a still-younger Tavin. With others, she made sure to mention that she had worked with Galvo since her own arrival in Sostavi, when he had already been a sventin. Galvo meant experience, reliability, certainty.

Through the delicate dance of trying to influence the vote while saying nothing direct, her last talk with Ardinas echoed in her head. *Trouble with Lassar. Shurik.* Ardinas's own feeling that neither of the two obvious candidates, the exact two they had, would be an ideal choice.

Goddess hear me, neither am I.

On the following Tretdina morning, the day of the final vote, Valda got to the Council meeting room early. The autumn fog from the harbor had come in thicker than ever this morning, dense and gray, swirling through Sostavi's streets and leaving clinging mist on the windows. Valda's brown robes felt too thin to keep out the damp chill. The hearth fire in the meeting room flickered uneasily.

She took her seat and set the unwrapped pine box and the *Rituals and Duties* on the table in front of her. Alone, with only the sound of the fire, she closed her eyes and offered a prayer.

Goddess who guides us, be with us now. Help us to choose Your servant wisely.

Footsteps and voices pulled her back to the room. The Council members came in in twos and threes, some talking quietly, some silent. Lesvin came in alone. Valda saw he looked as pale and anxious as he had a week ago. Galvo looked solemn, but Valda felt sure she read confidence in his face too. She hoped she did. Whatever anyone might say about him, she hoped that within the hour, she would declare him the Tavin-elect. Most of the other faces had the clarity that came from a decision firmly made, but Valda did see a couple of troubled expressions.

When everyone took their seats, Valda didn't have to raise her hand for quiet. All the faces turned to her, expectant, waiting.

"Council," she said. "In the sight of the Goddess, today we ask for Her guidance as we choose a Tavin to lead Her people."

She could only hope, now, that her indirect conversations, and whatever manipulations Galvo had managed, had done enough. She led the Council in the ritual prayer. "In Your wisdom, Kenavi, help us to choose that member of our fellowship who shall most faithfully serve You, and shall most willingly carry out Your wishes for Your people. Tebena."

Her colleagues echoed the last word back to her. *Tebena*: so be it.

The vote began. The Council members came up one at a time, alphabetically by patronymic, to place their stones in the box. The lid had a round opening just large enough to admit a closed hand, so that neither Valda nor anyone else would see what color each sventin put inside: blue for Galvo, white for Lesvin, or gray to abstain. The clatter of the stones against the wood made the only sound in the room. No one spoke a word.

The last Council member placed his stone in the box and went back to his seat. Now Valda must open the lid, lift the stones out, and count them for everyone to see. In the last moment before she did, she offered one last prayer that she would see what she hoped. Blue and white stones only, one color clearly outnumbering the other. She didn't care which.

The lid creaked as she raised it. She lifted the stones out. As soon as she saw them, her throat closed over.

Gray stones. Three. From the sounds around her, nothing as audible as a gasp but clear whispers of air as people caught their breaths, she knew everyone else guessed the same thing she did. There were not enough blue or white.

As the rules required, Valda separated the stones into three groups, naming and numbering each vote. Her voice sounded steady and clear. "For Sventin Galvo, one vote. For Sventin Galvo, two votes." Her hands didn't tremble as she moved the stones into groups. "One vote to abstain. For Sventin Lesvin, one vote."

The count went on until she gave the final tally. Eight votes for Galvo. Five for Lesvin. Three to abstain.

No majority.

No one spoke. Valda thought it might have been better if there had been arguments right then, accusations, even curses. She could not look at either of the candidates. She could only stare straight down at the stones on the table.

No.

The word filled her head. She wanted to close her eyes, let the word swallow her, open her eyes again and find that none of this was true.

She was Tavo Balsa. She had a duty to finish. As if watching from a great distance, she saw her own hands pick up the *Rituals and Duties* and open it to the correct page. Her voice sounded as steady and clear as before as she read the words that governed the Council now.

"If the Council shall not by specified majority determine the next Tavin, that the nation shall not lack leadership, the acting Tavo Balsa shall be installed as Tavin, thereby to serve the Goddess and Her people."

Goddess hear me. Goddess help me.

She closed the book and laid it aside. Now she raised her head and made herself look her colleagues in the eye, around the table, one after the other. She saw Eldin's anger, Rano's triumph, Lesvin's unmistakable relief, and Galvo...Galvo's inscrutable stillness, his veneer holding up even under this disastrous disappointment. One vote too few. From some remote place, Valda admired him.

"Council of Sventine," she said. "By the authority vested in me, and by the stated rules of election, I declare myself, Valdena Filtraikas, Tavin-elect of Namora."

Into the silence she spoke the final word: "Tebena." From around the table, sixteen voices spoke it back to her, sealing the result, echoing her own disbelief.

That afternoon, Valda sat alone in her chambers with the door latched and a servant stationed outside, instructed to let no one in. She had a piece of paper, a pen, and her wax seal on the little table in front of her. For now, these chambers still belonged to her. Too soon, she would have to move into the ones that belonged to the Tavin, where Ardinas had lived for so long.

After the vote, after she had sealed and declared the results, the Council had shaken off its shock and buzzed like a hive of disturbed bees. Everyone wanted to know who had abstained. No one would admit to it. Lesvin and Rano hadn't hidden their satisfaction. Eldin, and a couple of Galvo's other most outspoken supporters, hadn't hidden their anger.

At least three of her colleagues had seen Valda as the least of the evils on offer. They had disliked both candidates enough to risk putting in a Tavin who didn't have the majority or the Goddess's sanction. Valda wished it helped to know that.

Tradition said that the new Tavin must be installed in Ketva, the Fourth Month, after the high holy months of Akena and Algima, and after the busyness of the spring planting season in Ivesta. Valda would not wait that long. She wouldn't have any overblown pageantry or celebration for the result she had never wanted. She had told the Council at the end of the morning's meeting that she wished to be installed in Tyla, less than a month from now. No one argued with her, but Valda knew the arguments would come thick and fast, soon enough. Once the House of the Tavin actually belonged to her, her authority would look as fragile as an old clay pot.

Right now, she had to put the vote aside. She had to do something she had wanted to do since the instant when she'd put the voting stones on the meeting room table and known what they meant.

She dipped her pen in the clay inkpot and held the heavy paper steady. *Raimaté, Zhinin Ribas,* she wrote.

It probably wasn't wise to write to him. He might not understand hearing from her now, out of the blue, and the Goddess knew he might not welcome it, but he was there, in that mountain village. Three hundred miles didn't seem so terribly far when you thought about it as a week's journey in a good coach.

You must be surprised to hear from me, she wrote. *I regret that it's been so long.*

In the back of her mind, she remembered Galvo's face after the vote. She hoped he didn't blame her for what had happened. He had said he knew her better than that, but...

I should have written to you years ago. When I first arrived in Sostavi, I thought of you more than you can perhaps imagine.

It certainly wasn't wise to dredge up the past. She couldn't make herself crumple the paper and start over. Every hour of every day, she hid her thoughts and measured her words in front of her Great House colleagues. Now, if she was going to deal with the overwhelming reality the Council had handed her today, she would have to create a more perfect mask than she'd ever worn before. First she had to talk, the way she had talked to the boy who had sat at her lonely table and made himself her friend.

I won't take up as much of your time, or as much paper as it would need, to tell you all the history of my time here. Try as she might, she couldn't keep the distant, formal tone anymore. *I'll only say that in many ways, it hasn't been what I imagined when we were at the viduris together.*

The words came easily now. She wrote about dagira politics, about her colleagues who had schemed and grubbed for votes while their leader of so many years was dying. She wrote about the hours she had spent at Ardinas's bedside and how quietly the old priest had finally let go of life. She wrote what she had told no one else: how she ached every day for the old man who had always been kind to her.

He was a good man. We couldn't have asked for a better leader.

Through it all, she could see Ribas's face as if he were sitting across from her at the table again. She could see the sympathy in the blue eyes. *And now the election. I can't believe what's happened.*

She wrote candidly about Galvo and Lesvin and the failed vote. She knew how much the news would surprise Ribas; she could see him holding the letter, re-reading the last part closely, taking it in. *Sventin Galvo may still think I wanted this.* A tiny, detached corner of her mind wondered if she ought to consider Galvo for her Tavo Balsa. It would be an ironic twist for them both, but no one was better qualified. On the other hand, he wouldn't want the position if he still held any hope of becoming Tavin one day, and Valda thought wearily that she didn't know how long she might last in the job. She wrote, *I think you'll understand that I didn't want it at all. I want it even less, if that's possible, given that it happened because my colleagues couldn't agree on a candidate.* Not having the Council's sanction was bad enough. Right now, she couldn't even begin to think about whatever trouble might come from Lassar.

She told him that she planned to have the High Installation in Tyla instead of Ketva. Then she found herself writing something she hadn't intended.

Would you consider making the journey?

She stopped and looked at the words. The first winter chill was already settling on Namora. The weather in Tyla never got as harsh and bitter as it did in Akena, but the cold still bit deep, and storms could swirl up without warning. He wasn't strong. She didn't know how much, if at all, he could travel, especially in risky weather.

She let the words stay and added the exact truth. *It would mean so much to have you and Maryut Ribenis here.*

She understood the size of the honor she was handing him. The Tavin-elect personally inviting a zhinin from a backwater village to a High Installation: you could almost call it a command. What subservient dagira would refuse that summons?

He had refused something like it before. And this wasn't the

Tavin-elect speaking. This was one mosevin asking a favor from another.

Do you remember when all of us, you and Matevas and Niala and Andrin and I, had our installations in our different Circle Houses? They had been eighteen years old, close friends, finished with their apprenticeships and taking on assignments as full members of the dagira. It had been a busy, joyful, overwhelming time. *I remember your installation in Lida so clearly.* She didn't write about the pang it had given her to watch him trade the red mosevin's robes for the sea-blue robes of the zhinin, or the deeper hurt she had felt when frail old Zhinin Odilas presented him to Lida village as its new officiant. In those moments, she had fully understood how far away they would be from each other from that day on. Instead she wrote, *Those were such proud times. If you could be here for another ceremony now, I might be able to see it through.*

She had no right to send him any such thing. "Might be able to see it through," as if he should have to help her do that, as if she didn't know her duty. She had been the one who stopped writing to him once their lives went in different directions. She had cut off that part of herself when she came here from Paret. So-called honor or not, what made her think she could ask him to go through the trouble and hassle of a long winter journey, as a favor to someone who'd had nothing to do with him in years?

She kept writing, telling him that if he and Maryut did come for the Installation, they would be welcome to lodge in the Great House's House of the Zhinine. Finally she wrote, *I hope your life in Lida has been all you wished for. Your people are so fortunate to have you. I send you and Maryut my prayers and all best wishes.*

She ended it using the usual form between members of the dagira: *Yours in the fellowship of the Goddess Kenavi.* Though it felt stilted and wrong, she signed it *Valdena Filtraikas.*

After she folded it, slipped it into an envelope addressed to *Zhinin Ribas Silvaikas, Lida village, Kalnu region,* and pressed her seal on the back, she thought she might not send it after all. She'd done what she needed in writing it. No doubt she'd be much wiser not to trouble him.

She still found herself going to the door of her chambers with the letter in her hand. The servant stood at attention outside. Valda handed him the envelope. "Please send this by courier at once."

The servant bowed. Valda had closed the door again before she remembered that Galvo had seemed too interested in Ribas, that night when they'd spoken on the square. For a moment she thought she should get the letter back. But when she thought of it on its way, flying southeast as fast as a horse could run, she couldn't bring herself to do it.

8

———————

BEREG

Before he left Cheremay with his new detachment, on Impera Shurik's orders to find the Pala Vaia winter camps, Silde Bereg Orlon had to write to his family back in Thysidich. He had to tell them he wouldn't be home in a matter of weeks after all.

The Commission of Roads hadn't given him any gift with words. Gravel didn't need gentle talk; stones and border planks didn't ask for sympathy and concern. In his room in the great barracks in Cheremay, Bereg could see his wife and daughter's faces so clearly that he had to stop several times while he scratched out his single-page letter to wipe the tears out of his eyes. He had almost gotten back to them. He wanted to tell Nela and Ania how deeply he felt the delay, but his pen wouldn't do what he wanted.

Wife and daughter, I must tell you not to expect me when I said. He at least had the round clean hand all soldiers learned in school. No one had to work to recognize his clumsy words. *Impera Shurik has given me new orders. I have to travel south for a while.*

He could have told them he missed them. He could have told them how much he wanted the crisp cool air of home instead of the too-warm softness of the southern plains. He could have said that he'd been counting the days until he would be with them, and this new count felt much too high, but he would think of his family every single day until he made it back.

Instead, his pen wrote something else. *No one can disobey orders. The Impera has given me and others an important job, and I must do it before I can come home.*

Bereg thought Nela would understand him, after all their years together. But Ania...surely Ania knew her father too. Didn't she?

Ania, you must take good care of your children, and help your mother at home, but don't work too hard. I want to see you healthy when I come back.

Maybe that would tell her how much he cared. He couldn't seem to find the words to say that in his mind, she was still the little girl whose laugh had wound around his heart the way her fingers used to cling to his hand. He couldn't tell her what he would give to hear her laugh again.

Impera Shurik has graciously assured me that I'll have my retirement when I finish this task.

That news was the real prize. Bereg had meant to write every detail of what Shurik had promised him. "It will be my pleasure to send you home in the spring with all the compensation a soldier of your stature deserves." Shurik himself had said that. Bereg should send the Impera's exact words to his family, so they could hold onto that comfort.

He couldn't do that either. Not, this time, because his thoughts felt too clumsy and heavy. Because other words kept getting in the way.

I know he thinks he bought you, but that doesn't have to be true.

Bereg pushed the reproach out of his mind. He should have forgotten it by now. He wrote, *Both of you take care of yourselves. Walk with Mesha's protection until I see you.* He signed it, *Yours faithfully, Bereg (Father).*

He had to obey his orders. If he wanted to go home in the spring, he must accept the detachment assigned to him and take it out of Cheremay to hunt for the Pala Vaia camps.

He had followed orders all his life. He could follow this one. He knew no harm of the Pala Vaia, that was true, but surely the impera knew best. Especially when Shurik believed so absolutely that the orders to destroy the tribal people came from Lord Mesha Himself.

Why, then, Bereg wondered, out of all the soldiers carrying out this mission, why must he have Silde Fisa Vasem as the other officer with his detachment? Silde Vasem, the only soldier who seemed to have any opinion of the orders at all.

He told us to kill men and women who haven't harmed him or us. He told us to kidnap their children.

Bereg could still feel Silde Vasem's hard fingers gripping his arm. He could still see her gray eyes, dark with bottomless anger.

Ask your conscience, Silde Orlon, if you still have one. Ask it what happens to children who see their parents murdered.

He must not listen. He must not think. Bereg mailed his letter home to Thysidich and packed for the new journey, trying not to feel Silde Vasem's words lodged like a bone in his throat.

The detachments left Cheremay two days later. Autumn was deepening in the capital. Bereg knew that at home, the air would already have the clear sparkle that tasted of winter coming. He and his detachment headed south, into the plains, where the grass still waved tall and green and late-blooming yellow poppies looked like spilled butter under a too-open, too-wide sky.

They rode through Kovik Thydia and into Tsvavyest, one of the regions Shurik wanted most thoroughly reconnoitered. Their horses were the stocky, brown and white, strong-bodied breed the military favored. They didn't have the grace and elegance of the horses some wealthy folk kept for pleasure-riding, but they could cover dozens of miles a day, gallop with the weight of a fully armed soldier on their backs, and keep up their pace with minimal food and water if the grazing got thin.

Bereg had always liked the comradeship you got with a good mount. On this journey he knew, long before the detachment got out of Adin, that his horse's comradeship was the only kind he was likely to have until they got back to Cheremay.

Silde Vasem said very little to him. That, at least, came as a relief. She rode in almost perfect silence from day's end to day's end, only giving the young soldiers in the detachment a curt order now and then about breaking camp faster and not chattering so much on the road. In the evenings, while the young soldiers swapped jokes and stories about their sweethearts back home, Silde Vasem sat quiet with her supper plate on her knees and her eyes on the flames of the cooking fire. Bereg thought with some satisfaction that she must have seen the sense of following orders after all. She must have seen they had no choice. Certainly she could follow them as well as anyone.

The young soldiers said nothing to Bereg either, other than "yes, silde" and "no, silde" in response to his commands. No Lasska soldier would try to chat or gossip with a superior. Apart from that, he was too old to interest them. They talked and laughed amongst them-selves on the road, as much as they dared under Silde Vasem's smile-less presence and clear gray stare. Bereg knew that as far as they were concerned, he was the elderly parent who deserved respect but not liking.

As one long day followed another, and as the miles stretched out behind them first through Adin and then Thydia, Bereg found himself missing the old camaraderie of the Road Commission more and more. That branch of the military had as good discipline as any, but soldiers on the Road Commission were engineers and craftspeo-ple, hard workers who knew how to use their brains and hands both. They'd all understood one another. Bereg had made any number of friends in the Commission over the years. The long days of work they had all put in, backbreaking physical labor and all, had been nothing like the days of silence he slogged through now.

Every day, the plains opened up wider around them. Every day, the distance between Bereg and home got longer.

Then came the morning they crossed the invisible line that marked the border between Kovik Thydia and Kovik Tsvavyest: the Fourth and Twentieth Claws of the Bear. Only a tiny metal sign by the road showed the change from one Claw to the other. The impera believed the search detachments would be likeliest to find Vaia camps here, in the remotest and warmest part of Lassar.

Bereg's detachment left the road at the Tsvavyest border and struck off into the plains. The Vaia kept away from Lasska roads and settlements, so following the road farther would be no use. Bereg felt a pull of regret as they abandoned the solid pavement which, for him, was a link to the life he missed.

The young soldiers, though, were eager and excited. They reminded Bereg of the hunting dogs his grandfather had bred back home. Off duty, the dogs might gambol and play like puppies, but let them lead a hunter into the woods and they became wild creatures, sharp-eared and quick-eyed, padding noiselessly through the brush with all senses alert for prey and muscles tensed to spring.

Two young soldiers, a wiry narrow-faced boy named Dimik Kuzen and a tall girl named Lada Egem, unshipped their vinduli from their supply packs as soon as they crossed the Tsvavyest border. The vindula, the long-barreled firearm that could shoot three rounds before reloading, was a Lasska soldier's most powerful and dangerous weapon. Kuzen and Egem both slung their vinduli across their saddles, ready for action, as they led the column out into the tall wild grass.

Bereg rode up beside them. Even up here, he could still feel Silde Vasem's chilly presence at the back of the column.

"Egem," he said. "Kuzen. You know we are not to engage with the tribal people unless they attack first. Impera Shurik's orders."

Both young soldiers saluted him respectfully, crossing their right palms to their left forearms. Lada Egem said, "Of course, Silde Orlon, but we must be ready. The strenyi are treacherous."

Strenyi. Bereg had gotten used to thinking of them as Vaia. The Lasska word, "strangers," sounded odd. Lada Egem said, "Our weapons will be no use to us in our packs, if we should meet an ambush."

Reasonable enough, though as far as Bereg knew, none of them had any reason to anticipate trouble from the Vaia. The tribes wouldn't have any idea of Impera Shurik's plan.

The sun spilled down on the riders. Bereg's coat felt stiflingly heavy, and his back ached more than he liked after these days in the saddle, but the two young soldiers showed no signs of discomfort. Both of them were younger than Bereg's own Ania. Lada Egem had twisted her fair hair up in a knot at the back of her head, the way most Lasska women soldiers did, but a few strands had escaped and blew loose in the breeze. Her face looked round and smooth, girlish. Something about it made Bereg's chest tighten.

She must have noticed his expression. "Please don't be concerned, Silde Orlon. We will keep a good lookout." She nodded at Dimik Kuzen, who sat straight and tense in his saddle. "We have good judgment."

She smiled. For an instant Bereg's heart went out to her completely: she really was only a girl, too much like the one he missed. At a second glance, though, her smile felt wrong to him. Again he thought of the hunting dogs with their eager eyes and sharp teeth.

On the third night in Tsvavyest, Silde Vasem sat guard by the embers of larger of the two cooking fires, after the rest of the detachment turned in for the night. She had taken more than her share of guard shifts since the beginning of the journey. Bereg suspected she did it not to be helpful, but because she welcomed the time alone in the dark, with her own silence wrapped around her.

Bereg turned restlessly on his bedroll. He wouldn't admit it, but his bones protested against the hard ground more than they used to. He hadn't written to Nela and Ania since leaving Thydia and the military roads. Out here, until and unless they ran across another detachment headed back to Cheremay, he couldn't send a letter or receive one. He missed his link to home like a pulled tooth.

Finally he gave up on sleep. He didn't want Silde Vasem's companionship, and she certainly didn't seem to want his, but right now she was the only creature who might listen to him. He wanted to hear his own voice before it dried up and blew away.

She sat cross-legged on the ground beside the fire pit the young soldiers had dug, her eyes on the flickering coals. He went over and sat beside her.

"Silde Vasem," he said. "Thank you for taking guard duty again."

Her head bobbed, acknowledging him. Since the journey began, she had looked exactly the same every day: the same gray uniform jacket and pants, her hair twisted in the same knot at the back of her head, the same expressionless face. He wondered if she ever smiled. He had trouble thinking she could.

Insects shrilled and rustled in the grass. The dying fire popped softly as the coals cooled. One of the tethered horses pawed the ground with a hoof.

Abruptly, Silde Vasem turned toward Bereg. The fading red firelight barely touched her face. A hood of shadow seemed to cover her, but her eyes gleamed out of the dark.

"Silde Orlon. Tell me about your family."

The question sounded hard and angry, as if someone had jerked it out of her. She had never seemed to care about his family before. Why now?

He said, "I have a wife and daughter." Whether Silde Vasem actually wanted to know about them or not, Bereg felt relief in just saying their names out loud. He told her about Ania's widowhood and told her the names of his three grandchildren. When he finished, he said, "What about you? Do you have children?"

He found it impossible to imagine that, so he wasn't surprised when she said no. "I've never had a family," she said. "I never will."

Without wanting to, Bereg remembered her words in the square in Cheremay. *He thinks he's bought you.* Bought him because of

Bereg's love for his home. Maybe Silde Vasem's anger came from loneliness: she hadn't married when she was young, maybe, because the military life kept her too busy, and she regretted that now.

If that was her trouble, it might not be too late. Bereg knew she probably couldn't bear children anymore, but some men didn't mind that. She might find a widower who only wanted the comfort of shared meals and a warm bed at night. He wondered if he dared to mention that possibility to her.

Then she said, "My name isn't Vasem, you know."

The flat, expressionless words caught Bereg off guard. "What do you mean?"

"My parents were Voseg and Ina Leben." She spoke to the fire, not to him, in the same tone he'd heard when she had answered Shurik's questions about the Vaia. As if she were reciting a lesson she had learned. "I was born in Kovik Feyst, in a village in the mountains. I was four when Mangevar's soldiers came."

Kovik Feyst. Bereg had thought she was from Tyi; that was what she had said back in Cheremay when they had first met. And what was this about Mangevar's soldiers? If she had been four years old, that must have been some forty years ago. Right at the beginning of Mangevar's rule.

She said, "They were a company of fighting troops. I don't know what they were doing there. They came through the mountain pass near the village and quartered with us. I remember the tall men in their gray coats."

Why are you telling me this? Bereg's stomach felt tight. He felt certain, somehow, that she was going to say something he didn't want to hear. He couldn't bring himself to interrupt her. He had never heard her say anything about herself before.

"It was winter," she said. "We didn't have much food in the village. Not enough to satisfy them, I suppose. To make up for it, some of the soldiers decided to have sport with the women."

Her level, steady tone didn't change at all, but Bereg felt the words like a hand gripping his throat. In all his years in the quietly busy Road Commission, he had never heard of anything like this. Soldiers were disciplined, mannerly, trained to be from their first days in the army. Trained to be, in fact, before they were soldiers, as boys and girls in school.

"My mother was pretty, you know," she said. "I don't look like her. I remember how she used to laugh. Once, I was scared of a picture I saw of the God Mesha, and she told me not to worry, because bears could be fierce but they could also be gentle. She said a bear wouldn't hurt a little one like me."

Bereg wished he could tell her to stop. He didn't want to hear any more. He couldn't find his voice.

With no more expression than before, she said, "That day, when the company came, I found out she had lied. The soldiers with their flags of Mesha did what they wanted. Two of them were in our house. My father didn't want my mother used that way, so he died. When the two men were through with my mother, she died too."

Bereg felt sick. Somehow he managed to say, "Impera Mangevar couldn't have known. No soldier would be allowed to…"

"As far as I know, Impera Mangevar never knew or cared." Even then, her voice held no anger, only that horrible coldness. "The company leader found me in the house, with my parents' bodies. He felt responsible, I suppose. He lined up the company in the middle of the village and told me to point to the men who did it. When I did, he called the two of them out in front of everyone and shot them himself, one shot each to the head. Then he took me with him and said he would do right by me. His name was Arik Vasem."

Bereg couldn't say a word. She finished, "He was from Tyi. He took me home to his wife and the two of them raised me. The army was their life, so it became mine too."

Bereg felt as if he were trapped in ice. He had never served in a fighting force. Maybe they were different from the men and women he'd known all his life, but he didn't want to believe it.

What happens to children who see their parents murdered?

He managed to swallow. Somehow he managed to say, "Were they good to you, Vasem and his wife?"

She laughed. The bitterness in it stung like lemon juice on raw skin. "They tried to be, but they weren't my parents. I never loved them. I never loved anyone."

Bereg heard himself say, "You told Impera Shurik about the Vaia. You told him what you knew about the tribes."

Her shadowed face turned to him again. "Yes. Sometimes I disgust myself."

"You didn't know what he wanted. We have to follow orders."

Her eyes stayed on his face. He didn't know what she saw there, or thought she saw. She said, "Vasem and his wife named me Fisa. They said I should have a new name so I could have a new life. My parents called me Tama."

Tama Leben. Bereg didn't have to ask why she had wanted him to know all this.

She stood up. "You should get some rest, Silde Orlon. We have another long day tomorrow."

She set off to patrol the circuit of the camp. Bereg sat where she had left him, alone in the dark.

He didn't sleep that night. He had no idea what Silde Vasem's —Silde Leben's, he couldn't help thinking — village in Feyst would have looked like, but he pictured something like his own. He saw the row of gray-coated soldiers lined up in the square, and the dark-haired little girl staring at them, raising her small hand to point to one and then another. Had she cried then, Bereg wondered? Or had the coldness he knew already settled on her for good? He saw the two soldiers step forward. Had they been frightened, or had they thought their commander would give them only light punishment, a slap on the wrist for bad behavior? He saw the faceless commander, Arik Vasem, shouldering his vindula, and he heard the shots, one after the other. He saw the bodies crumple onto snow-covered flagstones.

How frightened had the little girl been? Bereg wondered if she had wanted to stay in her village, if she had cried or struggled when the commander lifted her onto his saddle in front of him. Maybe he'd had to hold her tight, clamp an arm around her or even truss her up in a blanket to keep her from getting loose, so he could go through with what he thought was right. Or maybe she had gone willingly enough, now that she had lost everything that mattered to her. Either way, she had left home and family behind forever.

She had been so young. Only four. Bereg thought about his own grandchildren. If they had to, could they learn to answer to new names, love other parents who tried to raise them as their own?

I never loved them. I never loved anyone.

Dawn came, and he still hadn't shut his eyes. Aching, he dragged himself up into the saddle. Silde Vasem rode at the back of the detachment as before. She said nothing to him, as if last night's confidence hadn't happened.

All morning, the detachment saw nothing but open grassland with a few scattered trees. Clouds sometimes briefly shadowed the sun. They heard the wind whispering in the grass and the calls of birds swooping overhead. Once or twice, a rabbit startled out of the grass and disappeared with a flash of its dark tail. Bereg began to hope that all their searching through this region would yield nothing more than what they saw now. It was much too soon to think that might happen, but if they found nothing, Bereg could take a blank map back to Impera Shurik. Orders followed with no harm done.

When the sun stood high in the sky, they stopped by a creek to water the horses and eat a few bites of dried beef and fruit. Bereg made the mistake of lying back on the grass in the shade. He didn't realize he had dozed off until someone shook him awake.

"Silde Orlon!"

Wiry Dimik Kuzen crouched beside him. Bereg pushed himself

up, rubbing the sleep out of his eyes. His head felt foggy, his tongue too thick in his dry mouth. "What is it?"

"Silde Orlon, look!" The boy pointed toward the west.

Bereg shaded his eyes and followed the pointing hand. A cloud of dust rising from the grass showed, yes, a column of riders coming toward them, fast.

They weren't Lasska horses. Heavy certainty settled on Bereg as he made out the small, lightweight mounts, more like wild horses than carefully-bred work animals. He couldn't see the riders' faces, but they looked dark-skinned. Near the front of the column, one of them wore a bright white shirt.

Pala Vaia. No question. Bereg wished he could appreciate the wonder of setting eyes on a people he had never seen before.

He dragged himself to his feet. Six or seven horses, it looked like, and five riders. Not a full tribe. Maybe they were scouting for land for their camp. *Stay out of these lands*, Bereg wanted to call to them. *Don't stop here. It's not safe.*

Dimik Kuzen said, "What should we do?"

Bereg doubted the column had even seen the Lasska detachment. Certainly they made no move to attack, or even turn in the soldiers' direction. They were heading straight west as fast as they could. Bereg had the sudden strange idea that they were running from something.

Impera Shurik had made his orders clear. "We do nothing," Bereg told Kuzen. "They aren't interested in us."

The rest of his detachment had seen the riders too. The young soldiers scrambled for their weapons. Silde Vasem, Bereg saw, held her own vindula. She looked through its sights and glanced around at him.

"Vaia," she said.

"Yes." Bereg would have liked to look through his vindula's sights too, to get a better view of these people, but the weapon was in his pack, on the other side of the little creek. He called out to the young soldiers. "Stand down, all of you. They don't mean us harm."

The column flew on, straight west. Soon they would be well past the Lasska detachment. The young soldiers obeyed Bereg and lowered their weapons.

All except one. Lada Egem stood off by herself at the edge of their temporary camp. Bereg saw her lift her vindula and sight through it.

"Egem," he snapped. "Stand down."

"There's a witch-woman!"

The eagerness in her voice brought acid up in Bereg's throat. She thought she would get a reward for killing the white-shirted rider. Bereg found himself willing the Vaia riders to go faster yet, get out of reach.

"Egem," he repeated, making for her. "Stand down now. That's an order."

Either she didn't hear him or didn't care. She peered through the vindula's sights, aiming. The column wasn't out of range yet. If she shot one of their riders, no doubt she would bring trouble down on them, but the Lasska soldiers outnumbered the Vaia column more than two to one. Those five Vaia would die here.

Bereg caught his breath. Before he could open his mouth to shout another order, he heard the roaring report of another vindula and saw Lada Egem collapse.

Silence clamped down on the company. Blood spread across the back of Egem's gray coat and ran down into the grass.

The young soldiers stared at Bereg, and past him, at someone else. Bereg forced himself to turn around.

Silde Vasem lowered her weapon. Her face looked so cold it frightened him.

"Lada Egem disobeyed two direct orders from her commander." Her quiet words fell into the silence. "She disobeyed the orders of Impera Shurik himself, who bid us not to engage with the Vaia unless provoked. We will not tolerate such treason."

She was right, of course. Again Bereg pictured the dark-haired child in the village square, pointing at the men who had killed her parents.

He knew what he had to do now. "Silde Vasem is correct," he said. "You, Kuzen, and you, Ilim, will dig a grave." His hand did not shake as he pointed at the two soldiers standing nearest. "Let all of you remember this lesson today."

His voice sounded as firm as Silde Vasem's. No one would know how the little food he'd eaten threatened to climb back up his throat at the sight of the mangled body. The young men moved silently to get camp shovels from their packs. No one said a word.

The Vaia column hadn't turned. Bereg looked out over the plain and saw them still riding west, outracing the movement of the sun across the sky.

9

KHARI

Khari gladly let her sister's man, Radavan, head the search group on their journey west to Namora. The two hunters, Handan and Mand-hani, wouldn't likely have listened to Khari's orders if she had taken the lead. They respected the Lodestone's brother and gave him no trouble.

Radavan was steady and deliberate in everything he did. He set their course every morning, traveling as directly west as possible while keeping to the open plains. The Lasska hadn't settled the grass-land very heavily. They seemed to favor the colder weather in the north. Radavan's southwest route let the group stay clear of towns and villages.

Khari trusted her sister's man's leadership, but she worried for him. Radavan kept himself a little apart from their evening cooking fires, sitting with his hands on his knees, quietly watching the flames. He never spoke a word about the days ahead, or Dahila and the chil-dren left behind. Khari didn't need words to hear what he was think-ing. She knew that, like her, he wished he could look back to the northeast and see the shapes of Pradesh and Vatiri leading the rest of the tribe into the plains. She guessed, too, that the firelight showed him Dahila's face, and she guessed at how much he longed to reach out and cup his wife's cheek in his palm.

For twenty days, they met no Lasska soldiers. They left the region the Lasska called Vyest and moved across the one called Syetch and into Tsvavyest. The warm air of the plains, the wide-open skies and sweet-smelling grass, and above all, the fact that they'd seen no hint of pursuit, made Khari feel more hopeful.

On the twenty-first day, Mandhani rode out in front of their little column, scouting ahead. He had the sharpest eyes: he could spot a bird in flight and tell what it was, when it was so far away that the others only saw a darting shape. Radavan followed some distance behind him. Handan rode at the back, keeping an eye out for anyone who might be tracking them. Khari and Rahul rode in the middle of the column with the spare horses.

Khari hadn't known Rahul very well before they'd started this journey. He stood out in the tribe the same way she did, young but with higher status than most of the elders. Since they'd been traveling together, Rahul had told Khari how he'd caught Pradesh's notice when he was still a child. The tribe had quartered closer to a Lasska village than usual, one particular spring, and Rahul had picked up the Lasska language just from overhearing talk between some of the villagers and some of the Vaia men. By the end of the season he spoke it fluently, much better even than Pradesh himself. A good Lodestone had to recognize ability in his people where he saw it. Pradesh had never been backward in that.

Now the tribe respected Rahul as one of its best thinkers, not just for his skill with Lasska. He took in ideas and made decisions faster than deliberate Radavan, but he had learned thoughtfulness and perspective from old Bakar, and had no trace of Handan's and Mandhani's hotheadedness. Everything he did had good sense about it. Khari liked to talk to him on days like this when they rode together.

Today the weather was clear and warm for autumn, the air fragrant with the scent of the grass and the swathes of yellow poppies that still brightened the plains. They had ridden for a little while in silence when Rahul said, "Sometimes I forget why we're out here, and I'm only glad we are."

"I'd like to forget," Khari said. "It's beautiful."

She thought about what this journey would be like without the constant fear of Lasska soldiers, and the weight of her own pathdream in her mind, and the questions she couldn't stop chewing over every night when she tried to fall asleep. *How much farther to the mountains? If we get across, will we find the man I saw? Will he know how to help us?* She had done a ride like this one every autumn, with the whole tribe, on the way to a winter camp. She had never known, then, how lucky she was to be able to delight in the sunlight and the strength of the horse under her. Everything simple and safe.

Rahul said, "You're carrying a heavier load than any of us."

Khari understood what he meant, but she didn't think so. "Radavan misses his family," she said. "Handan and Mandhani will have to fight for us, if we run into trouble."

Rahul laughed. "Don't worry about those two. They want to meet some Lasska. They're looking forward to it." He rode up closer beside Khari. Their horses' hooves thudded in rhythm against the hard ground. "We'll make it to Namora, Khari. We'll find the man from your dream."

On the worst nights, when Khari lay beside the last coals of the cooking fire and imagined herself back in the tent with Vatiri, the idea crept into her head that there might not be a man at all. She still didn't see how her dream could save them when Vatiri hadn't seen any hope for the tribe. On those nights, she would lie awake for hours, hollow and sick.

Now she said, "I wish the dream made more sense." She hadn't let herself admit that aloud to anyone but Vatiri. "Pradesh was right. How do we think we can find one person out of everyone in Namora? We don't know who he is, or where he is." Some nights, Khari had begged the Moon Woman, sender of pathdreams, for another dream to explain the mysteries of the first. No answer came. "Even if we found him, what could a Namoran do for us?" She had thought that over too, again and again, her mind gnawing at it like a toothless old dog trying to get purchase on a bone. "A Lasska might argue with the impera, maybe. If we found one who cared enough. But Namorans don't have anything to do with us."

She shouldn't have said all that out loud. If Handan and Mandhani heard it, they'd want to turn around and ride straight back to the tribe and tell Pradesh she'd been wrong. And Radavan, who already had too much to bear, shouldn't know what Khari was thinking.

Rahul didn't seem worried or angry. He rode for a while in silence, looking thoughtfully out at the horizon. Khari found herself watching his profile. He was about a head taller than her, slimmer than the two hunters, his face still boyish but mature for his age. He sat easily on horseback, his fingers twisted in the horse's dark coarse mane. Unlike the Lasska, who used saddles and bridles and bits, the Vaia rode bareback, with no barrier between horse and rider. Not everyone in the tribe rode comfortably or well, but Rahul seemed to take the same pleasure in it that Khari did.

Eventually, he broke the silence. "Lamps don't show everything. At night, a lamp only shows you the ground in front of your feet."

"I know that." Khari heard how impatient she sounded. "How does that help?"

When he smiled at her, mischief lit up his face. "If you want to find the path, you have to carry the lamp and start walking."

Khari narrowed her eyes. *Clever.* He reached over. His fingers closed briefly around hers, where they held onto her own horse's mane. "I trust you, Lamp-Carrier."

His touch made something jump in Khari's chest. For a moment, she wasn't a Lamp-Carrier and he wasn't one of the smartest men in the tribe; they were a girl and a boy, nearly the same age, companions on this strange journey. Then Mandhani's voice reached them.

"Soldiers! A dozen bowshots ahead!"

Khari's heart scrambled into her throat. Rahul pulled his horse up. Khari did the same, barely able to make her suddenly-icy hands draw back on the horse's mane.

The hunter came galloping back toward the rest of the column with Radavan at his shoulder. Handan saw the commotion and raced up from behind. The three closed in around Khari and Rahul. To Khari, the noise of the horses' hooves and breath seemed to fill the whole world.

Soldiers. In her mind, Khari saw the Lasska graycoats. The burning river in Vatiri's dream, flowing out unstoppably from Cheremay, destroying everything it touched...

Radavan was angry. He pulled his horse up and rounded on Mandhani. "Don't shout, boy. What were you thinking of?"

The tension in his voice woke Khari out of some of her own fear. Mandhani's face flushed dark. Radavan said, "How many soldiers?"

Mandhani collected himself. "Not many. Maybe a dozen. Maybe fewer."

A dozen was still far too many. Khari thought of the Lasska weapons that hurled hard metal to tear bodies open.

Mandhani said, "Two of them looked old, a man and a woman. The others all looked young. Probably fighters."

Radavan said, "Did they see you?"

"No. I'm sure they didn't. They were resting."

Khari swallowed. On the flat, wide-open plains, she couldn't believe the soldiers wouldn't spot her group if they went past anywhere near. Seven horses would raise enough dust to get attention.

Radavan sat erect on his horse, his hands steady in its mane. "But they would see us now, if we keep on the same path."

Handan said, "We could fight."

Rahul spoke up before Radavan did. "We don't have enough weapons. If your brother is right, and there are a dozen of them, we'd be killed."

Handan's jaw tightened. Khari knew he didn't like getting back-talk from someone younger than himself, no matter how much the rest of the tribe thought of Rahul. "We'd have to ride too far south to stay away from them," Handan said. "And what if there are others out there?"

Khari didn't like to admit it, but he was right. On the smooth, flat plains, with nothing to offer concealment, the soldiers might be able to see as far as Mandhani could. Their metal-throwing weapons could kill at far greater distances than a bowshot. Khari and the others would have to ride well out of their way to stay safe, slowing their journey west, and it was true, other soldiers might be waiting anywhere.

In a flash of terror, Khari saw Shurik's forces as pincer arms coming from every direction, trapping her group and squeezing them to death before they ever got near the mountains. Suddenly the sunlight wasn't the warm hand of the Sun God. It was a terrible danger, glaring down on the Vaia, leaving them nowhere to hide.

Radavan looked out in the direction Mandhani had come from. "We'll keep on as we are," he said. "We'll ride at full speed."

Khari felt as if her body had turned to clay, stiff and ready to shatter at a blow. Radavan formed up the column: himself at the front, Rahul in the middle with the spare horses, Handan and Mand-hani behind. "If they come after us, we need you two back there ready to fight." He told Khari to ride in the middle of the column beside Rahul. Khari lifted her chin and refused. If they went straight into a front-on Lasska attack, no one would say she let anyone else do her fighting for her. Radavan looked as if he wanted to argue, but she moved her horse up beside his, keeping her eyes on the path ahead, and he let it go.

Handan and Mandhani both carried bows and throwing spears. Rahul and Radavan had the long knives used for skinning and cleaning game. Khari had a long knife too, but she preferred the short dagger she carried in her boot. With it, if she was fast enough, she could pin a darting lizard to the ground.

All of them readied their weapons. At Radavan's signal, they rode out together at a full gallop.

Vaia horses were small and tough and moved as if riding the

Breath of Winds itself. Khari's fear dissolved in the speed. As the horses flew across the plain, Khari felt the distance ahead of them melting away. If only they could travel this fast, hour after hour, day after day, she would believe they could reach Namora and find what they so desperately needed.

Then she saw the dark shapes in the distance. The Lasska camp looked tiny, but the shapes resolved into people, other horses, a couple of small trees near the line of a creek. Fear closed in on Khari again like a blanket wrapped too tight around her chest. The soldiers would see them soon. Vaia horses could outrun the heavier Lasska mounts, but nothing could outrun those metal-throwing weapons.

She heard Radavan's voice beside her, over the noise of rushing air in her ears.

"Keep going. Don't look."

Khari gripped her horse's mane tighter and kept her eyes on the horizon. She called up the picture of the man from her dream: the silver in his brown hair, the lines at the corners of his eyes, the color of those eyes themselves, the same blue as the sky that met the plains far ahead. She would know his face anywhere. He was there in Namora on the other side of the mountains. She must find him.

The Lasska camp flashed up alongside them and fell behind. When it disappeared from the edge of her vision, Khari let herself breathe. Too soon.

A noise she had never heard before roared out behind them, louder and sharper than a clap of thunder or the crash of a falling tree. It tore the sky and left strange echoes bouncing in its wake. Khari heard Radavan shout, "Run!"

Behind her, Mandhani shouted something back, but Khari couldn't make it out. She hadn't thought they could go faster, but their horses, scared of the noise too, found another spurt of speed. The gold and green world blurred around them and the wind whipped tears from Khari's eyes.

Radavan didn't slow the pace until they were many bowshots away. The Lasska group hadn't set out after them. Finally Radavan slowed his horse to a trot and led the group to the shade of a small stand of orena trees.

Orena had soft pale wood, not much good for carving or burning, but their sap made decent pitch and their late-blooming purple flowers had a sharp sweet smell. Khari breathed the scent deep. She hoped the others didn't see how she almost fell off her horse's back. Her legs trembled so much they couldn't hold her up.

She stumbled over to one of the trees and collapsed under it. Its trunk felt comfortingly solid against her back. A little way away, Handan and Mandhani seemed to be arguing. Khari stared up at the tree's purple flowers and the amazingly calm blue sky above.

Rahul came over and sat down next to her. His dark face had an ashy cast. "It must have been one of those weapons," he said. He hugged his knees to his chest like a little boy. "I thought they'd caught us."

Khari had thought so too. She'd expected to feel the metal from the weapon tearing into her body, ripping skin and muscles apart.

Mandhani raised his voice. "I'm telling you what I saw!"

Rahul glanced at Khari. Now that she could think a little, Khari realized she didn't know when she'd heard the hunter brothers argue with each other. With anyone else in the tribe, yes, but the two of them always stood together.

Rahul got up first and held out his hand to help her. She felt so sick she didn't know if her legs would carry her, but when his warm fingers closed around hers, her head cleared just enough. Rahul kept her hand in his as they went over to the others, at the far end of the stand of trees.

They got there in time to hear Handan say, "That makes no sense. Why would one Lasska kill another?"

Radavan was listening to the talk, not interrupting to challenge or question. Mandhani said, "I don't know." His face looked hard, angry. Rahul let go of Khari's hand. "That's what happened," Mandhani said. "One of the older ones, the woman, she had a weapon and she used it to kill a young one."

One Lasska soldier had killed another? Khari didn't know how Mandhani had managed to see it when the group was moving so fast, but his eyes didn't lie. Why would a Lasska do that?

Handan said, "Then she made a mistake. She was aiming for us. They can track us here and they'll come after us in no time."

Sickness swamped Khari again. He was right. The soldiers wouldn't have any trouble following their track. She braced her feet hard on the ground; she wouldn't let her knees buckle in front of the men.

Handan said, "We have to go back and finish them."

He said it as if he actually thought they could do it, the handful of them with their few weapons. Handan had always been reckless, but to Khari, this sounded like madness.

Radavan said, "We can't go back." His voice sounded strangely sympathetic. "The Lasska didn't hurt us. It doesn't matter what the woman was trying to do."

Handan's face looked tight, but not flushed. He stood erect, face to face with Radavan, his arms rigid at his sides. "They want to kill us. You're telling me not to fight. What use am I?"

Maybe it was Khari's own fear, but something shifted then in the way she saw Handan. He wasn't only Pradesh's arrogant, bullheaded nephew. Khari looked at him now and saw the tribe's best fighter, who saw the terrible danger coming down on them all and wanted to put his own body as a shield between the Lasska and his people.

All his strength couldn't save them. Khari knew he understood that, whether or not he wanted to, and she knew how he had to feel. Out of her own sleepless nights, and the emptiness she felt when she thought her dream was nothing more than a useless fancy, she reached out for him.

"They could have come after us by now," she said. She talked straight to him, as if the two of them had been alone. "They must not be interested in us."

He rounded on her with his hands clenched into fists. "Vatiri said

Shurik's men want to kill us. Why wouldn't these soldiers do it if they got the chance?"

Khari didn't know. Something in her mind nudged her, something strange and elusive, like a movement you caught out of the corner of your eye, that vanished when you turned to see it.

The older woman killing one of the younger soldiers. Khari didn't understand it any more than Handan did, but there was something about it. Something she couldn't quite catch.

No, she thought, it wasn't like a barely-seen movement. It was more like light. A pinpoint of light that disappeared when you tried to look straight at it, like the faintest stars, or the moon in its newest, thinnest sliver, so faint you could barely find it in the night sky.

Radavan said, "We won't go back. We'll rest here a little while. Then we'll keep going."

The moon.

Handan turned on his heel and went away from the group, out into the open plain. Mandhani started to follow him, but Radavan stopped him. "Leave him alone."

Khari barely heard any of it. The moon.

Night after night, she had prayed to the Moon Woman for a new pathdream. Night after night, she had seen nothing, but something was coming to her now. She felt it, clear and brilliant, like a shaft of pure white light from the great low-hanging moon at the time of autumn harvest.

Moon Woman. Forgive my doubt. You heard me and you are answering.

She didn't know what else any of the men said to each other. She didn't know if Rahul stayed near her or not. She went back to the orena tree she had leaned against before and sat down. The dream came even before she closed her eyes.

A clearing in a deep forest. Khari saw the tall, strong trees, their thick branches twined together overhead. The cover was so dense that even in the clearing, no sunlight found the ground.

Khari herself seemed to stand at the edge of that narrow oval of open space, all gnarled tree roots stubbling the ground under a thin skim of moss and pale twists of grass. She knew she was dreaming, but when she made out a shape near her in the dark, she caught her breath.

A bear. An old male, stretched out at the foot of the nearest tree. His silvering muzzle had scars running back and forth across it, marks from many fights. He lay so close to Khari that she could have reached out and touched the rough fur on his flank. That flank rose and fell slowly, the only sign of life in him.

But there was more movement in the shadows. The shape of another bear loomed out so suddenly that Khari had to force herself not to step back. She must not fear her dream or do anything that might pull her out of it. Her hidden eye was wide awake, watching; she had never seen anything so clearly before, not even the man in Namora.

The second bear was female, younger and stronger than the male. She paced restlessly back and forth, back and forth across the clearing, shaking her head and growling softly as bears did when they were angry. Khari thought she felt the hot gusts of breath as the great head passed near her.

Rustling in the trees. A strong wind. Now the branches parted enough for a shaft of sunlight to hit the ground, bathing the clearing in light so bright it dazzled Khari's eyes. Every bump in every root stood out. Each individual frond of moss cast a shadow.

Movement from somewhere else, out in the deep forest. Something was crashing through the underbrush, coming toward the clearing from the opposite side. Khari made out the shape just as the newcomer stepped into the sunlight.

A third bear. A female in her prime.

The older female turned and raised her head. It seemed to Khari that she knew exactly what was about to happen before it did. She forced herself to stand perfectly still as, in one smooth motion and with no sound of warning, the older female launched herself at the young one.

The young bear was strong and healthy, but the older one was wily and savage with anger. The two fought back and forth across the clearing, snarling, clawing, tearing at each other. Their heavy paws trampled the dirt and their blood sprayed the ground. Khari did not move or breathe as the noise of their fury broke around and over her.

The male bear did. He opened his eyes and pushed his front paws underneath his stiff body, dragging himself up into a sitting position. His dark eyes followed the fight, but he made no move to stop or join it.

As suddenly as it had begun, the fight ended. The young bear lay on the ground with her throat torn open. The older female stood over her, triumphant.

The wind moved again in the trees. More branches parted. Now the sunlight pooled in the clearing and made a wide path that led away into the deep forest.

The female bear came up to the male. Khari saw her lower her head and rub her bloodstained muzzle against his scarred old face: a startlingly gentle motion after her savagery. Then she stepped back into the sunlight and followed the swath of it out of the clearing.

For a long time, the old male sat motionless where she had left him, looking away toward the place where she had disappeared into the trees. Khari knew she must not pull out of the dream. She must wait and see what he did.

Finally, slowly, he pulled himself to his feet. His legs seemed reluctant to hold him up, but he limped into the path the sunlight made. He left the body of the young bear behind and followed the older female's lead into the dark woods, which swallowed him.

Khari woke out of the dream so sharply it felt like jumping into an icy stream. Certainty, as bright as the sunlight that had filled the clearing in the woods, ran through her body.

Moon Woman who guides us all. Thank you for what you have given me.

She scrambled to her feet. "Handan!"

He was off by himself, sitting on the ground near the grazing horses. He'd found a stone and idly tossed it into the dirt, picked it up, tossed it again. Khari ran up to him.

"Handan," she repeated. "You were right. We have to find those soldiers again."

"What?" He dropped the stone.

The other men had heard her call out. They hurried over. "What is it?" Radavan said.

Khari no longer feared or doubted her pathdreams. Nothing had ever felt so clear to her. She didn't care that Handan looked incredulous and Rahul worried. She knew exactly what they had to do.

She turned to Mandhani. "You said an older Lasska woman killed a younger one. And you said you saw an older man too."

Mandhani looked as confused as his brother, but he answered at once. "From what I saw, the man was the oldest one there. Too old to be a fighter, really."

It all made sense. Khari said, "Those two, the man and the woman, will help us. We have to go back and find them."

Now Radavan looked as if he thought she had lost her senses. "Lasska soldiers help us? Why?"

Khari had once thought she could never stand to share a raw pathdream with anyone but Vatiri. Now, without hesitation, she told the others every detail of hers. The bears, the fight, the sunlight, how the surviving female left the clearing and the male followed her.

"The woman soldier will come with us," she finished. "The man will come too, but she'll have to convince him."

All of them stared at her. "Khari," Radavan said, "we can't walk back into a Lasska camp. Are you sure this was a pathdream?"

His question didn't even make her angry. "It's the clearest one I've ever had. Mandhani saw the man and the woman. We know the older woman killed the younger one. The sunlight stands for the God and the Vaia. The Moon Woman is showing us what to do."

Radavan still didn't look convinced. Neither did Mandhani. Rahul looked simply worried, as if he thought Khari might be sick or dizzy.

Unexpectedly, Handan spoke up, from where he still sat on the ground. "I believe her."

The others looked down at him. Mandhani said, "But she's asking us to go looking for the people who want to kill us."

Handan stood up. "I know what she's asking. I don't like it either." His eyes moved to Khari's face. "But I believe she's telling the truth."

Khari met his eyes. Suddenly he smiled, a grin of comradeship and mischief.

"Why not?" he said. "Maybe it's harder not to kill a Lasska than kill one. If you put two old ones in front of me, you'll have to tie me up."

Khari found herself laughing. "That woman is dangerous," she reminded him. "I think she could put up a fight."

Now Radavan looked like he thought they were both crazy. "The old Lasska have young soldiers with them. Fighters," he said. "We know what kind of weapons they have. We can't go into their camp."

Rahul said, "One of us could."

Khari's laughter stopped. Rahul said, "I speak better Lasska than any of us. I could go into their camp alone and talk to the old ones."

Khari wanted to say, *No, let me do it.* She wanted to put her hand on his arm, physically stop him if she could. Handan said, "I should do it. If they want a fight, I'll give them one."

Mandhani said, "If you're going, I'm coming with you."

Radavan cut off the argument before it could start. "No." He looked at Rahul. "If anyone goes, he needs to be alone and unarmed."

He didn't say, but Khari heard, *That's the only chance he'll come out alive.* She knew he was right. The Lasska wouldn't hesitate to kill an armed enemy who looked like the least danger to them.

Again, she wanted to offer to go into the camp herself. She couldn't. She was their only Lamp-Carrier, and besides, she only knew a few words of Lasska, nowhere near enough. In spite of the dream and everything she knew, she hated to see Rahul stake his life on her judgment.

He looked at her. His eyes told her he guessed at least some of her thoughts. "If Khari is sure about this," he said, "then we need to do it."

She made the only answer she could. "I'm sure."

"Then I'll go."

The group circled back and quickly picked up the Lasska trail. They found the camp again in the early evening. While the rest of them stayed well back, Mandhani went forward alone to see what he could. As the sun set, he came back with the report that most of the soldiers had bedded down for the night, but that the older woman soldier was awake, standing guard.

They couldn't hope for a better chance. As they waited for the safety of full night, Radavan told them all to rest and eat. No one could be sure what would happen once Rahul got to the camp. They had to be ready to run, or to fight as best they could if they had to try to save him.

Khari managed a few mouthfuls of flatbread and a swallow of water. No one else seemed to want to eat much either. Rahul sat with his head down and his eyes closed and didn't touch any food at all. Khari knew he was praying. If only they could have done this in the daylight, she thought; if only the Sun God could have guided him. But if it was dangerous enough to walk into the camp after dark, with most of the soldiers asleep, walking into an alert and armed Lasska regiment would mean certain death.

The Sun God could not guide Rahul. The Moon Woman could. As the dark settled around them, the bright white moonlight made lines of shadow behind each blade of grass. Khari looked up at Her face and felt the certainty of the pathdream rising in her again.

Finally Radavan said quietly, "Go, Rahul. May She walk with you."

Rahul got to his feet. No one spoke, but Rahul met Khari's eyes again and seemed to find some kind of assurance there. Only for her, he smiled.

He swung up onto his horse. Khari and the others watched him ride away until the darkness hid him.

They waited. No one spoke. Khari stared into the night as if somehow the Moon Woman would make a path for her to see all the way into the Lasska camp. She barely felt the hard ground under her or the rough grass against her palms. In her mind, she repeated a prayer, over and over, to the Moon Woman whose white light surrounded them.

Bring him back.

Mandhani saw him first. "He's coming!"

The words barely made more noise than the breeze that rustled the grass, but Khari felt them like a shock of lightning through her body and back down into the soil. Now she, too, saw the shape of the Vaia horse and its rider, and only a little distance behind them, a second rider on a taller, heavier horse.

The Lasska woman. Khari's dream had told the truth.

10

RIBAS

On the morning of Sesdina, Sixth Day, almost a week after the news came from Kunin Dergo about Tavin Ardinas's death, Ribas attended at a birth in the village. The new weaver's young wife was having her first child.

As early as it was, and as much as he wouldn't have minded another hour or two of sleep, Ribas savored the short walk to the weaver's house. Mist rose in plumes off the gravel roads as the first yellow rays of sunlight burned off last night's hard frost. Smoke from the first hearth fires hung in the air. Ribas breathed deep, tasting the sweet darkness of the smoke in the clear cold morning.

In this part of the village, the houses stood shoulder to shoulder, each with a small plot of land behind. Their front doors gave directly onto the road. Ribas turned onto the weaver's street and saw Lida's healer, Tayo Nevas, waiting in front of the house.

The zhinin always had to attend a birth, to perform the ceremony of bringing-in that must happen as soon as a child took its first breaths. Most families only called the tayo in if there was trouble. Ribas quickened his pace.

Tayo Nevas took his short wooden pipe out of his mouth as soon as Ribas got within earshot. ""Ribé. What do you think you're doing, coming up here on foot?"

The tayo had known Ribas since childhood and had cared for him during the illness that, as he still said, Ribas had only survived because he was too stubborn to know when to quit. Now Nevas was past fifty, his hair entirely silver-gray.

"Good morning to you too, Nevé," Ribas said. "What's the trouble here?"

The tayo, a head shorter than Ribas, frowned up at him. "It's getting too cold for you to be walking," he said. "I don't need another patient at this hour of the morning. Truth be told, I shouldn't have any patients at this hour of the morning."

"Tayo, tell me what's wrong here."

Nevas clamped the pipe in his mouth again. "Nothing. They need you, not me."

Ribas relaxed. He had served at plenty of difficult births over the years, but it never got easier to wait by those bedsides. Nevas went on, talking around the pipe, "She's panicking, and her husband isn't much better. Some people could do with more sense."

"Shouldn't you be in there anyhow?" Ribas said. "They did send for you."

"You don't need to remind me." Nevas drew on the pipe and blew the smoke out in a fragrant cloud. "I was waiting for you. The man's nattering on like a distracted chicken. I couldn't stand it anymore." Ribas swallowed a laugh. Nevas acted as if all the villagers were troublesome children who invented illnesses and injuries to annoy him, but Ribas had good reason to know how diligent the healer really was. "And now," Nevas said, "I find you out in the cold as if you lost the sense you were born with."

"It's four blocks, tayo. If I can't manage that, you might as well start digging a hole right now."

"We might have to do that anyway, you keep on like this."

Nevas opened the door and pointedly stood aside. Ribas heard the order the tayo didn't give him out loud: *Get yourself in the warm.*

The house had the same layout as all the others in this part of the village. The front door opened into a small hallway with a staircase leading up to the second floor. Off to the side, a single brick-floored front room connected to a kitchen at the back, with a door that gave out on the yard. Most villagers had vegetable plots, a few had fruit trees, and all had herbs and flowers that would turn the yards into a patchwork of color in the spring. The weaver's house had plain furnishings, but the walls were impeccably whitewashed, bright curtains hung at the window in the front room, and a warm fire in the front room had taken the morning chill out of the house. Ribas saw a clay vase of late-blooming ramunas, the starlike pale blue flowers with deep purple hearts, on the fireplace mantel.

The weaver himself came running down the stairs as soon as Nevas shut the door. Luvo Azulaikas was in his early forties, small and thin, with quick hands and shoulders starting to show a permanent hunch from all the time he spent over the loom. He and his much-younger wife, Alayut, had moved to Lida from Paret only a few weeks earlier. Luvo had told Ribas that town life had gotten stale for them. They wanted to raise their child in a place where they could hear the birds in the morning and the crickets at night. Ribas suspected the weaver had wanted that considerably more than his wife, but she wouldn't deny him.

"Zhinin," Luvo said now. "Goddess be thanked."

In spite of the warmth in the house, Luvo's hands felt icy as he caught hold of Ribas's. Out of the corner of his eye, Ribas saw Nevas shake his head and cast a long-suffering glance at the ceiling.

"I've been so worried," Luvo said. "Please, come right up."

Ribas followed Luvo up the narrow stairs, with Nevas coming behind. The house was a couple of generations old and the wooden planks creaked underfoot. As they went up, Ribas said gently, "The tayo tells me there's no trouble."

Luvo stopped in the upstairs hall. His eyes looked hunted. "I hope so," he said. "But Alya...well, she's having a hard time."

The upper floor had two bedrooms, a larger one for the family and a smaller one for a guest. A homespun runner covered the length of the short hallway. Luvo went into the larger bedroom.

"Alya, love," he said. "We're all right now. The zhinin's here."

They need you, not me. Some people thought Ribas had even more power than the healer, but he couldn't do anything to make sure a birth went the way it should. He hoped Nevas was right today, that his skills would be enough here.

The bedroom was as plain as the downstairs, but bright and warm with its own small hearth fire. The single window looked out into the back yard, now bare except for the straggling frostbitten remnants of the summer's flowers. The big bed in the middle of the room dwarfed the small, dark-eyed woman who lay propped up there on a thick pillow.

Alayut Luvenis was barely twenty, young to have a baby. Ribas knew that Luvo, who had at one point resigned himself to dying a bachelor, thought himself extraordinarily lucky that she'd agreed to have him. She reminded Ribas of his sister-in-law Virta, with darker eyes and hair but the same delicate prettiness.

She wasn't crying, but Ribas could see that she had been, very lately. "Zhinin," she whispered.

Ribas felt her terror, thick as fog in the room. He sat down in the straight-backed chair beside the bed and took her hand between both of his.

"Everything's fine, Alya. The tayo says you're doing well."

She and Luvo were still getting used to the life of the village. Ribas knew she was shy, and doubly withdrawn because of her pregnancy. She hadn't made friends yet. Her eyes filled with tears again when she heard him use her nickname; probably no one else in Lida had yet.

Her fingers tightened around his. "Zhinin, I..." A spasm of pain crossed her face. "I miss home."

Luvo was hovering by the foot of the bed. "Alya, love. This is our home."

Ribas caught Nevas's eye. The healer said, "We'll wait outside."

He took the weaver's arm and marched him to the door. From the hallway, Ribas heard Luvo protest and Nevas say, "The zhinin will take care of this. He'll call if he needs us."

At births and deaths, the times of greatest upheaval, people couldn't hold onto any masks they wore. Ribas knew what kinds of truths could come out at those bedsides. Alayut's feelings had weighed on her more than the child inside her.

She was crying now. "Luvo doesn't understand," she said. "He loves it here. I can't tell him I'm so lonely."

Ribas held her hand in one of his and rested the other on her hair, the way he would have comforted a sick child. "We're glad you've come to Lida," he said. "I know it's very different from what you're used to. Paret's a beautiful town, isn't it?" She sobbed agreement. Ribas said, "But I've lived here all my life, and I can tell you, it's the finest place in the world."

Her sob turned briefly into a laugh. "Is it?"

"I promise it is. You don't see it at its best this time of year, but just wait for spring, when everything's in bloom. And we'll have you feeling at home long before that."

"I wish my mother could have...but my father's not well." She swallowed hard. "He couldn't travel, and she couldn't leave him by himself."

Of course she wanted her mother here now. Ribas said, "We'll take good care of you, Alya. Your mother and father will be so glad to hear about their grandchild." He felt her clinging to the words as tightly as she gripped his hand. "And in a few weeks, we'll have the ceremony of welcome at the Circle House." That was the first public ceremony of a child's life, when the whole community turned out to greet a new arrival. "Everyone will be there for you and Luvo and your baby."

That idea made her sob again. "They will?"

"Of course." Ribas smoothed her hair. "We take these things very seriously in Lida. If anyone missed a welcoming, they'd hear about it from me."

She met his eyes and tried to smile. Ribas saw the same trust in her face that he saw in Asira's, when she was frightened or hurt and came to him for help.

Goddess above, let me always be able to help.

Pain washed over her. Her fingers dug into Ribas's hand. "Zhinin. I'm so scared."

He didn't often have to use the gift at a birth, but Alayut needed more than words now. "May I help?" he asked.

She understood the question. Her face gave him the permission he needed. He called on the gift and closed his eyes.

It showed him a mass of fear, exactly as he had expected: bruise-blue lines intertwined with the hot orange of hurt. This cut would take a lot from him. More than he should give, maybe, but he had to help.

He called on as much strength as he dared. When he made the cut, the room spun, but he opened his eyes and saw the wonder in Alayut's face. "Zhinin." Her voice sounded stronger already. "I..."

The pain came back. The baby was coming. She didn't want to let go of his hand – "please, zhinin, stay right here" – so he called for Nevas's help with the delivery. The tayo came in pretending to grumble about "perfectly simple births," but Ribas knew how glad he was to make himself useful. The healer told Luvo in no uncertain terms to stay where he was in the hall.

Ribas cut Alayut's fear twice more before the baby, a healthy girl, arrived into Nevas's waiting hands. The tayo bathed the squalling baby in water warmed over the fire and swaddled her in the waiting blanket.

"A fine child," he said. "Healthy lungs."

Alayut didn't let go of Ribas's hand until he had to take the baby from Nevas for the bringing-in. The tayo stuck his head out into the hall.

"Luvo Azulaikas. Come meet your daughter."

The weaver came in looking as if he'd survived several lifetimes over the past hour or two. Ribas didn't feel much better himself. The three cuts certainly had taken more than he should have given. His heart raced and a dull, throbbing ache radiated out from it, through his chest and up his spine. He hoped no one noticed how much effort it took him to reach out for the baby and settle her in the crook of his arm.

The Namoran faith said that, before a child was born, its soul waited out in the wholeness of the world. It must be welcomed in and joined with the body at birth, in the same way that it would later be released back into the world after death. The baby quieted in Ribas's arms. He asked the ritual question: "What is this child's name?"

Alayut's tired face was full of light. "Tiesa."

Ribas put his hand on the tiny head. "Tiesa Luvaikas, by the authority vested in me as a servant of the Goddess Kenavi, I welcome you into Her earthly family."

He had done this shortest, most powerful ceremony so many times. The wonder of welcoming a new soul never faded. Ribas heard the weaver catch his breath at that word "Luvaikas," the name that told the world this was his child.

The baby squeezed her eyes tight shut and pursed her little mouth, as if she wanted to tell the zhinin to hurry up with this business. Ribas smiled. "Long may you thrive, daughter of Kenavi," he said. "Tebena."

Alayut, Luvo, and Nevas all answered, "Tebena." Ribas put Tiesa into her mother's arms. The sun stood well above the horizon now. A warm shaft of light fell through the window and across the bed.

Alayut looked as if she didn't remember what loneliness meant. She took her eyes off her daughter's face long enough to say, "Thank you, zhinin."

This family would be all right. Ribas got to his feet and managed not to hold onto the chair for support. He and Nevas made their goodbyes and saw themselves out.

Out in the street, with the door safely shut behind them, Nevas gripped Ribas's arm. "You look terrible."

He'd been right after all. Ribas shouldn't have walked up here. "I didn't think I'd have to do that," he said. Nevas knew that meant the gift.

"You didn't have to do it. You decided to."

"It's only four blocks home." That seemed much farther than it had this morning.

"You're not going alone," Nevas said.

The village was awake now. Full daylight warmed the streets. The smells of baking bread, the voices of neighbors calling out to each other, and the clop of horses' hooves filled the air. Ribas didn't like people to see him when he felt this weak. Everyone knew about his heart, but the zhinin ought to be strong.

He tried not to lean too heavily on Nevas. The healer said, "Don't be an idiot. I can't fix that heart, but I can be a crutch." Ribas knew how much it frustrated him that he couldn't "fix that heart." He had wanted to since Ribas was a child. "I don't know what Marya's going to say to you," Nevas said.

Ribas had a feeling he did. When they got to the priest's house, Maryut was out front sweeping the porch. She took one look at her husband and dropped the broom. "Goddess hear me."

"I'm all right," Ribas said.

In two steps she reached him and took charge of him from Nevas, wrapping her arm around his waist, leading him up to the house as if he were an ancient grandfather. "Tayo," she said, "how bad was the birth?"

"It wasn't," Nevas said. "Your husband did more than he had to. As usual."

"Nevé," Ribas began.

"Don't you deny it," the tayo said. "Marya should scold you as much as she wants. Alayut Luvenis could have managed all right."

I couldn't let her suffer like that. Ribas didn't have the energy to argue. Nevas told Maryut about the delivery, the healthy baby, and how much Ribas had done to help the scared mother. In the front hall, Maryut looked up at her husband with the love and exasperation he knew so well. "Ribas Silvaikas, you're going to bed this minute. I'm closing this door and latching it."

"Marya..."

"I don't care who wants what from you this morning. You need to sleep."

Nevas said, "Do what she says, Ribé. And take that pain medicine."

Ribas tried to look stern. "I do have some sense, you know."

"Then try to act like it," Maryut said. "Go upstairs right now, or do you need help?"

Ribas wouldn't accept help to get up the stairs in his own house. He heard Maryut and the tayo still talking as he made it to the bedroom and measured out a dose of the willow bark tincture Nevas made up for him. He swallowed it and pushed off his shoes. Then the room, the daylight, the voices, and the angry ache in his chest all faded as he sank onto the bed and let sleep claim him.

He woke at midday when Maryut sat down on the bed beside him. "Love. Danya's here with some sort of letter."

Ribas sat up cautiously. His chest had stopped hurting. "Letter?"

"She said it came by courier. If you don't open it soon, she's liable to turn inside out."

Danya had changed quite a bit since the Pirdina service. She wasn't a frightened little mouse anymore. Maryut sized him up. "You've got some color back."

"I'm fine."

"So you say. When are you going to stop doing too much?"

He touched her face. "I'm sorry."

He did try to be careful. He knew he shouldn't take more risks than he had to, but he didn't know how to walk away from trouble he could solve.

Maryut said, "I think I know you by now." She drew his head

down and kissed his forehead. "You need to eat something too. Come on."

In the kitchen, Danya was sitting at the little round table with a mug of tea. "Raimaté, zhinin," she said.

Ribas bowed, mock-solemn. "Raimaté, mosevin."

She had kept her promise to tell him when she felt her troubles closing in. Since he had cut the net around her, she had started looking people in the eye, moving around the Circle House with assurance, chatting with the villagers, and – best, to Ribas's way of thinking – laughing often. She and Jano were becoming quite a pair. Sometimes Ribas had to remind them to quit joking around and get their work done.

His greeting made her laugh now. She held out a heavy parchment envelope. "A courier came to the Circle House a little while ago. He said this needed to get to you right away. It's from Sostavi."

Sostavi? Ribas took the letter with a new feeling of misgiving. He hadn't had any communication from Sostavi in fifteen years, since Tavin Ardinas had put a stop to Sventin Galvo's letters.

Maryut said, "Zhinin, you don't open that until you eat something." She put a plate of cheese and warm new bread on the table, along with a mug of strong tea with a spoon of honey in it. "Sit."

Ribas obeyed. Danya said quickly and unconvincingly, "I should go back to the House."

She didn't take her eyes off the letter. Ribas couldn't help smiling. "No, you can stay, mosevin. We'll find out what this is about." Surely, he thought, Sventin Galvo hadn't decided to renew his requests to have Ribas come to Sostavi, now that Tavin Ardinas was gone. The sventin wouldn't think it was worth his while to open up that old discussion again.

As he ate enough to satisfy Maryut's watchful eye, he looked at the seal on the back of the envelope. No, it wasn't Sventin Galvo. Ribas had never seen this seal before, but he knew who used it. The amber-colored wax seal with the Great House insignia belonged to the Tavo Balsa.

A strange quiet settled on him. Valda? After so many years?

Ribas put empty the plate aside, broke the seal, and took two closely-written sheets of parchment out of the envelope. Sure enough, on the second page, he saw her signature. *Yours in the fellowship of the Goddess Kenavi.*

Maryut said, "What is it, Ribé?"

She had sat down next to Danya. Ribas said, "It's from Valdena Filtraikas."

Danya gasped. "The Tavo Balsa wrote to you?"

"Yes."

Maryut's jaw set. "What does she want?"

Ribas put the letter down and reached over to touch her hand. "Marya, it was, what, sixteen, seventeen years ago? I think you can forgive her. And me," he added.

She smiled reluctantly. "I forgave you a long time ago."

Danya did look as if she might turn inside out with questions. Ribas said, "The Tavo Balsa and I were students at the viduris together. We were close friends in those days. For a little while, we were more than that, but it didn't last." He glanced at Maryut. "Somebody made it clear that I was hers."

Danya blushed. "You and the Tavo Balsa...you were..."

"We were both mosevine then, remember. Younger than you and Jano are now."

Maryut said, "I straightened him out. He had no right to look at another girl."

Danya's cheeks looked ready to ignite, but she laughed at that. Ribas said to Maryut, "You were furious, as I recall."

"You deserved it."

All the sting and confusion of that time had long since blown away. They had all been so young. Ribas had been sixteen, Maryut fourteen, with her pick of the village boys. Ribas couldn't have imagined life without her any more than he could imagine losing a hand, but he'd always assumed she would go on being the sister he'd never had. She deserved a healthy, strong husband.

When his friendship with Valda trembled briefly into something new and strange, Maryut had set him straight. His first visit home, after his letters had mentioned Valda in the new way, Maryut had given him a massive serving of ice and then dished out all the fire her naturally quick temper could muster. At first, he had been baffled and hurt. Then, one afternoon, she had cornered him alone in the apple orchard, taken his face between her hands, and stood on tiptoe to administer a kiss that left him breathless. Afterward, she looked him in the eye. "Now you know, Ribas Silvaikas."

He had known, all right. He belonged to her, then and always.

Now she gestured at the letter. "So why is the Tavo Balsa writing to you?"

She still didn't sound terribly forgiving. Ribas let it go and picked up the letter.

Raimaté, Zhinin Ribas,

You must be surprised to hear from me. I regret that it's been so long. I should have written to you years ago. When I first arrived in Sostavi, I thought of you more than you can perhaps imagine.

Those words brought back the girl she had been. He had hated knowing how much he hurt her, when he'd had to explain that he'd made a mistake and his heart wasn't his to give. He was sorry to see she had carried that hurt to Sostavi. As he read on, though, the other news of the past fifteen years sank in. Her rise through the ranks of the dagira, her service as the Tavin's right hand, her disappointment and disgust with her colleagues during Ardinas's last illness.

I was ashamed of them. Scheming and grubbing as if his life and death didn't mean a thing, except that his death left an open place they were ravenous to fill.

Sostavi bred its own brand of snakes. Ribas had certainly gotten a taste of that in all those letters from Sventin Galvo. And that was putting aside whatever had happened to his own father in the Great House, long before Ribas was born.

Many people do grieve for Tavin Ardinas and remember him as he deserves, she wrote. *They miss their leader, as they should, but I must tell you that the person I grieve for is the old man who was unfailingly kind to a young woman trying to find her place here. He was a wise ruler. He was a good man.*

Ribas felt her sadness as if it had seeped into the paper along with the ink. He could guess, after all, why she'd written to him now. But then she mentioned the election. *I can't believe what's happened.*

Maryut said to Danya, "I wish he'd read faster." Danya laughed, a quickly stifled sound. Valda had written about the vote. Ribas had to read it twice before he could take it in.

Eight votes for Sventin Galvo. Five for this Sventin Lesvin that Ribas had never heard of. Three to abstain.

A deadlocked vote. Ribas knew what that meant. Every member of the dagira did.

Maryut said, "What is it? Goddess hear me, Ribé, tell us."

He looked at her and managed to say it. "She's Tavin. Valda is the next Tavin."

Her mouth dropped open. Ribas couldn't take the time to explain. He handed her the first page of the letter and went on to the second. Out of the corner of his eye, he saw Danya lean over to read over Maryut's shoulder.

Valda wrote, *Sventin Galvo may still think I wanted this. I think you'll understand that I didn't want it at all. I want it even less, if that's possible, given that it's only happened because my colleagues couldn't agree on a candidate.*

Of course she didn't want it. What a position to find herself in. Suddenly she was Namora's new leader, but she hadn't chosen that, or reached for it, or had any real reason to believe it would come to her. And now she had to accept it not because the Council had approved her, or the Goddess had blessed her, but because the vote had failed.

She told him she wouldn't wait until Ketva or hold a great celebration for her Installation. She wanted to have it in Tyla, as soon and as quietly as possible.

Would you consider making the journey? It would mean so much to have you and Maryut Ribenis here.

He put the page down. Maryut had flipped to the other side of the first page. She and Danya were scanning it intently, but she felt his eyes on her and looked up. "What is it now?" she demanded.

"She wants us to come to the High Installation."

Danya gasped. Maryut snatched the second page from him and read as if her eyes would suck the words off the paper. "In Tyla," she said. "Goddess hear me. Of all things."

Danya said, "Of course you have to go, zhinin. Jano and I can take care of things here."

"I know you can," Ribas said automatically. Technically, what Valda had written wasn't an invitation so much as a summons. No backwater zhinin had the right to refuse the Tavin's personal request. And who in his right mind would turn down the chance to see a High Installation?

Maryut finished reading and looked up at him, wide-eyed. "What should we do?"

The Great Circle House Ribas had never seen loomed up in his imagination. Sventin Galvo was there, to be sure, the man Ribas had managed to avoid meeting fifteen years ago. Worse than the living sventin, Ribas thought, there might be shadows hiding in the great city. He didn't want to stumble on any memories of his father.

"You should go," Danya said again. "You can't miss that."

"We'll have to think about it," Ribas said. "Danya, thank you for bringing this over. When you go back to the House, please don't say anything about it to Jano yet."

She understood he was dismissing her. "Yes, zhinin." She bowed to him and Maryut and left the kitchen.

Maryut still held the second page of the letter. "A High Installation. But..."

She could guess about the things Ribas didn't want to find in Sostavi. She didn't know, yet, how serious things were with Gedrin. The evening at the Sheaf and Barrel, and that terrible Capture game, stood as sharply in Ribas's memory as if they'd happened yesterday. Could he leave Gedrin here alone?

"I know," he said. He took another swallow of tea, remembering the lonely girl at the viduris who had looked up from her book with frightened eyes. *If you could be here for another ceremony now,* Valda had written, *I might be able to see it through.*

That evening, Ribas and Maryut went up to the farm for supper. They hadn't told anyone else about Valda's letter, though Ribas knew it couldn't be long before the news about the next Tavin spread from Sostavi out into the farthest reaches of the country. No doubt he would get a letter from Kunin Dergo soon, telling him what he already knew. Whether or not Valda had won a vote, Ribas could imagine the old kunin's pride at the thought of one of his students moving into the House of the Tavin.

At the farmhouse, Ribas kept a close eye on his brother. Gedrin talked and laughed, swung Asira up on his shoulders when she asked him to, sat down at the Capture board with Raulin before supper. Ribas sat with them and saw no signs of impatience while his brother reviewed the basics of Capture with the little boy and played a short easy game with him, letting Raulin do moves over when he made mistakes. Gedrin didn't believe in losing deliberately, but Raulin didn't get frustrated or disappointed when his father scooped up his white Master. After the game ended, Raulin examined the pieces and reviewed moves with a seriousness that reminded Ribas of himself at that age. Ribas told him, "You'll be able to beat me in no time, Raulí," and Gedrin joked that he hoped any child of his could do that.

Supper was Virta's barley and vegetable stew, with biscuits Asira had helped roll out and cut. After everyone had pushed their empty plates and bowls aside and settled back to enjoy the warmth of the fire in the old farmhouse kitchen, and after Raulin and Asira had run down to the front room to play, Ribas told the family that he and Maryut needed their advice.

Gedrin propped his elbows on the table, cheerfully curious. "What's going on, brother?"

Wait till you hear. A lot of this decision would depend on how Gedrin took the news. Maryut had brought the letter. She took it out of the pocket of her dress and set it on the table while Ribas told the family about the election.

Mama looked stunned. "Valda Filtraikas as Tavin."

She remembered Valda very well. Virta, too, looked astonished. She had never met Valda: she'd been a little girl when Ribas was at the viduris, and hadn't met Gedrin until several years later, but she was from Paret too. Ribas saw her taking in the fact that a girl from her own town was going to be their new leader.

Mama reached out and picked up the letter. She skimmed it as Ribas explained about the Installation. "Valda wants Maryut and me to go," he said. "That's why we need advice."

On the one hand, he said, it would mean him leaving the Circle House for weeks, longer than he'd left it since his installation, and winter would be on them soon. On the other, it was a High Installation, and Valda was asking with the right of an old friend who needed help.

Mama glanced up from the parchment. Her eyes met Ribas's. He knew she had many of the same thoughts he did, not only about the trip and the possible risks, but about Sostavi itself. The same shadow hung over the city in her mind. She had never known what had happened to Silvas there. Ribas didn't think she wanted the past woken up any more than he did.

Gedrin said, "I don't think you should go."

Ribas looked at his brother and saw exactly what he had hoped he wouldn't. Gedrin's face looked hard, his jaw tight. He spoke quietly enough, but his voice had a dangerous undercurrent in it, like a fishing line pulled to the snapping point.

Ribas kept his own voice calm. "Why do you say that?"

"Because of everything you just said. You'd be gone too long. It's almost winter. It'll be Akena soon and that's your busiest time."

The edge in his tone got sharper with every word. Mama heard it too. Ribas saw her pass the letter back to Maryut. She sat still, her hands quiet on the table, but her eyes went back and forth between her sons.

Ribas knew he had to see for himself how far this would go. He wasn't a child anymore, facing down the father who had turned into something else. "My mosevine can take over at the House for a while," he said. "We'd be back before the end of Tyla. There would be plenty of time to get ready for the Akena services."

A dark flush climbed up into Gedrin's cheeks. Virta was watching him closely, Ribas saw. In her eyes he read a fear he'd never seen before.

No, Gedrí. Not you.

Maryut said, "It's a High Installation. We may never get another chance to see one." Ribas heard her impatience. To her, Gedrin was acting like a spoiled child.

Gedrin said, "My brother's place is here." His hand came down flat on the table. "Here, where we need him."

He wasn't shouting, not yet, but anger thickened and curdled his voice. Virta looked very pale. Ribas said, "What's worrying you, Gedrí?"

Then it came. Ribas was ready for it, thought he was ready for it, after what he had seen at the inn so recently, but when Gedrin surged to his feet, when his hand swept his empty bowl off the table to smash on the floor, every instinct Ribas had screamed at him to back away, to run.

He had not run from Silvas, no matter how much he had wanted to. It took every ounce of his self-control to sit still now.

"Don't you talk to me like I'm a child!" Gedrin snarled, and it was a snarl. Rage twisted his face. "You belong here, not in Sostavi, not someplace else where we can't reach you! I don't care what this woman wants! You shouldn't either!"

Beside Ribas, Maryut drew a sharp breath. Ribas knew she wanted to give Gedrin a piece of her mind. Without breaking eye contact with his brother, he touched her arm and shook his head.

Gedrin saw it. "Why do you always think you know so much? You always know what's best for everyone, you always..."

Mama started to say something, but Ribas got there first, gently but firmly interrupting his brother. "I'm supposed to know," he said. "What kind of zhinin would I be if I didn't?"

He held onto a picture of much-younger Gedrin, a little boy, wanting to know why his brother couldn't stay and work the farm. He held onto the memory of that little boy's tears. This was still the same Gedrin. Ribas must not forget it.

At the Sheaf, Gedrin had pulled himself out of the fit, or it had stopped on its own. This time it didn't stop. Ribas had time to see that Virta was crying, and then his brother was coming around the table with his anger like a fire around him.

Seldo could have defended himself if he'd had to. Ribas was no match for Gedrin. His brother would never try to hurt him, but his brother wasn't thinking now.

He got to his feet. Mama stood up too. Ribas had time to see the vivid blue of her eyes in her too-pale face.

A long time ago, a child had tried to protect his mother from hurt. He hadn't been able to do it, he had been too small, too weak, and his father's anger had ripped the world apart. Now Ribas had to let his brother's anger fall on him so it wouldn't touch anyone else in this room. The zhinin couldn't be afraid.

The gift showed him the livid red lines of the net. They seared against his own mind, too hot and strong. He should not do this. Gedrin had told him not to, before, but now he had no choice.

The lines had no weak places he could find. Knowing what the gift would take this time, he reached in with all the strength he could call up.

Cut.

One line snapped. The net began to unravel. As it fell away from Gedrin, the strands lashed against Ribas's mind, burning.

He had one moment to know it had worked. Gedrin stopped, his face frozen in confusion. Then pain came for Ribas and the room went dark.

He opened his eyes to see a very familiar ceiling. His bedroom, when he was growing up; Raulin's now.

His chest throbbed again and his body felt cold and clammy, as if he'd been sick. He knew he was lucky he didn't feel worse. He shouldn't have used the gift that way, especially after this morning.

Maryut's icy voice reached him. She told someone, "Don't you dare. You've done enough as it is."

Ribas tried to sit up on the bed, but the room started to spin. That felt worse than the pain. Someone put a hand on his chest. "Lie still."

He leaned back against the pillow and turned his head enough to see Mama sitting by the bed. The lines on her face and the silver in her hair stood out in the lamplight.

"I'm all right," he said. It hurt to talk, but he knew that would pass. After so many years, he ought to be resigned to his weakness. It still frustrated him every time. "I'm sorry your boys were fighting," he added, to see if he could make her smile.

She didn't. "Gedrí didn't mean it."

"I know."

"You shouldn't have done that, my dove. Gedrí wouldn't forgive himself if you got hurt."

"I'm fine, Mama. Besides, he'd have taken it worse if he'd hurt me himself."

Her face told him she knew that too. Her hand stayed on his chest and he willed his still-racing heart to slow down. She said quietly, "What are we going to do about him?"

He didn't know. From somewhere outside the door, he heard his brother saying, "I need to know if he's better!"

No doubt Maryut wouldn't let him in. Ribas managed to speak up enough for her to hear him.

"Marya."

She was beside the bed in an instant. "How are you feeling?"

"I'm all right. I just need to rest a while. Let Gedrí come in."

Her face tightened. "Please, Marya," he said. "I need to talk to him."

Maryut glanced across him at Mama. Mama looked intently into Ribas's face before she nodded and stood up. "Let's let them talk." To Ribas she added, "If you need anything, my dove, you have your brother call us."

"I will."

The two of them went out. Ribas heard Mama say, "He wants to talk to you. Be careful, now, and don't tire him out."

Gedrin rushed in. He took Mama's chair and caught Ribas's hand. "Goddess hear me, Ribé. I'm so sorry."

Ribas checked carefully in on his brother's mind. He had guessed what he would see, but that didn't stop the pang of new frustration when the gift showed him the lines of the net still there, slack and drooping, like the tendrils of a hardy vine that only needed water and light to flourish again. How long before they did? Could he stop it?

He smiled up at Gedrin. "When you want to cause trouble, you do it right. Breaking things, shouting at people. I thought you had some manners."

"I told you not to do that for me."

"I was going to let you knock me into next week? I don't think so, little brother."

Gedrin didn't smile back. "I'm scared, Ribé."

He hadn't been willing to admit that much at the inn. Now Ribas heard the tears in his voice. Of the two of them, Gedrin had always been much quicker to let everyone see what he felt, laughter or sadness or anything else. Mama said that was like their father too.

Ribas said, "What do you think happened there in the kitchen?"

"I don't know. I don't know why I got so angry. Goddess hear me, I wanted to hurt you. I felt like I had something inside me..." Gedrin motioned helplessly at his chest. "Something biting at me, tearing into me. It wouldn't stop."

Ribas found himself wondering if Silvas had felt the same thing. How much strength had it taken for him to manage his anger, however much he could? Had he felt the same shame Gedrin so clearly did?

The fear in his brother's eyes hurt Ribas more than the pain in his chest. He reached up to touch Gedrin's face. "You didn't hurt anyone."

"I would have, if you hadn't stopped me. I'd have hurt you."

"But you didn't. What do you think made you angry?"

They could have been boys again. Gedrin had grown up without a father, but Ribas, almost seven years older, had filled that place as well as he could. Gedrin had always trusted his brother to make things right.

He said, "You were talking about going away. I thought I couldn't stand it if you did. I..." He broke off, staring at the opposite wall, still gripping Ribas's hand. "Something's wrong with me," he said. "I know that. And I still don't want you to use that gift on me. But I thought, if you weren't here..."

Ribas understood. Gedrin looked at him again. "If you want to go to Sostavi, you should." He tried to sound cheerful. "Marya's right. When would you get to see another High Installation? And you knew Valda at school. I shouldn't stop you."

"You're not the only one around here who needs their zhinin. A lot of people might not like me going away."

"That's because you spoil us. You help us too much."

That was so exactly what Nevas and Maryut had said that morning that Ribas laughed, which made his chest hurt more. To keep Gedrin from noticing, he said, "What do you mean, something's wrong with you?"

He thought he knew what the answer would be. He was right. Gedrin said, "I'm turning out like Da."

The hopelessness in the words cut at Ribas again. He and Mama had always been very careful of what they told Gedrin about the father he didn't remember. After Silvas's death, everyone in Lida knew how he had been treating his wife and older son, and everyone knew what had happened because of it. Mama and Ribas hadn't wanted Gedrin to grow up with the shadow of old grief on him. They had tried, as much as they could, to protect the boy from the darkest things.

Now the dark had come for him anyway. "I know you and Mama were better off after Da died," Gedrin said. "I know I was, too. I don't want my family to have to say that about me."

"Gedrí," Ribas said, "no one will ever say that about you."

He still didn't have any answers. The best the gift could do, or the best he could do with it, couldn't fix his brother's trouble for good. *Goddess,* Ribas thought, *what am I to do here? How can I take care of him?*

Valda's letter came back into his mind. Sostavi: the one place any new member of the dagira would be expected to visit, but the one place Ribas had avoided when he'd traveled north to the coast before his installation in Lida. And Sventin Galvo, the man Ribas had barely been able to tolerate with half the country between them. In spite of the reasons to avoid all of it, a new, startling idea took shape.

If you could be here for another ceremony now, I might be able to see it through.

He decided to take it as an answer. "I can tell you what you're going to do over the next few weeks," he told Gedrin. "You're going to come with Marya and me to Sostavi."

"What?" When he realized Ribas was serious, Gedrin laughed: a warm, real laugh. "Go with you? I didn't get an invitation."

"You just did. I'm inviting you."

"But I can't..."

"You can." Ribas called up all his older-brother authority. "The farm's quiet this time of year. If my mosevine can take care of the House, Mama and Virta can take care of things here. We'll be back by the end of Tyla. And you could use the change."

He saw Gedrin's thirst for adventure waking up. Gedrin had so rarely left Lida that Sostavi felt like another world. Of course he'd want to see it. "I'll talk to Virta," he said.

Ribas had a feeling his sister-in-law wouldn't stand in Gedrin's way. Maryut might be another matter. She wouldn't especially like Ribas making this decision without her, and she might not like the idea of the two of them having to look after Gedrin for three weeks, but he felt sure it would be worth it.

"You do that," he said. "Now I'm going to take a rest before we head home."

Gedrin went out and shut the door quietly, leaving Ribas with his tangled thoughts. *You and Mama were better off after Da died. I don't want my family to have to say that about me.*

After Da died. Irresistibly, the words brought back that horrible night. Gedrin had never heard all the details of it. He had only grown up knowing about an accident and an injury their father had never recovered from.

Well, it *had* been an accident. Gedrin didn't need to know it had only happened because, that night, Silvas had decided to attack his six-year-old son.

Gedrin's life would never devolve into the same darkness. *Not you, Gedri.* Ribas thought the words as if they were a prayer. *Not while I'm living.*

11

VALDENA

During the two weeks after Valda sent her letter to Lida, the news of the election results spread through Sostavi and out into Namora. Soon, everyone in every town and village heard that Valdena Filtraikas would be the next Tavin only because the Council had failed to agree on a candidate.

Valda didn't let herself think about her letter once it had gone. She didn't expect Ribas to come to Sostavi and couldn't allow herself the weakness of hoping for it. The most she might get would be a return letter, a few lines from him, with a taste of the kindness she remembered. That would be more than enough of a gift.

Meanwhile, she must prepare herself for what was coming. As she went through the days, still serving in the Great House as Tavo Balsa, standing in for Tavin Ardinas, she kept herself rigidly calm. She told no one how surreal it felt to know she would soon wear the brown robes permanently. As a concession to her new role, she ordered two new sets of brown robes made: one woolen and the other linen, both richly embroidered, to maintain the right appearance. No one must see fear or uncertainty from the Tavin-to-be. No one should know how the hours slowed to a crawl for her every night, when she shut her chamber door on colleagues and petitioners and sat alone with only her thoughts for company. No one must ever guess at how often she cried during her prayers.

She prayed to the Goddess, of course, asking for help and strength and guidance in the days to come. Just as often, she found herself talking to Tavin Ardinas. Kenavi, Mother of Namora, was somewhere beyond human knowing, and the woman she had been had died centuries ago, but Ardinas had sat in the same chambers Valda did and stood on the dais in the same House. His hands had held the same crystal pitcher and bowl and the same richly carved box of salt. Maybe he hadn't entirely left the place he had served for so long. Maybe he could still hear her.

Sometimes she talked to him about the Installation. "I wish I had seen yours, Tavin. I wish had asked you how it felt to get ready for it." His Installation had come as the culmination of months of planning, during which all of Sostavi and the rest of Namora had eagerly looked forward to welcoming their new leader. She wanted hers to be over before most people had a chance to notice.

She could have handled it differently. She could have stepped into the role as proudly as if she'd won it with the Goddess's blessing. After all, she had served so close to Tavin Ardinas for the past six years; she had at least as many qualifications as Lesvin, though she didn't have Galvo's long experience. Lesvin's Council faction had apparently preferred her to Galvo. But she didn't want the role. Not this way, not now or ever.

Early on Setdina morning two weeks after she sent her letter, a servant knocked at Valda's chambers. "Letter for you, Sventin Valdena. Came by courier."

Letters arrived all the time. The most practical dagira in Sostavi and nearby towns had started angling for the Tavin-to-be's attention, knowing that a Tavin was a Tavin, no matter how she got there, and they should lay groundwork for alliances as soon as they could. Valda took the envelope. It was plain thin-pressed paper with a sea-blue wax seal on the back, the standard Circle House seal that countless zhinine used.

A courier, though. Valda tamped down on the hope that rose in her: this could still be anything. "Where did the courier come from?" she said.

"I don't know, sventin."

"Very well. You may go."

Valda took the letter into her sitting room. She broke the seal and took out the contents, one page, front and back, written in a strong, fluid hand. Her eyes moved on their own to the signature. *Yours in the fellowship of the Goddess Kenavi, Ribas Silvaikas.*

The page blurred. Valda swallowed hard. For a moment, she was thirteen again, looking up into a friendly face.

She sat down in the chair by the hearth. The page cleared as she read.

Raimaté, Sventin Valdena,

I am honored to receive your letter and your invitation to the High Installation. I write this as a zhinin to his new Tavin, but to go on, I'm afraid I must set formality aside.

She could already hear his voice in her mind. This was exactly the gift she'd hoped for, and she was so glad he'd addressed her by name instead of as "Tavo Balsa."

I must tell you, first, how much I admire everything you've accomplished in Sostavi. When you were named as Tavo Balsa, I was so glad to hear that news. Even in a place as difficult as Sostavi must be, it seems that sometimes, those who deserve rewards receive them.

That made her smile. She could see him smiling, too, as he wrote it. And he admired what she'd achieved? Those words made a glow around the rank that she had long since accepted as a burden.

Tavin Ardinas's loss must be very difficult for you, who knew him so well and worked with him so closely. I'm very sorry for your grief. And I am most sorry that you've had to face it alone, with colleagues who haven't been able to share it with you.

The page blurred again. *Yes, Ribé. I wish you were here.* She wished it so immediately and fiercely that she wanted to skim the letter in the desperate hope he might tell her he was coming to the Installation. But she must not think that, or rush through what he had written.

I have good reason to remember the Tavin's kindness to a young zhinin he had no particular call to notice. Please know that I grieve with you for the loss of the leader who was, as you say, a good man, who guided us and Namora surely and well. My thoughts are with you always, for whatever comfort that might bring.

That was exactly like him. Valda had to dry her eyes on her sleeve before she could keep going. She wondered if he had any idea that she would understand his reference to Ardinas's kindness to him. *He didn't have reason to notice you, Ribé? Oh yes, he did.*

Now he came to the election. Valda tried not to notice how her heart sped up.

The news about the vote of course comes as a shock. It must feel terribly daunting to step into such a role under these circumstances. At the same time, I can't help thinking that if the vote had to fail, we are very fortunate to have such an intelligent, discerning, and strong-hearted Tavo Balsa. We couldn't ask for anything more in our next leader.

Was he trying to make her cry? He might as well be. *Drat you, zhinin,* Valda scolded in her head, mopping at her eyes again. The Tavin-to-be shouldn't act like this. Thank goodness no one else was here to see it. But she had told him off the same way at the viduris when he'd made her laugh at the wrong time, for instance during one of those solemn Akena-month dinners when they were supposed to eat their mystery fodder in reverent silence. Ribas had never had to say a word out loud. His eyes, as he prodded a serving of some indeterminate casserole – *let's see if it grabs the fork* – held all the wicked humor in the world. Thinking of it now, she laughed again through the tears.

And then...

Maryut and I will be honored to come to Sostavi for the High Installation.

Valda stopped reading. She went back and looked at that sentence again. *Honored to come to Sostavi.* As the truth of it sank in, a great blaze of gladness swept over her, as if the sun, walled in for too long behind banks of clouds, had burst free.

Somehow she kept reading. *If I may risk an impertinence, may I ask the great favor that my brother Gedrin also be allowed to attend? Family concerns have made it necessary for him to come with us to Sostavi. He would be most gratified to see the ceremony.*

Of course. That would be no trouble at all. She raced through the rest. *If all goes smoothly on the road, we should arrive in Sostavi about two weeks after I post this letter. We will be glad to accept lodging in the House of the Zhinine, if that won't inconvenience our hosts. As one mosevin to another, I will be so glad to see you again; and as a member of the dagira, I will be honored to serve our Tavin.*

Yours in the fellowship of the Goddess Kenavi,
Ribas Silvaikas

Two weeks from his posting the letter. It would have taken about a week for it to reach her. Another week, then, and she would see him again.

It was more of a gift than she had dared to dream about. Valda folded the letter carefully and slipped it back in the envelope. *I thank You, Kenavi, Mother of us all. I thank You with all that is in me.*

Valda notified the heads of the House of the Zhinine that they would host three guests of hers during the week of the High Installation. When she gave them Ribas's name, she knew Sventin Galvo would probably hear the news within a matter of hours. She still didn't understand his interest in Ribas, but she found she didn't care about it, any more than she would have cared if someone had objected to the House of the Zhinine hosting three people from a backwater village at such a busy time.

In the days after she got Ribas's reply, she felt as if no impertinence, annoyance, or difficulty of any kind could touch her. Her younger self, the one who had believed in all the possibility and beauty of Sostavi, seemed to come to life again. More than that: she felt as if she had actually found the life she'd hoped for when she had arrived in the capital.

On the evening of the same day when she spoke to the heads of the House of the Zhinine, Sventin Galvo came up to her after the Great House service. Ever since the vote, his manner to her had been unfailingly friendly and polite. If he still held her at all responsible for the result, he never showed it in his words or behavior.

"Tavo Balsa," he said. Lately, he had used her formal title more than usual too, stressing his respect. She had no doubt he was working out how to turn the situation to his advantage, and intending to use that respect as leverage. He said, "I understand you're expecting visitors for the High Installation."

"Yes," she said. "I invited my old friend from the viduris and was delighted he accepted." No need to mention Ribas's name; they both knew who she meant. "He and his wife and brother will arrive in the city soon."

The Great House had emptied after the service. Subordinate dagira had gathered the prayer stones and cleared away the water and salt. Valda and Galvo stood alone on the dais, where only one lamp still burned next to the great hearth. Darkness lay over the rest of the House. Galvo's white robes and silver hair gleamed in the dim light. By contrast, in her brown robes, Valda felt as if she could have become part of the shadows and the holy quiet of the building.

Galvo said, "I would be honored to meet Zhinin Ribas. I do hope we can arrange it. There's so much I'd like to ask him about his work."

"I'm sure he would be pleased to speak with you." Valda couldn't help feeling sure of exactly the opposite, given what Ardinas had said about the many letters Galvo had sent to Lida. "I suspect," she said, "he might have to limit his engagements during his stay here. His health may not be very strong."

"Yes," Galvo said. "I remember his heart trouble. Most regrettable. How fortunate, though, that he's able to undertake a journey at this time of year."

If he wanted to know why Ribas would do such a thing for her, Valda had no answer, except that she'd asked for help and he had given it. She said, "Yes. I'll be very glad to see him again."

She didn't know what Galvo might have gleaned from the conversation, but he seemed satisfied. He gave her a correctly respectful good night and left her alone in the House.

The following days passed too quickly. The Installation reared up ahead of her like a wall too high to scale. All the Council together would perform the ceremony in the Great House. They would choose a representative to recite the same prayers and questions that made part of every installation ceremony in every Circle House in Namora. Valda would repeat the same words she had spoken when she first traded her red mosevin's robes for the blue ones of a zhinin, but this time, in trading her white for the newly made ceremonial brown, she would take a step only a handful of Tavo Balse had ever taken in Namora's sixteen-hundred-year history.

She didn't know if she could have gone through with it without Ribas's letter. His words made a lamp in her mind. She would admit that to no one, intended to say nothing about it to him either, but she followed their light forward, one step at a time.

Two days before the Installation, a servant from the House of the Zhinine arrived in Valda's chambers in the late afternoon to tell her that her guests from Lida had arrived. Valda sent him back immediately with a message. "Please ask Zhinin Ribas if he and his wife and brother will join me for supper in my quarters this evening." Galvo would doubtless hear about that too. Valda didn't care what he made of it.

The servant came back in short order and said that yes, the zhinin said they would be honored, they would look forward to waiting on her that evening. As Valda made arrangements for supper, her joy struggled against an increasing and unwelcome flush of memory.

That last year at the viduris. Valda didn't remember whether the summer before it had already felt different. She and Ribas would have written back and forth then, the same way they had during other breaks. Had she missed him more, that summer? Had he had started to intrude on her dreams?

She did remember seeing him again when they came back to school that fall, in Rudua. She remembered noticing exactly how blue his eyes looked against his sun-browned skin, and how the same sun had bleached his hair a shade lighter, and how much – oh, how very much – she found herself wanting to smooth that tousled hair with her fingertips, and touch the exposed triangle of his chest where his shirt collar lay open.

All long over and done with now. When it came time to dress for supper, Valda chose a simple dark-green sheath with lighter green embroidery at the neck and waist. Green, she felt, suited her as no other color did. She slipped the dress on and belted it, promising herself that the choice of color would be her only concession to the chaos inside her head.

She was the Tavin-to-be. Ribas was a well-respected and no doubt much-beloved zhinin who, as if Valda could forget it, had also been married for many years. Valda brushed her hair out and braided it with quick, impatient fingers. Time had no doubt changed him, in looks if nothing else. She coiled the braid and pinned it at the back of her head, slipping the pins in as if they could spear and extract her wayward thoughts. She had no time for nonsense. She would be grateful to see him again tonight as an old and dear friend, who had done her a great favor in coming here. That was all.

Two servants brought the meal in and set it out on the table in her front room. Valda made up the fire without help. It had just glowed into warm life when the knock came.

"Come in," Valda said. She linked her hands together behind her back, and then lowered them to her sides. She would not stand here like a mosevin waiting for an examination.

The door swung open. One of the House of the Zhinine's servants, a young blonde woman, stood outside. "Tavo Balsa, I have with me Zhinin Ribas Silvaikas, Maryut Ribenis, and Gedrin Silvaikas."

"Thank you."

The servant stepped aside and the three guests came in. Valda's eyes went to him at once. Goddess hear her, she would have known him anywhere.

He had new lines on his face, yes, and too much silver in his hair. He ought to be too young for that, he was no older than Valda, but no doubt his illness had caused it. He wore his hair shorter now too. Cropped closer, it looked less unruly than it used to. But his eyes. Nothing had changed those eyes, or his smile.

He bowed to her with his hand over his heart. "Raimaté, Tavo Balsa."

The same voice. *Then we're even. I know who you are too. Valdena, right?*

She wanted to say, *No, don't bow to me, not you!* She wanted to run to him and catch his hands in hers and prove to herself that he was real. Instead, with an effort that seemed to make every muscle ache, she bowed correctly in return. "Raimaté, zhinin." In some corner of her mind, she understood that whatever battle she had tried to fight tonight, she had already lost.

But she had a duty to perform. Now she could take in all three of them clearly: Ribas, and his wife, and the strong-built dark-haired man who must be Ribas's brother. Valda barely remembered Gedrin Silvaikas, whom she hadn't seen since he was a young boy. Ribas was saying, "Tavo Balsa, you remember my wife Maryut," and Valda stepped forward to shake hands first with the small vivid woman whose face she remembered very well. Her mind carried her back to Ribas's installation in that little village Circle House, and to the dark-haired girl who had run up to him after it was over, while Valda watched, and flung her arms around him in his new sea-blue robes, her face a study in joy and pride. That day, Maryut and Ribas had already been promised to each other.

Time had made small changes to Maryut too, but she still looked very much like the girl Valda had known. Tonight she wore a deep red dress, probably homespun but beautifully embroidered with interlaced rings of white flowers at the neck, sleeves, and waist. She returned Valda's handshake, head lowered politely. When Valda released her hand, Maryut stepped closer to her husband as if he were a shield.

Valda shook hands with Gedrin too. Both he and Maryut looked overawed; only Ribas seemed relaxed and easy, as though this place felt familiar to him as his own zhinin's house in Lida. Valda said, "None of you must call me Tavo Balsa." To Ribas she added, "You can't use my title when we were mosevine together." She was glad he hadn't worn his robes of office tonight, as a visiting dagira member might. They would have stressed the distance between him and her, which his simple, neatly-pressed shirt and pants didn't.

He bowed again. She heard the humor in his voice, clear as light. "As you wish, sventin."

That made her laugh, and now, finally, she let herself put her hand out to him. When he took it, she couldn't resist holding his, briefly, between both of her own. Yes, it was warm and strong and real. "Not that either, zhinin," she told him. "First names, please." She heard herself add, "I can't tell you how good it is to have you here. It's been a hard few weeks."

That wasn't the Tavo Balsa speaking anymore. He answered with the gentleness she remembered so well. "I can imagine. I'm glad to see you too, Valda."

Later, when she was alone, she would give her unruly feelings the punishment they deserved. Now she held herself together out of long habit. "You and Maryut haven't changed at all," she told Ribas as she led the way to the supper table. Ribas joked about his gray hair: "I didn't have that at the viduris, not for lack of trying on Kunin Dergo's part." Valda apologized to Gedrin for not knowing him as quickly. "You were a little shorter, I think, the last time I saw you." Gedrin sat stiffly at the table as if afraid to brush the fine cloth or touch the delicate pottery servingware. Valda was glad she hadn't asked any servant to help with the meal. After she'd been in Sostavi for so long, she'd forgotten that people in other places did things much more simply.

Supper was roast chicken with potatoes and a dressing made of brown bread, apples, and nuts. Valda passed the serving dishes around the table. Gedrin took tiny portions, as if he thought that was the only way he could be sure not to spill or drop anything. Ribas served Maryut and then himself. After he had set the last dish down in its place, he reached over and closed his hand briefly around his wife's. Valda couldn't see his face, but she caught Maryut's fragile smile and could picture the look Ribas had given her. *It's all right, I promise.* In spite of herself, her heart twisted.

She had never had his gift with people, but she pushed herself to try to help her guests relax. She asked about the trip; it had been uneventful, apparently, but Ribas said he'd been glad to see some of the country again. Since becoming a zhinin, he hadn't traveled farther from Lida than Paret. He talked a little about the route they had taken, more or less straight across the Kalnu region's northwest corner, east of the Isare Mountains in central Namora, and into the Jemtave region where Sostavi was. "I thought the trip might be hard, you know. My body doesn't always cooperate." He said it lightly, but Valda remembered how much trouble his heart had given him even at school. "Traveling seems to agree with me," he said. "Maybe it's good to get away from work for a while."

Valda was glad to hear it. She said, "I wrote you too much about what I've been doing. Tell me how everything's been in Lida."

He smiled. "Busy. Always."

Maryut said, with her eyes on her plate, "That's your own fault, Ribé."

Valda remembered Maryut as quick and outspoken. It surprised her to see her so shy now. Ribas said, "I don't know about that. Someone always needs something."

Maryut cut into a slice of chicken. "You don't always have to give it to them." She raised her head and her eyes met Valda's. "People come from all over to see him, you know. Not just people in Lida. He works much too hard, but he won't turn anybody away."

Valda heard her defiant pride. *You shouldn't be jealous of me, Marya. You won him long ago.* She knew how absurd that sounded. Maryut probably didn't feel jealous at all; Valda couldn't trust her own thoughts tonight.

She said, "I'm not surprised anyone would go to him if they could. He always was the easiest person I ever knew to talk to."

He said, "I'm glad." Those eyes. Valda couldn't make herself look away from them. At least her blush didn't rush into her face to humiliate her. He said, "Listening is one of my few skills."

Gedrin said what Valda was thinking. "Few? You've got more than a few."

Valda thought of the dovne kenavnis, the mysterious gift Ribas had never used during their time at the viduris, that only his closest friends, sworn to secrecy, had known about back then. She'd have liked to ask how he used it in his work now, but he had never liked to talk about it much. Besides, she saw something in the look that went between the two brothers.

Ribas said, "Sometimes I do." He seemed to be talking straight to Gedrin. "Sometimes I don't have quite enough skills, but you know I keep working on it."

Beyond question, the two of them shared some kind of trouble. Valda remembered what Ribas had said in his letter. "Family concerns" had brought Gedrin to Sostavi. She wished she could ask what was wrong.

Ribas turned back to her. "Tavo Balsa, since I can listen, I wonder if you'd like to talk."

She laughed. "What did I tell you about titles, Ribé?"

The nickname came out before she thought. She might have

heard an intake of breath from Maryut, but Ribas had already used her own nickname, and just for now, she wanted to let go of ranks and titles and the tangled mess her life had become.

His eyes were full of mischief. "Pardon me." Then the laughter disappeared. "From your letter, I thought you might need someone to talk to. I'd be very glad if I can help."

Of course he had understood what she needed. "I don't want to bore you."

"I can't imagine you would. It sounds like life here in Sostavi can be a little too exciting."

Valda couldn't resist the invitation. She had worn a mask for so long that she hadn't realized what a prison it had become. Now, as she told him all the details from the past weeks that she hadn't included in her letter, she felt as if a suffocating blanket wrapped around her had loosened. She hadn't known how badly she needed to catch her breath.

When she told him everything about Galvo's accusations, his face tightened. "He thought that? Does he know you at all?"

The anger under the words warmed her. "I wondered the same thing."

Maryut had been listening closely. She said, "I remember when this Sventin Galvo was bothering Ribé years ago. He sounds terrible."

Sventin Lesvin and his cronies apparently thought so. "He has a good side, believe it or not," Valda said. "He's been very kind to me over the years. The way his mind works, I suppose it's natural he'd think I'd want to steal the election if I could."

"Because that's what he would want," Maryut said. "He would think of cheating, but he had no right to say those things to you. If I see him here," she said with a glance at her husband, "I might have to give him a piece of my mind. Of course, somebody will have to point him out to me."

That made Valda smile, but something about it made her eyes sting too. Ribas said, "If you do that, love, I don't think he'll know what hit him."

"He'll deserve it."

Valda didn't miss that word *love*, or the look that went between husband and wife. She said, "I'll tell you something else. It's not easy for a Tavin to resign, but it can be done. I've been thinking about what I'd have to do."

Maryut said, "Don't let them make you do that."

Now she seemed like the confident girl Valda remembered. "I don't know," Valda said. None of her colleagues could know she had thought about it, of course, until and unless she decided to do it. "Maybe it would be best."

Ribas said, "You know what kind of a leader I think you'll be. I'm pretty sure I'm right, if I say it myself."

Intelligent. Discerning. Strong-hearted. Valda didn't know if she dared to tell him how much those words had meant. Gedrin helped her pass it off. "You're always pretty sure you're right, Ribé," he said.

Ribas's face looked perfectly innocent. "That's because I usually am."

Gedrin and Maryut laughed. Valda joined in, but a new thought seized on her mind.

She still needed to choose a Tavo Balsa. What if Ribas would do it?

At first glance, it looked impossible. He was a zhinin in a back-water village. But suppose she had him, the one person she trusted absolutely, as her right hand here in Sostavi. She had considered Galvo for the position. That seemed laughable now.

You shouldn't think of it. You know what you feel for him.

Valda pushed that voice away. Her Installation as Tavin would leave a gap in the Council. No one could object if the new Tavin made a strongly-worded recommendation that a particular sventin get the vacant Council seat. Ribas wasn't a sventin yet, but she could make sure he became one in time. As soon as she became Tavin, she would have the authority to promote him directly to that rank.

Plenty of the Great House's own dagira had spent years slavering for a chance at the Council, but they could go on waiting. A zhinin of

Ribas's ability more than deserved such a high promotion. And he had the dovne kenavnis. The dovne kenavnis on the Council: who of her colleagues would object to that? For the first time, Valda considered exactly how much her new authority might achieve. If he would agree to it. If he would so much as consider it.

She wouldn't say anything to him about it yet; not until she had thought everything through in detail. While they ate dessert, a dense sweet nut cake flavored with honey and cinnamon, they talked about Sostavi. Valda said, "I hope you'll enjoy the city when you have a chance to explore. It's very different from Paret, of course, but it's really quite lovely." Ribas mentioned that his and Gedrin's father had lived in the city years before. He said Silvas Jadraikas had actually served as a zhinin in the Great House. Valda didn't remember him ever talking about that at the viduris. She wanted to hear more now, but Ribas changed the subject right away, as if he didn't want to say anything else.

After they finished dessert, Ribas apologized for the tiredness he couldn't mask anymore. "I think I'd better get some rest. I'm not as young as I used to be."

He made it a joke, but Valda wished his illness didn't drag on him so much. "Certainly," she said. "I really can't thank you enough for being here. It felt..." She let herself say it. "It felt like home again."

Maryut offered her hand first. "We'll see you again soon." Valda caught an unmistakable sense of fellowship from her, one woman to another. She couldn't have been jealous after all. Gedrin, too, shook hands more easily than he had at first.

Ribas bowed to Valda, another correct salute. Before she could stop herself, Valda held out her arms to him. "For old times' sake?"

His smile twisted her heart again. "Gladly."

She told herself not to feel this too much. Especially, as she let her head rest briefly on his shoulder, with the smooth fabric of his shirt against her cheek and his arms around her, she must not think about how safe she felt. She must not think about how very, very much she had missed him, for so long.

After her guests had gone, Valda closed and latched the door. Servants would clear away the dishes in the morning. She had asked not to be disturbed tonight.

One clear thought stood out from the fog in her head. *My Tavo Balsa.*

It made good sense. She needed someone. She trusted him. The Council of fifteen years ago had apparently wanted him here, very much. Would they want him any less now? They would all realize soon that he wouldn't care about the position's downside. If he was still the man she remembered – and tonight had proven he was – he would have no interest in being a candidate for Tavin.

His health and his deep loyalty to Lida were both considerations. As a member of the Great House dagira, he would have attendance from the best healers in Namora. That could only be a benefit. Granted, to move to Sostavi, he and Maryut would have to uproot themselves in a way neither of them, especially Maryut, had ever experienced. Even if Ribas were willing to do it himself, he might not want to put his wife through it. As to Lida, no doubt losing him would leave those people in a serious bind, but Valda tried to believe they could find another good zhinin to put in that House. Ribas had apprentices already. Maybe one of them could do it, someone he had trained himself.

You shouldn't try this. Think of what you're doing.

Valda knew what she was doing. She knew exactly how dangerous it was, when she still felt his arms holding her. But that did nothing to make her stop wishing for the words that would convince him to stay where she needed him.

12

BEREG

After the death of Lada Egem, the young soldier who wanted to kill the Vaia rider, Bereg and the rest of his detachment spent the rest of the day traveling farther south in Tsvavyest. Bereg rode ahead, apart from the rest. The group of young soldiers behind him traveled in thick, curdled silence. Behind them came Silde Vasem, her presence as heavy and cold as stone.

The grass of the plains seemed to blur around Bereg. The afternoon sun beat down too hot; the blue sky looked hideously bright. He let his horse carry him and tried to look busy scouting a path, but he felt as if his brain was trying to crawl out of his skull.

The Vaia group they had encountered had kept riding west, in a straight line, as fast as their horses would carry them. Lada Egem, brought down by Silde Vasem's vindula, lay in the grave her fellow soldiers had quickly scraped out for her. The grave had no marker on it. Her family, if she had any – Bereg didn't even know that much about her – wouldn't know where to find her body. They wouldn't come to pay tribute to her if they did. Traitors deserved no honor or memory. Every Lasska knew that.

Bereg told himself to forget what had happened to her and focus on the job at hand. The light and heat around him made him feel sick. The sun felt like a monstrous eye boring into him.

None of this is right.

He should have stopped Silde Vasem. Somehow, he thought through the clouds of nausea, he should have realized what she was going to do, and he should have stopped her. How? Shot the weapon out of her hand? Cut her down, the way she had killed Egem?

Egem had disobeyed two direct orders from her commander. By extension, she had disobeyed the orders of Impera Shurik himself. That was treason. Traitors died.

None of this is right.

Bereg rode on, clutching the reins between his fingers. The leather strips, wrapped tight around his hands, dug into his skin. The rough pain kept him anchored.

He only had to see this job through. He felt sure the young soldiers wouldn't try to kill any more Vaia. They wouldn't risk Silde Vasem's immediate justice. Bereg simply had to finish the task in front of him. Then Impera Shurik would give him the promised reward and he would go home to Thysidich and his family, the business done, his hands clean.

He had never hungered for other men's blood. He had spent all his working life building roads, linking towns and cities together. Lassar's soldiers kept the empire's great heart beating and its people fed and cared for, but many of them had other skills too.

Afternoon slanted toward evening and the sunlight turned from hot yellow to deep gold. Bereg's mind wandered beyond his control, spinning out pictures of the second stage of Impera Shurik's campaign.

A thicket of tents in an open field. Dawn, maybe: a frosty winter dawn with the first light making splashes of rose and gold on the glittering grass. Cook fires sending smoke into the air. Pots bubbling; meat sizzling on spits.

Small-boned, dark-skinned women with long dark hair, tending the breakfast as it cooked. Men cleaning weapons, perhaps, and chatting together. Children running about: small dark children with bright laughing faces. Bent-backed, silver-haired elderly, sitting near the warmth of fires or in the shelter of tent flaps. Some enjoying pipes; some working at whittling with age-roughened fingers. Some, maybe, corralling a grandchild to lift into a lap, to savor the nearness of warmth and laughter and young breath against an old cheek.

The Lasska fighting force wouldn't ride straight up to the camp. They would stay out of bowshot range, keep to whatever cover they could find. They would surround the Vaia. Form a net around the camp.

The yellow-shirted leaders and the white-shirted witch-women first.

Silde Vasem hadn't said a word of warning. Lada Egem hadn't had the chance to put her weapon down or ask for mercy.

What happens to children who see their parents murdered?

"Halt!"

The word sliced through the noise in Bereg's head, the shattering report of dozens of imagined vinduli. Reflex made him rein in. In his mind, Vaia bodies bled on the frozen grass. Women screamed. Children stared, hollow-eyed, emptied out with fear.

What happens to children...

Someone rode up beside him. "Silde Orlon. It's getting late."

Silde Vasem. Bereg noticed, vaguely, that the afternoon light had faded. How had evening come so quickly?

The woman's face made a pale oval in the twilight. "We should make camp," she said.

"Yes." His voice seemed to come from somewhere else. Not out of his own living, breathing mouth.

The young soldiers worked quickly and silently, setting up cook fires and laying out bedrolls. Bereg sat off to the side, letting Silde Vasem keep everything under her eye.

A little girl raised her hand to point to two soldiers, one after the other.

He must obey orders. His thoughts felt as sluggish as fish in a half-frozen stream. He must not argue or question. Not if he wanted to go home.

None of this is right.

Mechanically, he ate the food one of the young soldiers brought him. Mechanically, he agreed when Silde Vasem offered to take the first watch again. He lay down and wrapped his blanket around him and tried to send himself back to Thysidich in his mind. Nela and Ania. The new grandchild he would hold in his arms, the small face he would look into for the first time.

In his mind, a Lasska soldier picked up a Vaia child who did not scream or struggle. The Lasska mounted his horse and held the child on the saddle in front of him and rode away from the camp. Maybe the child tried to twist around for one last look at the home and parents she had lost. Maybe she stared straight ahead, as the huge unknown world roared forward to meet her and the cold wind whipped tears from her eyes.

Someone shook Bereg's shoulder. He jerked out of a dark hazy dream to see Silde Vasem leaning over him with her finger to her lips.

"Come with me."

Bereg got up stiffly. She led him away from the fire and the cluster of young soldiers in their bedrolls. At the edge of the camp, beyond the firelight, she stopped and pointed.

Following her hand, Bereg made out a dark shape. Two. The moon hung full and round and a spread of stars glittered, showed him the outlines of a man and a horse.

Vaia.

Silde Vasem whispered, "He came into camp. He wants to speak to me. You'll come too."

A Vaia wanted to speak to them? Bereg didn't understand. He thought this might still be part of the nightmare.

"He was one of the ones we saw today," Silde Vasem said. "He says he's unarmed, but his friends may be out there."

Bereg tried to wake up. Maybe this Vaia and his friends had tracked the Lasska detachment and decided to mount an ambush. Bereg imagined a net of them, spread out around the camp, ready to move forward at a signal. But then, why would one of them walk in to give warning?

Silde Vasem moved away from the firelight, toward the man. Bereg followed her as if pulled along by an invisible rope. Neither of them had a vindula. Bereg did have a short knife in his belt.

The man stood quiet, waiting. As he and Silde Vasem got closer, Bereg made out that the Vaia was slim and young, not tall, about Bereg's own height. He wore leather breeches, leather boots, and a dark-colored shirt. His dark hair hung long and loose, past his shoulders. His horse looked small but strong-built, with a thick thatch of mane and a dark heavy forelock. Bereg couldn't see any saddle or bridle.

This man came from a world that intersected with Bereg's own, a world that Bereg had never looked into before. Bereg knew he ought to see him as an enemy. He shouldn't feel such a flash of wonder.

Silde Vasem spoke first. "This is Silde Bereg Orlon," she told the Vaia. Her low voice barely rose above the sound of the breeze moving through the grass. "Whatever you have to say to me, he will hear too."

"I am glad to know him," the Vaia replied. He spoke correct, strangely accented Lasska. "If he is the person I think he is, my message is meant for him too."

What message? How could the Vaia know who Bereg was, or have anything to say to him? Bereg wished his head would clear. He wished he had his vindula, something solid to grip and remind himself that he was a soldier and the Impera's servant.

Silde Vasem led the small group farther into the dark, away from the camp. Under cover of a small cluster of trees, little more than shrubs, she stopped. "Now," she said. "Tell us who you are and what you have to say."

The Vaia seemed perfectly composed. He couldn't be more than nineteen or twenty, Bereg thought. His dark-skinned face looked smooth, unlined and unbearded. He stood quietly, making no restless or nervous movements, resting one hand lightly on his horse's neck. The horse, too, stood still; no uneasy snorting, pawing, or head-tossing. For all the young rider knew, both Bereg and Silde Vasem could have weapons, and he knew their cohorts in the camp certainly did. It didn't seem to worry him. As if he and his horse owned these plains, Bereg thought, and the Lasska only meant temporary trouble, like biting flies.

The Vaia said, "My name is Rahul. My tribe winters on these plains, but this year, we are riding farther west. We know what your Impera Shurik plans for us."

Silde Vasem said, "What is it you know?"

The Vaia's calm tone didn't change. "Shurik is sending his soldiers out to find our winter camps and kill us. He wants to rid this country of the Vaia people."

Cold flooded Bereg. Shurik's plan depended on secrecy. Silde Vasem asked what he couldn't: "How do you know this?"

"Two of the women in our tribe are...in your language I think you would say Light-Bearers. Their dreams tell them what's coming for us. One of them saw Shurik's plan."

Bereg swallowed. *Witch-women.* No mortal person should be able to see the future. The Vaia people must have some dangerous dark magic. But why would this Vaia tell him and Silde Vasem this? Had they walked into an ambush after all, and this young man, Rahul or whatever his name was, only wanted them to know why they were going to die?

It occurred to Bereg he should deny what the Vaia said. He should say Shurik had no such intentions. Above everything else, the

Vaia tribes must not have the chance to prepare for the Lasska attack. In fact, Bereg realized, it was his duty to kill this young Vaia here and now. The man should not have the chance to spread his information any farther.

Silde Vasem said, "Why are you going west?"

"Our younger Light-Bearer had another dream."

Bereg should not listen to this. He didn't want to hear any more, but he couldn't make himself cut the young man off. He listened in increasing bewilderment as Rahul explained that his tribe's older witch-woman had seen the coming destruction, but the younger one had seen possible help. Rahul and a small group from his tribe wanted to get to the western mountains and across them into Namora. According to the younger witch-woman, they would find a man there who could help them.

What man? How could any Namoran help them? None of it made sense to Bereg. The Vaia's words buzzed in his head like bees trapped in a jar. He only knew that he and Silde Vasem had to do something: tell the Vaia his witch-women were lying, tell him Shurik didn't mean the tribes any harm, or else they should cut the young man's throat so he would never get back to his people. Bereg realized with slow and mounting horror that he couldn't do any of those things. He couldn't open his mouth to lie, and he knew beyond a doubt that even if the much younger, stronger Vaia stood still and let him do it, Bereg could never take out his knife and kill him.

Silde Vasem was listening carefully to everything the Vaia said. Surely, Bereg thought, she couldn't believe it. The Vaia did not honor the only true God. What had Impera Shurik said? The Vaia were primitive people who worshipped the sun, the moon...beings that weren't gods and never had been. Even the most faithful Lasska never got to glimpse the future. How could people who knew nothing of Mesha claim to have that kind of sight?

He realized Silde Vasem was speaking again. "What do you believe this man will do to help you?"

"Our Light-Bearer's dream did not tell her that," the Vaia said. "We only know he is our best hope. Probably the only hope."

"And you don't know his name, or where to find him," Silde Vasem said.

"Khari says we will find him if we can only get into Namora."

This Khari must be the "Light-Bearer," the witch-woman. Bereg couldn't picture the white-shirted rider Lada Egem had wanted to bring down; he had seen her too briefly, moving too fast. He did know that if the Vaia had to get to Namora to find help, then this man and his tribe, or however many were with him, had to be stopped. They could not reach the mountains.

Yes, a treacherous thought whispered to him. *But what will you do about it, old man?*

Silde Vasem said, "Why did you need to speak to me about all this?"

"This afternoon, we saw you kill the other Lasska."

Bereg had thought the dreamlike horror of all this couldn't possibly hold him any tighter. Now he listened to the Vaia tell how one member of his search party, someone with keen eyes whose name Bereg didn't catch, had gotten a good enough look behind, even as they fled, to see Silde Vasem shoot Lada Egem.

They should not have seen that. It shouldn't have happened. Bereg relived the afternoon again, all the worse and more sickening as the Vaia told it in his calm voice. Then the young man said, "Afterward, Khari had another dream. It showed her that you, Fisa Vasem, and you, Bereg Orlon, would leave your people and join us in our ride west."

The Vaia pronounced each of their names perfectly, inclining his head politely as he said them, as if he were a servant in Cheremay receiving them for an audience with the Impera. To Bereg, the quiet voice felt like a noose tightening around his neck.

Impossible.

He would not believe it. This girl, this witch-woman Bereg had only seen as a fleeing flash, could not know anything about him or his life or future. This was some sort of trickery, some sort of evil primitive magic meant to snare him.

Probably she couldn't see the future at all. Probably none of these witch-women could. Bereg clung to that thought like a drowning man clutching a slippery thread. Granted, they knew somehow about the Impera's plan, but they must have come by that knowledge another way.

What way? The small voice in his head woke up again. *Who would have told them?*

Bereg shoved the questions aside. He didn't care. Even if they did have some strange magic, even if this girl had seen something in her dreams, Bereg wouldn't listen to it. He would have nothing to do with this Vaia or his party. He would never abandon his detachment or aid the Vaia in any way.

None of this is right.

Ask your conscience, Silde Orlon...

Silde Vasem said, "How do you believe we can help you?"

She should have sounded incredulous, or angry, or dismissive. She should have told the Vaia she would listen to nothing he had to say. Instead, to Bereg's disbelieving ears, she sounded like a starving person being offered a meal.

The Vaia said, "Khari did not see that either, but she was very sure you can help us. She told us she has never had such a clear dream."

Bereg told himself that if these witch-women did have real dreams, the information they got from them had such big holes in it that it couldn't do any good. A road with holes that size would be dug up and re-laid. He said it to drown out the memory of his own dream, or vision, that evening, of the Lasska soldier carrying the Vaia child away from the ruined camp.

Silde Vasem said, "What do you intend to do to Shurik, if you can?"

The question came out as sharp and fierce as a whip crack against tender skin. When had the Vaia said they meant to do anything to Shurik?

"We don't intend to have anything to do with your impera. We hope we can find safety for the tribes, somehow, and that this man in Namora will help us. That is all we want."

"You people aren't fighters," Silde Vasem said.

The Vaia laughed, a surprising, warm sound. "You can be glad my tribesman Handan isn't here to hear that. He would want to prove you wrong, but it's true. We are not fighters, not like you Lasska."

When he finished speaking, silence wrapped around them. Insects sang in the dark. Bereg tried desperately to think what to do. He and Silde Vasem had to get away from this man and get back to the camp. He must remember the work. He must remember home.

Then Silde Vasem said, "I've served Shurik, and his father, because I had no choice. Now it seems I have one." Bereg stood frozen and silent as she finished, "I will help you. I will fight what Shurik is doing, every way I can."

She had just promised treason against the Impera. Bereg knew that if he had brought his vindula out of the camp, he would have had to take it up now and give her the same justice she had given Egem. He should still pull out his knife and do what he could, in the name of the Impera and Mesha Himself...but oh, Mesha guard him, he was old. He had no strength to stand against this fierce woman and her lifelong anger.

"Silde Orlon," she said. "You have a choice now too."

Bereg must tell her he had no such thing. He had to serve Shurik if he wanted any future at all.

I know he thinks he bought you...

The Vaia said, "The old bear will also come with us."

It took Bereg's torpid mind several seconds to realize he himself was the old bear. For no reason, he remembered the face of the bear on the throne in Cheremay. The scarred muzzle, the sad eyes.

No, he wanted to say. He did not want to harm Silde Vasem. He did not want to see Vaia die or know that Lasska soldiers had murdered parents and grandparents and dragged helpless children off into a world where they didn't belong. He did not want any of this to happen, but if he tried to stand against it, he would never see his home again.

Silde Vasem told the Vaia, "Silde Orlon and I are different. I have nothing to lose. He has people waiting for him."

The Vaia looked at Bereg, dark eyes shadowed in the dark face. "Then he understands that I do too."

Bereg understood, but he couldn't do anything about it. If only he had left the army long ago. If he had found a way to retire sooner, Shurik wouldn't have summoned him to Cheremay, and he would never have been part of all this.

Silde Vasem said, "If you won't come with me now, at least you'll let me go."

Bereg knew he couldn't stop her. In silence, he went back to the camp with her, watched as she quickly and quietly gathered her things and mounted the horse that would carry her away to the Vaia. She took three vinduli with her: Lasska weapons she would give to Shurik's enemies. Bereg knew that by letting her do all this, he had already made himself a traitor.

From the saddle, she leaned down. "Silde Orlon, if it helps at all, know that Silde Vasem isn't leaving this company. She doesn't exist anymore."

Bereg understood she was taking her old name back. She was Tama Leben now. She said, "I'll see you again when you want to find us."

He had never heard such joy in her voice before. He wanted to say, *I will never want to find you,* but he still couldn't open his mouth to say anything at all. She reached down from the saddle and briefly touched his shoulder. Her smile, the first time he remembered seeing it, gleamed out in the dark.

Then she touched her heels to the horse's sides. Bereg stood alone and watched her ride away into the night.

13

KHARI

Khari thought she had never known what relief felt like until she saw Rahul riding back toward them, out of the dark, with the Lasska woman on her own horse behind him. She offered a prayer of thanks to the Moon Woman out of the core of herself.

Handan got to his feet as the two riders came nearer. Khari saw he held a spear. The blade gleamed in the moonlight. Khari scrambled up, ready to put herself between him and the Lasska if she had to.

Rahul and the woman dismounted and came up to the group. Rahul's eyes found Khari first. "Lamp-Carrier," he said. "This is Tama Leben. She will help us."

The Lasska woman stood much taller than Khari, taller than any of the tribe. Only Radavan came close to her height. Her skin looked pale in the dark, and her strange stiff clothes, the gray coat and gray pants the soldiers wore, looked like the color of the night itself. Her hair, twisted up in a tight knot, had streaks of silver in it.

By speaking to Khari first, Rahul had given her permission to approach the Lasska before anyone else. Even Handan, still gripping his spear too eagerly for Khari's taste, watched quietly as Khari stepped forward and held out her hand, the way she knew Lasska did with each other.

"I am glad to see you," she said in Lasska. The words felt clumsy and awkward in her mouth.

The woman, Tama Leben, took Khari's hand and said something Khari couldn't follow. Her hand felt like any other hand: the skin a little dry, the fingers lean and strong. Khari could smell the dust and sweat on the woman's clothes and the musky scent of the fabric itself.

Rahul translated the woman's words. "She's asking if you are the one who had the dream."

Khari said she was. The woman said something to Rahul and went back to her horse. From the saddle, she took down three of the strange Lasska weapons, the ones that hurled metal. They looked long and awkward in her hands, like heavy branches. Khari knew this must be at least part of the help her dream had promised the Lasska would give. The sight of those tools of killing still made her feel sick.

Rahul said in Vaia, "Tama offers these weapons" – he carefully pronounced the Lasska name for them, *vindula* – "as gifts."

With no prompting from Rahul, Tama offered the first one to Handan. She could tell a hunter when she saw him. Khari tensed. Handan wouldn't know how to use it, but it felt like a mistake to put such a dangerous thing in his hand as he faced a Lasska.

He laid his spear on the ground to take hold of the new weapon. Hefting it, he stroked its long neck and peered along its length. Khari saw admiration in his face. When he looked up at Tama and jerked his head in a nod, the briefest possible thanks, Khari let out her breath in relief.

Tama did consult with Rahul about the second weapon, which went to Radavan, as the ranking member of the tribe and the closest they had to a Lodestone. Radavan took the weapon more cautiously than Handan had. Khari had a feeling he saw these Lasska things the same way she did: risky and dangerous, like a half-tamed horse that might turn on you and bite or throw you to the ground. Like Handan, though, Radavan admired the weapon, examining the wooden neck and the metal rods where, Khari guessed, the exploding powder went. In careful, formal Lasska, he said to Tama, "This is a fine thing. I thank you."

Khari expected the third vindula to go to Mandhani, as the tribe's other best hunter. To her surprise, Tama brought it to her instead.

Khari didn't want to take it. Her skin crawled at the thought of touching that smooth wood and cold metal. Tama looked into her face and said something. Khari shook her head. She would have to learn to speak better Lasska.

Rahul translated for her. "She says the Lamp-Carrier's dreams are a great gift. She says that such a woman deserves another gift to help her."

Khari heard his surprise. No Vaia would expect a soldier to offer a fine and valuable weapon to a girl, rather than one of the men, and especially to pass over a hunter like Mandhani. Khari felt all the men's eyes on her. She ought to accept the gift and show her strength, but she didn't want this thing. Mandhani should have it.

She looked up at Tama and tried to think of the right Lasska words to make the woman understand why she couldn't take the weapon. The soldier spoke first, this time slowly enough for Khari to follow.

"A strong woman needs a strong weapon. You must not be afraid."

Khari had the strange thought that Tama didn't just mean afraid of the vindula. Though the Lasska was nothing like Vatiri, Khari found herself thinking of her mother-in-truth. *Go, find help, and come back to us. You must do this.*

She reached out. The weapon did feel smooth and foreign in her hands. It was heavier than she'd expected; the metal gave it extra weight. Khari ran her hand along it.

Tama said, again slowly enough for Khari to understand, "I will teach you to use it."

Mandhani muttered, "What about the old man? Her dream said there would be two Lasska."

No doubt he felt sullen about the weapon and wanted to challenge the pathdream. Khari didn't much care, but Tama heard it. She looked to Rahul to translate and answered in a quick rattle of words. The Lasska language sounded much tighter and more cropped than Vaia, with strange dark vowels and sticky consonants.

Rahul said, "The man didn't choose to come tonight, but he let Tama go when he could have tried to stop her. She says she's sure he will follow. She says he stands against Shurik too, in his heart, but he doesn't know it yet."

Khari thought Tama must be wise, to understand what was in another person's heart. She wondered why this soldier wanted to help the Vaia. Khari thought she would have liked to ask her many questions, if only she could find the words.

Radavan said, again in slow and correct Lasska, "We must camp for the night. In the morning we go west."

They made their camp near the same stand of orena trees where Khari had dreamed of the Lasska soldiers. Tama made herself comfortable on the ground as easily as any of the Vaia.

In the morning we go west. Khari lay on her blanket with the new weapon, the vindula, near her. The next steps of the journey looked bright and clear.

For the next three days, the search party pushed on carefully. The time gave Khari a chance to learn more about Tama.

The Lasska woman had a strange darkness in her. She was quick to anger, ready to fight. On the second morning, Handan, who had watched her through the hours with the eyes of a hunter waiting for a predator's charge, demanded from her in broken Lasska why she would leave her own people to join his. His tone made it clear that the gift of the vindula hadn't changed his distrust.

Tama flared up at once. She challenged Handan to one-on-one combat – "or two on one," she said, and Rahul translated; "me against you and your brother both" – if he wanted to know whether she was a coward who would sell out the people she had come to help. Her temper, even hotter than Handan's, didn't stop the two hunters from wanting to take up the challenge. Radavan stepped in. "We must trust each other," he said in his careful Lasska. "Our Lamp-Carrier tells us this is right."

Khari did tell them so. She had her own suspicions about how the fight would have gone. She was glad Radavan hadn't let Handan and Mandhani make fools of themselves, but part of her would have liked to see it.

On the second evening, after they made camp, Tama took her and Radavan and Handan aside for their first lesson with the vinduli. Handan had already made some experiments on his own, blasting holes in the ground when the group stopped to rest, until Radavan told him to quit scaring the horses and stop wasting the black powder and the metal balls the vinduli threw. Khari knew the hunter didn't want to admit he had anything to learn from Tama, but he grudgingly imitated the Lasska in loading and unloading the vindula, then raising it to his shoulder and firing it at a distant shrub.

Of course he mastered the new weapon first. Radavan handled it more cautiously, but he, too, could soon hit the target shrub. Khari had more trouble. She could load the powder and ball into the chamber, but the when she pulled back and released the piece of metal Tama called a trigger, the noise of the explosion made her jump and the vindula slammed back against her like a kicking horse. She lost her aim and the vindula jerked toward the sky and spat its metal ball harmlessly into the air.

Handan laughed at her. Even Radavan suggested that Khari might be too small and light to control the weapon, and a man would do better with it. Khari knew he was thinking of Mandhani. Tama didn't listen to him. She sent the two men away and worked with

Khari alone while they still had the orange and gold light of sunset to see by.

"The vindula has a mind of its own," Tama said. "Sometimes you need to tame it." When she spoke slowly enough, Khari could follow her. Tama said, "A spear or a bow only has the strength you give it, but the vindula has its own strength too."

Khari found herself liking this idea. Tama said, "Sometimes you must set your strength against it. When you fire, the vindula will try to push you, but you must not let it. You must stand firm so its strength and yours will work together."

She had Khari set the weapon down and face her. "I will try to push you backward," she said. "You must not let me."

Khari didn't think that was fair. Tama was much taller and stronger. She could easily knock Khari off her feet if she wanted. Khari squared up as best she could, but Tama suddenly thrust forward and shoved her with both hands. Khari stumbled back.

"No," Tama said. "You must brace yourself."

Khari squared up again, clenching her hands at her sides. She and Tama faced each other. Then the Lasska again stepped forward and pushed, harder this time. Khari barely caught herself before she fell.

"No," Tama said again. "You are strong. You must show me."

Maybe I'm not strong enough. Khari could have pieced the Lasska words together, but something about the other woman's face stopped her from saying it. Tama was looking at her as if she wanted something, as if she was searching for something in Khari and she was determined to find it.

Again Khari thought of Vatiri. Vatiri, that morning in Pradesh's tent, fingering the white fabric of her own blouse to remind Khari who she was. She squared up again. This time she watched Tama's eyes and knew exactly when the push was coming. When it did, instead of trying to hold herself still, Khari pushed back against the woman's hands, forward and up like a rearing horse, with all the strength in her body.

This time Tama stumbled backward. Khari couldn't believe she had made the stronger woman lose her balance. Tama's smile lit up her face. "That's right," she said. "Now you have it."

She had Khari pick up the vindula again. Now Khari knew exactly what to do when she pulled the trigger. *Push back. Don't be afraid.* When the explosion came, she ignored the shock of the noise and set herself against the vindula's recoil. The shrub shuddered as the metal ball slammed into it at the base.

"Now you have it," Tama said again. Khari couldn't help grinning in triumph, though her body ached as if she'd taken a beating.

Tama touched her shoulder. "A strong woman deserves a strong weapon." The same words she'd said when she gave Khari the vindula. In her face now, Khari saw something unexpected. The older woman was proud of her.

The next morning, Tama came up to Khari as the group sat eating a quick meal of tea and flatbread before they broke camp. "I am worried for Silde Orlon," she said. "I would like to look for him."

Khari hadn't expected that. Tama didn't seem like the kind of person who would worry about a fellow soldier with a mind and will of his own. Handan overheard what she said. "Look for him?" he demanded, in Vaia. Like Khari, he understood Lasska better than he spoke it. "You mean you want to go back to those soldiers, and take us with you?"

Khari glared at him. He wasn't a complete fool, she knew that by now, but he never stopped testing Tama and didn't bother to control his tongue. Tama didn't ask Khari to translate what he had said. "Would you come with me?" she said. "Two of us could travel fast. The rest of the group could continue west and we would catch up with them."

She had chosen Khari instead of one of the men. Khari felt a quick thrill of pride at that. Handan, of course, didn't take it the same way. "Don't go with her," he told Khari in Vaia. "You're the most valuable person here. It could be a trap."

It must have been hard for him to call her that. "It isn't a trap,"

Khari said. "If she wants to look for the man, she has a reason. I'll help her."

Radavan gave his permission, reluctantly. He knew Khari trusted the Lasska soldier. When they broke camp, Khari and Tama turned back east, while the others went on toward the mountains.

It was a fine, clear morning. Tama had generally stayed quiet with the Vaia group, but now she seemed to want to talk. As they rode through the bright grass, she said, "Did I understand right that when you were a child, they took you from your parents?"

Rahul had explained a little to her about Lamp-Carriers. Khari shaped the Lasska words carefully. Already she could speak the language more easily. "I had to train with another Light-Bearer." She didn't know the exact translation of the word any more than Rahul did. "You have to..." She hunted for the right way to say it. "Give yourself to it. You have to learn to be a Light-Bearer, always. So I lived with Vatiri. She became my mother."

"Did you miss your real mother?"

"When my father took me to Vatiri's tent, I..." Khari couldn't think of the word for *struggle*, so she pantomimed kicking out with her feet and flailing at the air with one hand. Tama laughed. "And," Khari said, "I was not easy for my Amma. But I still saw my mother in the tribe, because everyone is together. And I soon loved Vatiri."

That thought brought her mother-in-truth's face up in her mind so clearly that she turned away from Tama before the older woman could see her face. For a little while, they rode on in silence. Then Tama said, "Did I also understand right that you might not have a family of your own?"

"Many Light-Bearers don't," Khari said. "We are busy. We have to take care of the tribe."

Tama turned in the saddle to look at her. "Would you like to have children if you could?"

Khari didn't know how to answer. Lamp-Carriers did what they had to do. She wondered why Tama wanted to know these things. "Someday," she said, "I will probably have a girl to train." If the tribe survived that long. If they could find help in Namora. "She will be like my daughter."

Now she wanted to talk about something else. "Why do you worry today about Bereg Orlon?" The name felt strange on her tongue, and she knew the words weren't quite right.

Tama said, "I'm not sure. I had a feeling." The grass whispered around them. "It was very hard for him, when I left."

Khari thought she understood. "You are friends."

Tama laughed again. "No, I don't think we are. Impera Shurik says those who go against him must die. Silde Orlon knew he ought to kill me."

Khari gasped. Surely she hadn't heard that right. "Kill you?"

"Yes. Because I was going to help you. He knew he should have stopped me."

Khari didn't understand. The Vaia didn't punish by killing. The worst punishment for any Vaia was banishment from the tribe, and the Lodestone would only order that after the worst possible crimes: theft, murder, betrayal of a tribesman or tribeswoman. Why would the Lasska ruler want his people to kill each other? That only left you with fewer people. The tribe's strength lay in its size.

She and Tama rode on through the morning. Then, when the sun hung directly overhead, they ran across a narrow trail through a patch of bare earth and scrub. It came erratically out of the east and veered north.

Tama reined in and dropped down from her horse's back to take a look. Khari joined her. The dust showed the blurred, almost obliterated print of a boot.

"No horse," Tama muttered. "And look here." She pointed to a long scuff mark. "He's hurt. Dragging his foot."

Khari lined up words. "Why is he going north? To follow us, he would come west."

Tama, still crouched on the ground, looked up at her. "For him, north is home." Her face showed a strange mixture of anger and pity. "He's trying to get there."

"Where north?"

"Thysidich." She spat the word. "The northern forests."

The forests? That was weeks of journeying away. Two mountain ranges stood in between. Khari thought Bereg Orlon must have gone out of his senses. Alone and on foot, he would never get there.

Tama mounted up. "He can't be far ahead of us. Come on."

They rode on. Khari knew they were close to the place where she and the other Vaia had first seen the Lasska soldiers. When had Bereg Orlon left the rest of his group? When had he gotten hurt? Fear for this man she had never met closed in around her.

Tama reined in again sharply. "Look there."

Her eyes must be almost as good as Mandhani's. Squinting into the distance, Khari saw a patch of green, maybe a spring, to the north, and a few low dark shapes near it. Shrubs, she guessed. She couldn't make out anything else, but as if they didn't have a moment to lose, Tama dug her heels into her horse's sides and took off through the grass.

Khari urged her horse into a gallop. The grass whipped at her legs. The green patch grew clearer, and then Khari could see a small glint of water in a clearing, and the spreading shapes of shrubs, and finally, sure enough, another dark shape huddled by the tiny pool.

The old bear. Khari thought of the bear in her dream, with its silvering face and scarred muzzle. How strong could this man be?

When they reached the clearing, Tama reined in so hard her horse pawed at the air. She jumped down and threw the reins over its neck. Khari followed, her heart pounding in her throat.

The old soldier lay near the pool, curled up on his side. He wasn't tall, Khari saw, not for a Lasska man, and though he had a stocky build, his hair was almost completely white and his cheeks, stubbled with white hair too, looked sunken. His eyes were closed. Khari couldn't tell he was breathing until she crouched on the ground beside him and saw the too quick, too shallow in-and-out motion of his chest.

"Stupid," Tama snapped. She picked up the old man's wrist and felt for his pulse with two fingers. "Stupid, stupid." Tearing at her shirtsleeve, she ripped off the cuff. "Here." She handed it to Khari. "Soak it in the water, and get my water skin too."

Khari obeyed. Tama turned the old man on his back and unbuttoned his gray coat and the shirt underneath. She snatched the wet cloth back from Khari and laid it on Bereg's forehead, then wiped it across his cheeks and down his chest, muttering under her breath all the time. Khari couldn't catch the Lasska words. Tama wet the cloth again and dampened the old man's hair. As she passed the fabric over his cheeks again, his eyes fluttered open and he caught his breath.

Khari hadn't realized she had been holding her own breath. Bereg stared blankly up at her and Tama. His eyes, she saw, were the gray of the sky during a storm.

Tama said, "Silde Orlon. Do you know me?"

The old man stared at her with no change of expression and Khari wondered if he had lost his mind. Then, so quietly she had to bend down closer to hear him, he whispered a name Khari didn't recognize.

"No," Tama said. "Tama Leben. You know that."

The old man whispered, "Yes."

Khari drew another breath in relief. At least he knew what Tama was saying. Tama held up the water skin to his mouth. "Drink," she ordered.

He took a deep swallow. "What on earth were you trying to do?" Tama said. The words had an edge on them like a spear.

Khari saw that the old man's left leg looked swollen against the fabric of his pants, especially around the knee. She nudged Tama and pointed to it. The woman nodded grimly.

Bereg Orlon said quietly, "I had to try."

Tama said something too fast for Khari to understand, but it ended in a question. Bereg replied. The two of them talked back and forth, question and answer. Then Tama rattled out something else. When Bereg nodded, Tama brought her fist down on the ground. This time Khari understood what she snapped: "Mesha guard us!"

Khari wondered what the old man had said to make her so angry. Tama looked around at her.

"Silde Orlon says he left the group the night after I did," she explained. Even in her impatience, she knew Khari hadn't understood what she'd heard. "He says he didn't know what else to do and he had to try to get home. He doesn't know where the group is, but if they were tracking him, he thinks they would have found him by now."

Khari thought that was probably right. But the old bear had thought he could get back to his northern forests alone? No, she realized; he had known he couldn't. She thought how much he must have hurt for that place he loved, that he would have risked such a journey anyway.

Tama said, "He says the younger soldiers wanted to keep on their search and he doesn't think they had much use for him anyway. They didn't respect him, but they were afraid of me." Khari could believe that. Tama said, "He fell two days ago and wrenched his knee. Today the pain got to be too much." Her mouth made a hard line, and she added, "He says he was waiting to die."

That explained why she had lost her temper. Khari said, "But he isn't going to die now."

Tama shook her head. She pulled out a knife and started cutting at Bereg's pant leg.

The old man focused on Khari for the first time. In slow, careful Lasska, he said, "Are you the one who had the dream?"

"Yes."

He asked her name and she told him. The unfamiliar sound of it seemed to confuse him. "I don't know how I could help you," he said, "but I am sorry for what my people are doing to yours."

Tama had cut the pant leg open. "Mesha guard us," she said again, quietly this time.

Khari looked. The sight of Bereg's knee turned her stomach. It was hideously swollen, bruised deep purple as if the blood were trying to burst through the skin. The swelling continued above and below the joint, with more bruises in ugly shades of gray and green. He had done worse than wrench this. And he had tried to walk on it for two days?

Tama said, "You won't walk on this again for a long time. Maybe ever."

Khari pitied him. A young man would have felt it more, but in the tribe, the elderly held onto their pride and mobility as long as they could. It would be hard for an old man to lose the use of a leg and have to hobble on sticks and have people help him from place to place. Tama said, "You'll ride on my horse now, and Khari will ride in front of you. He's strong enough to carry you both. I'll take her horse. We'll catch up with the rest of her people by evening."

Khari thought even the ride might be too much for the old soldier. She and Tama between them helped Bereg up onto the strong Lasska horse, but he winced and his face went even paler with pain as he had to bend the bad knee. Khari sat in front of him, the saddle unfamiliar under her body and the reins strange in her hands. Bereg put his arms around her waist. Khari willed him to stay conscious and hold on tight. Tama mounted the Vaia horse easily, seeming to find bareback riding natural.

"We'll get back to the others as fast as we can," she said. "Then we'll see what we can do for him."

Khari thought the old man was keeping himself upright by main will. She tried not to see the ugly colors of his leg or the ghastly swollen knee. They headed southwest directly across the open plains.

The horses loped easily, but Khari felt in her own body how each thud of the hooves against the ground must worsen Bereg's pain. She heard no sound from the old man except his rasping breath. She told herself that when they made camp, they would be able to help him. She and Radavan both had some skill with medicines and poultices. More than ever, Khari missed Vatiri, who had nursed her through childhood sicknesses and the pain of her first monthly bleeding.

She could imagine what Handan would say when she and Tama brought the dead weight of a wounded Lasska into camp. Khari didn't care. The distance to Namora still felt much too great, and the rest of the tribe following them felt too vulnerable and exposed, but in Khari's mind, something had shifted. The presence of the two Lasska soldiers with them, the truth of that pathdream, told her they still had hope.

She held onto that hope, along with the words the old bear had given her. *I am sorry for what my people are doing to yours.*

BOOK 2: THE ZHININ

in memory of Van Reiner

14

RIBAS

Ribas hadn't left Lida for more than a day or two, here and there, since he was eighteen. Back then, his family hadn't liked the idea of him traveling the country alone. It would have been all right for a healthy young man, but with his heart... Ribas's stubbornness had stood him in good stead in the face of all the fears no one said out loud. He could take care of himself, he'd promised Maryut and Mama, Tayo Nevas, and various worried friends. He knew how to manage his nemesis. And he must, really, see a little of the world – only a little, he promised that too, just a slice of the plains and a bit of the northern coast – before he settled down to village life for good.

It had been well worth it. Ribas had never hungered for more time away than those few weeks. Ever since that beautiful, adventurous summer, which had ended with his installation as Lida's zhinin, he had carried the memories of the purple flowers, cloudless skies, and fragrant grasses of the plains country, and on the far side of those lands, the ocean. The ocean alone, he had thought then and still thought now, was worth any amount of trouble and tiredness to reach. He had never tasted anything like those winds or seen anything like the power of the waves that flung themselves on the gray rocks and soft sand. If he never saw it again, as he never expected to, he would never forget it. He would taste the same wild joy in it again just by unwrapping the memories.

Now, though, with this trip to Sostavi, he would see the ocean again in life. Ribas didn't know what else they might find in the great city, but that, at least, gave him something to hold onto.

On the first night away from home, at an inn in Paret, he and Maryut stood out on the front porch after supper, taking in the air. The weather was chilly and raw, but the breeze smelled of evening fires and carried the sounds of the bustling life of a town. Maryut leaned on the porch rail and looked up into the dark sky. "Love," she said, "I feel as if somebody took the ground away from under me. I'm floating up in the air and I don't have anything to hold onto."

Ribas had enjoyed the first day's travel more than he'd expected. It hadn't been as tiring as he'd thought it might be, and he had loved watching the world slip past the windows of the coach that brought them from Lida. But Maryut had always been firmly planted back home. He knew how she felt, without the world she knew to anchor her.

He slipped his arms around her and bent to kiss the side of her neck. "I hope you have *something* to hold onto," he said.

She laughed and turned to see him. "Fair enough." In the circle of his arms, she reached up to put her hands on his shoulders. Her face was a round pale moon in the dark. "It's just..." He saw a suspicious glimmer on her eyelashes. "It seems like so long until we'll be back home."

"I know." He felt unmoored too, without the work that filled his days. Right now he didn't mind it. "But the time will go faster than we think," he said. "We'll be so busy, we won't notice how long we've been gone."

She hugged him and rested her head on his chest. "At least out here, I don't have to worry about people bothering you with all their problems. Whatever we find in that city, love, I want you to have a break."

"I will. And you wait until you see the coast. It's so beautiful, you can't imagine."

Her voice sounded muffled against his coat. "You and that ocean. I'm glad I got you back when you went out there the first time."

"You're glad?" Ribas touched her under the chin. "I'll show you who's glad."

The kiss, sheltered in the shadowy porch corner, lasted until the inn's door banged shut. "You two." Gedrin's voice was full of laughter. "It's indecent, I tell you."

"Indecent?" Maryut said. "Who's sneaking up on people, I'd like to know?"

"I made enough noise to wake up the lampposts. Come on back in, I could use a Capture game. With you, Marya," he added, glancing sideways at his brother.

Ribas laughed. Maryut was a much better Capture opponent than him. Gedrin couldn't have survived three weeks without a game, but he hadn't had to squeeze a board and pieces into his traveling bag, because every half-decent inn in Namora had them. "Good," Ribas said. "I'll do some reading."

Gedrin had seemed younger and happier from the minute Virta had agreed to let him come on this trip. Ribas knew it wouldn't solve his trouble permanently, but it gave them time. While Gedrin and Maryut faced off across the Capture board, Ribas sat off to the side in the inn's warm parlor, half-listening to the play and leafing through one of the books he'd brought along. Kunin Dergo had sent him this one, *The Campaigns of Lord Curin*, a few months earlier. The kunin always looked out for any Lasska-language books that might drift his way, few and far between though they were, and sent them on to Lida. He hadn't approved when Ribas had insisted on learning Lasska at the viduris. Apparently no other student in memory had tried it, but Dergo had given his troublesome mosevin all the help he could, and still did.

Ribas hoped to get in a visit to the viduris when they came back through Paret on the way home. Whenever he and Kunin Dergo saw each other, once every long while, the kunin never failed to greet him as if he were the same exasperating, too-curious mosevin from twenty years ago. *Rewrite the paper or accept the lower score. You make this difficult, Ribé.* For all Dergo's annoyance, Ribas knew what a compliment it was for him to unbend enough to use a student's nickname.

For now, he and Maryut and Gedrin had to get to Sostavi as soon as they could. They left Paret the next day and continued off into the plains country just east of the Isare Mountains, following the main roads northwest to the Jemtave region. Another six days' travel would bring them to the capital city.

On the third morning, Maryut said, "I can see why you like this, Ribé." It was fine, crisp day, overcast but brisk. The coach had left the Kalnu region and crossed into Jemtave. "There's something about it, isn't there?" she said. "You don't have to think about things. You can just watch."

Gedrin sat on the bench across from them, by the opposite window. They were sharing the coach with a family from Paret, middle-aged parents and three teenage sons, who'd said they were heading west through Jemtave to visit family in the Pajura region near the coast. They'd been curious to hear about the High Installation but, the father said, "We trust the dagira to take care of its business, and we take care of ours." *Fair enough*, Ribas thought.

Gedrin said, "I like this fine. It's good to know there's so much out here."

A week to the day after they'd left Lida, they arrived in Sostavi in the late afternoon. The coach that brought them from Aleta, a small town in southern Jemtave, took them into the city through the main gates.

Sostavi. The one place any new dagira member might be expected to visit; the one place Ribas had avoided when he'd had the chance to see it. As the coach drove through the gates, graceful wooden structures that stood taller than a person, Ribas felt as though the mouth of the city was opening wide to swallow him. What would he find here?

Maryut huddled against him as the coach drove along the busy street that led into the heart of the city. "It's too big," she whispered.

It was so big, Ribas thought, that Lida would disappear into it like a drop into a bucket. The buildings stood taller and closer together than any at home. You had to hunt for glimpses of sky in the gaps between the clay roofs. The coach's wheels rang on the hard cobbles. People thronged the sidewalks, everyone hurrying about some unknown business. So many people, so busy...how could they all have such important things to do?

But it was exciting too. Each of these people, more of them than Ribas could count, had a story. A history. It was like being caught up in a great web of life. He was only a tiny part of it, but he *was* part of it. He'd never felt anything like it before.

Maryut and Gedrin didn't feel the same. Gedrin looked uneasily out through one window, then the other, then at the coach's side door, as if he was thinking about making a run for it. Maryut sat still, but her fingers anxiously twisted the hem of her coat.

Ribas covered her hand with his. "We'll be fine, love."

The coach rattled into the main square. Ribas had a glimpse of a huge Circle House, bigger than any he had ever seen, and a tall building flying a Circle House standard and a sea-blue flag. Then the coach was pulling up beside a stone fountain whose jet of water splashed and glittered in the last afternoon sunlight.

"The Great Circle House of Namora," the driver announced, in his flat city accent. "House of the Tavin. House of the Sventine. Houses of the Kunine and Zhinine."

Ribas and Maryut and Gedrin collected their bags and got down with the knot of other passengers. The sight of the square made Ribas catch his breath. He knew what Sostavi looked like, he'd read descriptions and seen drawings, but this was grander than he'd ever imagined. The Great House reared up into the sky, its walls inset on every side with long windows made of colored glass: a breathtaking display of wealth. The four white Houses of the Dagira faced one another across the flagstoned square, each with tall double front doors and high clear windows, each displaying the Circle House standard and the colored flag that represented its rank. The square itself was thronged with people, city folk and visitors and, yes, Ribas saw robed dagira of all three ranks, no doubt here for the Installation too. Over the tangle of so many voices and unfamiliar scents of the city, Ribas felt sure he caught a taste of the ocean and a hint of the deep throbbing pulse of the surf.

The coach pulled away with a rattle of wheels and a jingle of harness. Gedrin backed up into the space it had left next to the fountain. "Ribé," he said, "we can't do this." He was staring at the building with the sea-blue flag, the House of the Zhinine, where they were supposed to stay. "We don't belong here."

Maryut agreed. "Let's find somewhere smaller. An inn, maybe."

Ribas put an arm around her. "No one's going to argue with us. The new Tavin invited us personally, remember?"

Gedrin said, "But the Great House priests live there, don't they?"

Yes, they did. Ribas understood what his brother was thinking about. Silvas must have lived here too.

Ribas ought to feel that shadow himself. He'd expected to. His father had been a zhinin in this strange thronged city, had worn the blue robes and stood on the dais of the huge Circle House with the brilliant windows. Somehow that past didn't catch at Ribas now. Sostavi had a huge restless heartbeat that drove it on into the future.

He said, "It'll be all right, Gedrí. It's been thirty-five years or so. This place has probably changed some."

Gedrin didn't look convinced. Ribas said, "Let's go see what it's like. If we don't like it, I'm sure we can find somewhere else."

Maryut gave in first. "We wouldn't have to pay, staying here. We'd have to pay for an inn."

"All right." Gedrin hoisted his bag, still unhappy. "We can look at it, at least."

Ribas felt daunted himself, walking up to those great glass-paneled double doors, though he tried not to show it. Inside the House of the Zhinine, they found bustling servants and groups of zhinine in robes more elegant than anything Ribas had ever worn. Ribas hadn't thought of wearing his own robes to travel. If he had, they wouldn't have helped him blend in here.

Maryut and Gedrin waited in a corner of the great front hall while Ribas went up to a table that seemed to be functioning as a kind of front desk. An elegantly-robed, blonde-haired zhinin, evidently another visitor, was haranguing the harassed young servant there about some trouble with the room she had been given. When the servant managed to placate her, he turned to Ribas and eyed his plain clothes with a distinct *Why are you here?* expression.

Ribas didn't care who thought he was countrified. He hadn't come here to impress anyone. "Raimaté," he said. "I'm Ribas Silvaikas, from Lida village. I'm told I have lodging here for the Installation."

The servant's expression changed the instant Ribas gave his name. "Raimaté, Zhinin Ribas," he said. "You do indeed. The Tavo Balsa requested the reservation personally."

I'm impressive after all. Ribas didn't let his face show his amusement. The servant called to someone else to take Ribas and Maryut and Gedrin up to the second floor, where their chambers were. "I'll notify the Tavo Balsa of your arrival at once, zhinin."

"I doubt there's any rush," Ribas said quietly to Maryut as they went upstairs. "She probably has enough on her hands right now." He wondered if they would see Valda at all, except at a distance during the Installation, or maybe in a brief greeting afterward with the rest of the visiting dagira. No doubt the Tavin-to-be wouldn't have much time to spare for her visitors from the village, as much as she had wanted them to come. Ribas hoped it would help her just to know they were there.

The House of the Zhinine was certainly impressive: wide hallways with rich carpeting and cloth hangings, ornate carving on the banisters, and those tall windows giving out on the square and the long slope that led down to the harbor. Ribas peered through one window they passed for a glimpse of that blue water far below, but he pressed Maryut's hand and whispered, "It's a nice house, but I like ours better."

The servant led them down to the end of the second-floor hallway and opened a door. "Here you are, zhinin."

Ribas couldn't help staring. These were guest chambers? The door opened into a front room with a hearth, more lush carpeting, and another of those beautiful varicolored wall hangings. The window here, draped with embroidered curtains, looked out over the harbor. The fire on the hearth was lit, filling the room with warmth and sweet wood smoke. The graceful table and chairs gleamed with polish. Ribas had a glimpse of two other doors that led into bedrooms. Then the servant asked if they needed anything, and Ribas managed to say no, thank you, and the servant went out and closed the door quietly.

Maryut stood perfectly still in the middle of the room with her hands at her sides. "I can't touch anything."

"I don't even want to walk on this carpet," Gedrin said. "I don't want to set my bag down. Ribé, we have to go somewhere else."

Ribas knew what he meant, but he said, "Come, now. We don't need to be afraid of this." He set his own bag down on the floor. "It's not that bad, is it?"

"Bad?" Maryut said. "No. It's too good."

That settled it, as far as Ribas was concerned. "It's not too good for us, love. You know that."

Gedrin said, "Ribé, you can't make me believe our da ever lived in a place like this. He gave this up and came back to Lida and married Mama and lived on a farm? It doesn't make sense." He looked around as if he thought the wall hanging or the curtains might reach out to grab him.

Ribas said, "We don't know what the regular rooms look like." He didn't want to think about his father living in any room in this building, or why Silvas had abandoned life here and gone back to the village. "Maybe the guest chambers are fancier."

Maryut said, "I hope so. I can't believe anyone has things like this every day." Some of her shyness faded as she glanced around again. "It's beautiful," she said. "I suppose it'll be comfortable, if I can make myself use any of it."

"I have a feeling we'll be glad to find out what the beds are like," Ribas said. "It's been a long day."

Gedrin didn't look convinced, though he set his bag on the floor too. "I don't know, Ribé. I still think..."

A knock on the outer door interrupted him. Ribas went to answer it. Yet another servant, a young red-haired woman, stood outside. "Zhinin Ribas Silvaikas?"

"Yes?"

"Raimaté, zhinin. The Tavo Balsa begs the favor that you and Maryut Ribenis and Gedrin Silvaikas will join her this evening for a private supper in her chambers."

A private supper with the Tavin-to-be? Ribas hadn't considered such a thing. Maryut came over to him. "I don't know, Ribé," she said quietly.

The servant said, "The Tavo Balsa is most eager to see you all. May I tell her you'll come?"

I'm sure you'd rather not tell her we won't. Ribas wondered if Valda had become the kind of taskmaster servants feared. He couldn't see it. "Would you give us a moment?" he said.

The servant backed away into the hall. As soon as Ribas closed the door, Maryut said, "Please, let's not. I can't face that."

It did change things. Ribas would have been glad to stay anonymous. Gedrin, surprisingly, disagreed. "If she wants to see us, she'll probably keep after us." He'd relaxed a little, as if the invitation made him think they might belong here after all. "We should get it over with. Besides, she'll probably give us good meal."

That was true. And if they didn't go, they would have to find somewhere else to have supper, or else go to the communal meal here in the House of the Zhinine. Ribas didn't think a meal with Valda alone could be harder than trying their luck in the city or eating with a crowd of these high-class dagira. Besides, Valda's letter had made it clear how much she might need someone to talk to.

Maryut said, "I don't think I can see her tonight."

Tavo Balsa or not, Valda hadn't sounded like she'd changed so much from the girl Ribas remembered. He said, "I think she'd probably just like to talk with us for a while. She's an old friend, you know."

Maryut folded her arms. "She's the woman who thought she had rights to you."

Gedrin laughed. Ribas didn't. Maryut's voice had no teasing in it.

"Marya, love," he said. "You know it doesn't matter what she thought. That was a long time ago."

Her eyes searched his face. Surely she knew him better than that; surely she knew she'd never had anything to fear from Valda. She seemed to see what she needed. "Fine," she said. "We'll get it over with."

Ribas told the servant they would be honored to accept the Tavo Balsa's invitation. They had time to rest for a while, and start to get used to the fine surroundings, before they had to dress for supper.

Maryut put on her second-best dress. The best one, royal blue with a pattern of paler blue flowers that Virta had embroidered on it, was for the Installation. She'd brought it to match Ribas's robes. The second-best was deep red with white embroidery.

"I hope this'll do," she said. "Goodness knows the Tavo Balsa probably has the finest dresses."

"You're beautiful," Ribas told her. He'd decided to wear plain clothes instead of robes, hoping Valda didn't plan to stand on ceremony. "I'll bet she doesn't have anything prettier than that."

Gedrin met them in the front room. "I hope she won't throw me out," he said. "I look like a farmer no matter what I do."

In his shirt, pants, and boots, with his hair a tangle of curls in spite of wetting and combing, Gedrin did look like he could have been out in the barn doing the milking, or in the orchard raking fallen apples. He was a solid anchor to home. Ribas said, "You look fine to me."

Gedrin looked him up and down. "You look pretty much like a farmer yourself."

"Glad to hear it."

Another attendant from the House of the Zhinine took them across the square to the House of the Sventine, where Valda lived. "I think we could have found it on our own," Maryut whispered on the way over. "It's getting on my nerves, all these people trying to be helpful."

The square was less crowded at night. Ribas thought the salt tang on the air tasted stronger. Tomorrow, he decided, they would have to get down to the harbor. He needed to see that water up close.

Maryut was right; they couldn't have missed the House of the Sventine. It was even bigger and more imposing than the House of the Zhinine, with the white flag flying over the grand double doors. The attendant took them up to Valda's chambers on the third floor. Ribas noticed curious looks from the few sventine they saw in the halls, and he wondered whether at some point they would have to deal with Galvo, who had almost been the next Tavin. Maybe the sventin had gotten over his far too active interest in the dovne kenavnis. Ribas he wasn't sure he thought so.

The attendant stopped in the third-floor hall and knocked at a door. From inside, Ribas heard, "Come in."

Maryut gripped Ribas's hand. Ribas felt a little nervous himself. Fifteen years was a long time, and Valda might have changed more than he thought.

"Tavo Balsa," the servant said, "I have with me Zhinin Ribas Silvaikas, Maryut Ribenis, and Gedrin Silvaikas."

"Thank you."

The servant stood aside. Gedrin was closest to the door, but he backed away with a look at his brother that plainly said, *you first.* Ribas obeyed. Maryut let go of his hand but stayed close behind him as they went in.

Valda stood waiting for them by her hearth. As soon as Ribas saw her, his nervousness fell away. She was older, of course, in an elegantly simple green dress that brought out the rich color of her hair, but the eyes that met his now were the same eyes he remembered from that breakfast table so many years ago.

Is it all right if I sit with you?

It was good to see her. Ribas was glad for her and everything she'd done, even though he knew what a hard thing she faced now. He smiled, one mosevin to another. "Raimaté, Tavo Balsa."

Just for a moment, he saw pure longing in her face. Then her polite mask settled back in place. "Raimaté, zhinin."

Fifteen years hadn't changed her feelings for him. Ribas didn't need to look into her mind to see it. He knew it again when she took his hand and said, "It's so good to have you here. It's been a hard few weeks."

He answered with all the sympathy he felt – "I can imagine. I'm glad to see you too, Valda" – but it hurt to see her look at him that way. *Valda, I'm sorry. I'd hoped you'd forgotten that a long time ago.*

Under the circumstances, the meal might have felt hopelessly awkward. Maryut and Gedrin were both nervous, and Ribas knew Maryut had noticed the same thing he had. At the supper table he took her hand, if the two of them had been alone, to tell her without words that he loved her.

He set himself to talk as easily as he could. It helped to remember Valda as the girl she had been, before things between them had shifted, back when they had studied together with their group of friends and argued about passages from the *Book of Kenavi* and joked about the viduris food.

Certainly there was no questionable food here. Gedrin had been right: the meal was excellent. The awkwardness, too, lifted faster than Ribas had hoped. Valda didn't let her face or voice give her away again, and soon enough, she gave Ribas an opening to ask if he could help her. "Since I can listen, Tavo Balsa," he said, "I wonder if you'd like to talk."

She laughed and scolded him for using her title. Then she took him up on the offer. "I mentioned Sventin Galvo in my letter, but if you don't mind, I'd like to tell you more about that."

She told the three of them how Sventin Galvo had come here, to her chambers, early one morning the week before the election. Ribas heard immediately how much she'd needed to talk about this. The words came out as if they had been choking her and she had to get rid of them to breathe.

"He sat there by the hearth," Valda said, "and he said to me, 'Do you know about Sventin Lesvin's plan?' As if he knew I did, he knew all about it, and he was going to scold me like a little girl he'd caught stealing cream out of his pantry." She kept her voice light, but Ribas could feel her anger. "And then," she said, "when I told him I had nothing to do with it, and I didn't want anything to do with it, he got a look on his face like the fox that swallowed the gosling, and he said, 'I hoped you would see it that way.'"

She cut into her slice of roast chicken. Ribas thought he saw a slight tremor in her hand holding the fork. "He *hoped*," Valda said. "He's worked with me every day for a dozen years or more, but he still only *hoped*. He wasn't sure I wouldn't steal the election."

Her voice didn't give her hurt away, but Ribas still heard it. Anger simmered in his chest. "He thought that?" he said. "Does he know you at all?"

"I wondered the same thing."

What a miserable business. If this was how the Great House dagira acted, Ribas wouldn't have wanted to spend a week with them, much less all of a working life. No wonder Valda hadn't wanted to be Tavin and didn't want to take what had been forced on her. No wonder she'd needed someone to talk to so badly.

He found himself thinking about his father again. Had Silvas run into something like this? Had some kind of treachery, or disgust with his colleagues, driven him back to Lida? Ribas glanced over at Gedrin, who had his eyes on his plate, concentrating harder than he needed to maneuver his knife and fork. Looking at him, Ribas could almost picture Silvas here.

Almost, but he didn't want to. He pushed the image away in time to hear Maryut telling Valda that Galvo had no right to accuse her. "If I see him here, I might have to give him a piece of my mind." Valda admitted she had thought about resigning as Tavin, whenever she could make that happen, and Maryut told her not to let anyone make her do it. Ribas was glad to see the two of them on the same side. As for Galvo, Ribas thought if he did run into the sventin, he might have to have a few words with him himself.

The only other hitch came after the meal. Valda shook hands with Gedrin and Maryut, but instead of returning Ribas's salute, she held out her arms to him.

"For old times' sake?"

He couldn't refuse when he saw how much it meant to her. She put her head down on his shoulder and held him as if someone had given her back some precious thing she had lost. It only lasted a heartbeat or two. Then they exchanged polite goodbyes, and Ribas and Maryut and Gedrin went back to the House of the Zhinine.

Gedrin put his head around his bedroom door to say goodnight. "This bed is so soft I'll probably drown in it. If I don't get up in the morning, you'll know why."

"Don't be silly," Maryut told him. Ribas said, "I'll check on you during the night. Make sure you're still breathing."

Gedrin laughed. "No, you won't. Get some sleep yourself. You look worn out."

Ribas had to admit he was. He and Maryut got ready for bed in their own warm room, changing into shifts and sliding gratefully under the elegant linens that, Maryut said, it was a shame to wrinkle. The bed certainly was soft. You could almost think you were floating, lying on something like this.

Maryut curled up next to Ribas and put her head on his shoulder. The delicate glass lamp on the bedside table cast a circle of gold light over them both. She rested her hand on his chest. "She hasn't changed much, has she?" she said. "Valda."

"She hasn't."

Her fingertips moved to the hollow above his collarbone and lightly stroked his skin. "She's still in love with you, you know."

"Yes. I'm sorry."

She raised her head enough to see him. "It's not your fault. And I don't blame her, really. But, Ribé…"

She hesitated for so long that he said, "What is it, love?"

"I know you don't have any regrets there," she said. "You didn't want to marry her."

"Maryut Ribenis, I should hope you know that."

"You'd be in trouble if I didn't. It's just, being here…" She hesitated again, stroking his chest thoughtfully. "You could have had such a different life, if you'd wanted. I can't help thinking about that."

Ribas cupped her cheek in his hand. "My love, do you think I could have wanted a different life?"

She smiled, but her eyes looked too bright in the lamplight. "You might have. If you were like your father, say."

So she had been thinking about Silvas too. Yes, if Ribas had been like his father, the same restless ambition might have brought him here. He might even have wished he had married the woman who was now going to be Tavin.

If anyone but Maryut had suggested such a thing, he would have gotten angry. He'd never been like Silvas in those ways. As the Goddess knew his soul, he never would be. He said, "I like to think I make better decisions than he did."

She knew, of course, what Silvas had been like to his family. "You do," she said. "I just want to be sure, zhinin, now that we're here with all this" – her eyes moved around the room – "you still like your decisions."

Now her voice teased him. He said, "There's exactly one thing in this room that I wouldn't trade for anything else in the world. I hope you know what it is."

"Goddess be thanked, Ribas Silvaikas, you never change."

She rested her head on his shoulder again. He turned out the bedside lamp and let the darkness cover them like another quilt.

The next morning, the three of them decided to brave the communal breakfast in the House of the Zhinine. Gedrin said, "We've had supper with the Tavin. We've got just as much right to be here as anyone. Besides, Ribé's probably a better zhinin than any of these people."

Ribas wouldn't have bet on that, though he did have one thing his colleagues here would want to know about, if they heard of it. He hoped that wouldn't happen. Valda knew about the gift, of course, and so did Sventin Galvo, but Ribas thought there was no real reason for the word to spread. His city colleagues certainly had no other reason to be curious about a zhinin from the mountains.

The dining hall had its own great hearth and a row of floor-to-ceiling windows that looked out on the square. Long tables at the front of the room held a spread of serving dishes. Groups of zhinine, some in the robes of office and some in plain clothes, sat at smaller round tables around the room's perimeter. Ribas felt the eyes on them as soon as he and Maryut and Gedrin went in.

The three of them found a table by themselves in a corner. The food made up for some of the strangeness: light new bread with butter, dense honey cakes, eggs and cheeses, platters with fresh apples and the dark purple grapes that came from the vineyards in southwest Namora. Fresh grapes at this time of year was a luxury. Ribas had heard of the greenhouses in the southwest, where fruit grew in boxes of glass and could thrive in any season. The Great House dagira must pay a good price to have the stock shipped all the way to Sostavi.

Gedrin started in on his plate with a good appetite, but Ribas saw the dark circles under his brother's eyes and the set lines at the corners of his mouth. "Gedrí," he said, "the bed didn't drown you after all, did it?"

"No. Don't worry."

Ribas pinned him with a look. "You've got something on your mind. Why don't you save yourself some trouble and tell me about it."

"You might as well," Maryut said. "You know he won't leave you alone until you do." She sipped the tea in her clay mug. "This is lovely. It tastes like flowers."

Gedrin said, "I don't want to bother you with it, Ribé. I do enough of that."

Ribas held his hand out, palm up. "Do we need to do it like this?"

Gedrin sighed. "Why do you have to be so stubborn?"

"Can't help it."

"Fine," Gedrin said. "I'll tell you." He took a bite of honey cake. "I didn't sleep much. I was thinking." He picked up the cluster of grapes off his plate and twisted at one, then another, but didn't pull them off the stem. "I kept thinking about how Da lived here. I know you said the place is probably different now, but do you really think it changed that much?"

Ribas had thought that might be it. He hoped bringing Gedrin here hadn't been a mistake after all. "I don't know," he said, "but thirty-five years is a long time. Longer than either of us has been alive."

"That's true. But..." Gedrin put the grapes back on the plate. "Ribé, you remember Da. I don't. Am I really like him? Besides the looks and the temper. Am I?"

His fear took Ribas back to a thunderstorm one summer night when Gedrin had been very small. Ribas had been about ten years old then. He'd woken up to his little brother crawling into bed beside him and huddling against him, shivering, while the lightning flared and the thunder growled around the house. *Ribé, will it hurt us?* Ribas had hugged him close. *No, Gedrí. It's just rain.* As the thunder ebbed, the rain had rattled on the roof like handfuls of thrown gravel.

Hear that? The Goddess is watering the orchard for us. We'll have lots of apples this year.

Ribas knew what Gedrin needed to hear now. He also knew he could only tell his brother the exact truth. "Gedrí, I don't remember him very well." He couldn't make himself say *Da*. "I only remember he was angry and cruel. Are you that kind of man? Absolutely not."

Gedrin blinked and looked down at his plate. "Then what kind of man am I?"

I'm turning out like Da, Gedrin had said before they'd left Lida. That wasn't true. Ribas said, "Gedrí. Look at me."

Gedrin raised his head. No, Ribas would not let this thing in his brother's mind keep hurting him. He would find a way to fix it, if it was the last thing he did. He said, "My brother is kind and warm and smart. He's a good husband and father, and an excellent Capture player. Nobody says bad things about him in my hearing and gets away with it. Understand?"

Gedrin bit his lip. He looked very young. "I understand." Then he cleared his throat. "But wait a minute. I'm an 'excellent' Capture player, but only a 'good' father?"

"Well, we don't want your head to get too swelled up, do we?"

Gedrin laughed and wiped his eyes with the back of his hand. "Fair enough."

Maryut glanced out at the room, over Ribas's shoulder. "Ribé. Somebody's coming."

Ribas turned around. A small-built, gray-haired sventin, easily identifiable by his white robes of office, had come into the room. As he walked toward the visitors, Ribas noticed eyes at other tables following him, as if he were someone significant.

Ribas had an uneasy feeling about this. So did Maryut. "Ribé," she said, "do you think that's...?"

Gedrin's hand closed into a fist on the table. "If it's that Galvo, we don't want him here."

"I'll take care of this," Ribas said. He wanted nothing to do with Galvo either, but politeness was the only option. He got to his feet.

A few feet from the table, the man stopped. Ribas saw the strangest expression cross his face. He wasn't just startled, but shocked, as if he had seen something he had never imagined and couldn't believe. The look disappeared in an instant, but Ribas knew he had seen it. What was that about?

The sventin came up to them. "Zhinin Ribas Silvaikas?"

"Yes, sventin."

The man smiled. "My name is Galvo Dendraikas. I'm honored to meet you at last."

Honored? Ribas thought about the sheaf of letters this man had sent to Lida, and how just a couple of weeks ago, he'd accused Valda of wanting to sabotage the election. Here in this room, in front of these other dagira, Ribas couldn't say what he'd have liked to.

Sventin Galvo had almost become Tavin. He was a high-ranking member of the Council of Sventine, and he had gone out of his way to come here this morning and find a visitor from a backwater village. Ribas knew some zhinine, maybe most, would have seen that as welcome patronage. "Sventin Galvo," he said. "The honor is mine." The right words, but they stuck in his throat.

"I'll only keep you a moment," Galvo said. "I wanted to give you my own welcome to Sostavi. I also wanted to make you an apology, zhinin."

"An apology?"

"Quite so. For my behavior when you were first installed in Lida. It was inappropriate, and frankly unconscionable, for me to pressure you as I did to come to Sostavi instead."

Ribas hoped his face didn't show how off-balance he felt. Galvo said, "When you've served on the Council for a while, I'm afraid, you begin to think your rank entitles you to whatever you want. You were right to stand up to me. I'm sorry I behaved as I did."

Everything about his manner said friendly, warm, genuine. None of it fit with Ribas's idea of him. "There's no apology needed, sventin," he said, "but thank you."

Galvo said, "I also wanted to see if I might offer you and your family my services, in a small way. I thought you might enjoy seeing the Great House during a quiet time. I've made a bit of a study of the history of the building and its artwork, particularly the windows, and I'd be glad to give you a tour of sorts."

This went beyond politeness. The gift nudged at Ribas. He would have liked to look into Galvo's mind, to try to understand what the man really wanted, but he didn't want to risk Galvo noticing.

He said, "That's very kind." Galvo's mention of his family gave him the opening for introductions. The sventin bowed politely to Maryut and Gedrin, who both looked as suspicious as Ribas felt himself. Ribas saw Galvo focus on Gedrin, the quick eyes briefly but intently studying his brother's face. Why would the sventin be interested in Gedrin?

Galvo said, "Might I propose we meet in the Great House an hour before this evening's service? I'd enjoy the chance to speak with you further."

Ribas didn't see a polite way to refuse. Maryut's face told him she didn't either. Gedrin looked unhappy. It was only be an hour in the sventin's company, though, and whatever Galvo really wanted, he probably could share some interesting history about the Great House.

"It would be our pleasure," Ribas said. "Thank you."

"I assure you, zhinin, the pleasure's mine. I'll look forward to seeing you later."

With another bow, Galvo left them. The eyes at the other tables followed his progress back across the room.

Ribas sat back down. Gedrin demanded, "Did you have to say yes?"

"I didn't see a way not to."

What was Galvo after? Ribas wished he knew. He would be glad tomorrow, when the High Installation would be over, and they could get ready to go home.

～

In the sun, Sostavi Harbor was a spread of turquoise crowded with fishing boats and the pleasure craft of the city's wealthy. Above the water, on the hillsides, the light turned the city's buildings into clusters of white crystals. Ribas breathed the fresh cold air off the water and remembered why coming here had been worth it.

Maryut leaned against him with her arm around his waist. "You were right," she said. She closed her eyes and tilted her face to the sky. "I like this."

"I don't know about all that water," Gedrin said. "I like fields that stand still."

Ribas said, "When we leave Sostavi, we'll go along the coast a little, and you can see the real breakers. Then you'll know why the Goddess loved this place."

When Ribas was eighteen, he'd had to come to the coast to see for himself what Kenavi had seen, what she had gone out to meet, when she walked into the water to offer herself to the old gods. He had seen the ocean in pictures and read countless stories and texts about it, about gentle Kenavi and rebellious Klaya both, but Ribas had still had trouble imagining those "fields of water" and believing in the power and authority of the gods of sun and wind and water.

When he saw the ocean, he understood. An infinity of water stretching away to the horizon. Waves rolling in, rearing up, crashing against the sand in a heartbeat huge enough to belong to the whole world. The size and power of it all took Ribas's breath away. He had wondered, many times, what Kenavi had actually felt on the day she decided to lay her life down. The stories all said she did it with pure courage and self-sacrifice, to earn the reward the old gods had granted her. Ribas himself had always thought she must have felt afraid, even if only a little, even if she didn't want to admit it to herself. When he saw the ocean, when he stood on the sand and let the wind tug at his clothes and rake through his hair, he knew he had been right. She must have been afraid, but she had also given herself to that water gladly. She had walked forward into that enormousness and let it swallow her. In that moment, she had felt joy. Ribas knew it, because he felt it himself.

Now, after he and Maryut and Gedrin took in the harbor, they went back up into the heart of Sostavi. Shoulder-to-shoulder houses and shops lined the narrow cobblestoned streets, so close together you couldn't see daylight between them. Back home, no building stood taller than two floors. Here, Ribas saw that some buildings had third and even fourth floors added: you could see the join work that linked new stories to older ones, like stacking books in a pile. Houses on top of houses, weaver's shops with grocers above, wine sellers perched above jewelers. The shade of the buildings felt like a burrow.

It was Tretdina, Third Day, which at home would have meant a quiet village square as everyone went about their usual business. Here, people seemed to have time to run in and out of shops, gather in groups to chat, stop to buy apples and roasted nuts and tea from vendors with their carts and baskets. To Ribas, it felt like market day in Lida, except the market spilled into every street.

They all had to admit the shops were interesting. At a woodworker's, Gedrin examined Capture boards and talked to the shop owner about wood varnishes and grains. Maryut turned her back on an elegant milliner's but chatted for a while with the woman in the shop across the street, which sold servingware and cook pots. Ribas let the other two go on wandering without him and spent a while in the remarkable haven of a bookseller's.

They got lunch at a small inn – "not bad," Gedrin said, "but the Sheaf is better" – and explored a little farther before going back to the House of the Zhinine. "I'm going to need a bath and a rest," Maryut said. "Otherwise I'm not going anywhere near that Great House tonight."

Ribas didn't know what to expect from the hour with Galvo, but at least the service afterward would wash away the bad taste. When it was time to leave in the evening, Ribas dressed carefully in the simpler of the two sets of robes he'd brought. This was one of the everyday sets he wore at home, made of homespun cloth and dyed a perfectly even sea-blue. The other set, for high holidays and for the Installation tomorrow, was made of linen. It had a wider collar and embroidered white cross-hatching on the hem, sleeves, and belt.

Maryut had put on the red dress from last night. "You're the prettiest woman in Sostavi, you know," Ribas told her.

"Don't you flatter me, zhinin." Her eyes laughed as she gave him a once-over, straightening his collar and reaching up to smooth his hair away from his forehead. "You look presentable," she said.

"Not like a farmer this time," Gedrin agreed, coming in. "I do, though. At least you two look like you belong in the Great House."

If the Great House had ever been the place where Kenavi had lived as a woman, no one ought to wonder if they belonged there. She wouldn't have turned anyone away. Ribas wondered if any of the dagira here remembered that.

The last of the late afternoon sunlight washed across the square and lit up the building's colored windows. The Great House stood open all day, the same way Lida's House did, but the similarity ended there. Ribas, Maryut, and Gedrin stepped inside, into a hush and grandeur like nothing they had ever seen.

It was beautiful. Much, much more than that. Ribas took in the interior in one long stunned look. Light fell through the jewel-like windows, making them glow and patterning the silver-gray marble floor with splashes of color. The long benches were made of some kind of golden wood. Intricate carvings of vines and flowers covered the back panel of each bench and ran down its sides. No carpets covered the floor, no tapestries hung on the walls; none could be needed, with those windows to draw the eye and fill the space with color. At the front of the House stood the great dais. The oval table that stood on it was made of the same kind of golden wood, polished to a sheen. No cloth covered it now; Ribas could see the same carvings of vines and flowers running around its wide edge and down its single central leg. The broad hearth, made of the same gray stone as the walls, was the plainest part of the House. With no ornament of any kind, its very plainness suggested great age and sanctity.

This place had been built to honor the highest. No one walking through its doors, Ribas thought, could doubt the grace of the Goddess to Whom it paid tribute. The very air felt holy.

He closed his eyes to breathe it in. As he did, he realized another truth about this House. His father had served in it. Silvas had walked along these aisles, his footsteps echoing on the marble. He had looked up at these windows. He had stood in the place where Ribas stood now.

Ribas hadn't felt his father's presence so vividly since he was six years old. The shock of it forced his eyes open. Grief and anger would have followed – Ribas felt them roaring down on him, a wave about to crash on the shore – but then a door somewhere near the House's dais swung open and quick footsteps came down the center aisle.

Sventin Galvo. Ribas heard Gedrin clear his throat impatiently. Gedrin wasn't any happier about this meeting than he'd been this morning. Ribas called on all the self-control he had cultivated all his life to push his own feelings aside and make the proper bow.

The sventin came to meet them, smiling. "Please, no ceremony, zhinin. I'm so glad to have the chance to talk with you."

If Ribas hadn't known anything about Galvo, he would have seen a small-built, aristocratic-looking man whose gray hair suited him as well as his immaculate white robes; a man who was clearly used to authority and commanded great respect, but who unbent with honest friendliness to make outsiders feel welcome. It was unsettling. Ribas didn't believe Galvo's motives could be as transparent as they looked, but the sventin had obviously had long practice at letting others see only what he wanted them to.

He also knew how to get people to trust him. Ribas knew his own abilities there, and he had to admit, reluctantly, that the sventin was an expert. No doubt Galvo knew that Ribas didn't have reason to like him, and that Maryut and Gedrin would follow Ribas's lead. The sventin laid himself out to take their suspicions apart.

"I remember your heart sometimes gives you difficulty, zhinin," he said, as he led them to one of the windows closest to the hearth. "I hope the journey here didn't prove troublesome."

"Not at all," Ribas said. "We enjoyed it very much."

"And how do you find Sostavi?"

"Truthfully, it's a little overwhelming. Beautiful, though."

"It does take some getting used to," Galvo said. "I came here from Laiva, you know, more years ago now than I want to remember." Laiva was another bustling harbor town, the capital of the Pajura region to the west. "I thought I was ready for Sostavi, but I was mistaken."

Maryut caught Ribas's eye. Her expression said she didn't know, any more than he did, why the sventin was so eager to be friendly. They followed Galvo up onto the dais, to the window to the left of the hearth. Standing on the Great House dais felt surreal.

Galvo said, "I thought we'd start here, while we have the light. This is the finest window in the House. At least," with another disarming smile, "I think so."

Ribas could see why. The glassmaker had used the tall, slender window as a canvas to draw a picture of the ocean meeting the shore. Ribas had never known glass could do so much. The colors of the water, greens and blues and violets, swirled into one another and curled toward the pale gold of the sand and the hard gray rocks. With the sunlight behind it, the colors looked so alive that Ribas almost thought he could reach out and feel the chill of the water on his fingers.

Maryut said, "It's beautiful."

"It was commissioned a hundred years ago," Galvo said, "to celebrate the fiftieth anniversary of the election of the Tavin of that time, Pedras Azulaikas. I'm sorry to say that in other respects, Tavin Pedras was less than an ideal leader, but he had fine taste in glasswork."

Gedrin said, "He'd been Tavin for fifty years? He must have been ancient."

Galvo laughed. "He was quite old, in fact, well over ninety. From what I've read, the Council regretted electing him in part because of his notoriously bad memory, which wasn't only a product of age. They had many other reasons, too."

Ribas wondered how they'd come to elect him at all. Galvo told them more about the glassmaker, a woman named Rasena Eldraikas. "She was one of the finest artists in Sostavi. Her apprentice, Liana Ranaikas, took over her workshop and created the window on the other side of the hearth."

He told them about the window opposite, and about the hearth itself, and about the different times when different parts of the House had been built. He had clearly studied its history in detail, and he knew how to talk about it. Everything he said was interesting. Ribas found himself asking questions, eager to hear more in spite of himself. Before he knew it, he and Galvo were talking about the texts that had inspired the designs of the two oldest House windows. The texts were two obscure stories about the Goddess written in the First Tongue, Pirlevis. "Are you familiar with them, zhinin?" Ribas wasn't. "You should read them. I can give you copies if you like. You might be struck, as I was, with similarities between Kenavi as she's described there, and our folktale heroine Klaya."

They talked about the story "Fourteen Stones" and a Pirlevis story of the Goddess with some of the same elements. Ribas hadn't expected to find such a sharp, thoughtful reader in Galvo. He certainly hadn't expected to enjoy talking to him.

Maryut and Gedrin had left them to their talk and wandered ahead to look at the other windows. Galvo motioned Ribas off the dais. As they went down the center aisle, Galvo said, "Zhinin, I'd like to ask you a question. I learned something about you quite some time ago, which I've been curious about ever since."

This had to be about the gift. Ribas braced himself. He shouldn't have forgotten that Galvo would want a return for all this kindness.

But the question wasn't what Ribas expected. Galvo said, "When Kunin Dergo at the Paret viduris wrote to the Council about you, just before you were installed in Lida, he mentioned that you had made a study of the Lasska language. Is that true?"

The kunin had told the Council about that? Ribas hadn't known. Dergo had said that the powers-that-be in Sostavi would have to know about the gift, because Ribas should be able to use it in his work, but it was such a rare thing that it couldn't stay private for long. Dergo had said he would notify the Council about it, and he was going to have to let Ribas in for what he knew would be a certain amount of trouble. Ribas wondered if the kunin had known or guessed that Sventin Galvo, in particular, would cause most of that trouble.

But Galvo wanted to know about Lasska. Ribas couldn't imagine why, but at least it wasn't what he'd been afraid of. "Yes," he said. "The kunin was kind enough to help me learn it, as much as he could."

Galvo stopped and looked up at him. "That's most interesting. Are you proficient?"

"I wish I were. I can read it pretty well, and speak it a little, but it's been a long time since I practiced. I don't know if a native speaker would understand me at all."

"I know very little about your kunin, but I got the impression that he didn't favor students who made their own rules."

He had such a knowing look, as if he'd actually been there to hear some of the arguments, that Ribas couldn't help smiling. "That's true."

"But he made an exception in your case. Learning Lasska on your own couldn't have been easy. Why did you want to do it?"

Ribas wondered if he could ask why the sventin cared. "We didn't learn much about the faith of Mesha, but I decided I'd like to be able to read what his people wrote about themselves, if I could."

"Why so curious?"

"We'd studied some Old Namoran and Pirlevis by then. We'd seen how our own stories sounded different when we translated them into modern Namoran." Ribas hadn't talked to anyone about this in a long time; not since he'd made his case to the kunin. "I couldn't help but think that when Namorans translated Lasska stories, the few we've got, we probably changed them too. I wanted to see how they were originally written."

The sunlight had faded by now. Attendants were moving around the House to light the lamps on the walls. In the warmer, softer lamplight, Ribas saw a puzzling expression on Galvo's face. It looked wistful.

The sventin said, "I hope you'll forgive my impertinence. I must tell you, your father would have been proud of you."

Ribas froze. His chest ached as if cold hands had closed around it. "You knew my father, sventin?"

"Oh yes. We served here together. First as zhinine, but we both made kunin, you know, before Ardinas became Tavin."

Silvas had made kunin? Ribas kept his voice steady. "I didn't know that. I don't know much about my father."

Maryut and Gedrin were examining the carving on one of the benches near the House's front doors. Ribas wished he could call them to come back. He didn't want to listen to whatever Galvo might say now.

The sventin's eyes stayed on his face. "When Kunin Dergo wrote to us about his student Ribas Silvaikas," he said, "I hadn't heard Silvas's name in many years. I wrote back to the kunin to ask if you were in fact the son of my old friend, and to see if he might have any news of your father. He told me that, yes, you were Silvas Jadraikas's son, and your father had died when you were quite young, and you didn't have much reason to remember him kindly. I was sorry to hear it."

Ribas realized the sventin might well know why Silvas had left Sostavi. If Ribas asked, he might finally get an answer to that old mystery. He wouldn't do it. He didn't want to hear any more than he had to. "Yes," he said evenly. "My father was very unhappy. He tended to take it out on his family."

"A shame." Galvo looked as if he meant it. "But I must tell you, zhinin, it's a great pleasure to see that you've inherited his strengths. You have the same kind of mind."

Ribas couldn't stop himself, though he knew Galvo wasn't entirely wrong. "I beg your pardon. I'm nothing like him."

Galvo didn't look offended. "I'm afraid I must disagree." Through his own rising anger, Ribas saw startling gentleness in the sventin's expression. "I knew Silvas very well," Galvo said. "Your brother, of course, has his looks. That's why I was so surprised to see him at breakfast this morning. But you, zhinin, you think as he did. Your temper is quite different, I can see that, but your curiosity and intelligence are the same. He would have appreciated you very much."

Ribas couldn't get out of this conversation soon enough. At least Galvo couldn't see into his mind. The sventin said, "The service will be starting soon. I need to go back to my chambers for a moment beforehand, but I hope we might talk again, perhaps after the Installation tomorrow."

Ribas didn't hope any such thing. He didn't say so. He and Galvo rejoined Maryut and Gedrin, and the sventin gave them all a polite good evening. "Do enjoy the service. I'm sure I'll see you again soon."

As soon as Galvo was out of earshot, Gedrin said, "He's not what I expected. Not as obnoxious, for one thing."

People were coming in for the service. The House was filling up. Maryut looked into Ribas's face. "Are you all right, love?"

Shadows. Memories. Exactly what Ribas had hoped not to find in Sostavi. He pushed them away as hard as he could. "I'm fine."

Gedrin said, "We'd better get seats before they're gone."

They sat in the third row of benches, near the center aisle. Ribas wanted to let his mind go quiet and let his soul bow down to the sanctity of the place. Galvo's words kept intruding.

Your father would have been proud of you.

What had the sventin really wanted? Why had he told Ribas those things, and why, yes, had he seemed so different from what Ribas had expected, especially when he talked about Silvas? This Galvo didn't seem like the man who had harassed a young zhinin or thrown accusations at the Tavo Balsa. But what had he wanted from Ribas fifteen years ago, and what did he want now?

Valda stood on the dais, in the brown robes of the Tavo Balsa, leading the service. Ribas wanted to listen to the prayers and offer his own prayers for her Installation tomorrow. He couldn't drive Galvo's voice out of his head.

You have the same kind of mind. He would have appreciated you very much.

The House of the Zhinine might have changed in thirty-five years, but the Great House had not. You could feel Time in its very stones. In Lida, Ribas had been able to wall off the fact that his father, too, had been a zhinin. Silvas had been a farmer there. Here, in Sostavi, he had been a priest.

The grief Ribas had held back only an hour ago rolled in to claim him. Grief for everything that had happened, for the man who had been here – Ribas could see him now, that strong-built, dark-haired man in robes so like the ones Ribas wore tonight – and who had, for what reason Ribas didn't know, abandoned this place and the life he had built. Grief for the woman who had married him later and for the children born to them. Grief for the loss of that man, too young, to his own uncontrollable violence and all the hurt he had caused.

On the dais, Valda was giving the final reading. Ribas wanted to hide his face in his hands. He closed his eyes and willed himself to stay still, stay quiet.

Maryut's hand closed around his. "Love," she whispered. "What's wrong? Are you hurting?"

Not the way she meant. Not his heart. Ribas managed to whisper back, "It's all right. I'll tell you later."

Later, he hoped, he could tell her what Galvo had said, and the shadows wouldn't choke him anymore. For now, he prayed the only prayer he could.

Goddess. Have mercy on my father's soul, and mine.

15

VALDENA

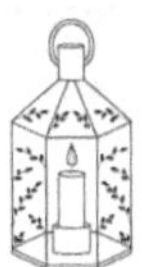

On the morning of her Installation as Tavin, Valda woke up out of a light doze to a sharp knocking at the outer door of her chambers. Outside, the sky had shaded from gray to rose and pale blue. Who would bother her so early?

In too few hours, she would have to stand up in the Great House and repeat the vows that would make her Namora's leader. She had slept no more last night than she'd expected. Every movement took too much effort, as if she were swimming through honey.

The knocking came again, louder this time. Valda wrapped a robe around herself and went to answer.

One of the House's servants, a boy with freckles and a shock of dark hair, stood outside. He held out an envelope. "Apologies, Sventin Valdena. This just arrived. It's from Cheremay."

Cheremay? Valda wrapped her robe more closely around her and took the envelope, willing her hands not to shake. The boy said, "The courier here thought it might be urgent, else I wouldn't have disturbed you so early. We know we don't get many letters from Lassar."

"Thank you."

With the door securely closed again, she looked at the envelope. It was addressed in a neat but rather jagged hand to the Tavin of Namora, Sostavi, Jemtave region. When she turned it over, she saw a red seal imprinted with the head of a bear. Its mouth hung open, showing rows of sharp teeth.

Today, of all days. Had Impera Shurik somehow known of Valda's Installation and timed this letter accordingly? She doubted it. Breaking the seal, she took the letter out, thinking through the cloud of uneasiness that she hoped at least he hadn't written in Lasska.

He hadn't. Valda unfolded the single page and took in the few lines.

To the Tavin of Namora, greetings from His Highness Shurik, Impera of Lassar and Servant of the God Mesha.

The Impera wishes respectfully to inform the Tavin that he will, in accordance with the wishes of the God, shortly undertake a campaign within the bounds of his own land to subdue a portion of his population known as the Pala Vaia. These are aliens and enemies of the God, his Highness, and the Lasska people.

In his wisdom, the Impera considers that these fallen people may seek refuge outside Lassar's borders. The Impera wishes to remind the Tavin of the long and peaceful relationship between their two countries. He also wishes to indicate that should Namora be known to harbor enemies of Lassar, the Impera will, with regret, find it necessary to address this circumstance.

The Impera looks forward to hearing shortly that the Tavin respects and concurs with his intentions. He and his people unite in wishing the Tavin good health and long life, and lasting prosperity to Namora. In the name of the God Mesha, signed this day by His Highness Shurik of Lassar.

Valda stared at the black ink on the parchment. The lines seemed to drift apart into single letters, then meaningless shapes. Two words held together in her head: *It's come.*

It might have been worse. Shurik could have shown much less respect and much more hostility. Valda knew, though, that this message meant Tavin Ardinas had been right in one of the last things he had said to her.

Lassar's impera, young Shurik, will be trouble.

I wonder what he may think his god wants from him.

Valda had never heard of the Pala Vaia. Whoever they were, if Shurik intended to "subdue" them, and if they might "seek refuge" outside Lassar, it took no great effort to guess what they faced. And if Namora dared to oppose Shurik's intentions, even to allowing refugees across the border, Shurik would, *with regret,* turn the weight of his mighty army against his tiny neighbor.

Valda's tiredness burned away. Her thoughts felt as clear and cold as ice. She dressed quickly in the brown robes of the Tavo Balsa and summoned another attendant.

"I require all members of the Council to join me in our meeting room in an hour. Send servants to wake them. Say that the matter is urgent, but they must say nothing to anyone outside the Council until we meet."

The servant, a young girl with long reddish hair, looked scared. Maybe she knew about the letter from Cheremay; news tended to spread quickly among the dagira and their servants. She bowed. "Yes, Tavin."

Valda had another idea and acted on it at once. "Send a servant to the House of the Zhinine as well. I request their guest Zhinin Ribas Silvaikas to join this meeting." She must have his good sense with her now.

"As you wish, Tavin."

Alone again, Valda forced herself to eat a little bread and drink some strong dark tea. Then, and not before, she realized that the girl had called her Tavin.

The Council convened in a cluster of confusion and argument. Valda had gotten to the meeting room early, taking Shurik's letter with her.

The sventine arrived in small groups, debating among themselves why she had dragged them here so early.

Most of them had taken the time to put on their white robes and render themselves as imposing as possible. Valda had put on her own robes of office for the authority they gave, but she saw the contrast between those who had dressed up and the three or four who hadn't. It did not flatter those who had.

Ribas was one of the ones who hadn't. He came in alone, between two of the groups of arguing sventine, and paused by her chair. "Valda," he said, too quietly for the others to hear. "Forgive me, but why am I here?"

He looked as if he'd gotten no more rest than she had. Last night, which already seemed to be part of a different lifetime, Valda had seen him at the Great House service. He had looked tired and drawn then too. She had wanted to find him afterward, to ask if anything had happened, but he and Maryut and Gedrin had left too quickly.

"I'm sorry, Ribé," she said. She wouldn't have apologized to anyone else. "I need your help. When you hear what's happened, you'll understand."

She motioned him toward the chair she had sat in when Tavin Ardinas had presided here. It was the only empty seat, of course, because each member of the Council had his own, but it was the Tavo Balsa's chair. Now more than ever, Valda knew she must find a way to convince him to accept that post.

The sventine noticed the newcomer quickly. When Galvo came in, his eyes went at once from Ribas to Valda and back again. Valda couldn't read his expression. The other sventine didn't know who Ribas was. More muttering and whispering went up and down the table as they tried to decide why he was there.

When everyone had taken their seats, Valda called the meeting to order with a single sharp word. "Council."

Her own voice sounded different in her ears, as cold and ringing as stones striking ice. "This morning," she said, "I received a letter from Lassar's Impera Shurik. Its contents have given me much concern. I have called you here to determine how we must respond to it."

Shurik's name set off another wave of murmuring. Galvo's eyes stayed on Valda. Ribas's did too; she saw him lean forward attentively. She raised a hand to cut off the talk.

"I have the letter here. I will read it in a moment, but first, I must explain why we have a non-Council member with us this morning." She motioned toward Ribas. "This is Zhinin Ribas Silvaikas of Lida village, in Kalnu. He is here in Sostavi by my invitation and at this meeting by my request. His perception, intelligence, and sense have my unqualified trust."

A few of the sventine seemed to recognize Ribas's name. Some of them, like Galvo, must have been here when the news about Lida's young zhinin first got to the Council. Valda knew what she had to say next, and she knew how little Ribas would want her to do it. *I'm sorry, Ribé.*

Galvo spoke up first. "I also have reason to know that Zhinin Ribas likely has greater familiarity with Lassar's traditions, language, and history than any of the rest of us in this room."

Valda wondered what he was talking about. Then she remembered, and couldn't believe she had forgotten.

"Yes," she said. "Zhinin, I'm correct, am I not, in remembering that you undertook private study of the Lasska language while we were at the viduris?"

How often they'd teased him about it, she and Niala and Andrin and the rest of their group of friends. No one but Ribas would have taken on all that extra work for no extra credit of any kind. No one else could have talked the kunin not just into letting him do it, but helping him. *Always so stubborn.*

Ribas met her eyes. "I did. But I must mention that it was a long time ago."

That might be, but Galvo was right. For the first time, Valda realized how truly foolish it was that senior dagira didn't learn more about Namora's vast neighbor to the east. No one should reach the

Council without at least a basic grounding in Lasska language and politics.

Galvo said, "It might have been a long time ago, zhinin, but I can say with confidence that no one else here has any such background."

When had Galvo learned about Ribas's studies? The two of them must have talked. Did that have anything to do with Ribas's tiredness at the service last night? Valda saw Ribas's face tighten now, as the sventin looked at him, as if he wanted to push something away. And Galvo...Valda couldn't be sure, but for a moment, Galvo seemed to be reaching out, hoping to take hold of something before it was gone.

Sventin Eldin, who had nominated Galvo for Tavin, put up a hand. "Tavo Balsa," he said, "is this the same Zhinin Ribas Silvaikas whom the Council heard of some time ago?"

Here it was. Valda didn't look at Ribas. She could only hope he understood why she must bring this out in front of them all.

"Yes," she said. "Some of you already know this, but for those who do not, it may interest you to learn that Zhinin Ribas also has a unique place within the dagira. He holds the dovne kenavnis."

"The dovne kenavnis?" Faces turned toward Ribas again, eager, questioning. Valda saw that Sventin Lesvin looked especially fascinated. People asked one another if it was true. "Can't be," Valda heard someone say. "That hasn't been seen in Namora since I don't know when."

Galvo spoke up again, cutting through the noise. "I can vouch for the zhinin's gift. I learned of it many years ago."

Valda knew the debate would start up again as soon as everyone recovered from this new surprise. Before it could, Ribas said, "Sventine."

All the heads swiveled back to him. Valda thought distantly that her colleagues would have sore necks before this meeting ended. Ribas said, "Tavin Valdena is correct. I do have the dovne kenavnis, but I respectfully submit that we must hear what news she has from Lassar."

He sounded absolutely calm, but Valda thought she still saw

tension in his profile. He'd had no more warning of this than the rest of them, no reason at all to think he would be brought into such a Council, and no wish to have his gift made a topic of discussion for these dagira. He carried himself with as much composure as anyone in the room. Valda had never doubted he belonged here. Everyone else must see it too.

Tavin Valdena. The Council could argue about anything, and Valda distinctly heard a whisper or two about how the ceremony hadn't taken place yet. Galvo interrupted them. "My colleague from Lida makes an excellent point. Tavin, we are at your service." If it cost him an effort to call her that, he didn't let anyone see it. "Please tell us what you've heard."

"Thank you, sventin." Valda picked up the letter. "Allow me to read what Shurik sent us."

She read the letter dispassionately, even as its contents seemed to bring a cold fog into the room. Beyond question, this meant trouble of a kind Namora had never seen before.

When she finished, silence gripped the room for a handful of seconds. Then the debate burst out again, loud and angry. Only Galvo and Ribas said nothing. Ribas sat quiet, his face as calm as before, his attentive eyes on Valda. Galvo, too, looked composed. Every other face in the room showed confusion, fear, and anger.

Valda held up a hand. "Council."

The room came back to order with surprising speed. She turned to Ribas. "Zhinin, I would like you to tell us anything you can about the people Shurik references here, or anything else about Lassar and its people that may help. As we know, you are the only one of us with any relevant background."

"I'm afraid I don't know much either, Tavin, but any knowledge I have is at this Council's disposal."

His steady, quiet voice settled the room, an anchor that Valda knew everyone felt. He said, "The Lasska texts I've seen say very little about the Pala Vaia. I understand they're a tribal people, wanderers, and they worship much older gods. It's believed they were the first people who lived in any of the countries in this part of the world."

Sventin Rano said, "Do we have them in Namora?"

"I don't think so." Ribas spoke as easily as if he were talking to friends in his own Circle House. "It's possible they did live in Namora at one point, but left here, or were driven out, a long time ago. The Lasska call them *strenyi*, strangers. In Namoran they would be *klayine*, wanderers. They seem to be outcasts everywhere."

"And why is that, zhinin?"

The question came from Lesvin, who leaned across the table toward Ribas. "Are they lawless? Do they cause trouble?"

"I don't know, sventin. The texts I've seen suggest they're peaceful people who keep to themselves. It seems no one knows very much about them."

Lesvin said, "But they might be vagrants, for instance. Lawbreakers. Thieves, perhaps."

"I can't answer that."

Galvo said, "Zhinin, would you do me the favor of telling the Council what you told me yesterday, about why you wished to study Lasska?"

So Valda had been right; they had talked yesterday. If Ribas didn't know why Galvo brought this up now, he didn't show it. "Certainly, sventin. At the viduris, the little we learned about the Lasska faith suggested we have nothing in common with the worshippers of Mesha. But we only saw Namoran translations of a very few Lasska stories. We know our own stories about the Goddess may sound different in Old Namoran and modern Namoran. I didn't believe we could be as different from the Lasska as it seemed, so I wanted to learn how to read their stories as they told them."

Only you, Ribé. Valda knew no one else would have made such an effort. No one else would have cared. She hoped he understood now why she needed him here this morning.

Eldin grumbled, "I fail to see what we could have in common

with bear-worshippers." Someone else said, "How does any of this help us?"

Lesvin leaned forward again to catch Valda's eye. "Tavin," he said, "I think that what Impera Shurik chooses to do in his own land is, to put it briefly, none of Namora's business. He says these people are the enemies of his God. He has the right to treat them as he sees fit. Namora cannot and should not interfere."

Enemies of his God. Valda felt no surprise that Lesvin had latched onto those words. Unbidden, her mind whispered, *Imagine if he had won the election.*

At his words, the talk broke out again, louder than ever. Valda heard voices agreeing with him. "That's right. Not our concern." "Tell him he can do what he wants." "He could overrun us in a day. Nothing we can do to stop it."

Ribas brought his hand down flat on the table, not hard, but the sound cut through the talk like a knife through a spiderweb. "Council," he said. "Tavin Valdena. Permission to speak?"

No one else here knew him well enough to see his anger. Valda recognized the stillness in his face, the slight pallor that made his eyes more brilliant than ever. She had never seen him lose control. He had told her, once, that he tried never to lose his temper in front of anyone, because he knew how much damage that could do.

She said, "Of course, zhinin."

"Shurik, like his father before him, is an autocrat." He didn't raise his voice, but Valda felt the undercurrent of anger in every word. "His country runs on its military strength. He can do whatever he wishes, and he expects total obedience from his people." All of that was exactly what Valda had discussed with Ardinas. Another village zhinin might not have known as much, but Valda felt no surprise that Ribas did. "Now," Ribas said, "he says he wishes to 'subdue' a people he doesn't care for. I don't believe it takes much imagination to think what that could mean."

He had never had any tolerance for cruelty. He said, "Do we have the right to ignore what Shurik does? The Pala Vaia are people, just as we are. If it comes to that, so are the Lasska. If you could take apart the barriers that the imperi and the rules of Mesha and whatever else have built around them, you might find we can understand each other. Can we turn our backs on people who need our help?"

Valda wanted to say then and there, *Ribé, you must stay here in Sostavi. You have no idea how much I need you.* Sventin Rano said, "But the plain fact, zhinin, is that we can't stand up to Shurik. With respect, you come from a tiny village. We can't expect you to understand international politics."

Now it was Valda's turn to get angry. Before she could tell Rano off, Galvo interrupted.

"Any of us could have taken the trouble to educate ourselves about Lassar, as Zhinin Ribas did. None of us chose to." Galvo looked around the table, impressing his words on each Council member. "Given that, I believe we owe the zhinin's views more consideration than my colleague has just demonstrated."

Undoubtedly Galvo was playing politics in this, knowing as he did that Ribas had Valda's support, but Valda couldn't quite shake the idea that Galvo meant what he said. The sventin's expression as he looked at Ribas showed genuine respect and something else, some deeper emotion that Valda couldn't quite define.

Lesvin said, "That's all very well, but does nothing to answer how we could oppose Shurik's army. We cannot afford to deny him what he wants."

He sounded openly hostile. No doubt he was ready to fight with Galvo because of the election, but Valda felt sure his religious fervor took a part in it too. *Enemies of his God.* She thought, *You told me once that you would listen for the will of the Goddess.*

Galvo said, "I don't suggest we try to oppose Shurik immediately. I suggest instead that we take more time to consider this. He can't expect a reply at once, coming as it would from such a distance." He looked at Ribas again. "And we must also remember that we have a particular asset here, in the dovne kenavnis."

Another stir from the room. Valda tensed. Galvo had always had far too much interest in Ribas's gift.

Ribas said calmly, "You give me too much credit, sventin. Given my gift's limitations, I don't think it could help."

Galvo opened his mouth, but Valda would not let a debate about the dovne kenavnis begin here and now. Lesvin had shown one extreme, Ribas the opposite, and Galvo had suggested a reasonable compromise; she had to give him credit for that. She said, "Thank you, Council. I believe Sventin Galvo has shown us the correct way for now. Meanwhile, we must get on to the business of the day." Her own Installation, which would happen in a matter of hours, felt remarkably small and secondary.

Lesvin started to protest. Valda cut him off. "I realize we have not reached any decisions, but we will reconvene tomorrow to discuss this further. Meanwhile, I ask you all to make no reference to it outside this room, or amongst anyone except ourselves." The last thing they needed was for the news to spread through Sostavi, dragging panic with it. "I value the initial thoughts you've given me. For now, this meeting is closed."

They obeyed her, willingly or not. As chairs pushed back, Valda said, "Zhinin Ribas, please wait a moment."

She had to do this now. She could see how tired he was, how little he wanted to be here, but he must, must listen to her. She must make him understand.

When everyone else had left the room, she shut the door. Ribas hadn't gotten up from his seat. He smiled when she sat down beside him.

"I'm afraid I was rude to your colleagues," he said.

"Not at all. They needed it."

"Valda, I'm so sorry. I know you thought I could help here, but I don't know any more than what I told you. I have no idea what you should do."

He had never changed. He was the same gentle, honest man she had known, and she needed him now. She took a breath and said what she must. "I can tell you how to help. Join this Council as my Tavo Balsa."

The words rang in the silence that followed. Valda heard her own heartbeat in her ears. For a moment Ribas's face looked absolutely blank. Then he shook his head.

Valda put her hand on his arm. "Don't answer now. Talk about it with Maryut and your brother and see what they think."

He didn't move a muscle, but she felt him withdrawing from her, calling on that rigid self-control. "Valda, no. I can't join the Council."

She wouldn't let him refuse so quickly. "Please listen, just for a moment. I need someone here I can trust, not only because of the Lassar business. I thought of this as soon as you came to Sostavi." Without thinking, she let go of his arm and put her hand on his, where it rested on the table. "Ribé, I can't tell you what a help it would be to have you here."

"But I'm not even a kunin," he said. "I can't..."

"Your rank doesn't matter. Please let me explain." She laid out everything she had already thought of: how she could promote him herself; how, given his record in Kalnu, no one could deserve such a promotion more; how he had, this morning, already demonstrated to the Council that he belonged here. "You said more useful things in an hour than most of them could manage in a month. I know; I've been listening to them for years." And he had faced them down as easily as if he had sat in these chambers all his life. "We need your voice here," she said. "Your mind."

"My gift?"

He must not think that. Valda's fingers tightened reflexively around his. She forced herself to let go and sit back. "Not as far as I'm concerned," she said. "I know Sventin Galvo wanted that, and he probably still would if he thought you would join us. That isn't what I need, though." *I need you here because there is no one else like you.* "I need you here because the Tavin must have a Tavo Balsa who can act and speak for her. I would trust no one with that duty more readily than you."

He was silent for a long moment, looking into her face. Valda wondered if he was reaching into her mind too. If he did, how clearly would he see what she felt for him? How much would that color his answer?

Finally he said, "Valda, you know my life is in Lida. I don't see how I could leave."

The idea hurt him. She saw that, she hated to see it, but he wasn't pulling away from her now, and he hadn't made another flat refusal. "I know it would be hard," she said. "I understand, and again, I don't want your answer now. Talk to Maryut and Gedrin." She laid out more of what she'd considered: how of course, if he agreed, he would have time to go home and settle affairs, and how the Council would help when it came time for him and Maryut to re-settle here in Sostavi. They needn't live in the House of the Sventine, which she felt sure they wouldn't want. The Council could help them find a house of their own. She said, "By all means tell Maryut and Gedrin about Shurik's letter, but please ask them not to say anything to anyone else. I'd like them to know why it would help so much to have you here now."

"But I don't know what I could do." He wasn't arguing with her, only making a point. "As your colleague said, I don't know much about international politics."

That smile. She must not let him see how it made her heart leap. She said, "You had the only useful knowledge of Lassar and the Lasska in this room. We ought to know more, every one of us. We'll have to change that as soon as we can, but meanwhile, you have to agree you do have something we need. Most importantly, I need someone here who thinks the way you do. Someone who remembers that, in the end, we're discussing the lives of people."

By the time she finished, he was shaking his head again. "You do me too much honor, Tavin."

The tiny undercurrent of humor in the words gave her so much hope. "Not at all," she said. Best to end this talk now, before he could give her that final refusal, or before she could give in and plead with him as she knew she must not. She stood up. "Please think about it. I'll see you this evening. You and Maryut and Gedrin will stay for the feast, of course."

The feast after the Installation. Only a day ago – less than that – Valda hadn't been able to imagine the Installation happening at all. Now it seemed to have no more weight than a grain of sand.

He understood the dismissal. "We'll be honored." He stood up and saluted her, and she returned it, wishing with all her heart she could give him his new rank here and now.

That evening, in the Great House, the Council performed the ceremony that installed Valda as the new Tavin of Namora.

The House was packed. People wanted to see the excitement of a High Installation, with or without all the traditional pageantry. Valda knew that Ardinas, like other Tavine before him, would have made a grand procession through the streets of Sostavi, letting the crowds greet and cheer for him. Opulent carriages would have carried him and the Council. Everyone would have worn their finest robes, and the high-stepping horses would have been curried and groomed until every one of their hairs lay exactly in place. Ardinas would have arrived at the Great House in a whirl of elegance. He would have made a final procession out of his walk down its central aisle, to meet the dagira who waited for him on the dais.

Valda arrived at the House on foot, walking across the square from her quarters in the House of the Sventine. Galvo had insisted on walking with her, as had Lesvin, probably out of determination not to let Galvo outdo him. Valda had conceded to the occasion by wearing her best white sventin's robes over a simple dress, but she hurried across the square without much ceremony. It vaguely surprised her to see how many people stood out in the cold, their breath forming clouds in the late-afternoon light, to watch her go into the Great House.

Inside, the press of so many bodies warmed the space, as did the fire burning on the hearth. As soon as she stepped inside, the rest of the Council, waiting on the dais, stood up. The murmuring and whispering in the House stopped at once. All the heads turned toward the great doors.

Valda walked down the central aisle with Galvo and Lesvin behind her. She felt the pressure of all the eyes. A day ago, she would have had to call on every ounce of self-control to keep her professional mask in place. Today, with the weight of Shurik's letter in her mind, and the massive unanswered question of what to do and what was going to happen to them all, she barely felt the length of the walk or the hard marble under her shoes.

Standing on the dais, she looked out at the House. The faces and fine clothes blurred together, but she scanned the room for the sea-blue robes of zhinine. There were many, too many, but just as she began to think she wouldn't be able to single out one person from the throng, her eyes found Ribas. He sat with Maryut and Gedrin a few rows back from the front, near the side aisle. He saw her looking at him and smiled.

Beside him, Maryut sat very straight, her shoulders squared as if she, too, was preparing to face a great challenge. On her other side, Gedrin leaned forward on the bench. Valda thought his face looked tense. Had Ribas told his wife and brother what she had asked of him? Did he have an answer for her?

Did she want to hear it?

The ceremony began. In all the times Valda had imagined this during the past weeks, she had pictured the words of the ceremony drifting past her like snow, thin and cold and inexorable. She had thought time would seem to stop as the rites went on, suspending her like a fish trapped in winter ice, caught in the fate that had never been meant for her.

Instead, time began to move strangely fast. The council had also chosen Galvo and Lesvin as the two main officiants for the ceremony. It seemed only fair. Galvo addressed the House with the traditional words of welcome, and then the sacred words so rarely said in this place: "Today it is our honor, our joy, and our most solemn duty in the sight of the Goddess, to install Her servant as Tavin of Namora." Valda thought briefly how difficult it must be for him to say those words, which he had expected someone else – perhaps Valda herself, as his incumbent Tavo Balsa – to say over him.

He led the House in prayer, calling on the Goddess to witness today's ceremony and grant Her love and guidance to Namora's new Tavin. Valda knew how much Galvo enjoyed lengthy, flowery prayers with elegant turns of phrase. He certainly hadn't held back today. He had a good voice for it, steady and resonant and compelling.

When he said the final "Tebena" – *so be it* – and the House echoed him, another member of the Council stepped forward to read from the *Book of Kenavi*. The passage was the familiar story of the Goddess's sacrifice, read at every installation ceremony in every Circle House, as a reminder of the duty any member of the dagira accepted in serving as Kenavi's priest. Valda tried to listen, but time seemed to shift forward again, running away with her.

Lesvin came up to the front of the dais to ask her the traditional questions. Valda had answered much the same questions years ago when she first became a zhinin; for this far different occasion, they changed only slightly.

"Valdena Filtraikas." Where Galvo had spoken smoothly and confidently, Lesvin's voice sounded tight and strained. Valda couldn't tell whether he was nervous about performing this ceremony, or whether he still ached that he hadn't won the election. "Do you," he asked, "willingly submit to the guidance of the Goddess, which has ordained that you shall be Tavin of Namora, bearing upon your shoulders responsibility for the well-being, safety, and health of all the Goddess's people, and caring for them as She wills?"

The guidance of the Goddess. Had that brought her here? "I do," she answered.

Lesvin said, "Do you pledge to serve the Goddess in your

thoughts, words, and deeds, listening for Her guidance, submitting to Her will, and honoring Her always in your service to Her country?"

I pray She will guide me, Valda thought. *I need it so much.* "I do."

"And will you, to the best of your ability, exemplify Her caring in all your doings for Her children, remembering Her devotion to the land and people She loved, and embodying that love as an example to all who look to you for aid and guidance?"

Valda had answered that question almost verbatim at her first installation. Ribas had answered it too. *If I can serve half as well here as he has in Lida.* If she could have the chance to ask him the same question again, when she raised him to sventin rank. "I will."

Lesvin led the House in another prayer. Valda's robes had begun to feel heavy, almost chokingly warm. She kept her eyes down, her hands folded in front of her, and gave thanks that the only people in this room who knew the news from Lassar were the ones on the dais with her, and the three out in the House. She didn't, yet, have to carry all the fears of everyone in Sostavi; of everyone in Namora, if and when the news spread that far. *Kenavi, Mother of us all, grant me the strength to bear that burden.*

Lesvin's prayer was shorter and less flowery than Galvo's. Another final "Tebena," and another sventin reading a different passage from the *Book of Kenavi.* Then Galvo faced Valda again.

"Valdena Filtraikas, I ask you now to kneel in the presence of the Goddess."

Now it became real. In the next moments, they would complete and seal the ceremony. For the first time, Valda felt time slow down around her as she knelt on the dais.

The marble floor felt hard under her knees, chilly even through the woolen dress she wore under the heavily embroidered white robes. She spread the skirts of the robes out carefully around her, in preparation for the last part of the ceremony.

She had done exactly this before, as mosevin, as zhinin, and once more as kunin. It did not, could not feel the same now.

Galvo dipped his hands in the bowl of water on the dais table and rested them on her hair. "By the authority vested in me as a servant of the Goddess Kenavi," he said, "and by the power of the water that recalls Her sacrifice, I hereby install you, Valdena Filtraikas, as Tavin of Namora. May you honor the Goddess and serve Her people faithfully in thought, word, and deed, for as long as She shall so call on you to do."

As long as She shall so call on you to do. Valda remembered how, not long ago, she had wondered how long she might have to wait before she could resign. That felt far away now. Nothing held much weight anymore, compared to the news from Lassar.

Galvo said, "Tebena."

So be it. "Tebena," Valda answered.

A sound came from the House: a collective murmur, or sigh, like the movement of wind over the ocean. They had finished the most official part of the ceremony. Namora had a new Tavin. Again Valda thought of Ardinas. In this moment, had he been afraid? Excited? Daunted by the weight on his shoulders, or eager to lift and carry it? Valda couldn't imagine he felt as she did now, as if she were one single grain of sand on a vast beach, her life so small compared to everything around her that she could almost disappear.

Now came the final part of the ritual. Lesvin came up behind Valda. She knew he carried her new brown robes, the ceremonial ones, grander than what she had worn as Tavo Balsa. She undid the belt at her waist and loosened the collar of the white robes. Then she lifted the skirts of the robes around her, and Galvo took the fabric from her and drew it gently over her head and away.

Another sventin took the white robes. Galvo accepted the brown ones from Lesvin. Valda raised her arms slightly, and Galvo spread the fabric and lowered it carefully over her.

At the viduris, so long ago, the mosevine had joked and cringed about terrible stories of flustered new zhinine trying to put their heads through the sleeves of their blue robes, having to be helped out by the officiant while their new congregations choked on their laughter. The robes were loose, especially with collar and belt undone, and there should be no trouble if the officiant knew his or her business, but the mosevine had all practiced with each other in the weeks leading up to their installations. Of course you couldn't actually wear the blue robes before you were installed – no mosevin would risk jinxing him- or herself forever – but you could trade one set of red robes for another. Valda remembered that all the practice in the world hadn't stopped the nightmares, where you jerked out of sleep imagining you were suffocating in a tangle of blue fabric in front of a crowded House.

No such misadventures now. Galvo knew his business. No matter what he might feel about this ceremony, he would not risk the reputation of the Great House itself by allowing a mistake to happen. The brown fabric settled around Valda's body. The wide sleeves encircled her arms and the skirts draped on the floor.

Still kneeling, she closed the collar and tied the belt. She had worn exactly this shade of brown many times, standing in for Tavin Ardinas, but it was not at all the same now. When she had finished, Galvo said, "You may rise."

Valda stood up. Her knees felt stiff. She faced the House again with the weight of the new robes on her.

So many years ago, she had watched Ribas face the House in Lida at the end of his own installation. Valda remembered his smile, and the look in his eyes: that shy, eager, beautiful look as he took up the life waiting for him. He took it up with worry and humility, a profound wish to do good with the skills he had, and with that extraordinary gift. It was all of a piece with everything she loved in him. It was all of a piece, she had thought on that day, hoping the heartbreak didn't show in her face, of everything she would always love.

She didn't let herself find him in the House again now. Her eyes moved over the congregation, making out individual faces. She promised them all, without words, that she would do the best she could for each one of them.

Galvo said, "People of Namora, I present to you our Tavin, Valdena Filtraikas. Tebena."

The answering word filled the House. "Tebena." And then it was done.

Valda didn't know how long the feast lasted. The crowd filled the great meeting hall off the House and spilled out into the passages. Valda met face after face, bowing to countless dagira, greeting elegantly-dressed well-wishers. She ate and drank things, but didn't notice what they were or how they tasted. Fatigue lapped around her.

Tomorrow morning, she would meet with the Council again. That fact felt as hard and solid as a prayer stone in her mind. Along with it sat the question, no less urgent, of whether Ribas would join them as their future Tavo Balsa.

News about the zhinin with the dovne kenavnis had apparently spread. Valda knew she couldn't have expected the Council not to gossip about that, and she hadn't asked them not to. If Valda herself was the main point in the crowd, with lines of people radiating out from her, Ribas and Maryut and Gedrin formed another point, not much smaller.

Valda knew this must be hard for him: for all three of them. They hadn't asked or looked for such notoriety during what they had believed would be a short stay in the city. Valda knew, though, how kindly Ribas would deal with everyone who approached him. She didn't glance often in his direction, but she knew exactly how each person who spoke to him would respond to his warmth. She prayed he would see how well he fit here. She prayed he would understand that he should occupy the place that waited for him.

Slowly, slowly, the crowd began to thin. Servants moved around in the room, collecting empty plates and serving dishes. Outside the windows, the sky had long since turned dark.

Finally, when the only people left were knots of dagira deep in talk, and the room had quieted enough that Valda could hear the wind outside, Ribas came up to her. "Tavin," he said, "may I speak with you?"

As if she had wanted anything else. New energy flowed through her, lifting her out of her tiredness. "Of course."

They left the meeting hall. In the passage outside, she said, "Did Maryut and Gedrin leave already?"

"They did. The crowd was a little much. Marya was pretty tired."

"I understand. I'm sorry not to have seen them, though."

She couldn't add that she hoped she would see them again before they left Sostavi. That would make it sound as if they wouldn't be back any time soon. Too much seemed to hinge on these next few minutes.

She let them into the Council meeting room and tried not to think about how few hours she had until she would be back here, trying to decide what to do about Shurik's letter. The two lamps in their sconces by the door lit the room, but nighttime chill had settled on it.

They didn't sit down. Valda faced him, trying not to let herself feel nervous about what he would say. She saw no hint of a smile on his face or in the blue eyes.

Long ago, they had joked about how zhinin's robes would match his eyes, "my only good feature," he'd said. He'd said that was why he could never be promoted higher. Of course the real reason was that Lida's little Circle House didn't need a kunin or sventin. If only his love of home wouldn't blind him to how much good he could do here.

He said, "I talked to Marya and Gedrí about what you said. I have to admit, they didn't like it." Valda had more or less expected that. He added, "To be honest, Valda, I didn't like it either."

His voice held no annoyance or resentment. "I understand," she said.

"I know what an honor it is. I know no priest in his right mind should turn down a promotion like that." He did smile then. "And Sostavi is beautiful. It isn't that I couldn't stand to live here, or anything like that. But Lida is home."

"Yes. I know." If he was going to say no, she would hear it out and take it as she should.

"We came up with a compromise. I told them I would ask you what you thought."

Valda tamped down her hope. "A compromise? Please tell me."

"We understand that the biggest trouble is Shurik. I still don't see how I can help you there, but we agreed I couldn't help at all if I were in Lida. Here, we thought I might be able to do something, if there's anything to do."

Valda controlled her face. She must not let herself feel too glad yet.

"Marya saw why I wanted to try. She hated to hear what Shurik's doing. Gedrí wasn't so sure. He doesn't want me away from home."

Valda could understand that too. But surely, Gedrin could see that his brother could do more – *deserved* to do more – than take care of the endless daily round of villagers and their troubles. Ribas was far too good to spend the rest of his life there.

"Marya and I can't imagine leaving Lida for good." Valda saw a flicker of pain cross his face then. She would not see him hurt for anything, but if only he could realize Sostavi had merits too. "But," he said, "we thought, if you would let me, I could serve as your Tavo Balsa just for a while, until we find a way to resolve things with Lassar. I realize that's incredibly impertinent."

Impertinent? Yes. No other priest would have presented such an idea. So many Great House dagira would have snatched at the position and clung to it with both hands, and probably feet too. And she had no guarantees that they could find any way to resolve the situation with Lassar, or how long it might take, or what Shurik might do meanwhile.

Valda knew he understood all that as clearly as she did. "Certainly," she said. "I would be glad to have you."

He looked surprised at her quick agreement. "I'd need to go home for a little while first," he said. "I would also ask that we agree that as soon as possible, I would take my old rank and my old duties back."

He would want a demotion back to zhinin, whenever this was over, and the freedom to exile himself back to his village. To be sure, she had never known anyone else like him. But if he served on the Council, if he saw how respected and valued he could be here in the highest House of them all, couldn't he change his mind enough to stay for good?

She said, "Ribé, if you're willing to do this, you can set the terms. I've already told you how much I need you on this Council."

"Then I'm at your service, Tavin." Did she hear regret in the words? "I wish I thought I could be more use."

Valda reached out before she could decide not to. She took both of his hands in hers. "Your presence here will be plenty of use."

Her mind raced ahead. In the morning, then, he could join the Council again. At the meeting, she would make her "strongly worded recommendation" that the Council accept Ribas's promotion and his addition to their ranks as her Tavo Balsa. No one had to know, yet, about the position's temporary nature. Right after the meeting, she would perform the promotion ceremony herself. They would keep it brief and simple, the traditional questions and prayers only, without extra readings or the pageantry with the robes. Maryut and Gedrin would witness the ceremony, of course, and Valda could bring in Galvo and Lesvin as well to represent the senior dagira.

Ribas was watching her now. Memory rushed in: the day at the viduris when he had caught her looking at him in the new way, after everything had changed. She hadn't been sure what he would think if he knew how she imagined touching his face, his hair, running her fingers down the length of his tanned forearm. He hadn't needed his gift to lay her secrets bare.

Now she let go of his hands and stepped back. "Thank you, Ribé. Please thank Maryut and Gedrin for me too, for their understanding."

"I will." He went to the door, but stopped and turned around. "I've said this before, so forgive me for saying it again. We're very lucky to have you as our Tavin." Then he was gone.

16

BEREG

Bereg had never experienced this kind of pain. His knee had gone through agony to numbness while he lay beside the pool, but now, as the Vaia horse jolted under him, the fresh stabbing in the swollen joint made him sick to his stomach. He clamped his mouth tight shut to keep from moaning, or throwing up the little water he'd drunk, and kept his arms around the waist of the Vaia girl in front of him.

He had never thought he might get so close to a Vaia. Her white blouse smelled of dust and sweat. Strands of her long hair, pulled back and tied at the nape of her neck with a piece of white yarn, blew around him and tickled his face. It felt awkward to hold onto her, but if he loosened his grip at all, he would probably fall off the horse and break his neck.

Two days ago, he had walked out of the Lasska camp before dawn, with a flask of water, enough dried meat to last for a day or two, and his vindula. He hadn't actually planned to hunt. As far as he had planned anything, he had meant to get as far toward home as he could and then wait for Mesha to take him. He shouldn't be alive now, much less riding toward a Vaia camp.

He had told Silde Vasem – Tama Leben now – that he had been

trying to get home. Obviously he had known he would never make it. But when he had let her leave the Lasska detachment, he had made himself a traitor and forfeited his own life, and he knew the world had no place for him anymore. Even his family would want nothing to do with him. Ania and Nela would still love him, he didn't doubt that, but they couldn't keep ties with someone who defied the Impera. He would walk until he couldn't walk anymore, and then accept the punishment that was rightfully his.

He thought back now to the relief he'd felt when he abandoned the detachment's camp. Anything, even that, was better than concentrating on the motion of the horse and the agony in his leg. When he gathered up his few things and left in the dark, he'd realized how profoundly he didn't want to hunt Vaia or try to lead the group of young soldiers anymore. As he had told Tama, the young soldiers never had respected him much. It had come as a shock, once he was alone, to realize that he didn't care. No doubt they had gone on following their orders. They had probably chosen a new leader and decided not to worry about his old hide.

Alone, he'd welcomed the empty plains, the heat of the sun, the dust and distance. He had known he would never see the mountains in Thydia, much less the great northern forests, but he had the image of them in his mind to carry him along. He felt great peace. No more orders, no more struggle, only the long walk for as many days as his body could carry him, and then the endless darkness after. He had felt as light as a particle of dust, as if the wind could carry him away to the great horizon.

When some root or bramble caught at his foot and he went down with his knee twisted under him, the pain told him immediately that he shouldn't try to walk. He had dragged himself back up anyway and gone on. It didn't matter. It only meant the end would come sooner.

He had given way next to the little pond and closed his eyes, not expecting to open them again. When light came back, and pain, and the sight of Tama and the Vaia girl bending over him, he had wanted to shut it all out and go back to the darkness and peace.

Bereg longed for that peace now. Tama and the Vaia girl were dragging him west toward the Vaia camp, both apparently determined to keep Bereg alive. He didn't know why they should bother. He was old and tired; he might have mangled his knee so badly he would never use that leg again. The girl's dream had said he would help her people, but Bereg knew she must have been wrong. He hated what his people were doing to hers. He had told her so. But he, himself, could do nothing to help anyone.

Time went past. Bereg focused on the texture of the girl's blouse and the feel of her hair against his face to avoid fainting and losing his grip. After a while, his knee subsided into numbness again as his body decided it couldn't tolerate the pain anymore. His stomach, though, still seemed to know what was happening to the mangled joint. It jolted and turned over so often he thought he might never want to eat again.

The setting sun had turned the plains deep orange by the time Bereg heard Khari say, "There they are." Her Lasska sounded strange, heavily accented and halting. Bereg had been riding with his eyes shut, concentrating all his attention on staying conscious. He kept them closed as he felt the horse slow down underneath him, and still didn't open them when the motion stopped and he heard new voices around him. He didn't want to face whatever was here, as if ignoring it would keep it, for a little longer, from being real.

One of the voices was male, openly hostile, though Bereg couldn't understand the words. Where Lasska was sharp and distinct, the Vaia language sounded soft around the edges, different sounds running into each other. Bereg heard the girl in front of him snap something back at the hostile voice. Then he heard Tama, speaking Lasska. "He's hurt. We need to help him."

I don't want help. But Bereg found now that it cost a huge effort to open his eyes after all, as if his body had spent the ride gradually shutting down. When Khari dismounted from in front of him, it took all of Bereg's strength not to collapse against the horse's neck.

Tama came up. "Can you get down?"

The ground looked much too far away. In the deep gold sunset light, Bereg made out strange faces around the horse: four Vaia men. One of them, the youngest, looked familiar. Bereg recognized him as the one who had come to the Lasska camp.

Bereg knew he should probably fear them. They were strangers, enemies, and he was incapacitated, couldn't have held or used a weapon if someone had put it in his hand and clamped his fingers around it. As it was, he only wished he could get down in front of the men without needing help, like a child needing a step-stool. His tongue seemed to fill his mouth. When he tried to speak, no words came. Miserably, he shook his head, the only answer he could make to Tama's question.

One of the Vaia men muttered something. Bereg recognized the same hostile voice as before. Tama and another Vaia man, not the young one, got hold of Bereg's arms and half-lifted, half-pulled him from the saddle.

The bad knee gave way as soon as Bereg's feet touched the ground. He would have fallen, but Tama got her arm under his shoulders and held him up. Leaning on her, he managed to hobble the little distance toward a cook fire. Khari spread out a blanket on the ground and Tama lowered him onto it. Though he tried to sit up, his body refused, so he lay back and stared up at the sky.

Outside Bereg's line of sight, the angry Vaia was saying something. The man who had helped Bereg down from the horse had rolled up another blanket. He came over to Bereg, gently lifted his foot, and rested it on the roll of fabric.

Bereg lifted his head enough to see the man's face. He looked older than the Vaia who had come to the Lasska camp. Something about him suggested good sense and reliability. Bereg felt faintly encouraged, though he still wished Tama had left him by the pool.

The man held up a flask of water and Bereg drank gratefully. The water was warm and tasted faintly of leather, but he was too thirsty to care.

The girl, Khari, seemed to be arguing with the angry man. The man beside Bereg said something, not sharply but firmly, and the arguing stopped. Bereg wondered if this man was the tribe's chief. He managed to say, "Thank you."

The man answered in slightly accented but perfectly clear Lasska. "You are welcome. My name is Radavan. We will do all we can to help you."

Bereg wanted to tell him not to trouble himself, but Tama came over, holding a piece of cloth wrapped around something. She knelt next to Bereg. "We have to wrap this around your knee," she said. "It may not feel comfortable."

She worked quickly and efficiently, wrapping the cloth all the way around the swollen joint and tying it into place with two pieces of yarn, careful not to pull the yarn too tight. For a moment Bereg felt nothing. Then needles of ice seemed to drive themselves into his skin.

"Poultice of orena leaves and bark, and crushed mint," Tama said. "We have to get the swelling down. Khari's making you a tincture for pain."

Bereg gritted his teeth. Tama got up again and disappeared from his line of vision, but Radavan stayed where he was, kneeling next to the blanket. The man said, "You have already met my tribesman Rahul. The other two with us are Handan and Mandhani, our tribe's best hunters. Handan, I'm afraid, is not entirely pleased with your presence here."

So Handan was the argumentative one. Bereg felt sweat forming on his forehead from the ice around his knee, but he unclenched his teeth to make a civil answer. "I can understand that."

At least he could think a little more clearly than he had during the ride. He knew again that he ought to feel uneasy, even terrified, here in a camp of the Lasska's enemies, wounded and at their mercy. It seemed they meant him no harm, and besides, he was tired and aching and old. It didn't much matter what happened to him now.

Radavan said, "Part of our concern, you understand, is that we must reach the mountains as fast as we can. Khari is not sure how well you will be able to travel."

The man talked to Bereg like any person to another. Bereg found himself wondering why, exactly, Mesha would hate them the way Shurik had said. More importantly, he couldn't imagine sitting on a horse for however long it would take to reach the mountains.

"To be honest," he said, "I have no idea how your girl thinks I can help you. You would be better off without me."

Radavan studied him. Like the other Vaia Bereg had seen, he had strikingly brown skin, and eyes that looked as dark as coal. Bereg found that attentive look unsettling.

"Khari is not mine," he said finally. "Nor do we think of her as only a girl, though she is young. She is the sister of my wife, and she holds a particular and honorable place in the tribe."

Bereg heard that for the scolding it was. Radavan went on, "I agree with you. I do not see your place with us either, but I trust Khari's dreams."

Bereg still didn't understand the dream business. No one could foretell the future. And all else aside, he couldn't imagine how these people would manage to carry him at any speed all the way to the western mountains, probably another week's journey at least. Even if they could make a pallet or travois of some kind, he didn't know if he could stand them dragging him over the ground mile after mile. And once they got to the Senai, if they could, how would they get him to the pass? The Senai didn't have the altitude of the mountains north of Cheremay, but they were still formidable. Bereg had heard of boulder-strewn trails with sharp climbs and tight switchbacks.

Maybe the Vaia would get tired of trying to carry him and would leave him somewhere between here and Namora. That wouldn't be much different than if he'd found death by the pool, but somehow, the wish for darkness didn't feel as strong anymore. Unwelcome life reached out for him.

Khari came over and knelt next to Radavan. She held out a

pottery mug with something steaming in it. "You need to drink this, Bereg," she said, in her halting, accented Lasska. "It will not taste good. Can you hold the cup?"

Something about the simplicity of her using his first name touched him. "I think so."

Radavan helped him sit partway up. The liquid in the mug smelled strongly of mint, with something else mixed in, something that made his nostrils sting. When he sipped, the ferocious spice seemed to ignite his tongue.

He spluttered for breath. "What is this?"

"Pepper," Khari said. Her eyes, as dark as Radavan's, looked concerned. "You Lasska call it *vazhav*, I think."

Fire pepper. Yes. Bereg had never tasted it before. He'd always been sure he couldn't stand the heat. And it was supposed to help with his pain? Maybe the idea was that with his mouth on fire, he would forget the pain in his knee.

With Khari and Radavan both watching him, Bereg forced himself to finish the contents of the mug. He thought his head should have opened up to let the steam out. When he finished, Khari brought him plain water and a plate of some dried beef and a strange flat bread he had never seen. "Eat," she told him. "Eat and rest."

She and Radavan left him and went over to the other three Vaia, who sat a little distance away on the opposite side of the cooking fire. Bereg heard talk start up. It sounded reasonably peaceful.

Tama joined him with her own plate. She sat down cross-legged on the edge of his blanket. "I still want to know what kind of fool you are," she said. "Going off alone like that."

Bereg took a bite of the bread. It tasted good, flavored with anise. An hour ago, he hadn't thought he'd ever feel hungry again, but now his stomach demanded the food and he had to be careful not to stuff it all down and make himself sick. He heard himself say, with more spirit than he'd felt in a while, "I don't remember asking you to rescue me."

"So you would rather still be there? You probably wouldn't have died yet. Takes a while for thirst and starvation to finish you off, unless some kind of animal found you."

Bereg had never heard of large predators on the plains. In the forests, of course, you had the bears. Legend said that Impera Curin had realized the presence of the God Mesha when he had been alone and injured in the woods and a great bear had come on him and spared his life.

Bereg didn't feel like arguing. "No," he said, taking another bite of bread. "I don't especially want to die now." He sighed. "Not that I have any idea what life has left for me. Not home, I know that much."

Tama looked at him. Her face was expressionless in the fading light. "You don't know that," she said.

"We're traitors." He threw the word down, more sad than angry. "Traitors don't get forgiveness."

She sat quiet for a while, eating her meat. Then she said, "I used to think I would live and die as a soldier and a servant of the Impera. I hated it, always, but I couldn't see any other way. Now I know other things can happen." Her smile flashed out, startlingly bright. "If we want anything to change, we must do things differently."

Joining the Vaia had apparently given her hope. Not Bereg: he didn't have grievances of the kind she had, to make him hate the boundaries of Lasska life so much. "I only wanted to see my family again," he said.

"You might still do it, Bereg Orlon. Don't give up."

She had changed, he thought, changed so much even in the few days since he had last seen her. Her constant anger had redirected itself into energy. He could have told her what he'd told Radavan: he couldn't do anything to help the Vaia, he couldn't travel, he was an old man with nothing left to give. Instead he said, "Suppose we did manage to get through this. What would you do? Go back to Feyst?" Maybe she wanted to reclaim the place where she had been born, the same way she had reclaimed her name.

"No. There's nothing left for me there. I wouldn't want to see the village again."

"Tyi, then?"

"No. I want to find a place that belongs to me. A place I choose."

The mint-and-pepper drink did seem to help the pain. Bereg said, "Well, there's a lot to say for Thysidich."

She laughed, a simple sound of amusement. "I know you'll say a lot for it."

Suppose, Bereg thought, she could go there with him. Suppose they could go out on a fine, crisp winter morning and walk his favorite forest trails, with the snow underfoot and the warm scents of machia and pine in the air. Suppose, afterward, she could sit by his hearth with a mug of tea and a plate of Nela's cake, feasting herself on the warmth, and the richness of nuts and honey, and the chatter and laughter of Ania's children. She had never known any home like that. Suppose Bereg could give it to her.

He chewed the meat wearily. Might as well eat, keep himself alive for now. Who could tell what would happen next?

Tama finished her food. "You rest," she said. "Don't try to move around."

"I can't."

"Good."

She went over to the group of Vaia. Bereg lay alone, finishing his meat, looking up into the sky where the first stars had come out.

Bereg had a long, restless night on the blanket with his foot propped up. He couldn't turn over on his side. After a while, the pressure from the hard ground made his back ache. Before the camp went to sleep, Tama put on a fresh poultice and Khari gave him another dose of the pepper tincture, but neither helped to quiet his mind. He lay for a long time, staring up into the dark, trying to remember that the same stars hung over the cabin at home. For whatever good that did.

In the morning, Tama and the two Vaia hunters put together a travois. Apparently a lot of the Vaia discussion around the fire the night before had to do with how to move Bereg. No one had been able to come up with a better solution than this. The Vaia men went out early to find wood and brought back long heavy branches that they stripped with axes and tied together with rope. Tama lashed smaller branches across the main ones to make a rough kind of basket, which she lined with two blankets.

Watching them work, Bereg saw the resentment of the two Vaia hunters, especially the taller, stronger man: the one Radavan had called Handan. Most Vaia were small-built, but it seemed Handan and his brother Mandhani were tall and stocky for the race. Bereg saw clearly that neither of them, especially Handan, wanted to go to all this extra work to drag an old Lasska soldier along with them. He also saw that neither of them looked entirely happy to work with a Lasska woman, although Mandhani did seem cautiously friendly toward Tama. Tama had given the three extra vinduli she had taken from the detachment to Radavan, Handan, and Khari. Handan apparently shared his with his brother. The weapons, at least, got some appreciation.

Tama had given Lasska weapons to Vaia tribespeople and taught them how to use the vinduli. Bereg found he didn't feel as angry about that as he should. If no other Vaia knew how to use the weapons, it wouldn't make much difference that these three did. In fact, Bereg found, he didn't much care if they all learned somehow.

Autumn came late to the plains, but when it did, it came down fast. Dew lay thick on the grass this morning. The sun pushed feebly through a wall of cloud. Bereg knew that probably, in another few days or so, the rainy winter weather would set in.

When the group got ready to move, Tama and Radavan between them helped Bereg onto the travois and harnessed it to Tama's horse. Tama propped his foot up again and covered him with an extra blanket. When he told her not to fuss over him, she answered curtly that it was his own fault he had to go around half-naked – meaning his mostly ruined pants, because she'd had to cut the leg off – but she wouldn't see him catch his death of cold.

Bereg doubted he could catch cold after Khari had given him a third dose of tincture. When he asked how many more he would have to take, she looked at him gravely with those striking dark eyes. "As many as you need," she said.

Tama gave him his vindula to carry beside him on the travois, not that he thought he could do much good with it while he was jolting along over the ground. She had her own, and the three armed Vaia carried theirs across their saddles. The group set out before the sun had gotten well above the horizon.

The travois bumped and jounced over every stone and root, even on the reasonably flat and level ground. Every movement drove another needle of pain into Bereg's knee. When the group went through tall grass, he couldn't see anything but the dry crackling yellow and gold stems rising around him. He didn't like that temporary blindness any more than the pain, but he resolved that nothing would get any complaints out of him.

The group went steadily on through the morning. Then, as the sun climbed toward noon and the air tasted briefly of the summer that had gone, Bereg, facing backward in the travois, saw distant shapes coming up over the horizon behind them.

He didn't shout an alert at first. The shapes could be anything, or nothing: just tricks the light played over the flat distance. Bereg knew better than to trust his eyes. He fumbled for the vindula beside him and lifted it to look through the sights.

Soldiers. Bereg saw gray coats, horses, and what looked like a cart piled high with something. They were moving fast, headed directly toward him and the Vaia. Following them?

He still didn't shout. Instead, half-turning in the travois, he called, "Tama."

She turned around in the saddle. Bereg lifted his vindula to point toward the horizon. Already the shapes looked bigger. "Soldiers," he said.

She reined in. The travois jerked to a stop. The rest of the group stopped too. Bereg heard the two hunters muttering what sounded like questions.

In the saddle, Tama lifted her own vindula and peered through it. Then she turned to one of the hunters. "Mandhani." She passed the vindula to him. "What do you see?"

The hunter looked briefly through the weapon's sights, then lowered it and shaded his eyes to look out at the horizon. The shapes looked distinctly bigger now.

The Vaia said in halting Lasska, "Six or seven gray coats. Coming fast. Tracking us."

Bereg's heart sank. Tama said, "Tracking us? Are you sure?"

"Yes."

Bereg wondered how he could tell. It could be coincidence that the soldiers were on the same path, although the Vaia group had made its own trail, cutting across the open ground. He wondered if the soldiers could have joined up with his former company. Had they been sent to look for him? Did they know the party they were following had five Vaia in it? He remembered Lada Egem's eagerness. These soldiers might be after them for exactly that reason.

The other hunter, Handan, said something in rapid Vaia. Bereg heard Radavan answer something that sounded like a disagreement. He turned enough in the travois to see Tama. "What are they saying?"

She didn't know any more Vaia than he did. It was Khari who answered, riding up alongside the travois. Her face looked tight.

"Handan says we must get ready to fight, that there are enough of us and we have weapons. Radavan says he doubts we can face Lasska soldiers and he thinks we should try to outrun them." She paused, listening. "Now Handan is saying that we can't run fast enough because we are dragging you."

Then cut me loose and run. Bereg didn't say it, but he realized he did not want any of these people to pay the price of his life.

He tried to think. Handan had a point. This group could match six or seven Lasska soldiers in numbers at least. Bereg, Tama, and three of the Vaia had good weapons. That meant decent odds, at least on the surface, but the three Vaia didn't have much experience with the vinduli yet. Bereg himself was a good shot, but how much could he do flat on his back in this travois? Out of all of them, they could only count on Tama as a fighter. Even she wasn't fast enough to deal with six or seven well-armed enemies.

And this group couldn't run, not with the travois. Handan was right about that too. An easy solution, then, would be to cut Bereg loose and let the soldiers take him. Maybe they should do it.

Arguments were going on behind him in Vaia and Lasska both. Bereg looked up at Khari, the only silent one, holding her horse steady beside him.

"You should leave me," he said.

She shook her head. "You belong with us."

I don't. I am one of them. But that wasn't true anymore, was it. Everything had changed when he let Tama ride out of camp.

"You shouldn't try to fight them," he said. "You'll get cut to pieces."

She smiled, thought it looked strained, and lifted the vindula across her saddle. "Tama showed me how to use this," she said. "I think I could shoot once."

No. A new idea formed in Bereg's head. It took shape much too slowly, like ice crystallizing on the outside of a warm window. He tried to push it along faster.

Behind him he heard Tama say, "They are gaining on us. We can't afford to stand here and argue."

"Then if you will not fight, leave the old man and we run!" That was Handan, in heavily accented Lasska.

From beside Bereg, Khari spoke up, her voice strong and carrying. "We do not leave him. We need him with us."

Radavan answered something, but Bereg wasn't listening anymore. The idea in his head came together, clear and solid.

"Wait," he said. "I know what to do."

The company behind them had gotten close enough to see clearly without spyglasses or a hunter's vision. It was too late to get away, but Bereg would not watch the Vaia try to stand and fight.

Tama said, "What's your idea?"

The group gathered around the travois. Bereg explained quickly. They would wait to meet the soldiers. The Vaia must act as if they knew no Lasska and as if they had no idea how to use the vinduli they carried. Bereg knew it might be safer to ask them to give up the weapons for now, but if the plan went wrong, they should have at least a chance to defend themselves. He said he would tell the soldiers a lie they would probably believe. He didn't spell it out then and there, because he felt sure it would start time-wasting argument, but he did explain that they stood the best chance of succeeding if he knew no one in the group of soldiers coming, and if none of them had a rank equal to his and Tama's. He added that if all went well, he would also be able to get the Lasska cart.

"It's critical that you let me speak for all of us," he finished. He meant that for Tama too. "And Khari" – it was easiest to talk to and look at her – "you and Radavan and all of you must act as if you don't understand anything I'm saying. The soldiers must believe you are under my authority."

Rahul translated this, mostly for the two hunters. When he finished, another burst of argument broke out. Radavan motioned for quiet.

"I do not see another choice," he told Bereg. "We are trusting you with our lives."

Bereg knew that. "If it goes wrong, I'll fight with you." He knew what it would mean to have the blood of Lasska soldiers on his hands. He also knew that he had already gone so far that another act of treason couldn't matter.

The soldiers would be on them in a matter of minutes. Bereg said once more, "Remember. You must act as if you understand no Lass-ka." He meant that mainly for Handan, because he could imagine how the hunter would react to the lie Bereg was going to tell. "They have to believe what I tell them, or chances are, we're all lost."

Mesha guard us. Bereg didn't know what to think, anymore, about what the God wanted, but he offered that prayer in the privacy of his head. If his plan worked, no one had to die right now. That must count for something.

Soon enough, the company rode straight up to them. Bereg had an impression of heavy-built, strong horses raising a storm of dust. The strongest horse hauled a cart that creaked and rattled under a big load. From where Bereg lay in the travois, the mounted soldiers looked as if they were miles above him, as omnipotent as the God Himself. Bereg felt terrifyingly weak, like a beetle waiting for a boot to crush his life out.

But he did not recognize any of these faces, and all of them looked too young for Silde rank. Bereg scraped together the courage he had left and held it tight.

The soldiers reined in a short distance away. The column's leader, a man young enough to be Bereg's son, rode forward. Bereg saw the others unshipping their vinduli.

Bereg pushed himself up in the travois and snapped, "Halt, soldier!"

The young man pulled up, obviously confused. Bereg pressed the advantage. "State your rank and orders."

The other soldiers looked uncertain too. None of them, Bereg guessed, had expected this kind of welcome from an obviously injured old man, apparently at the mercy of if not the actual captive of a group of Vaia. The soldier said, "I am Captain Arteg Ivalon. My company is proceeding west to the border with Namora, to join another company there."

The Namoran border? Bereg knew his face must show no reaction. He wanted to know more about the group's orders. Captain Ivalon said, "Whom am I addressing?"

"Silde Bereg Orlon," Bereg said. "And that is Silde Fisa Vasem," he added, pointing toward Tama.

If by any chance the captain recognized their names, if he had met up with Bereg's company, trouble would start here and now. To

Bereg's relief, the captain saluted at once to the superior rank. He and his men looked more confused than ever.

"Silde Orlon, Silde Vasem, I ask your pardon," he said. "But..." He hesitated, showing his youth and inexperience. "Do you require our assistance?"

Now Bereg must lie. "Not at all, captain," he said. "These strenyi are our prisoners." He caught himself before he could say *Vaia*.

Not a sound came from Handan or anyone else. Captain Ivalon said, "But, forgive me, sir, I can't help noticing they are armed."

"They carry our weapons for us, but do not use them. Surely you know the strenyi don't understand sophisticated weaponry."

"Yes, silde."

Bereg could see the captain still had questions. He spun the rest of the lie, trusting in the long-ingrained Lasska obedience to superior officers.

"Silde Vasem and I were with a larger company that ran into a strenyi ambush. We had many casualties, but we won out and took these prisoners. As you see, we have one of the very valuable witch-women with us." He willed his hand not to tremble as he pointed at Khari. "We also have a near relation to a tribal chief." Khari had told him that Radavan was the brother of Pradesh, the man her tribe called Lodestone. "We anticipate great bounties for them," he said, "once we proceed with our orders and rejoin our forces to the west."

The captain looked convinced. Bereg had time to bless the Lasska habit of deference. Apparently it made sense to the young man that Bereg and Tama between them could keep five young, able-bodied Vaia prisoners subdued, even though Bereg obviously could neither walk nor ride, and the Vaia wore no ropes or chains. Apparently it also made sense that the "strenyi" wouldn't use the vinduli as clubs if nothing else. Everyone knew they weren't fighters, didn't they? And everyone knew that you believed what your superiors told you. Captain Ivalon said, "Do you wish us to ride with you, sir? Perhaps you need assistance with your wound?"

Bereg brushed off the second question. The first one gave him a chance to learn more. "Where are you headed, captain?"

"Northwest, sir. We are making for the southernmost pass through the Senai. Impera Shurik wishes to strengthen the border guard and establish more watchtowers, to make certain the strenyi cannot flee Lassar."

Captain Ivalon really was inexperienced. He should know better than to volunteer more information than asked for. He certainly shouldn't have discussed the next step of Shurik's campaign so openly. *Border guard,* Bereg thought. *Watchtowers.*

Lassar had always had a guard on the mountains, but the Senai themselves made a reasonably effective wall between Lassar and Namora. The Lasska generally wanted nothing to do with their western neighbors. Everyone knew the Namorans were an outlandish people who worshipped a Goddess, as if anyone could believe in such a thing, and held services in humble round houses rather than the kinds of temples a deity deserved. Furthermore, the Namorans were known to go out on the sea, which Impera Curin had expressly forbidden to his own people. Seafarers could not be trusted. On their own side of the border, the Namorans showed no interest in Lassar either. The two countries had stayed separate for generations.

Now Shurik was building a net on this side to be sure no Vaia could get through to possible safety. Bereg knew that his group wouldn't be able to use the closest pass, if they could get to the mountains at all.

He schooled himself to speak as if he approved of the captain's words. "We are going directly west," he said. "I will not ask you and your men to ride out of your way."

They would have to try to get across the mountains somewhere else. Bereg didn't know how they would do it. He said, "You can provide me with assistance, though, captain. I will requisition your cart."

The young man's face looked blank. He looked around at the

cart. "I...forgive me, Silde Orlon, but we are transporting materials to build a watchtower. I don't know if I can..."

Bereg pushed himself up again. "That is a direct order from a superior officer, captain. Unload your supplies and give me your cart at once."

Very faintly, on the edge of hearing, Bereg thought he heard someone stifle a laugh. Khari? The captain looked as if he wished he had never seen Bereg. "But, sir, I..."

"Captain Ivalon, you can see that I am wounded. Our orders are to proceed west with all speed. We cannot achieve any speed at all while I am trapped here. Now will you assist us, or will you stand against us?"

The words tasted sour in Bereg's mouth. At the same time, he felt a faint thrill of satisfaction at the young man's confusion.

The soldiers unloaded the cart, stacking its cargo of rough-hewn boards on the ground. Speaking as brusquely as he could and throwing in unnecessary gestures, as if they would not understand his words, Bereg ordered Khari and Rahul to unharness the travois and hitch Tama's horse to the cart instead. When they had done this, Tama moved the blankets over from the travois. She and Radavan between them hoisted Bereg up onto the cart bed. Bereg felt grateful for the thick wrapping around his knee, which might make the injury look less like an accident and more like a spear or arrow had gone through the leg.

He told the captain, "You can use the travois. It'll hold at least some of your load. You can build another one to haul the rest."

Ivalon looked resentful and his men sullen, but none of them dared to argue. Bereg said, "We must continue on. Mesha guard you, soldiers."

Ivalon saluted correctly. Bereg returned it, and then the cart was rolling underneath him, the Vaia group moving on and leaving the soldiers behind. From an increasing distance, Bereg could hear them arguing about how to haul the wood.

His group rode on in silence until the Lasska party disappeared behind them. Then Bereg heard Tama laughing, a clear, delighted sound, like a child surprised with a gift.

Khari rode up beside the cart and reached over the side to squeeze Bereg's hand. "Thank you."

Tama reined in. The group clustered around the cart. Rahul was laughing too. "I must tell you," he said, "I doubted that would work, but..."

Bereg didn't catch the rest. Handan, his eyes fierce, stared at him and said something loudly.

Khari smiled. "He says the old bear is cunning," she said. "He says all our enemies will know it."

Cunning? And *the old bear*, again. Well, old bears were cunning, it was true. They had to be. They had outsmarted many hunters and younger challengers.

After a short rest and some food and water, the group went on. Bereg lay in the blessed comfort of the cart and tried to feel pleased about what he had done.

Without touching a weapon, he had won out against this particular group of Lasska and inconvenienced them enough to slow down their progress west. Not one person had gotten hurt. The Vaia now thought he was worth something. He had made his own presence far less of a burden.

None of that changed the fact that the border guard would make it harder than ever to get across the mountains, if they could do it at all. And none of it changed the fact of his treason.

Mesha guard us. Old bears were not only cunning, but dangerous. Who had Bereg become?

17

KHARI

Khari doubted the old soldier would ever have the full use of his leg again, but once Bereg had tricked the other soldiers out of their cart, neither Handan nor anyone else complained again about "dragging" the "old and useless" Lasska with them. Khari helped Bereg all she could with the poultices and tincture. If Vatiri had been with them, Khari had no doubt the older woman could have done more.

The new respect Handan and the others had for Bereg and Tama made for easier travel. It helped to feel they were all working toward a common goal, and that Khari's pathdream had again led them well. Khari began to think they might actually reach the mountains.

She knew they would find more trouble once they got there. She had understood most of what Bereg and the Lasska captain had said to each other, and Rahul had translated all of it afterward. Shurik's border guard meant they wouldn't be able to cross into Namora at the closest pass. Khari didn't know what they would have to do to find another way. She didn't let herself think about how far out of their way they might have to go, or how hard it might be. They had to reach the mountains first.

The weather changed, autumn deepening quickly into winter, as it always did on the plains. One morning the sun didn't dry the heavy dew. The next morning, two days after the encounter with Captain Ivalon, they woke up to fog so thick it felt as if the clouds had come down out of the sky to nest on the grass. Droplets of water clung to skin, clothes, hair, and blankets. The damp wood on the cook fire smoked and didn't want to light. Khari knew the days of warm sun and quick breezes were over. From now on, they would have fog and mist, clouds and rain, with only short periods of clearing to let them catch their breath.

On that second day after they met Captain Ivalon's men, in the late afternoon after they set up camp, Handan came over to Khari where she sat mending a tear in one of Bereg's blankets. "We need more meat," he said. "Will you hunt with me?"

Khari's surprise almost made her run the needle into her thumb. She caught herself just in time. Vaia hunters didn't ask girls to go with them. Nobody expected Lamp-Carriers to hunt at all. Khari could use her throwing knife, fair enough, but she couldn't lift and aim her vindula fast enough to get any kind of decent shot at a moving target. She hadn't had time to practice since she and Tama had found Bereg. She would be more of a hindrance than anything else to a hunter like Handan, who had made himself an expert with his own vindula as fast as Khari had expected.

He might only want her vindula for Mandhani, but he didn't want to ask her straight out to lend it. He had been noticeably more polite to her since her last pathdream. She said, "Mandhani can have my Lasska weapon if he's going with you."

Handan frowned. He stood in front of her with his feet planted and his hands behind his back, as if somebody had called him over for a scolding. "I haven't asked my brother to hunt with me," he said. "I'm asking you."

A strange idea darted through Khari's mind. No, she decided; that wasn't possible. She didn't put the blanket down. "I would make it harder for you."

"You need practice with your weapon. We don't know what we'll find when we get to the mountains. We all need to be ready to fight."

He was right about that, but Khari couldn't help noticing he looked more than ever like a small boy caught in some mischief. In any case, he didn't seem willing to accept her no. She set the blanket aside and got to her feet. "All right, but I warn you, you'll need to be patient."

She got her vindula and the two of them left the camp on foot. Khari noticed curious glances from Tama and Mandhani. She and Handan doubled back toward a small creek they had crossed earlier in the day. The plains didn't have many great rivers, but narrow streams and creeks crisscrossed the land, and small springs and ponds dotted it. Enough water to support the Vaia tribes and the game they would count on during the winter months.

Near the creek, Handan chose a stand of shrubs as a screen and settled on the ground behind it, motioning Khari close to him. "Might get a deer," he said. "They'll come down to drink at evening."

Khari didn't need him to tell her that, as if she were a toddling child, but she let it pass. She lifted her vindula cautiously to her shoulder and practiced sighting along it. Undoubtedly Handan would get his shot in before she could. She didn't mind. She didn't trust herself to kill any game, and the noise of her missed shot would only frighten it off.

Handan said, "The two Lasska are useful. You did well, telling us to go back for them."

He had never given her a direct compliment before. Mist gathered in the air as it cooled, but his face stood out sharp and clear. The expression in his eyes made her earlier suspicion rush back in.

She didn't welcome it. Plenty of women in the tribe would have been glad for Handan's notice, but if she wanted a man, she wouldn't choose him. He was proud and touchy. If she turned him down, it could cause trouble.

"I didn't tell you what to do," she said. "The dream did."

"You stood by the dream when some of us didn't believe it."

He had believed it before anyone else. He had spoken up for her. Khari hoped he didn't intend to use that now to bargain with her.

He said, "The old bear is useful, but unhappy."

Khari welcomed the safer subject. "He misses his home."

It wasn't only homesickness, Khari knew. Shame troubled Bereg as much or more. The old soldier believed he shouldn't have gone against the laws of his ruler. Every day that he helped Khari and her people get closer to Namora, he felt he was committing another wrong.

Handan knew it too. "If a ruler makes a bad law," he said, "he isn't a fit ruler. Suppose Pradesh told us to ride out against another tribe that had never harmed us. We'd turn him out and have a new Lodestone."

He was right. Lodestones led the tribes, but they were not tyrants. Khari said, "The Lasska aren't like us."

Handan waved a hand as if brushing off a fly. "The Lasska say they have many dangerous fighting men, but look how easily the old bear fooled some of their fighters. If the Lasska were as strong as they say, they'd ride out against Shurik and take this bad ruler off his throne."

"Many Lasska agree with him." Khari thought of old Bakar saying that the Lasska had always wanted the Vaia gone from their country.

"Why should they care about us?" Handan said. "We don't harm them."

Khari didn't understand that either. "Their god doesn't like us," she said.

Handan shrugged. "We aren't Mesha's people. He shouldn't trouble himself with us at all."

Khari had no answer to that. For a while they watched the creek in silence. The sun slipped below the horizon and the sky faded to creamy, purple-tinged blue. Khari had trouble watching for movement on the creek banks. Her mind moved restlessly over the miles remaining before they reached the mountains. And when they did, if Shurik's guard was waiting for them, what would they do?

Handan touched her arm and pointed. Khari blinked. Two deer, vague shapes in the mist, had come down to the creek to drink. Both were does, with fine tapered heads and strong rounded bodies.

Handan whispered, "Take the shot."

Khari knew she would miss. She didn't want them to lose this chance. Handan whispered again, "Take the shot. You can do it."

Khari lifted her vindula reluctantly. She didn't completely trust its dangerous power, but she didn't want Handan to see her fail.

She sighted carefully, aiming for the lowered head of the closest deer. The vindula brought far-away things close, so close that Khari could see the doe's liquid eye and the flutter of her nostrils as she breathed. Khari didn't know if her shot would find its mark, but she sent a silent apology to the living creature whose life she would try to claim. *Forgive me.* All hunters asked forgiveness from the creatures they killed. *Thank you for feeding me with your life.*

She pulled the trigger. The vindula roared and kicked against her shoulder, but she pushed back against it with all her strength. The bullet flew straight to its mark.

The second deer flung its head up and disappeared in a fading drum of hooves. The one Khari had shot lay where she had fallen, her head in the creek and her body splayed on the bank.

Handan jumped to his feet. "Good."

It had been a clean shot. No time for the doe to feel pain; no need to follow a wounded animal until you could get close enough for the final thrust, the way Khari knew bow and spear hunters often did. She had always ached at the idea of the deer or bear trying to run, knowing its enemies were closing in behind it. The vindula killed quickly and mercifully.

Even so, as Khari stood over the doe's body, the sight of the mangled head turned her stomach. The bullet had gone in just above the animal's left eye, leaving behind blood and fragments of bone. The eye itself hung loose from the socket. The vindula felt warm in Khari's hands, like a living thing.

Handan had dragged the deer clear of the creek. Now he

crouched beside the body and looked up at her, his grin white in the dark. "Well done."

Khari tried to feel proud. She had gotten the meat they needed and proven she could use her weapon. The group had another decent shot with them. Against Shurik's border guard, they needed all the strength they had.

Handan stood up and slung the deer's body across his shoulders. On the way back to camp, Khari walked as far away from him as she could without getting separated from him in the thickening mist. She didn't want to see the doe's lolling head bumping against his chest, trailing its blood down his shirt.

On the flat plain, Khari could picture a border guard only too clearly. A long line of soldiers holding hands, like children playing fish-in-a-net, ready to catch anyone who tried to slip through. She knew they wouldn't actually line up like children in the game, but they would have plenty of warning of anyone creeping toward them across the flat, level ground. Khari pictured her tribe riding across the plains, a whole school of fish swimming straight into that waiting net.

When the Senai first came into view, Khari thought Shurik's soldiers would have no trouble catching her people there either. From a distance, the mountains reared up like the side of a bowl. They made a decent wall on their own. Each day, though, as Khari's group got closer to them, and the craggy peaks of the mountains stood out more clearly through the mist and drizzle, she saw more clearly how complex the land became.

The Senai didn't look like the mountain chain north of Cheremay. Khari had only seen those peaks once, when she was very small. They had seemed to reach straight up for the sky like a great bear rearing up against a tree, and they rose up out of the level land as if, long ago, the gods had made them by folding the earth like a piece of paper. Only a few passes cut through them. The Lasska military had built roads that climbed those slopes and crawled over the top and down the other side. The Vaia didn't use the Lasska roads, opting instead to take the weeks'-long journey around to the east or west.

The Senai were different. The land changed gradually over the days of travel. Grass and dust gave way to boulders and hummocks. They had to slow the horses and maneuver Bereg's cart around or over outcroppings of rock that could tear the wheels off. Sometimes they followed paths cut by deer and the wild goats that lived in this rough terrain. Sometimes they made their own trails, winding their way through land that quickly became foothills, the knees of the Senai slopes.

Khari had never traveled this far west before. Radavan had, once, but no one else in the group had any experience of this place. Handan was uneasy and Bereg, to Khari's surprise, was the most impatient of them all. He had begun to complain about staying in the cart. Once or twice, when they stopped for the night, he tried to hobble a little with the help of a thick stick. Even though his knee didn't look as swollen anymore, and he had managed to fit his spare pair of gray pants over it, it gave way if he tried to take any weight on the leg. When Khari and Tama ordered him to stay off his feet, he snapped that he didn't know if he could trick another captain and he wouldn't be the reason the group got captured. Khari knew he had as much to fear from capture as any of them. The closer they got to the mountains, the more he began to see soldiers behind every rock and stubby tree.

True, soldiers could find plenty of places here to wait in ambush, but Khari thought the bigger, heavier Lasska horses would have more trouble on this rough turf than the smaller, lighter Vaia mounts. And the Lasska themselves had never struck her as very graceful or agile people. Khari had the feeling they counted on their strength and their weapons, but couldn't dodge or run as easily as the Vaia could, or adapt themselves to the shapes of the land. Many Lasska lived out their lives in one place, a village or farm or in one of the great stone cities like Cheremay. They didn't know how to adjust to different surroundings.

Shurik wouldn't have an easy time guarding all of this. As they picked their way carefully toward the Senai's main slopes, Khari felt a light growing stronger inside her, despite the gray skies and chilly mist. They would have to find a way up those slopes, staying away from the known passes. That would cost them time and trouble. But somehow they would reach the top, and when they looked down from those gray boulders where patches of last year's dirty snow still hung on, they would see Namora.

The third day in the foothills, with the peaks closer but still far above, they had to leave the cart. Radavan said reluctantly that it was too conspicuous and clumsy and slowed them down too much. He and Tama had to help Bereg down from the back, though he tried to pull himself out. They helped him again onto the saddle of Tama's horse. Khari saw the pain cross his face as he bent his knee to fit his foot in the stirrup. Riding for days, for however long it took to get over the peak, would damage his knee more, but none of them could think of a better answer. Even the light-footed Vaia horses had trouble on some of the land they had to negotiate. Khari and the others, all except Bereg, walked more than they rode, leading the horses one careful step at a time.

As the peaks got nearer, Khari began to wish they could go faster. They had gotten so close to Namora, but their progress had slowed down so much that she began to feel like an ant laboring along, trying to climb a single stalk of grass. The light of certainty still filled her, but it crackled around the edges like lightning on the days when it was too hot and the rain wouldn't come.

All of them braced for trouble. Bereg and Tama agreed that if or when they met more soldiers, they would first try a trick like the one that had worked on Captain Ivalon. If the Lasska thought that Bereg and Tama were escorting five Vaia prisoners to some other company, they might let the group go on its way. Of course, now they would have a much harder time convincing anyone that the party was following orders. They were too obviously heading toward Namora. By making their own path instead of using roads, they showed too clearly that they wanted to avoid other soldiers.

When they first got into the foothills, Bereg had briefly raised the idea of trying the roads and hoping they could get away with the lie long enough. They might have to actually bind the Vaia, he said, to make it look convincing. Tama pointed out that it got likelier all the time that other soldiers would recognize hers and Bereg's names, now that Ivalon and his men had met them. Plus, people might know by now that both of them had walked away from their original detachment. Their young soldiers could have met other detachments. The lie might not hold up very long. Suppose it collapsed on a main road bristling with soldiers? Finally, Tama said, if they somehow did make it to the nearest pass, how could they explain wanting to go through it with a group of Vaia: the very people Shurik said could not leave Lassar?

So they kept to the original plan. On the fourth day, trouble found them, on the skirts of the Senai's main slopes.

They knew they were some distance south of the main pass, which Radavan said cut through the mountains into central-eastern Namora. Khari looked up at the slopes above them and wondered how they would ever carve a trail to the top. From a distance, the Senai looked like green swells dotted here and there with gray patches of rock and snow. Up against them, you saw the messes of boulders, sharp outcroppings, spreads of gravel, and here and there a sheer drop.

The rare, thin morning sun had burned off some of the mist. Khari wished she and the others could travel like the wild goats, who bounded away over the rocks as if the earth didn't pull on them at all. As it was, she led her horse carefully up the slope behind Radavan, who had found one of the goats' narrow trails to use as a guide. Mandhani had the best eyes for distance, but Radavan was the most skilled at tracing a path. Rahul and the two hunters came behind

Khari, single file. Bereg rode behind them and Tama came up at the end of the column.

Rocks littered the narrow path, some no bigger than a fist, others the size of a deer's skull. The trail itself wasn't much more than a few scratches in the dirt, where you could see dirt at all under the rocks and through the yellowing grass. Khari knew it took all of Radavan's skill to keep them moving along it. She couldn't imagine a group of heavy, clumsy Lasska soldiers doing the same.

She had that comforting thought a moment before a vindula roared out, shattering the morning stillness. A bullet smacked into the trail no more than a couple of handsbreadths away from her feet. Her horse reared, neighing, almost jerking the lead rope out of her hands. Khari hung on desperately.

Noise and panic swirled around her. Radavan's horse had tried to plunge off the trail into the underbrush. Radavan was gripping the lead rope and shouting at the animal to stop. Khari heard Handan yell behind her, "Soldiers! They're on us!" A clatter of hooves on rock told her another horse was trying to bolt. Then she heard Bereg's voice, loud and clear.

"Stop!"

The Lasska word cut through the terror. Khari's horse, as if it had understood the command too, stopped trying to pull away and stood still, trembling. Khari heard Bereg call out, "State your name and rank, soldier!"

Radavan, still holding his horse's lead rope, backed along the trail until he stood beside Khari. "My fault," he whispered, pointing. "I didn't see."

At first, Khari didn't see either. Then the watchtower, only a few boards for walls and some scrub branches for a roof, seemed to appear out of the side of the slope to the west, no more than a bowshot away. Now that she saw the structure, she saw the soldiers too. Four of them.

Khari had to give Shurik's men credit. They had camouflaged the structure so well you could almost touch it before you knew it was there. They had known that even this tiny trail, barely there, could make a path over the mountains for desperate travelers, and they had known that anyone following the trail would have to watch their own steps too closely to have their eyes everywhere.

Khari saw how much of a net Shurik had actually built. She willed herself to swallow her fear, stand still, and wait for whatever happened next. She knew better than to reach for the vindula tied with her bedroll on her horse's back, but she felt the way she thought a deer must when it caught the hunter's scent.

Bereg would try the lie now. Khari forced herself to listen. The soldier he had hailed called back, "I am Silde Varig Alyem."

Silde. Khari knew that was the same rank as Bereg and Tama. That meant trouble: Bereg couldn't rely on a subordinate officer believing him or obeying orders.

Radavan knew it too. Khari saw him reaching, very slowly, toward the vindula in his own bedroll. She wanted to stop him, but at the same time her mind raced forward, thinking of what would happen if the lie failed. Unless more soldiers were hiding somewhere, Khari and the others outnumbered the Lasska. They might have a chance.

The soldier Alyem called, "Who are you?"

Bereg answered, "Silde Bereg Orlon." Without looking around, Khari knew he would point at Tama as before. "This is Silde Fisa Vasem."

Khari felt at once that something was wrong. Time seemed to slow down. The air around her felt tight and thick.

Then Alyem called back, "Bereg Orlon. You stand accused of abandoning your detachment."

He said something else, but Khari didn't catch it. So the other soldiers had found out what Bereg had done. The lie wasn't going to work. The knowledge formed in her head with the sharp chill of ice.

When the soldier stopped speaking, everything seemed to stand still. Then motion and noise exploded.

Handan shouted in Vaia, "You won't take him!" Beside Khari,

Radavan snatched for his vindula. There was a roar as one vindula went off, on the trail, and then another as an answering shot came from the watchtower.

Horses screamed and plunged. Khari grabbed her own vindula and dropped her horse's lead rope. The animal clattered away over the rocks. Khari threw herself to the ground with her weapon in her hands.

Time seemed to slow down again. Sharp edges of stones pressed against her skin. She heard her own frantic heartbeat in her ears and felt the sharp rasp of her breath, but everything around her seemed sharper and clearer. She could see the four Lasska in their gray coats. One of them had fallen, sprawled on the ground by the watchtower. Whoever had shot from this side had gotten their mark.

We must kill them. Khari knew that if any of those soldiers got away, the news about Bereg and Tama and the Vaia with them would spread. This group of Lasska had found them by accident, but other searchers could come after them. Hunters on the trail.

Another vindula roared out to her left. Khari saw another soldier fall, clutching his leg. Handan, she thought. Beside her, Radavan lifted his weapon. When the shot came, Khari knew at once it had gone wide. She saw it bite into the side of the watchtower, harmless.

But now she saw something else. The first soldier, Alyem, lifted his weapon, aiming carefully at something well above the ground. Khari remembered that Bereg could not get down from his horse without help.

She sprang to her feet. In the length of time it took to catch her breath, she took in the rest of her company: Tama with her vindula on her shoulder; Rahul gripping a spear; Handan and Mandhani side by side, Handan with his Lasska weapon and Mandhani with his bow; two of the Vaia horses still standing in the trail; and Bereg, on the stalwart Lasska horse that apparently hadn't moved a muscle, lifting his own vindula, taking aim at Alyem...

Deep within herself, Khari felt what it would mean to Bereg to have to kill another soldier. It tore at her like a bullet passing through her body.

No.

She lifted her own weapon. Standing straight and firm, her feet planted on the dirt, she sighted on Alyem. His head through the sights looked as clear and sharp as the deer's had. She had never thought she would have to kill a man.

The trigger felt cold and hard under her finger. She drew it back. In that moment, something bit into her side. Pain scorched her ribs, but she held steady and fired.

Through the sights, she saw the bullet find Alyem. She saw him fall. Then the pain rolled over her in a burning wave. Her legs gave way.

She felt rocks pressing against her spine, against the back of her head. She felt the vindula fall from hands that could no longer grip. Then shadows swam across the sky.

When Khari opened her eyes, at first she still saw only darkness. She was lying on her back, with something soft under her head. Then she made out distant pricks of stars and light from what seemed to be a fire. She could smell the wood. With every breath she took, a knife drove into her side. Lines of fiery pain radiated through her chest and back.

Someone bent down next to her. "Khari. Can you hear me?"

Khari tried to turn her head. Her neck felt stiff. The dim shape crouching beside her, silhouetted in red-orange firelight, resolved into Tama. With the light behind her, Khari couldn't see the woman's face.

"I hear you," Khari whispered. Her tongue seemed to fill her whole mouth.

Tama touched her shoulder. "The bullet hit you in the ribs. We haven't had time to stop. We had to get as far from that tower as we could."

Tower. Khari remembered the four Lasska. She remembered pulling the trigger. "Did we get them all?"

Tama nodded. "We had to keep going in case others came. Bereg says you were the one who shot the silde."

"I didn't want him to have to," Khari whispered.

"I know." Tama touched Khari's shoulder again. "You're a good shot."

Khari wanted to ask if anyone else had gotten hurt. She couldn't make her mouth shape the words. Tama said, "I have to get the bullet out. It won't be easy."

Khari tried to nod. Tama's shape moved away. Khari heard distant talking, and then Tama was beside her again, with two others. Khari recognized Handan and Rahul. "I need you to drink this." Tama bent down and held a cup to Khari's lips.

Khari sipped the hot liquid. It tasted of musky orena and fiery pepper. Tama said, "I'm not as good at tinctures as you are. I hope this will help."

She was going to take the bullet out. Khari knew, distantly, what that would mean. For a moment she wished Vatiri was there, but she didn't have strength to feel afraid.

"You've lost a lot of blood," Tama said. "But I think you'll be all right if we can clean out the wound and get it bandaged."

She didn't sound certain. Khari tried to nod again. Her body felt as heavy as a fallen tree. She wondered what had happened to the horses, if Tama and the others had managed to find the ones that had run. She wondered who had carried her here, to wherever they were, and she wondered where that was, how far they had gotten since the fight. She couldn't shape the words to ask anything.

Handan and Rahul knelt beside her now too, Handan on her left and Rahul on her right. Tama held a small sharp knife. Its blade glowed red. Khari knew she must have held it in the fire. Tama said to the men, "You need to hold her tight."

In case Khari tried to fight. Khari didn't think she had the strength to move even a fingertip. Strong hands pinned her wrists; knees pressed her legs against the ground.

Tama cut into her side. Khari felt the knife, heard it sizzle, smelled her own flesh burning.

Khari screamed and thought her throat would rip in two. A tiny corner of her mind told her not to struggle, she must be brave, but oh, she could not be brave now. Her soul would fly out of her body if this pain didn't stop.

She heard Handan swearing and Rahul chanting something that sounded like a prayer. She heard Tama saying "I'm sorry." The words barely reached her. She dragged her strength together, straining against the hands holding her, fighting to get away.

There was no escape. The agony wrapped around her like a suffocating sheet. Then somehow, blessedly, it faded.

Maybe the Moon Woman had decided to take her. Khari couldn't feel anything anymore: not the knife, not the hands holding her down, not the hard ground underneath her. The shapes of the people near her faded too. Only the dark stayed, closing around her again.

If you are calling me, Moon Woman, I will come. Khari didn't know if she thought the prayer or tried to say it out loud. She wished she could have seen Vatiri again.

"We can't move her."

"We have to. We can't stay here. Soldiers could come."

Khari heard the voices, but they came from a long way away. She seemed to float alone in an endless dark sky.

"She can't lose any more blood. She'll die."

"What good would it do to get to Namora without her?"

Khari couldn't tell if time went past or not. Once, she thought she felt someone lift her, but she couldn't see anything but darkness. She couldn't tell whether she opened her eyes or not. There was pain, or maybe an echo of pain, something she remembered or dreamed.

More time passed. She thought someone held her; someone's strong arm wrapped around her waist, someone's body supported her, but she couldn't see anyone. She had a faint sense of movement, but the darkness around her stayed even and constant.

"She killed him so I wouldn't have to."

"Yes."

"A soldier all my life and I've never killed a man. She's only a girl."

"Yes."

More darkness. Khari didn't know if she slept or woke, if she stayed in one place or if the movement she thought she felt, the darkness slipping past like a stream on either side of her, was real. Waking or sleeping, she dreamed.

The doe lowered her tapered, delicate head to drink from the stream. The weapon roared like a beast and the doe fell. Her blood ran into the water.

After more time Khari couldn't measure, the pain crept closer to her, a hunting beast in the dark. It drove into her like a hot knife. The darkness began to burn.

But in a different twilight, the doe didn't die. The arrow or the spear hit her in the haunches, in the side, in the neck. The doe ran, with the hunters following.

The pain made a haze around her. Haze like the smoke around a cook fire. Flames, orange and red, licked up into the dark. Someone was there, she thought: someone held her, someone's hand rested on her forehead...but she could not be sure. She couldn't tell where her own body began and ended.

The doe ran, with the hunters following. The arrow fell away, or the spear, but the blood ran from the wound. A seed of pain sprouted and grew.

Someone was saying something. Khari tried to hear.

"Mesha walk with us. Mesha guard us."

The doe ran. The smell of the hunters filled the air, and they were closing in, and the doe felt so heavy, so tired. Every motion hurt beyond bearing.

Now, out of the trees, or out of the grass, or out of the air, another shape came. Huge, with teeth and claws.

"Mesha protect this girl. You must save her if I can't."

The hunters closed in behind the doe. Before her, the great bear, dangerous and unimaginably vast: the enemy. The doe knew the bear would tear her life out with a single sweep of its paw. It wanted her blood. It wanted her dead on the ground before it.

The darkness began to give way. Khari thought she saw flames, real ones, on the edge of vision. She thought she felt hard ground underneath her body.

Someone held her. Someone lay beside her with an arm across her chest.

The doe fought for life, running. All her enemies closed in around her. With her last desperate breath, she flung her head up…

"No!"

The shout was her own. The voice was her own. Khari felt the scrape of it in her throat. The darkness lifted, and she saw the fire, and the smoke, and the face so near hers.

"Khari." The arm held her tight. Tears streaked the face silhouetted in the firelight. "Khari, child, it's me. It's Tama."

Tama. Khari stared up at her.

The great bear sprang forward. The doe watched, with the last of her strength, as the bear bore down on the hunters. Its huge paws scattered and crushed her enemies.

The doe collapsed, but the bear lifted her. It lent her its strength and gave her its huge bulk as a shield.

Tama said, "Khari. Do you know me?"

Mesha. The great bear.

He is not my enemy…

Khari tasted the grief in Tama's voice. In the firelight, the Lasska face could almost have been Vatiri's.

Yes, I know you.

Mother.

The words wouldn't come. The dark drifted back in, carrying Khari away.

~

In a clearing in the woods, an old bear and a young doe.

"Are you sure?"

"I can't do anything but sit in this saddle. I'm no damned use, but I hope I can hold up someone as small as she is."

"Then we'll ride ahead. If you need help, call."

The doe's wound had almost taken her life. Now she opened her eyes and saw sunlight filtering through the leaves.

The old bear sat beside her. His scarred, graying muzzle moved back and forth as he tested the air for danger. The doe knew there was none. She knew, too, not to fear him, nor his kind.

Mesha...

Khari felt movement underneath her. She was sitting upright with someone supporting her, someone's body like a wall behind her and an arm holding her securely. Pain made a distant fog around her, but not so heavy or so thick that she couldn't open her eyes.

Sunlight. When had she last seen it? The shapes of trees: spiky, dark green conifers; a canopy of orenas with orange leaves. Rocks and yellowed grass. A narrow dirt trail.

The movement under her was a horse. Khari saw the mane and neck and dark ears, and then took in the elderly, work-roughened hand in front of her, gripping brown leather reins. Only one hand, because the rider's other arm held Khari around the waist.

She knew who it was. "Bereg."

The hand jerked on the reins. The horse stopped. Khari pulled herself straighter in the saddle, wincing as her side ached.

Bereg's voice came from just behind her. "Khari. Child. Mesha guard us."

Khari heard joy and disbelief and the beginning of tears in his voice. She tried to turn to see his face, but her side shouted a protest.

The horse stood stock-still on the trail as Bereg dropped the reins. "Khari." For a moment she felt him shifting in the saddle, and then, "Damn this wretched knee. Child. Can you look at me? Mesha guard us, are you better?"

She turned her head as far as she could. He held her now with both arms around her, as if he couldn't let go.

He leaned forward to peer into her face. She could just see his storm-gray eyes. Her tongue felt like a thick slab, and her voice had cobwebs on it, but she said, "Yes. I'm better."

He gave a shout. "Tama! Radavan!"

A clatter of hooves behind them announced another rider. Dust rose on the trail in front of them and two more horses came into view. Khari realized what she hadn't before: the trail was narrow enough, but the ground here looked nearly level. The two horses coming toward her and Bereg could run side by side.

Tama's voice reached her. "What is it? Is she..."

Khari remembered the night by the fire. *Khari. Do you know me?* She found enough voice to call, "I'm all right, Tama."

Then they were there. Tama and Radavan; Handan and Rahul; Mandhani, who had kept a rear guard at the back of the column. They clustered around Bereg and Khari, all of them wanting to see her, wanting proof that she had come back to them.

Her side still hurt. She tried not to show how much, at least not while Tama watched her with tears standing in her eyes. Khari had never thought of the Lasska woman crying. Handan said gruffly that he'd known she would pull through, and Mandhani added that otherwise they wouldn't have bothered dragging her along day after day, trading her from one saddle to another like an extra bedroll. Khari kept herself from laughing because she knew how much it would hurt. Rahul gave her a long wordless look that sent the blood into her face.

Radavan came close and put his hand on her hair. "I can't tell you how glad I am," he said. "Do you know what your sister would have done to me if I had lost you?"

Dahila. Khari's eyes stung. She saw her sister's swollen body and wondered if the baby had been born yet, if Dahila wrapped the newborn every day against the journey over the plains, while she prayed that her family would come back together one day so that Radavan could hold his youngest child.

Tama passed Khari a water skin. "Drink." Her voice sounded as hard and curt as Khari had ever heard it.

Khari swallowed the dusty-tasting water gratefully. Bereg still held her close. She remembered shooting the silde: killing a man. No Vaia did such a thing without the greatest need. Khari would pray for the Moon Woman's and the Sun God's forgiveness, but she could not regret having done it for the old bear's sake.

She said, "Where are we?"

Tama and Radavan glanced at each other. Tama asked Khari, "Can you ride with me, do you think?"

Khari could. Radavan dismounted and lifted her down from Bereg's saddle. To her shame, Khari couldn't get her legs to hold her up, but with his and Tama's help, she re-mounted in front of the Lasska. It hurt to move, but not as much as it might have. Radavan explained, "Tama and I were riding ahead to see what was coming. You should see it too."

Tama held her as close as Bereg had. Khari thought about saying she could sit up well enough on her own, but she wasn't certain she could, and in any case, she remembered Tama's face in the firelight. The face of a woman who had lost her own family, who had never had another to help her heal.

Mother.

The horses went back along the level trail. Khari saw only trees and grass and the gray stone that made up so much of the Senai. Then they rounded a curve and the land fell away in front of them.

The trail went on, edging diagonally down the face of the mountain, but down below, the land stretched out in green and gold. Khari saw dark forests, and spreads of golden fields, and a blue disk that must be a pond, sparkling in the rare late-autumn sunlight. She even made out a cluster of houses. A village.

"Namora." She whispered the word. If she said it aloud, this beautiful place might disappear.

Tama said, "We made it."

Khari turned her head enough to see the woman. She herself was crying, she couldn't help it, but Tama was crying too, smiling through the tears like sunlight breaking through clouds.

They still had to get down onto the flatland. Once they did, they had to find the man from Khari's first pathdream. With Lassar and Shurik and his soldiers safely behind them, Khari felt as if they could simply lift off the mountain's face and float down into those fields below.

"We made it," she answered. Tama leaned forward. Khari felt a brief, gentle kiss on her forehead.

18

RIBAS

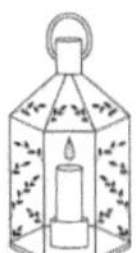

The morning after Valda's Installation, Ribas joined the Council meeting again. He hadn't slept much the night before. Exhaustion fogged his mind. Underneath it, a slow current of anger swirled.

He had let himself hope Valda would turn down the compromise he and Maryut and Gedrin had come up with. He'd tried to believe she would need a Tavo Balsa who could stay in Sostavi for good. When she told him he could hold the position on his own terms, he had hated having to go back to the House of the Zhinine and tell his family he had to do it.

Now he hated being here. The lifelong habit of self-control let him keep his face and voice calm as he sat at the table and listened to the people who would soon be his colleagues in fact, not only under the broader heading of dagira. Valda had said the sventine could argue about whether or not the sun came up in the morning. Today he saw that in full force.

"I still say we cannot consider doing anything that will bring Shurik's anger down on us," one of the Council was saying now. Ribas hadn't gotten his name yet. He was one of the oldest members, thick-bodied and white-haired, in an elaborately embroidered white robe. "I don't believe we can afford not to give him the assurance he wants."

Ribas hadn't worn his own robes to this meeting. He knew how plain and countrified he looked. He preferred that to the pompous, oily look of the sventine who had dressed up, preening over their fine robes, worrying about the safety of their own skins as of the highest importance in facing the threat from Shurik.

Valda sat at the head of the table. Today she wore the ceremonial brown robes of the Tavin. Her face looked pale but calm. She hadn't given Ribas any particular attention when he had come in, but he knew what would happen later in this meeting, and how much it would mean to her.

Another, younger Council member said, "What would you suggest, then? We should write and tell Shurik we will do what he wants, turn a blind eye to whatever he decides to do to his people?"

The first speaker said, "I don't see how we can do otherwise."

The anger pulsed harder against Ribas's temples. Another sventin said, "Colleagues, how much does it matter what we tell Shurik? We can tell him we will cooperate, but we might be able to do something different."

"What could we do?" That was young Sventin Lesvin, who had argued with Ribas yesterday. "All of us know the size of the military force Shurik has at his disposal. Surely we aren't willing to risk him unleashing it on us because we try to save people who are no concern of ours. And they *are* no concern of ours." The young man threw the words down as if daring anyone to deny it. "They are Shurik's subjects. I still believe we must stay out of his way and let him do as he sees fit."

A babble of talk broke out. None of it sounded any different from anything Ribas had heard the day before. No doubt the Council could circle around and around an argument, not deciding, not finding a way forward.

The anger battered at Ribas's temples. He didn't want to be here, didn't want to be in this place with these people. Home seemed much too far away.

"Sventine," he snapped.

Yesterday he had seen how, whether they wanted to or not, the Council listened to what he had to say. They gave the priest with the dovne kenavnis at least grudging respect. Valda seemed to think they also respected him for the work he did in Lida, for the kind of priest he was, although he didn't know whether to believe that or not.

Well, let them see right now what kind of priest he was. Let them see what they would have, if Valda had her way, as their Tavo Balsa.

The talk had stopped. All the faces turned to him. Ribas took a breath and gripped his self-control tighter.

"We've discussed what Shurik wants and whether or not we should give it to him. Have we stopped to consider what the Goddess wants?"

Sventin Lesvin looked angry, Sventin Galvo smoothly polite, other faces confused or stubborn or questioning. Ribas's eyes went to Valda. Her expression didn't change at all, but he had the feeling that he was saying exactly what she wanted to hear. He said, "Make no mistake, Shurik intends to kill the Pala Vaia. He intends to exterminate that part of his own population." It took an effort not to let his hands clench. "If we stand back and let him do it, have we asked ourselves what that makes us? Have we asked ourselves whether it makes us the people the Goddess calls us to be?"

He wished he couldn't feel Valda's profound gladness, or the way her heart reached out to him the same way she had reached out to take his hands last night. Now she spoke into the silence his words left behind. "The zhinin makes an excellent point. We must also consider what the Goddess expects of Her servants."

"But I don't see what She *can* expect of us!" Sventin Lesvin again. This time the words cracked at the edges. "How can She ask us to stand up to the greatest military power in the world? Would She have Shurik's army invade this country and destroy it?"

That got murmurs of agreement from around the table. The

young sventin's face looked pale, his green eyes feverishly bright. "Zhinin." He faced Ribas directly. "The Goddess calls on Her people to look after *each other*. The Pala Vaia are not Namora's people. They are not of us. They don't belong to Her. Why would She ask us to risk ourselves, risk this land She loved, to try to help strangers?"

Ribas's anger ebbed away in the face of the sventin's too-obvious terror. *Imagine if he were our Tavin.* He thought of Shurik again. They could talk about dangers and demands and military forces, but Ribas found himself remembering that the Impera was another very young man in a position of power. A very young man who had recently lost his father.

Ribas answered Lesvin quietly. "The Pala Vaia aren't Namorans, it's true. But where do we draw the line that says which people deserve to live, and which don't? Would the Goddess want us to make that choice?"

More murmuring. Lesvin held Ribas's eyes briefly and then looked away. Ribas didn't need to look into his mind to feel his shame.

Another sventin spoke. "Zhinin Ribas, I agree with everything you say. Without question, yours is the most right-minded argument we've heard, and the most faithful to the character of the Goddess as we understand Her. But I still cannot see how we might help these unfortunate people. How could we begin to stop Shurik from carrying out his intentions, much less protect ourselves from his retribution?"

Valda spoke before Ribas could say anything. "Council, I would like to make a proposal to you."

Ribas knew what was coming. He tried to brace himself to accept it.

"As you all know," she said, "the Tavin must choose a Tavo Balsa. This person must serve as a trusted advisor, a leader within this Council and a fit interpreter of the wishes of the Goddess. In the difficult times we face now, the Council, and the Tavin, would be fortunate to have a Tavo Balsa whose skills extend beyond those normally found even among the elite dagira."

Ribas felt the eyes on him again. He kept his own on the table in front of him. No doubt most of the Council had already guessed what she was about to say.

"As you've all heard," she said, "Zhinin Ribas has rare, even extraordinary qualifications. We noted yesterday that he has the only working knowledge of the Lasska people and culture we can claim. He has the dovne kenavnis – an ability which," she went on, over the muttering that immediately started up, "has limitations, but none-theless gives him unparalleled insight into the minds of others. Also, as Sventin Rano noted just now, he has shown himself to be a faith-ful, thoughtful, and wise servant of the Goddess." Ribas heard her warm approval. "I submit that we could not ask for better help in the times ahead. Therefore I propose that this Council assent to Zhinin Ribas's immediate promotion to the rank of sventin and his installa-tion as my Tavo Balsa."

Ribas didn't raise his head when she finished. The Council could refuse, argue her down. Who had ever promoted a village zhinin to that too-high post?

Sventin Galvo spoke first. "By all means, Tavin. My colleague from Lida is the ideal candidate for the position. I will be delighted to have him join us."

Ribas looked up then to see the sventin watching him. No doubt Galvo wanted everyone to notice him supporting the Tavin's ideas. That could only help him politically, and Galvo also had reason not to want the Tavo Balsa position for himself. But Ribas didn't under-stand why Galvo had told him so much about Silvas, and he didn't understand the look on the sventin's face now. Galvo needed, or wanted, something that had nothing to do with the Council or Lassar. Ribas didn't know what it could be. He didn't want to find out.

Some of the other Council members argued against Ribas's promotion, but they didn't oppose as strongly as Ribas had thought they might. The idea of his gift had dug into all their minds. No matter what anyone said about *limitations,* they probably couldn't help hoping that the gift would give them some extraordinary and unlooked-for solution to this impossible problem. Sventin Lesvin held out longer than the others, but the rest of the Council overruled him soon enough. A unanimous vote approved Valda's proposal.

"Very well," Valda said. "I will perform the zhinin's promotion ceremony myself this afternoon. Thank you, colleagues."

She didn't bother to hide her satisfaction. Ribas wished, for her sake and his own, that he could share it.

A few hours later, Ribas and his wife and brother went back to the Great House for the ceremony that would make him a sventin.

Maryut and Gedrin had taken the news about the vote as well as they could. Gedrin had said, "If they have to have you, we can't do anything about it." Maryut had tried to hide her tears. Before they left their chambers for this ceremony, she had done her best to smile, and she had told him she was proud of him. "Not that you need me to say it, I hope." He had put his arms around her and held her until Gedrin said they shouldn't keep the Tavin waiting.

Now Valda met them at the Great House with Galvo and Lesvin, who would witness the ceremony on the Council's behalf. Galvo welcomed them scarcely less gladly than Valda herself. Lesvin looked as though he had recently been force-fed green apples. Ribas followed Valda up to the dais as the others took seats in the first row of benches in the empty House.

He hadn't worn his robes of office for this either. It would have felt better, but they couldn't perform the robe-changing when he had no white ones yet, and he must not end this ceremony as a zhinin. Except he would always be a zhinin. He would let nothing change that.

He stood on the dais and listened as Valda recited the traditional prayer. "In the sight of the Goddess...that Her servant Ribas Silvaikas shall be raised to the rank of sventin...continue his service to Her honor and by Her will..."

Her words wove around Ribas like cold mist. This should not be happening.

What could they do about Shurik? What possible answer could they find to his demand? Ribas had promised to serve here in Sostavi until they did find an answer, but what could he himself do, gift or not, knowledge of language or not? What could he change about any of it so they could find a way through?

So many dagira would have given anything to stand where he stood now. He would have given anything he had not to. When would he go home for good?

Would he?

Valda faced him. "Ribas Silvaikas, do you willingly accept the rank of sventin, with its privilege and responsibility, to serve here in the Great House of the Goddess, caring for Her people as She wills?"

He had answered almost the same question long ago, when Zhinin Odilas installed him in Lida. He had meant his answer then. He gave the same answer now, though the word *willingly* made his chest ache.

"I do."

"Do you pledge to serve the Goddess in your thoughts, words, and deeds, listening for Her guidance, submitting to Her will, and honoring Her always in your service to Her House?"

"I do."

"And will you, to the best of your ability, exemplify Her caring in all your doings for Her children, remembering Her devotion to the land and people She loved, and embodying that love as an example to all who look to you for aid and guidance?"

Ribas had done that as well as he could for the past fifteen years. If the Goddess needed him to do more now, he would have to try. He didn't know how much more he could give.

The zhinin could not refuse to give help. He couldn't back away; he couldn't say, *Kenavi, Goddess, haven't I done enough?* In the echoing space of the Great House, Ribas felt anger and sadness pushing, pressing, straining against the walls he had built in himself.

He propped the walls up with all his strength. "I will."

Valda said, "I ask you now to kneel in the presence of the Goddess."

Ribas obeyed. The marble floor of the dais felt cold through the fabric of his pants. Suddenly and vividly, he had an image of his father kneeling in this same place, receiving the promotion from zhinin to kunin.

Now that he saw it, Ribas couldn't push it away. Silvas's brother and sister dagira members would have been here, filling at least a few benches in the Great House, witnessing and supporting him in his rise. He would have worn blue robes and traded them for gray. It would have been, Ribas had no doubt, a moment of triumph and happiness, the culmination of years of hope and work.

And Ribas had never known that the moment had happened. His father had never said a word, at least not that Ribas could remember, about any of what he had done here in Sostavi. But Silvas had knelt here in this place, and the officiating priest – had it been Tavin Ardinas? a member of the Council? – had done exactly what Valda did now, dipping his hands in the waiting bowl of water on the dais table, stepping forward to complete the ceremony.

Now Ribas felt the cool water on his scalp and the light touch of Valda's hands as they rested on his hair. She said, "By the authority vested in me as a servant of the Goddess Kenavi, and by the power of the water that recalls Her sacrifice, I hereby raise you, Ribas Silvaikas, to the rank of sventin, to serve in the Great House of Sostavi."

Grief and sorrow and anger blended together. Thoughts and pictures tangled in Ribas's head. Home. His own Circle House he missed so much. The robes he wished he could have worn today. The trouble facing everyone in the days to come. Valda herself. The memory of Silvas.

For the first time Ribas could remember, in all his years of training and service, his mind settled on the image of the priest his father had been.

Da.

He had not applied that word to his father since Silvas's death. In this place, with the past coiling around him, he couldn't back away from it.

Da. Would you be proud of me today?

Valda said, "May you honor the Goddess and serve Her people faithfully in thought, word, and deed, for as long as She shall so call on you to do."

Ribas had never thought of making his father proud. He had spent his life making sure he was nothing like the man who had caused so much pain. The great space around him swam. His throat closed over.

"Tebena," Valda said.

Ribas forced the syllables out to seal the prayer. "Tebena."

It was done, finished. He was a sventin now, serving in this House. That fact hurt more than his heart ever had.

"You may rise," Valda said.

When he faced the House, he looked at his brother first. Gedrin's face was closed off like a locked room, but Ribas knew how scared he was, thinking he would have to face whatever was happening to him alone, while Ribas stayed impossibly far away in Sostavi for some length of time they had no way to measure. Ribas ached to promise his brother that in a certain number of weeks or months he would come home, and they would fix Gedrin's trouble together. He couldn't promise anything.

Valda said, "Witnesses. In the sight of the Goddess, I present to you Sventin Ribas Silvaikas. Tebena."

Maryut and Gedrin, Lesvin and Galvo answered together, "Tebena." Ribas saw Maryut dabbing at her eyes. Gedrin turned away as if he couldn't stand this anymore.

Ribas stepped down from the dais. Galvo got to him first. "I congratulate you, sventin."

Zhinin, Ribas corrected in his head. As Galvo's equal in rank now, he didn't have to bow. "Thank you, sventin."

"Your official presence on the Council will be a great asset. I value your views very much."

Again, that expression that Ribas couldn't quite explain away as smart politics. What did Galvo want? No doubt Ribas would find out soon enough, once he was serving with the Council.

Lesvin came up and gave Ribas a brief nod. "I look forward to working with you."

He certainly didn't mean it, but Ribas said, "Likewise." Lesvin's fervor could do good things if channeled in the right direction. *We don't need another Shurik here, sventin, but I think you are better than that.*

Maryut stood beside the front-row bench with her face hidden in a handkerchief. As Ribas went to her, he noticed Galvo walk over to Gedrin.

Maryut wore the same dress she had worn for the Installation yesterday: the rich royal blue, embroidered at the neck and on the sleeves with paler blue thread. She had told Ribas that morning, trying to joke, that she hadn't thought she would wear it for two ceremonies on this trip, but she was glad she'd brought it because she should certainly wear her best at her husband's promotion.

Ribas put his arms around her. She leaned on him and hid her face against his chest. He stroked her hair, feeling the fine softness of it, and closed his eyes so that for this little while the two of them could be alone together. "I'm sorry, love," he said.

Her arms went around him and held on tight. "It's not your fault." The sobs she tried to stifle shook her. "I shouldn't act like this. Goddess hear me, I should be glad."

Neither of them had ever wanted anything like this. Ribas kissed her hair. From a little distance away, he heard Galvo saying something to Gedrin about Capture.

Valda stepped down from the dais. Ribas kissed Maryut again and said quietly, "The Tavin."

Maryut drew away from him, drying her eyes. Valda came up to them. Concern struggled in her face with the happiness she couldn't hide.

Maryut lowered her handkerchief. "I'm sorry," she told Valda. "I'm proud of him, I honestly am, but..."

She couldn't finish. Ribas knew how much she hated to look so weak. He kept his arm around her as she mopped at her face again.

"I know," Valda said. Ribas wondered how well she really could know. She had always wanted to get to Sostavi. She said, "I want to thank both of you again for this. I know it's hard."

Maryut said firmly, "People have to do what they can. He'll do his best, of course. But" – she looked up at him – "please, love, try not to be away too long."

They had talked about it last night. She didn't think she could leave Lida and their home and all the responsibilities of their life without knowing how long she would be gone. Ribas thought the pain in her face now would twist his heart into pieces. "Marya," he said, "if you don't come back here with me, I don't come back."

Through the tears, Maryut laughed. "That's not fair, *sventin*."

"I mean it. I won't do this without you."

Valda said, "Then you must come back, Marya. I need my Tavo Balsa."

Valda hadn't used Maryut's nickname before. Maryut looked surprised but not displeased. *Tavo Balsa*, though: Ribas wouldn't be that, officially, until the next time he joined the Council. The title would suit him no better than a heavy wool coat in the middle of summer.

Galvo's voice reached them. He and Gedrin had evidently gone on talking. "Sventin Ribas, I understand you leave for Lida tomorrow?"

"Yes. First thing in the morning."

The sventin turned back to Gedrin. "Then I wonder if you would favor me with a match this evening."

Gedrin told Ribas, "The sventin was telling me that our da was a good Capture player."

Ribas hadn't known that. "Oh yes," Galvo said. "Silvas was one of the best players I ever saw. I'm delighted to learn at least one of his sons inherited that gift."

At least one. Ribas might have smiled at that if Gedrin hadn't looked so tense. He wouldn't have wanted to hear about yet another thing he shared with their father. Ribas said, "Well, I surely didn't inherit it. Gedrí could beat me by the time he was six." He added, "One of the many reasons why he's always been the biggest nuisance I know."

To his satisfaction, Maryut and Valda both laughed at that. Galvo said, "Then, Gedrin Silvaikas, may I hope for the pleasure of a game with you, say after supper?"

Gedrin looked to Ribas for guidance. If Galvo played a good game of Capture, Ribas thought, it might help Gedrin get his mind off things. Ribas said, "Sventin, I have no doubt my brother will make you a worthy opponent. I just hope you don't mind him beating you."

For a moment, the sventin had the same expression Ribas had seen during their talk the other night. *Your father would have been proud of you.* Then he said briskly, "I will look forward to that, if he can indeed do it."

Gedrin and Galvo agreed to meet after supper at the House of the Sventine. Valda wished the travelers safe journey tomorrow, hugged Maryut, and held out her hand to Ribas. "I'll see you again soon, Tavo Balsa."

Back in the chambers, they finished packing. Gedrin said, "I wonder why the sventin wants a game so much."

Ribas folded his blue dress robes and put them in his traveling bag. "Better you than me," he said. This should have been the end of their time in Sostavi. For now, he would not think about having to stay in another set of rooms like this, in the House of the Sventine, too few days from now.

"Well, that goes without saying." Gedrin said. "Ribé, I want to be glad for you." His voice sounded tight enough to snap. "I feel like an ass."

Maryut, bending over her bag, looked around at them and then quickly away. "Don't you start, or I'm going to cry again."

"Why should you be glad for me, Gedrí?" Ribas said. "You know I don't want this either. It's only for now. Only a trick, really."

Maryut said, "Come on, now." She wiped her eyes impatiently as she got up. "We should eat supper so Gedrí can go have his game with the sventin."

"Defend the family honor," Ribas said. "Goodness knows I couldn't."

As soon as they went into the dining hall, Ribas felt the stares. Murmurs and whispers filled the room. He had met most of these faces only the night before, at the feast after the Installation. Everyone knew about the dovne kenavnis and everyone wanted to talk to the stranger who had it.

Ribas could guess what all of them were thinking now. *The gift will stay in Sostavi. It will belong to the Great House.* No doubt they hungered for it: exactly what he had wanted to avoid fifteen years ago.

Gedrin had his match with Galvo. It went late, so he didn't get back to the House of the Zhinine until after Ribas and Maryut had gone to bed. At breakfast the next morning, he told them, "We played six games. We each won three." He grinned as he buttered a slice of bread. "He's a good player. Smart, takes good risks. We thought about a tiebreaker, but we decided to leave it."

Anyone who could beat Gedrin three times had to be good. Ribas would have liked to hear more about it, especially more about why Galvo had brought up Capture in the first place, but breakfast was busy and crowded. Word had spread that Ribas was leaving Sostavi in a few hours. By now, all of the Great House dagira had also heard about Shurik's letter.

Yesterday, Valda and the Council had agreed to send a letter back to Shurik, acknowledging his communication and thanking him for his notice. They would neither promise to support his campaign against the Vaia nor oppose it yet. They would say that Namora had recently undergone a change in government, which, as Shurik himself had reason to understand, meant a period of transition, and they would assure the Impera that he would receive further word from Sostavi in the near future.

Everyone knew that sending such a respectful but vague reply could mean trouble, but it would take weeks for the communication to reach Shurik in Cheremay. Meanwhile, Valda and the Council, including its new Tavo Balsa, could plan a more solid response.

This morning, zhinine came over to Ribas's table alone and in groups, all wanting to talk to him and hear what he thought the Tavin and Council could do about Shurik. Ribas saw too much strain and fear on faces and in minds. He saw too much hope pinned on the dovne kenavnis, on help he might not be able to give. Over and over, he heard, "Tavo Balsa, I don't see what we can do."

He didn't either, but they called him by the new title, and they trusted him and his authority. The dovne kenavnis meant no more sidelong glances at the backwater zhinin or muttering about whether or not he belonged here. He gave the only help he could. "The Tavin and the Council will discuss everything again as soon as I get back from my village. We'll find an answer."

The right words, in the right tone: it seemed like he had always known how to do that. The dagira believed him, even though he didn't entirely believe it himself.

Afterward, in the chambers, Maryut took his face between her hands. "I'm coming back here with you, all right," she told him. "These people won't wear you out if I can help it."

"Good. You know I can't manage without you."

She blinked hard and brushed an imaginary piece of lint off his shirt collar. "I should think I know that by now, Ribas Silvaikas." He heard what she didn't add: *And I don't want to manage without you.*

One of the Great House's carriages took them from Sostavi to

Idria, about a day's journey to the southeast. All three of them had decided, without needing to talk about it, that they would enjoy the trip home as much as they could. Autumn was deepening into winter. Late Tyla and early Akena would bring the first snows. Ribas tried not to think about how soon he would come back over this same road, looking out at white-dusted trees and fields under the gray sky of winter. He would have a week at home, no more, to explain things to the village, and pile more responsibilities on his mosevine than they should have to deal with.

In Paret, only one more day's ride from Lida, Ribas and Gedrin walked to the viduris in the morning while Maryut went to the market. It was gray and chilly, the kind of day that hinted at snow but would only offer a scattering of flakes here and there. Cold enough that Gedrin wore his coat for once. Ribas didn't have time for the real visit to the viduris he'd hoped for: they had to catch the morning coach to get to Lida by evening. Kunin Dergo was undoubtedly in classes until midday. That was too bad. About the only enjoyment Ribas would have gotten out of his new title would have been the sight of the old kunin's face when he heard it.

Paret had grown up around the viduris and the Circle House it served. The main square had ended up a few blocks away, but the viduris had a square of its own, which at one time had been the heart of the little village that had eventually bloomed into the town. The viduris had two buildings: one for classrooms and the other for mosevine lodging. They were both long and low, set at right angles to each other, each one taking up a whole side of the square. They were whitewashed in the manner of Namoran houses, with roofs made of the usual gray-blue clay tiles. Small windows broke up the flat surfaces of the walls.

Ribas didn't need to look through the windows to remember the old desks, the scuffed wooden floors, the smells of dust and paper and ink. And the lodgings: tight square rooms with two narrow beds to a room, a narrow bookshelf hung on the wall above each bed so you risked your head every time you sat up in the morning, and barely enough floor space left over for a work desk and chair for each mosevin, and a place to put two trunks. Two people sharing a room like that ended up knowing each other well, whether they wanted to or not.

Gedrin said, "What are you thinking about?"

Ribas realized he'd been smiling. "Just remembering," he said. "Things were a lot simpler back then."

"You know, I always hated it when you'd come back here. You'd come home on your breaks, and it felt like the world was all right again, and then you'd have to leave."

The day when Ribas first left home to come to Paret, six-year-old Gedrin had refused to say goodbye. He'd run away as soon as he heard the coach coming. Mama had written to Ribas later that she'd found him hidden in the farmhouse loft, curled up under a pile of old blankets. "I only found him because he sneezed," she wrote. "You should have seen all the dust. But I have to tell you, my dove, he's not the only one who misses you."

Those three years of training had been hard on Gedrin. Ribas wished he'd been able to make them easier, and that he could make the coming weeks, or months, easier for him now. "I know," he said gently. "I'm sorry."

Gedrin brushed that away. "Ribé, I've been wanting to tell you. Sventin Galvo asked me something the other night, when we were playing Capture."

Gedrin had been more quiet than usual since leaving Sostavi. He'd often seemed lost in thought in a way that wasn't like him. Ribas had put that down to worry, but now the edge in his tone made Ribas wonder. "What did he ask?" he said.

Gedrin jammed his hands in his coat pockets. "Well, to start with, he talked a lot about Da. He told me how he and Da were good friends, you know, when they served in the Great House. He talked about how smart Da was, and he said he had a temper in those days too, and some people thought he was intimidating." Ribas could picture that. He wondered how often Silvas's fellow Great House dagira had seen that temper slip its bounds. Silvas must have had better control over it in those days, or the Great House wouldn't have wanted him. "But," Gedrin said, "the sventin said Da was funny and easy to talk to, and he was a brilliant Capture player."

Funny and easy to talk to? That was much harder to believe. Gedrin said, "And he said a couple of times how much I reminded him of Da. How I used the same kinds of strategies, and how playing against me felt so much like playing against his old friend."

Ribas had time to feel a wave of thankfulness that none of this had made Gedrin lose his own temper the way he had with Seldo at the Sheaf. It could have happened so easily. Ribas said, "Gedrí. Even if all that is true, it still doesn't mean..."

He wanted to say, *doesn't mean you're the same person*, but Gedrin interrupted. "And he said you reminded of him of Da too. Not to look at, of course, but the way you think."

Ribas had told Maryut about that, but he'd thought it was safer not to say too much about Silvas in front of Gedrin. Now he said, "He told me some of that too."

"Ribé, he asked me..." Gedrin hesitated. His eyes probed Ribas's face. "He asked me what happened to Da. Why he died."

Ribas's heart gave a sharp, angry throb, as if to remind him again where his nemesis came from and why he had to carry it. He wondered why Galvo hadn't asked him that question, if he had wanted the answer. He might have expected Silvas's older son to know more. *And if he had asked, what would I have said?*

Gedrin said, "I told him I had always understood there was an accident, something to do with work in the orchard or something. I said I didn't know exactly what happened."

The past rose up in a dark wave. Ribas and Mama had never told Gedrin the specifics of that night. They had given him a vague answer that didn't lie, but let him think Silvas had gotten hurt doing farm work, and that was another reason to be very careful when you were climbing trees and dealing with livestock and heavy tools. They hadn't wanted to burden Gedrin with too much knowledge about something he didn't remember. And the village had helped them protect Gedrin. All of Lida had known, in those days, what had happened to Silvas, and what he had been doing to his wife and son during the years before his death. All the truth came out after that single night when the world had shattered. But the village had wrapped itself tightly around Pelya and her sons afterward, as if to make up for what no one had known about before. Its collective memory had set Silvas Jadraikas aside in the past, so that no shadow would follow his sons into the future.

Except the shadow was still there. It had always been there; Ribas carried it every day. His chest ached again, the dull throbbing pain he knew much too well. *Not this*, he thought, knowing nothing would prevent Gedrin from saying the words he didn't want to hear. *Not now.*

He did hear them. Gedrin kept his voice level and casual with an effort Ribas could feel. "I'd never worried about it before," he said. "But...what did happen, Ribé?"

Ribas closed his eyes. He couldn't help it. The past wrapped around him with suffocating strength. *Why, Gedrí? Why now?*

It was true: Gedrin hadn't worried about it before. Ribas had sometimes thought that if his place and his brother's had been reversed, if Ribas had been the one too young to remember anything about Silvas, and Gedrin had been the one who had survived, Ribas might have pestered him for answers all along. Gedrin had always taken life more easily, getting on with the day-to-day, accepting what was in front of him.

Now Galvo had shown Gedrin how much he didn't know about the past. And right now, Ribas knew his own face gave too much away.

Gedrin's hand closed around his arm. "Ribé. What is it?"

Even if Ribas could have lied, if he had been willing to commit such a betrayal, it was too late. He opened his eyes.

"It was an accident, Gedrí. He fell and got hurt. That's the truth. But as for how it happened..."

After all these years, Ribas still hated to think about it. Yes, it had been an accident. Mama had spent a long time trying to get Ribas to understand that. Meanwhile, he had paid for it with health and strength, and would continue to pay for the rest of his life.

He said, "One night, after Mama had put you to bed, she and I were in the front room by the hearth. We'd had a bad day."

Gedrin knew enough about what Silvas had been like to under-stand what that meant. "He'd been...Da was in a bad mood?"

Ribas had to tell this, but he must not let his brother see how hard it was or how much it still hurt. "Yes," he said. "He used to be cruel to Mama on days like that. She was upset."

He had thanked the Goddess, many times, that Gedrin had no memory of those times. He had never seen Mama huddled in a rocker by the hearth with the tears slipping down her cheeks, her face and body aching with fresh bruises. She had loved Silvas; Ribas had understood that even then. And she hadn't known how to keep the anger from taking him. Gedrin didn't know, as Ribas did, the terror and rage of watching your mother, the heart of your world, taken to pieces. You would have done anything to help her, but you were so young and small, and you didn't know how.

Gedrin set his jaw. "And you. He was cruel to you too."

"He could be. But Mama would tell me to get out of the way when he lost his temper. She'd tell me to go outside or up into the loft."

She had never wanted her boy to get hurt. That hurt her worse than anything Silvas could do to her: Ribas had understood that too, even as a very young child. And he'd been afraid of his strong, powerful father, and that annihilating anger, though he never wanted to show it. He wanted to stand up for Mama.

Ribas made himself keep talking. They didn't have much time before they had to get the coach. "So that day, he was in a bad mood. He'd gone out to the barn, and Mama had told me to go to bed. She knew he wouldn't be any better when he came in." It had usually taken days for the storms to quiet down. "But she was so upset. I couldn't go."

He must not let himself go too deeply into the memory now. Oh, Goddess hear him, if he could go back and change anything...but what could he have changed?

Gedrin looked so young and scared. Ribas went on, "He came inside and he started in at Mama again. He was shouting at her about the horses, something to do with the feed, I remember. Mama told me again to go to bed. Usually I did what she said, but that night..."

That night, he couldn't. That night his own anger overwhelmed his fear, and he would not, *would not* leave his mother there alone.

"I said no," he said. It helped to hear how calm his own voice sounded. "I stood in front of her chair, so if he tried to hurt her, he'd have to get past me."

What had he honestly thought he could do? He had been not quite seven years old, small and thin in those days, long before the growth spurt that had given him his height. Even now, as hard as he tried to keep it at bay, Ribas felt the same terror that had filled him that night as he stared up into his father's face. But something else had filled him too: the icy certainty that this time, he would not back down, no matter what.

He said, "That made him angrier, I think. He told me to obey my mother and go to bed. I told him I wouldn't."

Sometimes he thought that might have been the single bravest thing he had ever done. Sometimes he thought it might have been the most stupid. Certainly, it had changed everything.

"He..." As calm as he tried to keep himself, Ribas had to struggle for the next words. "He said he would teach me to disobey, and he came at me. He wasn't thinking. I know that. He hit me in the face."

Ribas had never forgotten that either. His father's face, and the closed fist rising, and the blow that lifted Ribas off his feet. "I fell," he told Gedrin. He could still hear his mother's scream, but there had been no pain, not then. The pain had come later, and the blood where Silvas's fist had cut his cheek open. He had to finish this now, while he could. "I was there on the ground by the hearth, and he was coming at me again," he said. "The poker was under my hand. I picked it up and held it out in front of me."

He hadn't swung it, not that he could remember. He hadn't been thinking clearly enough to do that. He had only wanted to put some kind of distance between himself and the terrifying figure bearing down on him. "He didn't see it," Ribas said, and now his voice sounded distant and thin. "He was coming fast. He tripped over it and hit his head on the hearthstone when he fell." The hard, solid hearthstone, with its sharp edges.

Gedrin's face seemed far away. Gedrin, who looked so much like their father. The past had closed so tightly around Ribas that he felt an echo of the old fear as he looked into his brother's eyes. He said, "Mama and I took you and went to Marya's parents for help. The tayo came and got our father into bed, but he never woke up." He could not, would not say *da*. "The fall had hurt him too much. He died the next morning."

Gedrin's mouth had dropped open. Ribas closed his eyes again, briefly, calling on himself to remember where he was. This was here and now, in Paret, and they were going back to Lida, and then he had to go to Sostavi again as Tavo Balsa. He said, "I thought it was my fault. Mama did all she could to make me see it wasn't, but..." He shook his head, trying to push the long-ago horror away. "After that, I got sick," he finished, as gently as he could. "And I never quite got over it."

That was an understatement. He had been so sick that all of the village had thought Pelya was about to lose her son along with her husband. Ribas had a single memory from the long fever, of Mama holding him in her lap, her arms around him, her voice telling him that he was going to stay there with her, she wouldn't let him go. He remembered hearing the words through her tears and wanting to comfort her, but he had been so tired and everything had felt so far away.

Gedrin's eyes were full of tears. "Ribé." He shook his head slowly, as if trying to wake up. "That's why your heart..."

"That's why it's never been quite right."

Gedrin had always known that his brother had gotten sick as a child and the weak heart was left over from that. He had no memory of Ribas healthy. It had been so many years ago that Ribas himself barely remembered how it had felt to trust his body completely. But Gedrin hadn't known why the fever happened.

"And you tried to stand up to Da. You tried to protect Mama." Gedrin's fists clenched and unclenched at his sides in a way that, Ribas couldn't help thinking, would have meant trouble for Silvas if somehow he could have been there in front of them. "Why didn't you tell me? Why didn't I ever know this before?"

He was angry, but the grief was worse. Ribas touched his arm. "You didn't need to know. It was all over and done with. Mama and I didn't want you to have to worry about it."

"But that's what I'm turning into! I would have hurt you myself! I'd have done the same thing he did, if you hadn't stopped me!"

Ribas saw what the terror showed Gedrin: a picture of himself attacking Virta and the children. He reached out and pulled his brother into a hug.

"No," he said. He held Gedrin tight, as if loving him hard enough could solve everything. "You didn't hurt me. You aren't going to hurt anyone else."

Gedrin held onto him. Ribas felt his brother's tousled curls against his face and heard the rasp of Gedrin's harsh breathing. "But you're going away," Gedrin said. "Ribé, Goddess hear me, what am I going to do?"

It came out as a sob. *Goddess above us,* Ribas prayed, *show me how to help him.* He had asked it before. He would go on asking it every day, hour after hour and breath after breath, until he got an answer.

For a while Gedrin let Ribas hold him. Then he drew back and wiped his eyes on his coat sleeve. "And you know something," he said.

"If you'd told me all that before, at least you wouldn't have had to carry it by yourself. I could have helped." He looked up into Ribas's face. "You're always looking after people. Mama, me, the village. Now it's going to be all of Namora and half of Lassar too, it sounds like." He laughed, a tired sound with no humor in it. "Brother, when do you look after yourself?"

"I'm all right."

Gedrin glared at him. "I know when that's hurting." He touched Ribas's chest. "Even when you try to pretend it's not. And I know you get angry and upset and scared like anyone else, you just never talk about it." He gripped Ribas's shoulder. "When you get back from Sostavi, you're going to take better care of yourself."

Ribas managed to laugh. "Marya will be glad to hear it."

They had to get going. They couldn't afford to miss the coach and lose some of their precious time in Lida. Gedrin let Ribas lead the way back to the main square, where Maryut was waiting with the bags and a couple of packages from the market. "Are you two all right?" she said.

Gedrin gave Ribas a challenging look. *I'm sorry, Gedri,* Ribas thought. *I only know one way to answer that.* "We're fine," he said. "We were just talking about a few things."

The coach arrived in a jangle of harness and the noise of hooves on the flagstones. The three of them stowed their luggage and joined the handful of other passengers going to Lida. Ribas watched the familiar scenery slip past and wished, again, that they were going back to stay.

19

VALDENA

Early in the morning of Sesdina, Sixth Day, two days after her Installation, Valda got up before dawn. Around her she felt the stillness of her new lodgings: the House of the Tavin.

The fires in her bedchamber and the front room had burned down hours earlier. The chilly air of late fall seemed to seep even through the House's solid walls. Valda wrapped her dressing gown around her and shuffled into her thickest pair of slippers before she lit a new fire in the front room.

Last night, when she had finally gone to bed, she had thought of all the hours she had spent in the same bedchamber, sitting with Tavin Ardinas during his final weeks. The servants had moved Valda's own bed over from the House of the Sventine, but the same walls made a box around her, the same ceiling stared down, the same window showed the same view of the square. Ardinas had looked out that window day after day as he waited for the time when his soul would fly. Valda had found comfort in the idea of his soul staying near the Council chambers and the Great House, but here in the place where he had lived, it only made her grieve again. *I'm sorry*, she thought to him. *This was yours.*

Galvo or Lesvin probably would have taken possession of Ardinas's chambers as easily as they would buy a loaf of bread. As she brewed a cup of strong tea over the new fire, Valda thought how either of them, but especially Galvo, also would have made much more use of the servants. No stoking their own fires or making their own tea. Valda sat at the inlaid table by the front room window and sipped from the delicate cup, trying to picture Galvo crouching over the hearth with paper and matches. Had he ever had to do that? Valda imagined him lighting one match, then another, shoving them into the paper only to watch them die out in puffs of smoke, leaning in to blow on a fresh one and singeing his robes when the paper caught. She told herself she shouldn't laugh.

There wasn't much to laugh at now. Her work waited for her, the Council waited for her, and to the east there was the huge brooding presence of Lassar. But Ribas would be back in Sostavi soon: her best hope, far too much of a hope, as she knew perfectly well when she felt the blush climb into her face again.

She had been so happy, yesterday, when she performed his promotion ceremony. She had been so happy to give him the rank he richly deserved, but she had seen, perfectly clearly, what the ceremony cost him and Maryut both.

Maryut's tears had felt like a knife against Valda's conscience. She had wanted to say, *Aren't you proud of him? Can't you let him have this?* But he didn't want it. And Maryut was proud of him, she had said so, but neither of them wanted the life his promotion brought with it.

Ribé, Valda thought now, wearily. *I'm sorry.*

She would learn to be more careful. She needed him here, yes, but she wouldn't let her feelings intrude on the work. She had to let go of what she could never have. She should have done that long ago.

In the bedchamber, she dressed quickly, putting the simplest of her new brown robes on over a woolen shift. No one would be in the Great House this early. Valda needed time in the quiet, to pray and try to get her mind in order.

The sky had gotten lighter, but it didn't look like the sun would come out today. Typical weather for Tyla: the gray month of quiet led up to Akena, the month in which the Goddess had laid down Her life for Namora. Tyla created the solemn hush the Sacrifice deserved. In Algima, the month of Rebirth, the sun would come out again for longer and longer stretches, warming the earth for Ivesta, the season of planting.

And what would have happened by then? Valda wished she could guess.

When she stepped into the Great House, the dim light and silence wrapped around her. She breathed in deeply, feeling her soul waking up and reaching out into the holy place. Then a strange, unsettling sound caught her attention. Someone was crying.

From where she stood near the back of the House, she scanned the benches. The sound was tight and harsh, as if whoever was making it didn't cry often, and didn't want to now. She saw a figure sitting at the end of a bench, near the center aisle: a man in a plain light-colored shirt and plain brown pants. He sat with his gray head bowed and his clasped hands resting on the back of the bench in front of him. Valda couldn't see much of his profile from this distance, but he seemed to have his eyes closed.

He looked vaguely familiar, she thought, but she couldn't place him. Someone from the city, it might be, who needed quiet time to pray as much as Valda did herself. She wondered if a word from her would help. It might not. Right now, even the Tavin might be just another unwelcome person, intruding on his prayer.

Then his profile seemed to come into focus. With a shock, she realized who he was. He looked so different without his robes of rank.

Sventin Galvo.

Galvo, crying? Valda hurried forward, walking as softly as she could. Her shoes did make noise on the hard floor, but he didn't raise his head. He was lost in whatever sadness wrapped around him.

She had never thought he could need hers, or anyone's, pity or compassion. In the plain clothes, he seemed smaller. This wasn't the smooth, politically expert veteran who had risen so far and achieved so much. This was just a man.

Valda reached out. "Sventin."

The moment her fingers touched his shoulder, his head jerked up. The tears cut off at once. The raw anger in his eyes made her step back.

A mask seemed to come down to shield his face. "Tavin," he said.

It was almost the same polite tone as usual: almost, but not quite. His hands gripped each other on the back of the bench in front of him. Tears made tracks down his cheeks.

She stepped closer. "What's wrong?"

"Nothing I would trouble you with, Tavin."

She ought to give him his privacy. She could leave the House, although, if she told him she wanted time here alone, no doubt he would leave her to it. Instead she held out her hand, palm up.

She hadn't invoked this ritual in a very long time. Zhinine did it more often than higher-ranking dagira, because they dealt most often with everyday people. Valda had felt awkward about it when she'd first been installed. She hated pressing for a confidence.

Now she held out her hand with all the right of superior dagira to subordinate. The right, in fact, of the ultimate authority. Galvo's eyes challenged her. For a moment she thought he might try to refuse. Then, slowly, he unclasped his hands and reached out.

His palm touched hers. His fingers felt chilly when she closed her hand around them. "Tell me," she said.

With the ritual sealed, he had to tell her the truth. He knew it. His mouth turned up in a wry smile, acknowledging the position she had put him in.

He moved over on the bench so she could sit beside him. She felt the full strangeness of it: the Tavin and the one who had nearly been Tavin; the girl from years ago and the man who had been, it was fair to say, her patron. He had pulled a lot of his usual bearing around himself, but she saw how his fingers laced around each other in his lap, so tightly his knuckles turned white.

He said, "You have the advantage of me. I'd expected to be here alone."

"I expected the same thing."

He gave her an appraising look. "I wonder if you came in for much the same reason I did. Valda, I think you know what a burden love can be."

She had never wanted him to know so much. Color rose into her face, but here and now, they were only people, and she was forcing honesty from him.

"Yes," she said. "I do."

"I thought so. I've wondered about that for some time."

She would not show him more than she could help. She drew herself up straighter. "Forgive me, sventin, but I don't know what that has to do with your being here this morning."

"Fair enough," he said. Now he looked as self-possessed as always. Whatever had shattered his composure must have had to work for it. He said, "I only mention it because perhaps, in light of that, what I say to you next will make more sense."

He looked up toward the front of the House, apparently studying the dais and the hearth. Valda waited quietly, listening to the wind whistling outside. This evening they would light the hearth fire for the service, but for now, the House held the same chill she had felt in her chambers that morning.

"Last night," Galvo said, "I had a very strange experience. You may remember that yesterday I challenged Sventin Ribas's brother to a Capture match, and he accepted."

Valda hadn't expected any mention of Gedrin or Capture. "Yes, I remember."

"We played yesterday evening." Galvo kept his eyes on the hearth. "Gedrin Silvaikas plays extraordinarily well. If I say it myself, I am very difficult to beat. I only ever knew one other person who could do it as readily as he did."

Valda remembered some of the talk after Ribas's promotion ceremony. "Gedrin's father?"

"Yes."

Silence settled around them again. Valda waited. Then Galvo said, without looking at her, in the same polite voice as always, "You realize, Valda, I would not tell you any of this without the ritual."

"I understand. And you know, Galvo, that whatever you tell me will go no farther."

"Very well. Then I will explain that when I first met you, I had recently had word from your kunin at the Paret viduris. This was shortly after he had written to us about then-Zhinin Ribas and the dovne kenavnis."

When I first met you. Valda hadn't expected that jump into the past, but the words seemed to suggest a direct connection between whatever Kunin Dergo had said about Ribas and the fact that Galvo had met Valda.

Why, indeed, had he singled her out? "Yes?" she said.

"To make matters brief, you know that when I learned about Zhinin Ribas, I wanted him to come to Sostavi at once, but he refused. You may not be aware that I continued to correspond with Kunin Dergo for a while. In the course of that correspondence, the kunin mentioned that another of his students, a classmate of the young zhinin's, was in fact coming here. He told me your name and suggested I look for you."

Valda hadn't known that. Galvo said, "I will admit, Tavin, that my initial interest in you stemmed from your connection with Sventin Ribas. I thought that perhaps you stayed in touch with him, perhaps your views of Sostavi might encourage him to come here after all."

So simple, and yet neither of them had ever mentioned Ribas at the time. Valda matched Galvo's politeness word for word. "I'm afraid you were disappointed, then. He and I didn't stay in touch, in those days."

"Indeed not. As I said, my initial interest in you came from that. Selfish, I'm afraid. However, you quickly proved to be one of the most able young zhinine I had ever known, well worth attention and support."

Valda felt a surprising curl of pleasure at that. Then she thought of something else. "It paid off after all. I seem to have brought him here to Sostavi."

"Yes," Galvo said. "I won't trouble to deny my extreme satisfaction when I learned he was coming. Or my still greater satisfaction when you proposed him as your Tavo Balsa."

He didn't sound particularly satisfied right then, she noticed. Certainly not triumphant, as anyone might have expected. Before she could stop herself, Valda said, "Why does it matter so much? What do you want from him?" And what did any of this have to do with *the burden love can be?*

Galvo considered her. "Yes. Forgive me for saying that without the ritual, I would answer neither of those questions."

"I know that."

Galvo looked out at the hearth again. "I wonder," he said, "if you can imagine something. Suppose that you were, say, twenty years older than you are now. Suppose you had not seen Sventin Ribas in a very long time, and that, in fact, you would never see him again. You had learned of his death some time ago. And then suppose that, one day, you were to meet his son, and this son was the living image of him."

Valda set her jaw. The idea of Ribas's death made it hard to breathe, but she would not give in to that weakness in front of Galvo. *Ribas doesn't look like his father,* she thought, clutching anger as a shield. *He and Gedrin both said so. What are you getting at?*

Galvo went on, in the same level voice as before. "And suppose that it turned out that this son had one of the same abilities as his father. Suppose that you were able to sit with him and relive some of the best moments you can remember, or, at least, it would feel that way to you. You would feel as if, for that short time, you could see and talk to the person you had dearly loved."

Wait.

Stillness closed around Valda as she realized what Galvo was saying. No, Ribas didn't look like his father, but Gedrin did. Galvo had played Capture with Gedrin, the way he had once played it with Silvas. *Dearly loved.*

The burden love can be.

Valda didn't move a muscle, but her thoughts raced. *You loved him. You loved Silvas.*

Galvo said, "And then, if you will, suppose that the reason why you had not seen Sventin Ribas during the years before he died, and why, in fact, you had had no news of him at all for a long time, was that you had done a great wrong, and it had cost you his friendship."

No change in his quiet voice, but Valda felt as if the floor had dropped away. "Done a great wrong? What do you mean?"

She didn't realize she had said it aloud until Galvo turned to look at her. The gray eyes seemed to burn in his pale face.

"Silvas Jadraikas left Sostavi and the dagira because of me. Because he learned of something I had done. You will forgive me, Tavin, but ritual or not, I do not intend to share that particular confidence."

Valda tried to understand. Galvo had "done a great wrong" and lost someone he had loved. Yes, she found it all too easy to imagine what he had felt last night, facing Gedrin across the Capture board. She knew, too, what had brought him here this morning, stripped of all the trappings of rank and so much of his self-control. She had never thought she would pity him. She did it now, from her heart.

He had drawn his composure back around him. Valda wondered what kind of effort that had cost. He said, "As for what I want from Sventin Ribas. You won't repeat this to him?"

He had insulted her, suggesting she would break the privacy of this ritual, but she couldn't get angry. "No. You have my word."

Galvo looked around the House before he answered. Valda saw him taking in the walls, the beautiful windows, the dais with its table and the fine box of prayer stones. She wondered what kind of strength he might be asking for, as he called on this place and its stones and the presence of the Goddess.

He said, "I want two things. Whether or not the sventin can give them to me, I can't say, but I had intended to ask him about one of them when he and I spoke the other evening. In the end, I couldn't bring the conversation around to it."

Valda knew the city was waking up around them. Before long, no doubt, someone would come in and interrupt this extraordinary talk. Galvo said, "I wanted to learn more about what his gift can do. Specifically, whether he could go into my mind and erase Silvas's memory."

Valda stared at him. "You would want that?"

"Wouldn't you? Given what I've just told you?"

No anger in his face now, only a grief Valda could almost reach out and touch. Would she ever, under any circumstances, want Ribas erased from her mind, as if she had never known him? "It isn't the same," she said, "but I don't think I would."

Galvo considered that. "Perhaps not. And you might be right. I don't know yet whether his gift could do such a thing. Do you?"

"No. I don't know enough about it."

"Neither do I, but I would still like to find out. That was why I was doubly glad that you proposed his joining the Council. As for the second thing, which I suppose he would have to give me before the first. I would like to feel that Silvas might have forgiven me for what I did. He can't do it himself now, certainly, but perhaps his son would."

For all these years, Galvo had wanted Ribas to come to Sostavi for those two things: forgiveness and the gift of forgetting. Valda's pity threatened to swallow her. "I'm sure he would."

If she knew him, he would. But Galvo said, "It would mean telling Sventin Ribas what I've refused to tell you. I'm not entirely certain I can do that. And he might judge me, perhaps, in the same way he's judged his father."

Ribas, judge anyone? Valda said, "He doesn't..."

Galvo interrupted smoothly. "Yes, he does. I'm afraid he judged and condemned Silvas long ago. I don't blame him, given what I understand of his childhood, but unless I miss my guess, he hasn't forgiven."

If he hasn't, he has good reason not to. Valda kept that thought to herself. Galvo said, "And now I've told you all I can, Tavin. May I beg the favor of a few moments alone?"

Valda gathered her own self-control around her. "Certainly."

"Raimaté, Tavin."

"Raimaté, sventin." Valda's footsteps echoed in the great space. She went back down the aisle and left Galvo alone with his past.

20

BEREG

Bereg knew at once that the lie wouldn't work. The Lasska detachment at the watchhouse in the mountains knew who he was and what he had done.

"Bereg Orlon. You stand accused of abandoning your detachment."

Bereg knew what was coming. He sat perfectly still in the saddle as Silde Alyem's next words reached him. "In the name of Impera Shurik, I arrest you to stand trial for your crimes against his authority."

If he turned himself in and went quietly, maybe Alyem would let the others go. Bereg had time to think that and know how stupid it was. Tama was a traitor too. These Lasska soldiers would no doubt welcome the chance to kill Vaia or take them prisoner.

Then, from behind him, he heard a shout. He didn't understand the Vaia words, but he recognized the hunter Handan's voice. A vindula went off near him. Another answered it from the Lasska side. The fight had started.

Bereg felt no particular fear. At first, he felt nothing at all. He had known this would happen eventually. He knew what he had to do now.

If Khari and the others were to have any hope of getting away, Silde Alyem – the leader of the enemy force – would have to die. Bereg had never killed a man before. He knew how to shoot. Sitting on horseback, he had the best vantage point he could ask for.

Sitting on horseback also made him an ideal target. He knew if he tried to get down, his useless knee would give way. He would slow down anyone who tried to drag him to safety and probably cost at least one life.

He had to stay where he was. He lifted his vindula and got Silde Alyem in his sights, knowing each breath he took might be his last.

At a moment like that, when you were about to take your enemy's life, you shouldn't have time to think. Time shouldn't slow down around you. You shouldn't feel each separate movement as you lifted the weapon, sighted, adjusted it slightly. Bereg had never had blood on his hands. He knew, as he prepared to fire, that this would make a rift in his life that he would feel until he died. You shouldn't have time, even though you knew the enemy would kill you first if he could, to grieve for the life you had to end.

But then he heard the report of another vindula. He saw Alyem fall, and when he looked up the trail, he saw the girl Khari standing with her weapon still aimed at the place where Alyem had stood. Bereg saw her collapse in the dirt.

Time rushed back in. The fight ended soon after. The four Lasska soldiers were dead, and on Bereg's side, no one but Khari had taken a wound. The girl was unconscious when Tama and Radavan hoisted her up onto Tama's horse. They couldn't do anything for her until they got as far away from that place as they could.

That night, when they stopped, Tama got the bullet out. Bereg, to his shame, couldn't help. He wasn't strong enough to hold Khari down and, in fact, had to force himself not to put his hands over his ears to try to shut out her screams. The only thin comfort came from the fact that Radavan looked as sick as Bereg felt.

Afterward, Tama shook her head. "She's lost too much blood. I don't think she'll make it." The words sounded cold and flat, but Bereg saw the hard lines of grief on her face.

They couldn't stop traveling. The mountains might be crawling with soldiers by now. Radavan and young Rahul were afraid to try to move Khari, but eventually they agreed with everyone else that they had to risk it. If they waited, none of them might make it to Namora. Then, if Khari died, she would have given her life for nothing. Granted, they would be lost even if they did get there without her. None of them could be sure they would recognize the man from her dream.

Tama was brusque and cold, the woman Bereg had met in Cheremay again. At first, she would allow no one else to help with Khari. She supported the girl in front of her on the saddle as they rode, lifted her down in her arms when they stopped for the night, lay next to her by the fire and held her. They had to have fires, big of a risk as they were when there might be enemies anywhere. Tama needed to heat water to clean Khari's wound, and they couldn't risk the girl's body going into shock with cold when it had already taken so much damage. As far as Bereg knew, Tama didn't sleep. She kept watch over Khari as if she would fight off death itself.

On the third night after the fight, Bereg dragged himself over to the blanket where Khari lay with Tama sitting beside her. Tama glared at him like a mother bear guarding her cub.

"You can get some rest," Bereg said. "I'll watch her."

"No."

"I won't sleep. Don't worry."

Tama's eyes had bruises under them like smears of ink. Much more of this and she would collapse. Bereg said gently, "You need your strength too."

She looked from him to Khari and back again. Then she nodded curtly. "If you think you're going to sleep, wake me up."

"I will."

She lay down next to Khari with her arm across the girl's chest and fell asleep instantly. Bereg didn't lie back, but sat where he was, his injured leg stretched awkwardly out in front of him. He watched Khari's chest moving up and down. The motions looked too small and shallow, but she was still with them.

Something woke up in him then. Not hope: you couldn't call it hope, when he knew he was still a traitor and had nothing left to live for. But now he knew, too, that if nothing else, he would make it across the border into Namora. If the strength of his prayers could do any good, and the God would listen to one such as he, Khari would make it there too.

It seemed as if it should have taken weeks, even months, for the ground to level out and the peaks to come in sight. In reality, it hadn't been more than a week since the encounter with Alyem and his soldiers.

Everyone felt the change in the terrain. They had been vigilant all along, but now Bereg felt as if they all needed extra pairs of eyes. This close to Namora, they might run into more guards, even well off the main roads as they were. Bereg wouldn't put it past Shurik to stretch a line of soldiers shoulder to shoulder across the peak to keep his targets trapped.

One morning, Tama reluctantly agreed to let Bereg take Khari on his saddle while she and Radavan scouted ahead. Handan and Mandhani made up the rear guard, in case of pursuit coming up from behind. For days they had seen no living things except birds, ground squirrels, and the mountain goats that stared at them from rock outcroppings and then sprang away with a clatter of fleet hooves. Bereg tried to trust in the outriders and concentrate on keeping his own horse moving steadily over the trail. Carrying the injured girl, he felt as if every jolt must send a spearhead of pain through her. He had learned enough about that from his own injury.

The ground leveled out still more and became almost flat, the flattest Bereg had seen since the plains. Could they have found the peak? Bereg found himself daring to hope it when he felt Khari move against him. Not much louder than a whisper, he heard her say his name.

The world stopped. Bereg barely knew he reined in. He had to see her face and know if she really had come back to them. To do that, he had to get down, but the useless knee kept him trapped in the saddle, and he couldn't dismount anyway because he didn't dare let go of her.

"Khari, child." He remembered he shouldn't call her that. Hadn't Radavan scolded him for it, so long ago? "Child, can you look at me?"

She turned in the saddle, as much as she could. He saw her dark eyes and heard her saying she was better.

That afternoon, for the first time in more time than Bereg wanted to remember, he believed that the God did listen and hear him. Because no more soldiers came to stop them, no one except a few birds saw them at all, and they did reach the peak and looked down and saw Namora stretching out below them, green and gold under a clear afternoon sky. They had done it.

Over the next days, they aimed their careful descent toward the one village they could see from the peak. It didn't look like much: only a knot of buildings around some sort of square, with a few paths leading out like spokes of a wheel into the surrounding farmland. Mandhani scouted north and saw signs of real roads, but the group decided to avoid people while they could. The village might provide some protection if Namorans didn't automatically hate Lasska and Vaia. Bereg had no idea what the Namoran people might think or know about the people to the east of the mountains.

Tama didn't know either. One night by the fire, she said, "I wonder if they're as scared of us as we are of them."

"Are we scared of them?" Bereg said. "I've always thought we didn't think they were worth noticing."

Khari, sitting with them, laughed. Bereg saw her wince and put her hand to her side. She could sit horseback now without help and get herself in and out of the saddle, but the days of travel wore on her more than she would admit to anyone. Bereg hoped the Namorans had decent doctors, if nothing else. "You Lasska," Khari said. "Always thinking you're the most important."

Tama raised an eyebrow. "*We* Lasska? You're speaking decent Lasska yourself these days, my girl."

She had taken to calling Khari that. None of the Vaia, including Khari herself, seemed to resent it. "Only because you don't speak Vaia," Khari said.

Bereg, likewise, had picked up exactly no Vaia in all these days of travel. He'd decided that an old bear probably couldn't learn such a trick. Khari and the other Vaia all spoke good Lasska now, even Handan and Mandhani, who had resisted it at first. Bereg sometimes forgot that the Vaia came from a different people than Tama and himself.

Tama said, "If it comes to speaking, have we thought about how we're going to talk to this Namoran when we find him? I don't speak Namoran."

Khari said, "Neither do I."

Bereg had never learned Namoran either. Lasska schooling taught practically nothing about the countries on the other side of the mountains, apart from the fact that they existed and were inhabited by pagans who did not worship Mesha. Tama said, "I suppose we'll have to hope he speaks Lasska. Although then we'll have to admit Namorans are smarter than we are, learning our language when we don't learn theirs."

That got another laugh from Khari. In pain or not, Bereg thought, she seemed young and cheerful on this side of the mountains, in a way she hadn't always on the Lasska side. He found himself wondering what would become of her once they got through all this, assuming they did. Would she find the rest of her tribe again some-day? Would she train another girl to read dreams the way she did? Bereg still didn't understand how that craft, if it was one, worked, but it did seem that her dreams told truth. He had no particular right to know about her future, but he hoped he could witness at least a little of what she became.

Khari told Tama, "Then you must learn Vaia and prove you are at least as smart as I am."

"I might," Tama said, "if you didn't have such a ridiculously complicated language."

Rahul came up in time to hear that. "It's the oldest language there is," he said. He sat down beside Khari. "The mother of tongues."

Bereg said, "It doesn't sound anything like Lasska."

"Your people must have changed it a long time ago," Rahul said. "We were first, though. First people, first language."

"Don't brag like that to me, young upstart," Bereg said.

All of them laughed at that. Bereg wished that they didn't have to worry about the future or think about what was going on behind them in Lassar. Here, suspended outside the world, they had peace. In fact, they almost felt like a family: certainly the only family Bereg had now.

A couple of days later, they came out on the flatland, as much as you could call it that. On the Lasska side of the Senai, you had the plains, but this country seemed to be upland. There were forested hills and gentle swells of brown and green grasses. During the descent, Bereg had noticed several tiny blue lakes, not much more than ponds, dotting the countryside. The land looked rich over here. Bereg had never been a farmer, but he thought about what it might be like to drive a plow into this earth. The trees showed every sign of health and strength. No doubt other things grew well too.

To the north, they had seen a much bigger town, almost a city. They briefly debated changing course and aiming for it, on the basis that a larger place might give them a better chance of finding the man they needed, but Khari, in particular, argued against that. She hadn't had any more of what she called pathdreams, but she said they were right to keep making for the village. No one challenged her authority.

Once they reached the flatland, they spent one more night in the foothills of the Senai, in the peace of a solitary grove. They could make out the village's lights in the distance, but their small fire wouldn't draw any attention this far away. Bereg got Rahul to help him strap a thick stick to his injured leg. With that rough splint, and with another heavy stick to lean on, he did manage to hobble a little around the camp. Tama and Khari both told him not to strain himself. Bereg said flatly that he was damned if he'd stay useless forever. "I don't know what we're going to get into out here, but I'll face it on my feet."

The next morning dawned chilly and overcast. Khari wanted to go to the village at once, but when Handan said he and Mandhani should ride forward carefully and get the lay of the land, she agreed. "If we meet any Namorans," Handan said, "we can see what they think of us. Two of us can get away fast if there's any trouble."

Khari waited restlessly after the hunters had gone. Bereg saw her touch her side more than once, hurting again in spite of the pain tincture she'd taken that morning. Bereg's own leg ached after his experiments of the night before, but he didn't intend to admit it. He sat beside Khari, who had rolled up her bedroll and lashed her vindula to it, and now sat perched on it, waiting as if a coach would pull up at any moment for her to climb on.

That thought made him say, "Have you ever ridden in a coach?"

Her eyes looked as dark and liquid as a deer's. "No," she said. "I saw one once."

He realized, again, the differences between her life and his own. They were heading toward civilization now, however different it might look from the towns and cities he knew. He was getting back on familiar ground. She and the other Vaia were leaving behind the kind of life they were used to. He wondered if she was afraid.

He said, "This country doesn't look so different from Lassar. Not yet, anyway."

"I don't know what some of the plants are." She pointed at one of the trees, a spindly-looking evergreen. "That doesn't look like the trees at home."

Home struck him as a strange word for her to use. He knew her people traveled all over Lassar. To him, "home" was the place you always came back to, the one corner of the world that belonged to you. Maybe, to her, it meant the whole country. He found himself wondering if Shurik, in the Hall of the Bear, could have said the same.

She said, "I wish I knew what the man will do to help us. I wish the dreams had shown me more."

The words sounded as if she had held them back for a long time. Bereg had never heard her complain about the dreams. He said, "Khari, where do your dreams come from?"

"The Moon Woman." She said it as if it was obvious. "The Sun God is the ruler of all, but the Moon Woman must guide him. She chooses the Lamp-Carriers to guide the Lodestones."

Bereg had learned that "Lamp-Carrier" was the proper term for what she and Rahul had first called "Light-Bearers." "But why..." He hesitated over what he was about to say, because it sounded like heresy. Every Lasska knew there was no such thing as a Moon Woman. "Why did she choose you?"

"I don't know." She sounded tired. "No one knows how it happens."

She was so young. Only she, out of all the Vaia, had apparently gotten any guidance to look for help in Namora. The future of people she loved, and many others besides, might depend on her.

What a burden to place on this girl. Bereg wondered if this Moon Woman, if she did exist, had thought about that. Then he wondered if his own God had actually told Shurik to destroy Khari's people. Tama didn't believe it. Bereg knew, to his bones, that he didn't either.

Handan and Mandhani came back sooner than Bereg expected. Everyone gathered to hear their report. Handan said, "The place is quiet. We only saw a few people in the streets. They did look at us, but no one started anything."

Bereg noticed, again, how well Handan spoke Lasska. Maybe he and Tama ought to try harder to learn Vaia.

Tama said, "Did they seem friendly? Unfriendly?"

"Neither," Handan answered. "I think they were watching us to see what we would do."

Tama said, "In a place this size, I'm sure everyone knows everyone else. They would notice strange faces right away."

Mandhani said, "The Namorans we saw look a lot like you Lasska. Light-skinned and tall."

"They will certainly notice us, then," Radavan said. "I wonder if they know anything about the Vaia."

Khari said, "Probably not. The Lasska don't."

Bereg said, "We Lasska ought to know more than we do."

That made her smile. Handan said, "Khari. You told us Vatiri said the Namorans build round temples?"

"Yes. Or she said they used to."

"We thought we saw one," Mandhani said. "In the middle of the village. It's round, made of stone. The biggest building there."

Handan said, "We didn't see anyone near it, but we didn't go inside, of course."

Khari thought about this. So did Bereg. If the building was a temple, that would mean a priest. If Namoran priests were anything like the ones in Lassar, there was a decent chance that the one in this village knew everyone who lived here. And if, Bereg thought, by some miraculous chance, the man they needed was here – although why they would be so lucky, Bereg had no idea – a priest might direct them to him. The temple might be a place to start.

Khari evidently thought the same. "I'll go there now."

"You're not going alone."

Handan, Tama, and Bereg had all said it. Another time, Bereg might have laughed, but Khari's face showed too clearly what these next few hours might mean. Suppose they couldn't make the priest understand them, or he refused to help them, or the man they needed was in some other part of the country and they left here with no clues at all to guide them. They had come this far and gotten this close.

Tama fixed Bereg with a look. "Well, you're not going, old man."

"I can get along as well as any of you." On horseback, at least. Bereg thought of something else. "Maybe a silde – an *old* silde," he added for Tama's benefit, "would get more respect from these Namorans." Lasska valued the elderly, especially soldiers, for their experience and wisdom. Namorans might do the same.

"Or less respect," Handan said. "They may not like soldiers here."

Khari said, "I think Tama and Bereg should come with me. They look most like Namorans." To Radavan she added, "The rest of you should stay here. If these people don't like Vaia, we shouldn't risk us all."

Handan said, "You need protectors."

"I can do that," Tama said.

Rahul said, "Khari's right. More of us may frighten the Namorans. But if there's any trouble, you must come back as fast as you can. We'll be ready to help."

Bereg saw the way he looked at Khari. Handan would be a catch for her too, probably, given his skills as a hunter and fighter, but Bereg found himself hoping that if she chose either man, it would be the quiet, level-headed Rahul. He splinted his bad leg again, though it made riding more awkward, and brought the heavy crutch as well. Tama helped him struggle into the saddle and the three of them set off.

Late-growing mint lined the grassy path that led west toward the village. The air tasted of its cool scent. As Bereg and the others reached the outskirts of the village, the grass gave way to a dirt road. Namorans didn't take their road construction as seriously as the Lasska, Bereg noticed. They passed farmland, now bare earth and stubble, and a few tidy white houses with roofs made of unusual gray-blue tile. Then they came to the village square.

It really was a small place. The square was paved with cobble-stones and a few hitching posts stood on each side of it. Bereg saw what looked like more houses, and a few bigger buildings, undoubt-edly shops and businesses. One building stood out, though: the single one built of stone.

As Mandhani had said, it was the biggest one in the square. The eye went to it at once because of its strange round shape and, even more unusual to Bereg's eyes, the conical roof. He had never seen anything like it. What kind of work must it have taken to build a structure like that? He had never studied architecture, but he knew about engineering and design. Creating rounded walls like that, much less setting windows in them, must have presented a real chal-lenge. Bereg wondered why the Namorans had chosen this shape for their temples.

A few people were out and about in the village. On the near side of the square, a tall man with a bald head took wooden shingles down from the windows of a long, low building. Bereg couldn't read the sign that hung over the door, but it showed a picture of a barrel with sheaves of what looked like wheat standing in it. An inn, maybe. The man eyed the three riders curiously.

Khari said quietly, "I think we should go into the temple."

Bereg realized he didn't feel as comfortable with "civilization" as he would have expected. The square felt not unfriendly, but strange. The round building put him off despite his interest in it. He had never been in a temple built to any god but Mesha. There weren't supposed to be any other gods.

They dismounted at the hitching post closest to the temple. Bereg got down clumsily and winced as his bad leg tried to take his weight. The splint kept the knee from buckling. He leaned heavily on the crutch to keep himself upright.

Tama tied his horse to the post alongside the two Vaia mounts. "Are you all right, old man?"

"I can manage."

The building's tall wooden front doors stood open. Bereg saw

Khari square her shoulders before she stepped inside. He and Tama followed.

It wasn't a big space, but the round walls made it feel larger than it was. Bereg looked around. A central aisle ran down between rows of benches to a raised dais. A table stood on the dais, and behind it, a wide stone hearth. The whole place looked much simpler and plainer than the temples of Mesha that Bereg had seen, even the one in his home village in Thysidich. Somehow, the quiet of it appealed to him.

A noise came from up near the front of the room. A door near the dais opened. Two people came out into the temple.

They were both young – around Khari's age, Bereg guessed – slim-built and dark-haired. The boy stood considerably taller than the girl. Both of them wore plain, simple clothes: brown pants and a homespun shirt for the boy, a wheat-colored dress for the girl. They were talking, their voices echoing in the still space, but of course Bereg couldn't understand what they said.

Khari stepped forward, partway down the center aisle. In Lasska, she said, "Excuse me."

Her voice carried down to the dais. The two people stopped and peered out at the newcomers. Bereg saw puzzlement, and then the two exchanged a look that, to him, had alarm in it.

Next to him, Tama tensed. You couldn't bring weapons into a temple, obviously, and Bereg couldn't imagine these two young people causing any trouble, but he didn't know what kind of guards or soldiers a village like this might have. Would the boy and girl call for help? If they did, who would come?

No one shouted anything yet. The girl stepped down from the dais into the center aisle, with the boy following her. The two of them walked toward Khari.

Bereg limped forward with Tama beside him. His crutch would make a good weapon if he could prop himself up long enough to swing it. *Old man* was right.

Khari and the girl faced each other. Bereg saw the girl take Khari in, scanning her face and hair, her white blouse and leather breeches.

Bereg had gotten so used to the way Khari looked and dressed that it gave him a start to realize how different this girl, who could have been a young Lasska woman, looked by contrast.

The girl said something that sounded like a question. Khari shook her head and spread her hands: *I don't understand.* She said, in Lasska, "We're looking for someone."

The girl and boy exchanged blank looks. Obviously they spoke no Lasska. Bereg looked helplessly at Tama. *What do we do now?*

The boy stepped forward. He pointed at himself and said something that sounded to Bereg like "Yanno."

A name? Bereg nodded as if he understood. The boy pointed to the girl and said "Danya." Bereg caught his breath at how much it sounded like his own daughter's name. Then the boy pointed at Bereg. "Lassar?" he asked.

So they knew that much. Bereg nodded again. The boy and girl talked quickly back and forth in their language. Beyond question, they both sounded scared. Tama stepped closer to Bereg. "Trouble, do you think?" she said.

"I don't know." Bereg gripped his crutch tighter.

The two Namorans seemed to reach a decision. The girl pointed to the three travelers, then to herself, and then to the temple entrance. With one hand, she pantomimed walking. Then she asked something else that sounded like a question.

"Do they want us to leave?" Bereg asked.

"I don't think so," Khari said. "I think she wants to take us somewhere."

Where? Was it safe to go? The girl – Danya – was small, but suppose there were guards or soldiers waiting outside. Suppose this was a trap.

Khari said, "I think we should go with her."

Tama closed her hand around Khari's arm. "Are you sure?"

"Yes."

The Namoran girl, Danya, led them back out to the square, walking fast. Bereg had to struggle to keep up, even with Tama supporting him on his good side. They went down a side street only a short distance from the square. Just as Bereg began to wonder if he could stay on his feet after all, Danya stopped outside a house that looked like any of the others. She knocked on the door.

Tama glanced around uneasily. "Where are we? Whose house is this?"

None of them had any answers. Khari looked tense, but she stood quietly on Bereg's other side, watching the door.

They all heard footsteps coming from the other side. Then the door swung open to reveal a small woman in a dress that made Bereg think of the yellow poppies on the plains. She stood only a little taller than Danya, and she had dark hair and eyes and a pretty face in spite of her expression, which said, as clearly as any words could, that visitors were absolutely unwelcome right now, and probably would be for quite some time. Bereg found himself wanting to apologize and back away.

The woman and the girl talked back and forth. Bereg saw the same alarm in the woman's face that he'd seen from both young people. He caught the word "Lassar." The woman shook her head and pursed her lips, but said something else to the girl and then left the door open as she hurried away. Bereg thought he heard her call to someone inside the house.

In a little while, she came back again. The man she brought with her was considerably taller than she was. Like the boy in the temple, he wore plain slacks and a homespun shirt. Bereg noticed he was barefoot. Then Khari gasped and caught Bereg's arm.

The man stepped into the doorway. Now Bereg got a good look at his face. Lined and worn-looking, tired, but somehow not old. Brown hair heavily streaked with silver. Eyes the color of a cloudless autumn sky.

We found him. Bereg felt the absolute certainty of it, even before he heard Khari whisper, "It's him." The words of a prayer of thanks shaped themselves in Bereg's mind.

The man said, "Can I help you?"

He spoke Lasska, strangely accented, but perfectly understandable. Khari stepped forward. "Please," she said. "We have been looking for you."

The man looked taken aback, as well he might, Bereg thought. It struck him, though, that unlike the other three Namorans they had dealt with so far, this man did not look worried or scared. He said, "You need help from a priest?"

He was the priest here? Bereg had only known a few priests in Lassar, but even the one in his home village had always dressed with as much pomp as his modest salary allowed. He would never have thought to see one barefoot.

Khari shook her head. "We have been looking for you," she said again. "I must explain."

The woman in the yellow dress took hold of the man's hand. Bereg didn't need to understand the words that passed between them to know that she was the man's wife and she was worried for him. He had seen the same look, heard the same tone, from Nela when he'd had to set out to do jobs when he was under the weather. The memory sent a shaft through him.

The man touched the woman's face briefly and said something. Bereg knew what her expression answered. *Very well. If you must.*

The man turned to the travelers. "Please come in."

The girl, Danya, bowed to the man and went away. Back to the temple, Bereg guessed. The man held the house door open. Khari led Bereg and Tama inside.

The priest's name was Ribas Silvaikas, an awkward-sounding group of syllables on Bereg's tongue. His wife's name was Maryut. Bereg hadn't let himself make guesses about the man from Khari's dream; he hadn't dared to believe they would find him. Now that they had, everything about him came as a surprise.

To begin with, this Ribas knew that Khari was Vaia before she told him. In the house's small kitchen, they sat around a wooden table and Khari told Ribas baldly, with no preamble, that Impera Shurik wanted to destroy her people. Bereg thought she would have done better to take things more slowly – surely this backwater priest would have no idea about world affairs, and would have to scramble to keep up – but the priest took Khari's words as sorry confirmation of something he already knew. Shurik had written to the Namoran ruler in Sostavi, the capital city, and demanded Namora's cooperation with his plan. In his correct, bookish-sounding Lasska, Ribas said, "Our leader has asked me to help her decide what to do about the impera's request."

Bereg couldn't help staring. This was a tiny village. Why would a great ruler, as he assumed this woman in the capital must be, ask someone from a place like this to help with such a matter? The priest must have more to him than anyone would guess. But he was young, younger than his gray hair suggested, and his health, Bereg guessed, wasn't strong. He looked as if he had been carrying a heavy weight for a long time. Bereg thought that weight looked heavier with every word Khari said.

The only time he looked startled was when Khari told him, "Some of my people can read dreams. I am one of them. One of my dreams told me that we must come to Namora and find you, and you would help us."

Ribas spoke carefully. "Allow me to be sure I understand. Your dream told you to find me, in particular?" His Lasska, Bereg thought, certainly did sound like he had learned it out of books. Ordinary people didn't speak so formally.

"It was very clear," Khari said. "It showed me exactly what you look like. As soon as I saw you, I knew you were the right person."

"Did your dream say how I am to help you?"

"No," Khari said. Eagerness and anxiety mingled in her face. To Bereg, she looked very young. "It only said you would. It was very clear," she repeated.

Ribas looked more tired than ever. Bereg found his heart going out to the younger man. How could anyone know what to do about something like this?

All through this, Ribas's wife, Maryut, stood behind his chair and kept her eyes on him. Bereg couldn't help thinking she wanted to send some of her own health and strength into him. Ribas asked Khari, "How did you come to travel with Lasska soldiers?" Tama had briefly explained what Bereg could not: that she and he had both made themselves traitors, abandoning their detachments and Shurik's orders.

Khari glanced at Bereg now. Her Lasska probably wasn't up to the full explanation yet. He said, "It's a long story. I can tell you, though, that Khari and Tama saved my life."

Ribas looked as if he wanted to hear more, but Khari said, "There are four other Vaia here, not far from the village. Will they be in danger?"

"Not from us in Lida," Ribas said. "And probably not from anyone else, yet. Word about Shurik hasn't spread. My people know what is happening because I'll go back to Sostavi in two days. I needed to tell them why I am leaving."

Two days. Bereg felt a bead of sweat slide down his spine. If they had gotten to the village two days later, they wouldn't have found the priest at all. Bereg had no idea, yet, what the man might do to help them, and it seemed clear that Ribas had no idea himself, but he was still their only hope.

Ribas said to Khari, "It would be best, I think, if the other Vaia also come into the village."

Tama said, "You're sure your people won't make trouble?"

"They won't," Ribas answered. "We have a service this morning, in our..." The words he used translated as 'house in a circle,' which Bereg didn't understand, but decided he must mean the round temple. "I'll speak to everyone about your being here."

He had the authority to get his villagers to accept the presence of five Vaia and two Lasska soldiers, all of whom were at least theoretically Namora's enemies. Bereg felt impressed. Priests in Lassar got a certain measure of respect, but everyone knew soldiers had the final say in everything.

Ribas's wife, Maryut, put her hand on his shoulder and asked a question. He answered in their language. Out of the flow of words, Bereg only caught his own, Tama's, and Khari's names, Khari's several times, and the words "Vaia" and "Shurik," but he felt sure the priest was summarizing everything for his wife. Maryut's face changed as she listened. Shock, no doubt at the news about Khari's dream, turned into anger, which in turn gave way to sadness. When Ribas finished, she said something else, glancing at Khari as she spoke. Her hand still rested on Ribas's shoulder. Ribas covered it with his own.

"Maryut says," he told Bereg and the others, "she had hoped that Shurik would not do what he intended. She is sorry to hear of such cruelty. We'll help all we can." Bereg saw him press his wife's hand before he let it go. "Khari, can you go and get the others now, and bring them here?"

Tama got up also. "I'll go with her."

Maryut said something else to Ribas and left the kitchen too. Bereg started to push his chair back, thinking he should follow Tama and Khari, but Ribas stopped him. "You need help with your leg. Maryut has gone to send for our...the word you would use is 'healer,' I think."

Bereg wasn't sure about that. He would have felt better if the priest had said "doctor," but maybe they didn't have them in Namora. He said, "We've brought a lot of trouble on you."

"Trouble was already here."

Bereg wondered if that meant Shurik, or something else, or both. "I'm afraid your wife is worried," he said.

"She is. It's hard for us to understand why Shurik would do such a thing. And, to say truly, she wishes I didn't have to go back to Sostavi."

Bereg heard himself say, "My wife must have hated it when I got ordered to Cheremay. That's our capital, you know, a long way from where I lived." With another pang, he remembered the cut-and-dried letter he had sent. *How hard would it have been to tell her I love her?* "I was supposed to have left the army. I was going to retire and go home for good. But then all this started."

Ribas asked, "Where is your home?"

"It's called Kovkya Thysidich, the Fourteenth Claw of the Bear."

"I would like to hear about it, if you would like to tell me."

Bereg wondered if all Namoran priests were like this. Ribas either meant what he said, or knew how to act like it...but Bereg had the feeling that, over-formal speech or not, the Namoran didn't say what he didn't mean. Bereg found himself liking the priest's face. He wasn't handsome, certainly, except for those striking eyes, but he seemed both sensible and kind. For a moment Bereg remembered Shurik's pale blue eyes and the feverish color in his cheeks as he talked about the will of his God.

Bereg let himself talk about Thysidich and his family. At first, he thought the words might choke him, but letting them out eased a weight he had carried for too many weeks. Ribas's quiet attention made it easy to keep going. Sometimes he didn't understand a word or phrase Bereg used, but if Bereg spoke simply and a little more slowly, Ribas caught the line of the talk again. Before Bereg knew it, he was explaining how and why he had left his detachment, and how he didn't know how to live with himself once he became a traitor. "Khari and Tama and the others are all I have now," he finished. "I've gone against everything I ever believed in. I don't know what's going to happen to any of us."

Lasska soldiers didn't give way to tears in front of strangers. Bereg wouldn't let it happen here, but the idea didn't seem entirely shameful in front of this priest. Ribas said, "I find it hard to believe that your God hates any of his people so much, to want them killed."

He couldn't know anything about Mesha. Bereg still wanted to trust the gentle certainty of those words. "Shurik would say the Vaia aren't Mesha's people because they don't believe in Him," he said. "Maybe he's right. I don't know." He decided to change the subject before his grief had a chance to crawl up his throat after all. "Forgive me for asking, but do most Namorans speak Lasska?"

Ribas smiled. It lit his face up surprisingly, and for a moment, Bereg saw how young he actually was. "No," he said, "we don't. I hope my words aren't too terrible."

"Not at all," Bereg said. "You could speak a little less formally, but your accent is very good."

"I'm glad to know that. I haven't had much practice in a long time."

Bereg wondered how and why he had learned the language in this backwater, and who he had practiced speaking it with, and whether he had ever met any Lasska before today. Bereg also would have liked to ask about Namora's ruler. Lassar did not have women imperi. Before he could settle on one question out of the many, he heard the house's front door open again.

Maryut came into the kitchen with an unkempt old man who looked like he had just gotten out of bed. His long silver-white hair was uncombed and his shirt was shoved hastily into his pants so that one tail hung down in the back. He carried a brown leather satchel.

The man gave Bereg a glare and shot a question at Ribas. The priest answered. The man came over to Bereg's chair. Ribas said to Bereg, "This is our healer. His name is Nevas. With your permission, he will take a look at your leg."

Bereg didn't like the sound of that. This man was a doctor, or whatever Namorans called them? He looked like someone you would see on a street in Cheremay, holding out his hat to passerby for spare change.

Ribas seemed to see Bereg's thoughts. "He is an excellent healer," he said. "He and I work together often. He helped get me through a sickness once that I should not have survived."

That did give some reassurance. Bereg undid his splint and pulled up his pant leg. The healer knelt down beside the chair to eye the knee closely. He rattled out a question.

Ribas said, "He would like to know how you got hurt."

Bereg explained how he had fallen and how Tama and Khari had helped take care of the knee. Ribas translated for the healer. Maryut stood off to the side, watching and listening. Nevas, if that was his name, certainly didn't seem friendly, but he listened to everything Ribas said and examined and flexed the knee with a quick, deft touch. Now and then he asked another question: how often Bereg had tried to walk on that leg, how well he could move when he did, how much pain it gave him.

When the healer had heard enough and probed the knee to his satisfaction, he stood up and told Ribas something else in Namoran. The words sounded crisp and decisive. Ribas said, "He says that for you to be able to walk well again, he will have to..." He closed his eyes briefly, gathering words. "He will have to open your knee."

Bereg swallowed. "Do you mean he wants to cut it open? Operate?"

"Yes. He says you have torn something. I'm sorry; my Lasska isn't good enough. He says the thing that is torn can't heal on its own, so he will have to sew it back together."

Bereg didn't like the sound of any of that. "In Lassar, even the most experienced healers" – he used the word Namorans apparently understood – "don't like to operate. They don't think the body can heal well enough if you cut it open." It might be terribly rude of him to argue with these people, but how could he believe that a village "healer" knew more than a Lasska doctor? "Would you explain that to him?"

Ribas translated. Nevas snorted and answered with a fast and impatient-sounding stream of words. Ribas said something that sounded conciliating, but Bereg felt sure he heard the faintest hint of laughter behind the words. Nevas said something else, quick and firm.

Ribas told Bereg, "Nevas says that we do things better in Namora. He says if you will let him help you, you will walk again. Otherwise, you will not."

I can walk with a crutch. Bereg wanted more than to hobble and drag himself around with help from anyone willing to give it. But to do such a thing here, so far from home, to let anyone cut him open and "sew" something inside him back together...what kind of horrible maiming might he let himself in for?

"Do you trust him?" Bereg blurted the words out before he thought.

Ribas looked as if he heard everything Bereg hadn't said. There was no laughter in his voice now. "Yes," he said. "I trust him completely."

The healer said something else to Ribas. Ribas told Bereg, "He says for you to think about it, but think carefully."

Bereg didn't like taking orders from the brusque old Namoran. He bound the splint to his knee again, wondering how much he could trust anything in this strange country, no matter what the priest said, and whether he had a choice.

Shortly before the service in the round temple, Khari and Tama came back to the priest's house with Radavan and the others. Bereg could see the Vaia didn't like being closed in. In spite of Ribas's welcome and reassurance, Handan and Mandhani in particular eyed the walls and furniture as if expecting a trap.

Ribas told all of them a little about the service he would lead at the temple. "I would like you to feel sure of your safety here," he said. Bereg had a feeling the priest's smile was one of his more powerful tools, if you could use that word about something so genuine. It practically compelled trust. "Our goddess, Kenavi, calls her people to take care of each other. Our services remind us of that, and how she cared for us."

Bereg hadn't gone to Lasska services much more than a serving soldier had to, but all of them were full of bowing in the awful presence of the God and apologizing for your feeble human strength and abilities. These Namoran services sounded different. Ribas said,

"Our stories tell that Kenavi gave her life to help the people she loved. We remember that, and we are never lazy in looking after each other."

"Lazy" was a funny word to choose, but Bereg knew why Ribas had wanted them all to know this. He still wondered if the Namorans, much less their goddess, had any reason to "look after" outsiders.

Khari said, "Ribas, may I come and watch the service?"

If the question surprised the priest, he didn't show it. "Certainly. You'll be welcome."

Lasska teaching said there was no God but Mesha. Bereg had always accepted that. Now he said, "I'd like to come too, if that's all right." He had gone so far down the road of treachery and heresy already, another few steps to find out more about this Namoran goddess couldn't make much difference. What kind of god sacrificed itself for puny humans?

Tama said, "I don't know what you two expect to understand, when you don't know any Namoran," but in the end, she decided to go too. Bereg had no doubt she meant to keep guard over Khari. The three of them got to the temple early, with Ribas and Maryut. Bereg was glad they could take seats before more people arrived.

Maryut led them to a bench near the front of the temple. Bereg wouldn't have minded keeping to the back, but it seemed she typically sat up there during services and she wanted them to stay near her. They couldn't talk to her, which felt awkward to Bereg, but she was attentive and kind. She made sure they were comfortable and that the sitting didn't put too much strain on Bereg's leg. After she got them settled, she went to the entrance of the temple. Bereg saw her greeting villagers as they came in.

It seemed like everyone in Lida must come to services. The place filled up steadily. Ribas had explained on the way over that today was called First Day, and that most people did come to the First Day morning service. Apparently they would also have a meal afterward. Bereg wondered if he and Tama and Khari could quietly disappear during that meal. He didn't know what kind of welcome they would get, once Ribas had told the villagers about them and why they were here.

The temple worked strangely on him, though. It was a simple place. The uncarpeted floor was made of the same gray stone as the walls. The windows, spaced at even intervals around the room, were clear glass. The wooden benches were sanded smooth but not ornamented. Their seats and backs showed wear from the generations of people who had come here. A feeling of peace seemed to come out of the stone walls themselves. Bereg couldn't say he had ever felt the same thing in any temple of Mesha.

It turned out that the two young Namorans who had been in the temple that morning were Ribas's apprentices. They walked around the temple now, both wearing red robes of office, greeting and talking to the villagers. After a little while, Ribas himself came into the temple through the door back by the hearth. He wore white robes with no ornamentation Bereg could see. Bereg thought about Mesha's priests, their brown or gold vestments embroidered with elaborate pictures of bears' heads and teeth and claws.

When Ribas stepped to the front of the dais, the talk in the temple quieted down. The two red-robed apprentices went up to the big hearth, where a fire was laid but not lit, though the soot on the stones showed that one had burned here recently. The apprentices stood on either side of the hearth. Maryut came back to her seat beside Tama. Bereg watched as Ribas put his hand over his heart and bowed to the people with a greeting Bereg didn't understand. The villagers answered it.

Khari, sitting between Bereg and Tama, touched Bereg's arm. "He looks sad," she said quietly.

Bereg saw it too. He remembered Ribas saying that he had to leave the village in two days, that his wife didn't want him going to the capital city. Now that Khari had pointed it out, Bereg thought sadness seemed to rise up the walls of the temple itself, as if each person had brought a cupful of it with them, the way you could fill a cistern with water a little at a time. Ribas's people didn't want him to leave. Based on what he'd seen of the priest only this morning, Bereg couldn't blame them.

Ribas was saying something in Namoran. Then Bereg heard him switch over to Lasska. The priest looked directly at the bench where Bereg and the others sat.

"I am going to tell them now that you are here because of what Shurik is doing," he said, "and I am going to tell them what that is."

Bereg nodded. Tama, he saw, looked tense. Like him, she must be thinking about how all the people in this place might react to what they were about to hear. No one had really noticed them yet, the two Lasska and the Vaia girl, but that would change in the next moments. Khari sat forward, attentive, her eyes on the priest.

Ribas started speaking in Namoran again. Bereg caught the words "Lasska" and "Vaia," and then "Shurik." A whisper started up around the room. As Ribas went on, the whisper swelled to a murmur. Bereg caught an edge of anger in the sound. He gripped his crutch where it leaned on the bench beside him.

Tama leaned across Khari. "I want to know what they're saying."

Bereg did too. For all any of them knew, they might be trapped here, weaponless except for his crutch, with the entire village after their blood. No matter what Ribas had said about them not being in danger, about the villagers taking care of one another the way their goddess wanted them to, maybe these people resented the travelers for bringing their own trouble into Namora. Maybe they saw the arrival of Lasska and Vaia here as another reason why their priest had to leave them, and they wanted to take out their sorrow on easy targets.

Ribas stopped talking. The murmuring filled the temple, and you couldn't mistake the anger in it now. Bereg didn't dare look around at any of the faces near them in case someone took it as a challenge. Tama clenched her fists. Bereg knew she was ready to take a swing at anyone who came for them.

Maryut reached over and put her hand on Tama's arm. She

looked anxious, but shook her head. Khari said, "I think she means it's all right."

On the dais, Ribas held up his hands. The talk stopped at once. The priest said something else in Namoran and Bereg heard a swell of what sounded like agreement from the villagers. Ribas looked at the travelers again.

In Lasska, he said, "We will help you stand against Shurik." Again, Bereg read real sympathy in the too-worn young face. "What he is doing to your people, Khari" – the blue eyes rested on her – "is wrong. We will not sit by and watch."

Bereg felt himself relax. They were only words, but he could see that words had power here. Tama still looked suspicious, but sat back against the bench. Bereg glanced at Khari and saw a tear shining on her cheek.

Too much of a burden to put on her shoulders. It wasn't fair. They had come all this way, and found the priest, but neither they nor he seemed to have any idea how he could help them. And meanwhile, Khari's tribe was still on the other side of the mountains. No one knew what might be happening to them by now.

The service began. Tama had been right: Bereg didn't understand any of it. He watched the motions and tried to recapture the peace he'd felt here earlier. He tried not to think how he never, in over a half-century of life, could have believed he would find himself in a Namoran temple, listening to a Namoran priest go through a ritual to their foreign goddess. He tried not to think of the uncountable miles that lay between him and home.

One thing did stand out in the service. When Ribas began to read from a small book, Khari sat forward, her eyes wide. She listened as if hanging onto every word.

Did she understand it? How? Bereg whispered to her, "What's he saying?"

She held up a hand to silence him, never taking her eyes off the priest. When Ribas finished reading and closed the book, she sat back. Bereg heard her sigh.

"I couldn't quite understand it," she whispered, "but almost. I don't know what language it was. It sounded a lot like Vaia."

Vaia? Namorans spoke something that sounded like Vaia? Bereg puzzled over that during another reading, a prayer, and a ritual involving a pitcher of water and a box of what looked like salt. Then he recognized the end of the service, because Ribas had explained how it worked.

Each villager went up to the dais and took a stone out of a basket that stood on the table there. They each then went to one of the temple's eight windows and offered a prayer to Kenavi there. Bereg watched the lines of people moving up to the dais, and then away through the temple: men in working clothes, women in bright dresses, old people leaning on canes or the arms of younger ones, children holding onto a parent's hand. Bereg wondered at the meditative silence that still filled the great room. No one talked or whispered or coughed. Even the smallest children didn't giggle or run around. Bereg wondered if Namorans were always so quiet, or if this was part of the same sadness he had felt here earlier.

Bereg and Tama both stayed where they were on the bench, but when Maryut stood up to go to the dais, Khari followed her. Bereg watched anxiously to see how the villagers would react. He saw some curious glances at the Vaia girl, who stood out both for her clothes and her dark skin and hair, but no one approached her or said anything. When Khari took a stone out of the basket, Bereg saw Ribas smile at her. She went to the nearest window and stood quietly, with her head down, for several heartbeats before she put her stone in the smaller basket on the windowsill.

After the service, everyone moved toward the door by the temple's hearth. Bereg dragged himself off the bench to follow the others. They went down a short passage to the warm, crowded kitchen, where the big meal would take place.

No, Namorans weren't always quiet. The noise hit Bereg first: a babble of talk and laughter, the clatter of dishes, the scrape of benches on a stone floor. Then there was the warmth, and the smells of food, and the crackling of a big hearth fire. It felt as if the village were a single huge family all crowding into a home to share a meal.

Bereg, Khari, and Tama stood close together in the corner nearest to the doors. They could see long tables on the other side of the room, spread with food. The scents made Bereg's stomach growl – he couldn't remember eating a full, good meal since leaving Cheremay – but he didn't want to think about trying to get through this crowd.

He remembered what Ribas had called the temple: the "house in a circle." Maybe the village really was something like a family, and this temple was something like a big house that someone had thrown open to let everyone inside. He found himself wishing Nela could see it. She'd have been right up there by the big tables at the front, helping people fill their plates. Bereg cut the thought off, but not before the room swam.

Meanwhile, the villagers had closed in around their priest. If the village was a family, and the temple was a house, then Ribas was...not a father-figure, exactly, he was too young for that. But Bereg saw how the children pestered him for attention, and how the adults reached out for handshakes and hugs, and how some of them – the oldest ones – took hold of the priest's hand between both of theirs and held it as if they didn't want to let it go. Bereg's chest tightened at the memory of Nela holding Ania's hand exactly that way, just before Ania's wedding.

He had never seen anything like this with a Lasska priest. Tama saw it too. "They love him," she said.

Bereg needed to get off his feet. The splint and crutch could only do so much. Now, though, people were closing in around him and Khari and Tama too. Bereg saw a great deal of curiosity, but no hostility in the glances. There were smiles and friendly looks, more sympathy than Bereg would have dared to expect. The villagers couldn't speak Lasska, but face after face told Bereg that the travelers were, as Ribas had said, safe here.

"They're decent people," Tama said quietly. Bereg agreed. Khari said, "They also follow their priest."

Just as Bereg began to think he couldn't stand there any longer, Ribas detached himself from the group around him. He brought two people over to the travelers: a stocky younger man with dark curly hair, and an older woman with silver hair and eyes the same brilliant blue as the priest's own.

Ribas said, "This is my brother Gedrin, and my mother Pelayut. They have a farm on the north edge of the village. You and the other Vaia are welcome to stay there."

A farm? Bereg liked the sound of that. A place with open land, away from people. Tama said, "It will be safe?"

Ribas assured her it would be. Khari said, "Can we go there now?"

Ribas couldn't leave the temple yet, but the younger man and the woman agreed to go back to the priest's house first for Radavan and the others, and then take the group up to the farm. The woman, Pelayut, gave Bereg her arm to help him walk. To his surprise, she said a few halting words of Lasska.

"I am glad we can help you."

Her accent wasn't as good as her son's, but Bereg felt only too grateful to hear familiar words. "Thank you," he said.

He guessed she was only a few years younger than he was, but her height and straight-backed, graceful way of carrying herself made her seem ageless. In her face, he saw strength and what looked like the echo of an old sadness. He said slowly, articulating carefully in the hope that she would understand, "I am sorry we must trouble you like this."

"Not at all." She had the same smile as her son, too. It lit up her face. "We like visitors."

To Bereg's relief, she and the young man, Gedrin, had a cart waiting outside the temple. It had two benches in it. "You must sit," Pelayut told Bereg, motioning at the benches to make sure he understood. "Help your leg."

He obeyed. They went to the priest's house first, where Khari explained to Radavan and the others where they were going. The

Vaia mounted up and followed the cart, which Gedrin drove, up one of the small grassy roads away from the village square.

Pelayut sat on the bench next to Bereg. The bench faced backward so they watched the riders behind. Handan and Mandhani looked uneasy, out of place in these strange surroundings, scanning the fields for any sign of trouble. Rahul, Bereg saw, seemed fascinated by plants he didn't recognize. More than once, he held back to look at a tree or shrub and then had to hurry to catch up with the cart again. Radavan kept a steady pace some distance behind the cart; the rear guard, Bereg thought.

Khari rode close enough to the cart to talk to Bereg. "It's a beautiful place," she said.

He had to agree. Pelayut understood the words too. "We like it," she said.

Bereg asked her, speaking as carefully as before, "Did Ribas teach you to speak Lasska?"

Her smile told him he had guessed right. "Yes," she said. "When he needed practice. It has been a long time."

Bereg would have liked to talk to her more, but he didn't want to press her too far past her command of the language. Most of the ride up to the farm happened in silence. To Bereg, at least, it was a comfortable silence.

The farm had a long, low house, several outbuildings, and a big apple orchard. It looked nothing like the cabin in Thysidich, but somehow it didn't feel entirely different. A sense of home hung around it.

Pelayut had noticed that the travelers hadn't eaten at the temple. In the farmhouse kitchen, she gave them a meal of bread and some sort of soft cheese, tea, cakes made with what tasted like honey and cinnamon, and some of the finest apples Bereg had ever tasted. Pelayut noticed his admiration and proudly told him the apples came from this farm. Bereg decided he'd been right about the rich land here.

The Vaia didn't want to spend any more time indoors than necessary, so Bereg and Tama between them persuaded Pelayut not to worry about beds. The house seemed full already, with her and Gedrin and Gedrin's wife and young children, but Bereg had a feeling Pelayut never turned a guest away. She insisted on giving him her own room, making a pallet in the loft for herself. He couldn't refuse. His old bones would welcome a break from the hard ground.

Khari felt more comfortable inside the house than the other Vaia. When Ribas and Maryut came up to the farm later in the afternoon, Khari sat in the front room, by the hearth, talking with the two of them about the service. Tama had gone outside to explore the grounds, but Bereg stayed by the hearth too. Having solid walls around him and a comfortable chair to sit on felt like luxury.

Khari asked Ribas, "What was that language you used when you read? It wasn't Namoran."

"We call it *Pirlevis*." Ribas had changed out of the robes of office. He looked like a farmer in his plain clothes, and it suited him. He said, "In Lasska, I think you would say, 'First Speech.'"

"It sounded like my language," Khari said. "Vaia. Not quite the same, but almost."

"Really?" Interest made Ribas's face young and alive in the same way his smile did. "I never heard they were alike. I'm afraid I know nothing about the Vaia language."

Pelayut came in from the kitchen and joined them, taking the chair next to Bereg. Khari said, "I could try to teach you a little Vaia," and Ribas answered, "I would like that very much."

Pelayut's face was quiet, her hands still, but Bereg saw how she looked at her son. If Ania had to go away to face a danger, Bereg would want to make his own body a shield in front of her. He couldn't, and Pelayut couldn't, but she watched Ribas as if her attention could protect him.

Bereg felt certain, too, that Ribas had trouble with his health. The priest had mentioned *a sickness I shouldn't have survived*. A bad sickness could have left behind trouble that would account for the tiredness in his face, the lines around his eyes and the gray hair. Bereg thought that, like Khari, the priest had to carry too much of a burden. From what Bereg could tell, that burden would only get heavier in the days to come.

He came out of his thoughts in time to hear Khari say, "I want to come with you to the city. May I?"

What was this? Bereg hadn't considered going to Sostavi, wherever that was. Ribas looked doubtful. "I don't know what I will be able to do," he said. "And I don't know what people there may think about you."

He was right. A Vaia in the capital, with the threat from Shurik out in the open. Bereg knew it wouldn't be safe. Khari lifted her chin. "I think I should come. Please."

Bereg didn't know how she thought she could help. Ribas clearly didn't either. Before he could reply, someone knocked on the front door and walked in without preamble.

It was the old healer from the morning. Bereg wished abruptly that he'd gone outside with Tama. Nevas greeted Maryut, Ribas, and Pelayut warmly and then snapped a question. Bereg had a feeling he knew what it was.

Ribas looked like he was struggling not to smile. "Nevas would like to know," he told Bereg, "what you've decided about your leg."

Bereg felt trapped. What choice did he have? But how could he trust himself to this person when they didn't speak the same language? How much would a Namoran healer know?

Khari said, "Bereg, I think you should let him do it." Bereg had told her and Tama about the healer before the service. "I want you to be able to walk again."

When she looked at him that way, it was hard to refuse. "You're hurt too," he reminded her. "Would you let him look at your side?"

"Yes."

Bereg wished he had her certainty. Coming across the mountains had severed his last link with home.

But, right now, they had this farm, with its delicious apples. And they had gotten the friendly looks in the temple, and they had this priest, weighted and worn as he was.

"All right," Bereg said. He looked at Ribas. "Please tell the healer I would welcome his help."

Ribas translated. Bereg saw that Nevas looked grimly satisfied. At least he also looked a bit more reputable now, with his hair combed and both of his shirttails tucked in. Bereg probably ought to trust a man even older than himself.

And if they did this soon, if the healer cut his leg open, Bereg would not be able to travel any farther, probably for weeks. If Khari went on to Sostavi, he would have to stay behind.

This day had been too long. Bereg had sat in a foreign temple and watched people worship a foreign goddess, something he had heard all his life that Mesha would condemn His people for doing. He didn't know what to think about Mesha anymore.

I find it hard to believe, Ribas had said, *that your God hates any of his people so much.*

21

KHARI

Khari had not let herself believe they would find the man from her dream so quickly. She had hoped the village temple would be a place to start looking, and that the village priest might guide them, but she hadn't let herself think, during the walk from the temple to the priest's house, that the search might end here. When the priest stepped into the doorway and Khari saw his hair and lined face and those unmistakable eyes, she had thought the sheer relief might make her collapse where she stood.

Moon Woman. Forgive me my doubt.

He existed. She sat at his table and looked into the face that, by now, she knew as well as her own. She might have believed she was still dreaming, except for the ache where the Lasska had shot her, and cool smoothness of the tabletop under her palms, and the scent of the hearth fire and some unfamiliar Namoran spices. Khari explained why she and Bereg and Tama had come to Namora, and what was happening behind them, on the other side of the mountains. The priest, Ribas, understood Lasska. He replied in the same language and told her he knew of Shurik's plan already.

For those first minutes, it was enough. Khari felt as if she could take the journey of the past weeks, the pain of separation from the rest of her people, the encounters with the Lasska soldiers, the death of the silde by her own weapon, all the fear and strain and uncertainty, and roll it up like a blanket to lay at the priest's feet. Her part of this struggle had ended. If her pathdream was right – and it must be, because he was here – he would know what to do now.

That relief lasted only a short, precious while. Then Ribas asked her, "Did your dream say how I am to help you?"

But you know. You must. "No," Khari said. "It only said you would. It was very clear."

His face told her at once that he had no more answers than she did. Disappointment broke over her, as hard and fierce as a summer storm. After they had come so far; after she had trained all her hopes on finding him. It couldn't be true.

"How did you come to travel with Lasska soldiers?" he said.

Khari didn't trust herself to speak. She wouldn't let herself cry like a child in front of this man. Instead she looked at Bereg, who said, "It's a long story. I can tell you, though, that Khari and Tama saved my life."

Khari made herself ask if Radavan and the others would be safe here. She listened numbly as the priest said yes, and explained that the villagers knew about the Vaia because he, Ribas, was leaving in two days to go to the Namoran capital city. Two more days, and he would have been gone from here. Khari tried to conjure up her relief again, but it had fallen apart like a trampled spiderweb.

When she and Tama went to bring Radavan and the others into the village, Khari told the men candidly that they had found the person they needed, but she still didn't know how he could help them. She saw her own disappointment reflected in Radavan's face. Handan, though, shrugged it off. "But he's here. Your dreams have led us right so far."

Rahul agreed. As they rode back toward the stone temple, he brought his horse up beside Khari's on the narrow road. "At night," he said, "a lamp only shows you the ground in front of your feet."

He had told her the same thing on the day they had first seen Bereg and Tama, the day Khari had her second pathdream and Rahul himself went alone into the Lasska camp. That day, he had wanted to make her smile. There was no mischief in his face now.

She said, "I know." With Tama and the others riding ahead, it didn't feel so shameful to let her eyes well up. "I thought it would be simple once we found him." Only a child could have thought such a thing. "I should have known better."

He reached over and took her hand. "You've done well, Lamp-Carrier."

The warmth of his fingers around hers helped her blink back the tears. Ahead of them, Handan glanced around. Khari saw his eyes move to her hand and Rahul's, joined together. She didn't let go.

Vatiri had told Khari, so long ago now, *You'll find him. You'll get help for us.* The path ahead of all of them was still dark. Khari must keep carrying the lamp forward.

She set herself to learn about the priest. If she watched him, she might see what he could do for them. At first, her disappointment made it hard to see anything, but her mother-in-truth would expect better of her. Khari tried to clear the dust from her eyes and mind.

Ribas didn't seem strong. Khari thought at once that he must have some kind of health trouble. He wasn't physically strong, but – again she pushed herself to see more clearly, more truthfully – he had something else. He had listened to her story without fear or distrust. He had accepted her truth at once. He had told her and the others, with a simplicity that allowed for no doubt, that the Goddess he served called on her people to take care of each other, and he would see it done.

A different kind of strength. Khari went to the service at the round temple to watch him more. There, she saw how much his people didn't want him to leave them, and she began to realize the place he held in the village. He wasn't like a Lodestone, or a Lamp-Carrier either, but maybe a little of each, with something else besides. Lodestones commanded respect. Lamp-Carriers did too, sometimes with a side measure of fear of their power. This priest claimed love. Khari saw and felt it filling the temple.

When he told the village about the Vaia and Shurik, and angry voices rose around them, Khari saw Bereg's and Tama's tension. She herself wasn't afraid. Ribas wouldn't let anything happen. When he looked straight her and said, "We will help you stand against Shurik," and promised, "We will not sit by and watch," she knew he meant it. Hope rose in her again. She still had no answer to the question of what he could do, but she felt sure the answer was there, if she could find it.

At one point in the service, Ribas opened a small thin book and began to read from it. Khari hadn't understood anything before that, but at that moment, she felt as if some long-forgotten memory was trying to wake up in her mind. The words sounded almost, almost like the language she had spoken all her life. She wished Ribas would read more slowly, let her listen to the words one at a time, so their meaning might take shape...but the reading ended, and he was speaking Namoran again, and the picture she hadn't quite been able to piece together fell apart.

He had explained the prayer ritual that would end the service. When his wife Maryut got up to offer a prayer, Khari followed.

She still didn't entirely understand how a mortal woman could be a goddess, but Ribas believed it, and he belonged to this Kenavi. Maybe his goddess could help light the next steps of the path.

The prayer stones in the basket distracted her when she looked in. So many colors, all polished to gleam like glass. They were beautiful. Khari chose a small pure-white one that fit snugly in her palm. She waited in line, aware of the unfamiliar space around her and murmurs and whispers in the language she didn't understand, but nothing about the place or the people in it frightened her. When her turn came, she went up to the window next to the temple's hearth.

Gray winter fog lay over the village. Khari hadn't seen sunlight since that morning on the peak in the Senai when she'd gotten her first glimpse of Namora. Mist came in through the open window and dampened Khari's skin and hair.

She closed her eyes, aware of the smooth touch of the stone against her palm. *Kenavi,* she thought, *if you can hear me, you know I serve the Moon Woman. I do not belong to you, but Ribas does.*

Her side still ached from the Lasska bullet. Bereg might never walk again. All of them had paid, in different ways, for this journey into this country where they were all strangers. They had done it on the strength of Khari's dreams.

Ribas is supposed to help us. He carries a weight of his own.

She saw that weight in the tiredness in his face, the sadness that hid behind his smile. She liked his smile. She wished he were healthier.

Please guide him, Goddess. Please show us what we must do now.

She offered the prayer in Vaia, trusting that language didn't matter here. When she finished, she set the white prayer stone in the small basket by the window.

At the farmhouse, which belonged to Ribas's mother and brother, Khari watched the priest's family, learning how they moved and spoke and treated one another. She saw immediately how much the older woman, Pelayut, loved and worried for both of her sons.

Some kind of trouble hung over the younger brother, Gedrin. He didn't do or say anything out of place, but as Khari watched him, she found herself thinking of a roped wild horse, ready to lash out at anyone who came too close. She saw how Pelayut watched Gedrin closely and listened attentively whenever he spoke. Khari had a feeling that she wanted to hold him, wanted to wrap her care around him like a blanket to keep him safe and quiet.

With Ribas, it was different. Khari saw the way Pelayut's eyes followed her older son, never intrusive, always aware. Before the priest and his wife left the farmhouse for the night, Khari saw Pelayut take Ribas's hand and say something quietly. The look that passed between them told Khari that they shared some kind of sorrow that bound them together more tightly than any cord. She wondered what it was.

That evening, she and Radavan and the others had supper in the farmhouse kitchen with Pelayut, Gedrin, and Gedrin's family. The warm room with its big hearth could barely hold so many people. Radavan and Handan had talked about eating outside, in the camp they had set up on the edge of the apple orchard, but Pelayut wouldn't hear of it.

Namorans made good food. The hot chicken stew, seasoned with mint and a sweet, fruity herb Khari didn't recognize, drove out the winter damp. Khari thought she had never tasted anything quite as delicious as the golden apple cider Pelayut served out of squat glass bottles. It tasted the way sunlight would if you could pour it. Khari and the others found themselves laughing as they tried to communicate with the Namorans, using hand motions and a few Lasska words here and there. Pelayut understood a little bit of Lasska and tried to translate back and forth, but she tripped over words and got tangled up between the two languages. Gedrin pretended to scold her. Khari noticed how much younger and happier he looked when he laughed.

Gedrin's children, a little girl and a slightly older boy, watched the strangers with shy round eyes. Toward the end of supper, the boy got up and went around to Handan. When he tapped him on the shoulder to get his attention, Khari saw Handan start at the touch and look around at the child as if he might be some unusual kind of animal. The boy flexed one of his arms and mimed the motion of throwing something, and then asked a question in Namoran. Pelayut translated it carefully as, "He says you are strong, and asks if you can play..." She looked for the words. "Ball-on-post."

Khari didn't know what that meant. Handan obviously didn't either. Rahul had been leafing through a book Ribas had lent him from the temple, something rich with intricate pictures. He looked up and said in Vaia, "It must be a game of theirs."

Handan shook his head at the boy. "I don't know how to play."

Pelayut translated this. Khari saw the boy's disappointment. Handan apparently did too, because he said, "But I can hunt. You know?" He mimed the motion of shooting an arrow from a bow. The boy's eyes went wide and he said something eagerly. Pelayut told Handan, "He says he would like to try that."

The Vaia were strangers everywhere. Khari didn't quite know how to feel about this Namoran family accepting them, and Bereg and Tama, so readily. That night, the two Lasska slept in the house, but Khari and the other Vaia went out to the camp near the orchard. In spite of the cold, it felt good to see the sky up above and talk together in their own language.

Handan looked thoughtful. "I wonder what Namorans teach their children. If that boy will learn to hunt someday."

He hadn't said anything about Khari and Rahul. Khari was glad. Radavan said, "I doubt it. I think he'll be a farmer like his father."

"Farming." Handan made a derisive noise. "Why do people tie themselves to the ground?"

Rahul looked up at the spreading branches of the apple trees. They were bare now, but the cider from supper had shown what those trees promised next year. "I don't know," he said. "For fruit like this, it might be worth waiting."

"You'd wait years," Handan said. "You'd get tired of staying in one place."

Rahul didn't look convinced. Khari had never seen the appeal of owning one small patch of ground, instead of moving freely over the earth, but now she had seen and talked to people for whom *home* meant something specific and sacred. Home, for the Vaia, could be anywhere and everywhere. For the first time, Khari understood a different way of living.

That night, she moved her bedroll a little distance away from the others. They didn't have to watch for soldiers here. The peace of the farm and the orchard, with a light chilly wind moving among the bare branches of the trees, made a shell around her. When she slept, she dreamed.

It began with the ocean. Khari had seen the ocean only once, several years ago when the tribe had gone farther south than usual for the winter. Now, her hidden eye, the part of her that watched her dreams, called it up again in memory and she recognized it. A single great field of water that moved and glittered under the sun and spoke with its own voice.

The Mouth of Winds breathed on the water. The Sun God reached down for the hand of the God of the Sea. The young world drank the sunlight and the salt breeze.

A finger of land stretched out into the water. Rocks made a jagged coast around it, but inland, the earth was smooth and green. At the end of the peninsula, a hill curved up into the sky. Khari seemed to see all of it from above, as if the Sun God had lifted her high above the earth.

People lived here, on the finger of land. A village, a cluster of houses, started on the flatland and climbed up the green slopes of the hill. The houses were round, built of stone. They had roofs shaped like cones, made of bundles of branches lashed together.

Khari's watching mind saw the houses and knew where she had seen such a thing before. Then the eye of the dream moved closer, into the village.

A stone guarding wall separated the village from the causeway that led to the mainland. Men gathered together by the wall and clustered by the wooden gate. They were tall, rangy, with sun-browned skin and long hair that ranged in color from sandy-pale to soil-dark, except for one or two gray heads. They wore loose-fitting shirts and breeches that seemed to be made of hide. Some of them carried long spears. Others had heavy wooden clubs. A few had axes with heads cut from stone.

Khari seemed to stand on the guarding wall by the gate. The men's voices rose and swirled around her, loud and angry and running into each other. She couldn't understand the words, but she felt their meaning. The men knew of danger outside on the mainland. They were going out to hunt it and bring it down.

The eye of the dream moved again, skimming down the peninsula and back to the mainland. Here, people had made a camp, not far from the place where the peninsula jutted out from the shore. They had tents made of animal skins and cook fires where meat turned on spits. They had horses, small-bodied and compact, with dark manes and tails.

And the people themselves: Khari knew them at once. They were dark-skinned with long dark hair. Some had woven grasses and flowers into their braids. One of them wore a hide shirt bleached pure moon-white. Another wore a hide shirt dyed pollen-yellow, and it glowed under the sun like a flag.

The dream moved back to the village and the guarding wall. But now someone had come to join the men: a young woman, no more than fifteen or sixteen years old. She was slender but strong-built, with wheat-brown hair and eyes the color of a cloudless sky. She stood with her back to the guarding wall, facing the men, shouting something. Her words carried anger and grief.

The men argued against her. They shouted, hefting their spears and brandishing their axes.

The woman, the girl, scrambled to the top of the guarding wall, so close to the place where Khari seemed to be that Khari could have reached out and touched her sleeve. The Mouth of Winds tugged at the girl's long hair and made her hide skirt flap around her legs. Behind her, far below, the ocean crashed against the rocks. The girl stood fearless, with her arms folded over her chest. Her stance and her face said she would not let the men pass through the gate.

But now two of the men swung the heavy gate open. The thick logs scraped on the gravelly soil. The girl shouted again. The grief in her voice drove through Khari like the Lasska bullet.

The girl lifted her face to the sky and closed her eyes, and a change came.

Khari saw the men dragging the gate stop where they stood. Confusion filled every face. Weapons fell from hands that no longer wanted to hold them. Men looked at each other as if they did not know where they were or what they had been doing.

On the guarding wall, the girl swayed, her body suddenly no stronger than a reed in the wind. Khari reached out to catch her, knowing she couldn't do it. The girl's body passed through her hands as if it was made of mist. Khari could not keep from crying out, a sound no one heard, as the girl fell. The Mouth of Winds carried her down onto the rocks. The Sea God reached up to claim her.

The dream changed.

A place outside of everything. A great bear, bigger than worlds: paws the size of nations, teeth like the tallest trees.

Nothing should be able to hold such a creature. But a web traps it: lines of red and blue fire bind its legs, snare its head, grip its body. Fur scorches under the fire. Skin burns. The bear snarls in pain, but its teeth and claws cannot rend the net.

Then someone else is there, in this place beyond any place.

A man. His face is worn and lined; his eyes are the color of a cloudless sky. He is far too small and weak to face the bear, trapped though it is. For a time outside time, there is nothing else. Only the man with his tired face and the snarling bear caught in its torment.

Then, out of the surrounding dark, the ocean rushes in.

The great blue wave sparkles with the light of the Sun God and sings with the Mouth of Winds. It surges toward the man and lifts him up. The shapes of the swirling foam on the water hint at a woman's face and eyes and hands.

The man reaches out, not with hands or voice, but he reaches out all the same. The wave itself reaches out with him.

A shaft of white light slices through the net binding the bear. The lines of fire disappear.

And the bear is free, towering in strength, roaring with gladness. But the wave falls away, carrying the man with it. The white light vanishes. The dark pours in.

~

At first light, Khari went down to the village alone. The dream sat in her heart, heavy as stone.

Maryut answered her knock, dressed in a shift with a dark green robe wrapped around her. Khari grieved for the worry in her face. She wished she had the Namoran words to apologize for coming so early, but she could only say in Lasska, "I must see Ribas. Please."

Maryut seemed to understand. She let Khari in and led her to the kitchen, where she lit a fire in the grate, and said something in Namoran. Khari only understood Ribas's name.

Maryut left the room. Khari sat at the table. The dawn chill seemed to have wrapped around her and burrowed deep into her muscles. The fire quickly warmed the kitchen, but she shivered. Lamp-Carriers must not back away from the truth of their path-dreams. The Moon Woman had granted Khari great guidance on this journey. Khari must not question Her now.

Ribas came into the kitchen. He had dressed, but wore a robe over his clothes. The early-morning chill must bother him too. Khari said, "I'm sorry to come so early."

He sat down at the table with her. "That's all right. What is wrong?"

She had tried not to let her face show anything. He was too quick, and the kindness in his voice made it all the harder to say what she had to. "I had a dream last night."

She didn't know if he understood the dreams. She had tried to explain their importance yesterday, but Namorans didn't know about such things. He must not think she had woken him up so early because of a simple nightmare.

He didn't seem to think so. "Please tell me."

Khari steadied herself. Carefully, simply, as if she had been laying them out for Vatiri, she told him about both parts of her dream. The girl in the village who had done – *something* – so that the men would not go out and hunt the people that Khari knew must be Vaia.

And the second part, the great bear in the net, and how Ribas himself had done – *something* – so that the net had disappeared.

As she told it, she wished with all her soul that Vatiri had been sitting here with her. She wished that she, Khari, could lay these truths in front of the older woman, and Vatiri could dig into their meanings as calmly as she had with the dream in which Khari had seen Ribas for the first time. And then Vatiri could find some other meaning for the end of it, a different meaning than the one that made Khari feel as if the chill that had settled in her would never leave her again.

As she talked, keeping her voice as level as she could, speaking simply and slowly to be sure he followed, she saw Ribas's face change. At first, he was simply attentive. Then, as she described the girl and the village and the houses – round houses, just like the temple – the attention turned first to confusion and then astonishment. When she told him about the girl falling into the water, he shook his head; not, she understood, to deny what she said, but out of amazement. He didn't interrupt.

When she told him about the bear, though, and the lines of the net, she heard him gasp. His eyes narrowed and he looked at her so closely that she had to clench her hands in her lap not to stumble over her words. She told him about the wave and the white light that set the bear free, and then she told him about the darkness.

Her voice shook at the end. She couldn't help it. After she finished, Ribas looked at her for what felt like a long time. She saw nothing in his face now but a quiet, grave attention, but she still found it hard to meet his eyes.

The girl died. The man fell, and the light disappeared.

Khari wanted her people safe. She wanted to see her mother-in-truth's face again and feel those strong arms around her. She wanted to know that she and her tribe, and all the tribes, could live in peace in the land that had been theirs since beyond memory. The longing she felt for those things went beyond anything words or tears or prayers could express.

The pathdream might have shown an answer. Khari had to think it did, though she didn't understand that answer yet. But she didn't know how to lift the weight of it that lay before her. She didn't know how to hold and carry the knowledge that the price of her people's safety was the life of the man sitting with her now.

Ribas closed his eyes. Khari felt his breathing as if it had been her own. Did he understand the ending of the dream as well as she did?

He opened his eyes. "What you've told me...that is extraordinary."

If he did understand, Khari wondered at his strength of mind, to sound so calm. She herself was trembling. Treacherous memory showed her the Lasska silde in the sights of her own vindula. She had pulled the trigger. She had watched the Lasska fall. The Vaia did not take other people's lives if they had any other choice, but the silde had been an enemy. In the single day since she had met Ribas, Khari had seen who and what he was.

He said, "I was unsure what to think about your dreams. But you knew something about me that you had no way of knowing."

She would match his strength if she could. "I don't understand what I saw."

He smiled then, a sudden ray of light. "I have a strange...skill," he said. "I'm sorry. I don't know if my Lasska will let me explain. I can see into a person's mind, and sometimes I can change what is there."

Khari had never heard of such a thing. Carefully, with her help over some of the Lasska words, he told her about his skill – gift, he called it – and how it worked. He told her that when he looked at a person, he could see lines and patterns of light that told him what that person was feeling. The net around the bear sounded familiar to him. He had seen such things before. He said he could sometimes reach in and, for example, cut a net of that kind, to free the mind it trapped.

"It sounds as if that happened at the end of your dream," he said. "But when I cut a net, I have never seen white light."

Fascination overruled Khari's fears. She wanted to ask a handful of questions at once. Had he always had his gift? Had someone trained him to use it? How exactly did he cut the lines? But he had questions first.

"Tell me again about the net around the bear. The colors in it."

Khari described them. When she told him about the blue lines, he asked if they were a pure blue, and she remembered that in fact they'd had a grayish-purple cast, like a bruise. He told her that kind of blue meant fear, and the red was anger. "But I don't understand the bear itself," he said. "What does it mean?"

Khari didn't know either. "The bear always means something about Lassar, because of their god. Sometimes it can mean Shurik. Bereg and Tama were in my dreams as bears too."

He thought about this. She realized he was looking at it as systematically as Vatiri would have. That steadied her. "But in your dream, the bear was huge," he said. "Would that still mean only one person? Could it be Shurik?"

Khari didn't think so. Shurik had appeared as a bear in Vatiri's dream, but nothing like the size of the one Khari had seen. She told him something that sounded foolish inside her own head. "I wonder if it might be Mesha himself."

His face went very still. "Mesha. The god?"

He had just told her what he could do to minds. She said, "Shurik says it's Mesha's will to destroy my people. To help us, then, you might have to change the will of the god."

Could a mortal person hope to try such a thing and survive? The answer to that question lay dark and heavy in her mind.

"Khari, for the gift to work, I have to be able to see the person." His voice sounded gentle. "I can't see Mesha."

With the mind of a god, could his skill work in a different way? Did a god have a mind like a person? Khari meant to ask those questions, but instead she heard herself say, "When you use your gift, is it dangerous?"

Morning light came through the kitchen windows now; not warm sun, but the thin gray light that filtered through winter clouds. The lines on Ribas's face stood out more clearly than ever. "Yes," he said, "it can be. When the lines are strong, thick" – he mimed trying to pull something apart – "they are hard to cut. They need a lot of strength." He smiled, but it looked tired. "I'm afraid I do not have much."

Khari thought of the fiery lines that burned the bear's fur and scorched its skin. No net could be stronger than that. "If it was too hard to cut, what would happen to you?"

"The gift has a cost. Sometimes my heart..." He touched his chest briefly. "Sometimes it has trouble. I might be sick for a while."

Khari knew, without his telling her, that the consequences might be much worse. *The girl fell. The light disappeared.*

She hadn't told any of the men about this pathdream. They had all been asleep when she came down to the village. If they did know about it, she could hear Handan saying that there was no choice, the Namoran priest must sacrifice himself to save the tribes. Handan would see it as a simple matter. One life in exchange for many. Even Radavan, who understood Ribas's worth to his own people, would probably agree. He had Dahila and the children always in his thoughts.

Rahul might see it differently. He might know why Khari felt so sick and cold. And Vatiri? If she were here, what would she say?

Ribas said, "This will need some more thought. We need to know what the bear is. And I would like to know more about the wave too."

If the bear wasn't Mesha, what could it be? And the wave. Khari guessed the wave had something to do with Kenavi, but she didn't know what that meant for Ribas, or for what he might have to do.

He said, "I am also very interested in the first part of your dream. The girl." He looked past her, out the window behind her, and pieced words together. "Our stories tell us that Kenavi, the woman who was Kenavi, died because..." Again the pause to think. Khari listened to the fire crackling in the hearth. "Because the older gods were angry," he went on. "Her people did wrong things and the gods were going to harm the land. She gave herself up so the gods wouldn't punish her people."

His eyes came back to Khari's face. "But your dream says something different."

Khari wished for Vatiri so much she thought she might close her eyes and see her mother-in-truth sitting beside her in this kitchen. *Amma, you told me I would find help for us. I must do it. But what have I found? What will happen now?*

A Lamp-Carrier must never deny her pathdream. "I only know what I saw," she said. "I don't know anything about Kenavi. But pathdreams don't often have people in them. If a person is in a dream, that person is real."

"Your dream says that she died to save your people. And our stories also tell us that Kenavi had the gift I have, much stronger than mine." He rested one hand on the table. Khari saw no tremor in his fingers. "It sounds to me as if she died using it. To stop her people from killing yours."

Khari closed her eyes. She couldn't help it. The girl on the wall. Those vivid blue eyes.

Ribas said, as calmly as before, "If what you saw is true, I wonder if the older gods were angry because of what her people were going to do."

Khari didn't know. She made herself look at him again. He said, "You told me that our language Pirlevis sounds like yours. The oldest stories about Kenavi are in Pirlevis."

She didn't know how he could care about that right now, but it let her ask a question she hadn't gotten to ask yesterday. "The story you read, what was it about?"

"It was a very old version of the story we call..." For a moment it looked as if he was counting silently. "Fourteen Stones. All Namorans know it. You could say it's only a story for children, but those have truth in them too."

"What is it about?"

"A woman who isn't like other people. Her people aren't sure about her, but when she needs their help to do a great thing, they come together and do it."

Khari wished she had been able to understand it yesterday. Ribas said, "Did you need to tell me anything else about your dream?"

She had told him more than enough. "No," she said. "That was all."

He pushed his chair back. "I should probably rest a little longer. Today our healer will see about Bereg's leg, and he may need my help. Tomorrow we'll leave for Sostavi."

Khari stood up too. "I will come with you to Sostavi."

She had asked him yesterday. Now she was telling him. He said gently, "I don't know what we'll find there."

Khari lifted her chin. He was so tall he towered over her, so that she felt like a little girl talking back to an adult, but she said, "I can face it with you. You won't leave me behind."

She hadn't meant to say the last part aloud. Blood climbed into her cheeks, but she didn't back down. Neither this last pathdream nor any other had told her she should do this. She knew as clearly as she knew anything that she would not watch him leave the village, to go out to whatever waited for him, without such help or guidance as she could give.

He looked at her for what felt like a long time. Finally he said, "You and Marya will get along well." She heard laughter behind the words. "We'll be glad to have you with us."

Khari walked back up to the farm. Mist and drizzle turned the dirt into thin mud and beaded on the tall grass that grew along the road. Again she saw the Lasska silde collapsing in the dirt, the blood staining his gray coat.

He should not have to die for us. Not this man. But the dream gave her no other answer.

22

RIBAS

When the time came to leave Lida for Sostavi, Ribas could not do it unless he took the Vaia girl Khari's dream and locked it away tightly in the part of his mind that held his own fear and pain. He could not tell the people he loved what he faced. He could not say goodbye to them if he thought he would never come back.

Mama took his face briefly between her hands and said "Be safe, my dove," in a voice that had no tears in it only because she didn't allow them. Gedrin held onto Ribas as if he wouldn't let go, and finally muttered "Come home soon, brother," before he turned away. Danya and Jano promised to take care of the village, but reminded Ribas that Akena was coming, that in fact the month commemorating the Goddess's Sacrifice would be on them before Ribas reached Sostavi. As if Ribas could forget the high holy observances he had officiated over in Lida for the past fifteen years, to say nothing of the great celebration of Algima the following month, the Goddess's Rebirth. His Circle House needed its zhinin more than ever in those two months, but Ribas wasn't a zhinin anymore. The wrongness of the white robes he wore now was only one more twist of the knife that worked its way deeper every day into his heart.

If he told anyone about Khari's dream, even Maryut who should share everything with him, the grief would tear him apart. He couldn't find a clear thread of purpose in the Vaia girl's visions to show him what he must do. He only saw one certainty: if he did the thing that would save Khari's people, whatever it was, he would not see Lida again.

Maryut, of course, had asked him why Khari had wanted to talk to him so early on that second-to-last morning in Lida. "She looked terrible, Ribé. Was she sick?"

"No, love." The strain of all the changes in their lives had taken too much of Maryut's light from her. Ribas wouldn't add to the weight she carried until and unless he had no other choice. "She'd had a dream, one of those dreams that might help her see the future." Neither he nor Maryut really understood the "pathdreams," but after what Khari had told him about his own gift, Ribas couldn't doubt their truth. "She thought she might have seen a way to help her people, but she wasn't sure what the dream meant. Neither was I."

Maryut wanted to know more. "She thought she saw how you could help them? How?"

Ribas couldn't, wouldn't, open the door in his mind and bring the dream out in the open for her. "I want to think it through more," he said. "If I have an answer, I promise I'll tell you."

She didn't like it. Neither of them had known what to make of Khari's sudden appearance in Lida, or her insistence that her dreams had shown her that Ribas, out of all the people in Namora, could find a way to save her people from Shurik. It was too much, coming on the heels of his promotion to Tavo Balsa. Ribas didn't know how to keep holding up the weight of the terrible needs, and terrible hopes, that had poured in on him in the past handful of weeks. He only knew he had to.

Now, on the journey back to the coast, fear and sorrow made a choking fog around him. He woke up to it every morning and went to bed with it every night. Sometimes he wished he could give into it just once, let it overwhelm him and get off by himself somewhere to cry until he couldn't anymore for everything he stood to lose.

He couldn't do that. What right did he have to say that his life, just one life, was worth more than all the people Shurik wanted to destroy? Instead he made himself think of all the times when he was small, before he'd gotten sick, when he had tried to help his mother and protect her from Silvas's anger. *I have to be brave. I have to help.* He had told himself that over and over, to keep the fear from swallowing him. If he could do it then, he could do it now.

Khari and the Lasska soldier Tama Leben came with him and Maryut to the capital. Khari had persuaded the other Vaia to stay behind, in a place they knew was safe at least for now, but Ribas could see that none of the men liked it. Bereg Orlon didn't like being left behind either, but Tayo Nevas had done the surgery on his knee, with Ribas's help to control the pain. The Lasska wouldn't be able to get on his feet for weeks.

For the first couple of stages of the trip, from Lida to Paret and then into Jemtave region, the four of them traveled together in a coach. Once they got to Idria in Jemtave, they found a carriage from the Great House waiting again. Maryut took Ribas aside and asked if they couldn't hire a second carriage for the last leg to Sostavi, to have a little time alone.

They left Idria the next morning, Setdina, in the two carriages. They would make it back to Sostavi tomorrow, almost exactly three weeks after they had left it. Tama and Khari rode in the Great House carriage. Ribas and Maryut followed behind.

Maryut rested her head on Ribas's shoulder and put a gloved hand on his chest. The carriage had blankets inside and thick fabric over the windows to shut out the cold winter air. "Oh, my love." She sounded too tired. "How did we get into all this?"

He held her, stroking her hair. "I wish I knew."

None of it should have happened. They should have been back in Lida now, in the lives they'd always known, getting ready for the gracious, solemn beauty of Akena. Ribas had to shut those thoughts away along with Khari's dream.

"Khari's a sweet girl," Maryut said. "I probably shouldn't call her that. They think of her as a woman, it seems like."

Ribas saw Khari as a girl too, but her place in the tribe meant she was more than that. Nothing he had read about Lassar had told him about the Vaia Lamp-Carriers. He wished he could learn more about their gift; it was more powerful and much more fascinating than his own.

Maryut said, "I can't believe what she's been through. And she was *shot*, poor thing. Those Lasska weapons sound hideous."

They did. Khari certainly had been through a lot, from what Ribas had pieced together. Standing up to her tribe's leaders, who didn't know how much they should trust her dreams. Undergoing the long journey into Namora. Dealing with the danger of the Lasska soldiers and surviving the wound she had taken: Nevas had looked at that too, and said Tama had done as good a job treating it as he could have himself. Ribas had offered to help Khari manage the pain, but now that she knew more about his gift, she had refused. "You won't use up your strength on me," she'd said.

She had so much courage. Ribas could never let himself forget for a moment what kind of dangers her people faced. She had explained the other Lamp-Carrier Vatiri's dream: a picture of the kind of complete destruction that should only happen in nightmares. She had called Vatiri her mother-in-truth, and Ribas hadn't needed his gift to see how much she ached for this mother-figure and for all the people she had left behind. If he could somehow give her those people back, he could not hesitate.

Maryut sighed. "May the Goddess forgive me. I can't get used to all this. Pala Vaia. Lasska soldiers." She raised her head to look at him. "And you, the Tavo Balsa." She laughed, but he heard tears there too. "I don't know, love. Do you think we'll ever get back to how it used to be?"

It took all his strength to smile. "I hope so."

She looked into his eyes and reached up to touch his face. "I'm scared, Ribé. What's going to happen?"

Oh, Marya. I wish I knew. He had to be strong. "Well, first, Valda and the Council will meet again." For now, he could tell her what he wanted to believe himself. "It might help to have Khari and Tama with us. Tama is a high-ranking soldier. She can tell us a lot about how Shurik runs his army. That might give us some kind of starting point."

"But what can you do? You, Sventin Ribas. That's the part I don't understand."

It helped that she teased him about his new rank, though it made his eyes smart too. "I don't know either, love." He couldn't tell her yet that he would have to use the gift. Not when he didn't understand how he was supposed to use it. "Right now, all I can do is be there."

The bear in Khari's dream. She had thought it might be the god Mesha, but it couldn't be. Ribas didn't know how anyone could try to use the gift on a god, or what might happen if they did. Their best hope might be that it wouldn't work.

Maryut put her head back down on his shoulder. "I just don't understand what Shurik is doing." Anger tightened the words. "What kind of man is he? What kind of person does something like this?"

No Namoran ruler would, Ribas hoped. "It sounds like he's very young. Maybe he's trying to prove something. Maybe he's scared."

"That's not the way to prove anything, unless you want people to know you're an idiot, and a murderer besides. And what could he have to be scared of? Doesn't he have the biggest army in the world?"

Something woke up at the back of Ribas's mind. *Maybe he's scared.*

Khari had told him about the blue lines in the net around the bear. Fear lines. But the bear wasn't Shurik, Khari had felt sure of that, and Ribas somehow didn't think it was either. If it wasn't Shurik, and it wasn't Mesha, then what?

Ribas said, thinking aloud, "Bereg Orlon said Shurik believes their god is telling him what to do. But what god..."

The words trailed off as the thought in the back of his mind got more insistent. *Scared. Not Mesha.* Khari had said, *The bear always means something about Lassar.*

Maryut said, "If Mesha tells his people to do something like that, he's no real god. That's disgusting. They ought to get rid of the whole religion."

That's disgusting. No wonder the Lasska are so strange, if they go around believing stuff like this. Exactly what Ribas's friend Matevas at the viduris had said, the first time his class had gotten assigned a reading about the Lasska faith. Teeth and claws, blood and vengeance. The Bear was powerful, not loving, not merciful. The reading had said so. But Ribas had gone to class the next day and argued about it. He'd pointed out that the writer was Namoran. He'd said he'd like to know what the Lasska themselves wrote about their god, and what they wrote about themselves...

The bear, trapped in a net of anger and fear. Not Mesha. Not Shurik. *Something about Lassar.*

Maryut said, "I'm glad we don't believe anything like that. I wouldn't want you serving a Goddess who treated Her people that way."

Ribas said, "I don't think I'd want to serve Her." But he was thinking about the girl in Khari's dream. A girl who, if the dream was right, had given her life for *another* people, not her own.

Something about Lassar.

An idea began to take shape for him. It was so huge, so terrifying, he could only see the thinnest edge of it, as if his mind refused to look.

What if the bear was Lassar itself?

Maryut said, "I shouldn't be so tired, but I am. I'll see if I can sleep a little."

Ribas dragged himself out of his thoughts. He kissed the top of her head. "You do that."

She snuggled closer against him. "You should rest too, but don't let go of me, now."

"I won't."

If the bear was Lassar itself...Ribas felt Maryut's body relax more fully against him as sleep closed over her. He was tired too, but there would be no rest for him now.

If the bear was Lassar itself: Lassar, trapped in anger and fear, mired in beliefs its rulers had fed on and had fed their people on for generations. The histories said that the first impera, Curin, had raised the standard of Mesha and brought all Lassar under the rule of the Bear. But who had Curin himself been? What beliefs had he had? He had given the Lasska people a new God. Who and what had he told them that their new God was?

Tama had said she didn't believe Mesha wanted the death of the Vaia. Ribas didn't believe it either. What if Lassar's rulers, starting with Curin, had shaped the Bear into something He was not, had tangled their country and Mesha both in a net of their own making?

But what can I do? Goddess hear me, how can I help?

He could not imagine trying to cut the net that bound a nation. What would that mean? How could it be possible?

The wave in Khari's dream...she had said she saw a woman's face...

Kenavi. Is this Your will for me?

Kenavi, who had been a girl, who had given her life to save another people.

Of course, what Khari had seen in her dream did not agree with what Ribas had been taught at the viduris, what all the dagira had learned of the history of their Goddess, but he knew how stories could change over time. The same story was different in Pirlevis, in Old Namoran, in modern Namoran. Khari's dream had a core of truth he could not deny.

Grief broke over Ribas. He held his wife, his dearest love, in his arms, and fought with all his strength against the tears that wanted to engulf him. He must not grieve now. He must not burden his beloved with that.

Kenavi. Oh, Goddess.

If this was Her will, to cut the net that bound all of Lassar, She would help him do it. Ribas felt sure that was what the wave in the dream meant. But could he survive the effort?

The girl fell off the guarding wall. After the net was cut, the light went out.

Ribas didn't need to ask the question. He didn't need the dream to confirm the answer for him. He knew how hard it could be to use the gift on a single person, and this went far, far beyond anything he had ever done. It would take everything from him, if even that was enough.

He pushed back against the darkness with all his strength. *Oh, Goddess. Forgive me. This is more than I can stand.*

All through the last leg of the trip, Ribas held the darkness at bay. He had to keep it locked away with everything else, or he couldn't talk to Maryut and translate back and forth between her and Khari and Tama. Both the Vaia girl and the Lasska soldier, but Khari especially, had started to pick up a little Namoran, so communication was getting ever so slightly easier. But Ribas had to fight for every word he said, every smile he managed to give, and he knew Maryut watched him closely and more and more anxiously.

He must not think about what would happen to him because of this last and hardest use of the gift. Instead he must think about how exactly he had to use it. What did it mean, to cut the net that bound a country? A country had no face he could see, no eyes he could look into, no mind to open for him. And yet a net could trap it just the same. If Khari's dream was right, then the rules that had always applied to the gift didn't apply here. Ribas would have to find a new way to use it, do something he had never imagined before.

If Khari's dream was right. Through the final hours of the trip before they reached Sostavi, Ribas challenged the dream in his mind. Khari herself had said she hadn't always trusted her dreams. This one might be wrong...but every time Ribas caught at that possibility, his mind gave him the same answer. *She knew about you. She knew about the gift.*

They arrived in Sostavi early in the afternoon of Ashdina, almost exactly three weeks after they had left the city. The House of the Zhinine had seemed so huge and imposing only that handful of time ago. Now Ribas barely noticed the still-greater grandeur of the House of the Sventine.

A young, sandy-haired man in the by-now-familiar servant's robes met them as soon as they set foot in the building. "Raimaté, Tavo Balsa." He bowed to Ribas. "Tavin Valdena has sent a messenger to ask that you wait on her as soon as possible."

Ribas wouldn't actually hold the Tavo Balsa rank until he joined the Council again and received their final, official sanction. The title put him worlds away from home and the zhinin he had been, but right now, it felt no heavier than a fly. "Thank you," he said. "Please send her word that we'll come as soon as we're settled."

The servant looked curiously at Tama and Khari, who were obviously strangers to Namora. Tama still wore her Lasska military uniform for lack of better clothes, but she had stripped the bear's-head insignia off it and wore it like any jacket and pants. Khari, dark-skinned and in blouse and breeches, looked as noticeably different as Tama. Ribas explained that the two women had traveled with him and Maryut. "I hope the House of the Sventine might offer them its hospitality."

"Certainly, Tavo Balsa." The rank had its uses.

As soon as they put their luggage in their chambers, the four of them went to wait on Valda together. Ribas knew he would have to tell the Tavin everything he knew and guessed. She needed answers, anything he could give. The thought of telling her about Khari's dream made him feel as if he had fallen through ice into a winter lake, but he must lay it out for her.

The House of the Tavin felt too large for one person. Under different circumstances, Ribas would have admired the high ceilings, the ornate wooden cornices, the huge tapestries of pure color displayed on the walls. Generations of Tavine had added their own touches and flourishes here. One of the servants showed them into the front hall before going to announce their arrival to Valda.

Tama and Khari looked around the space. Khari looked stunned and Tama skeptical. The Lasska woman said to Ribas, "Your priests live in fine style."

"Most of us don't live like this," Ribas said. It took so much effort to keep his voice even. "Only the rulers do." The Lasska word "ruler" didn't quite describe what the Tavin and senior dagira did, but he didn't know a better one. He said, "The impera has a grand house, doesn't he?"

"The palace of the imperi is simpler than this," Tama said. "Lord Curin didn't believe in excess in the service of Mesha." Then she gave one of her brief, sudden smiles. "But I shouldn't criticize your priests. Priests of Mesha have as much finery as they can carry. People forget the standards of Lord Curin when they can."

Maryut stood close to Ribas. He felt her worry and love reaching out for him all the time. She knew him much too well for him to hide everything he felt from her, no matter how hard he tried.

She would hear about Khari's dream at the same time Valda did. Ribas didn't know how he could stand to say what he had to, in front of her, but he never could have done it without her there. *Oh, Marya. Forgive me.*

Footsteps announced the return of the servant, who bowed and said, "Tavin Valdena." Then Valda came quickly and impatiently into the hall.

"We don't need the formal announcement every time," she said, but she was smiling. She didn't have on her robes of rank. In her plain, dark blue dress, even with her hair elegantly braided and coiled, she looked girlish. She held both hands out to Ribas. "Tavo Balsa."

He took her hands and lowered his head. "Raimaté, Tavin."

"That's the last time you'll use my title in private, Ribé," she said.

She pressed his hands and let them go. "It's so good to have you back. And Marya; I'm so glad you're here."

Then she saw Tama and Khari. The servant evidently hadn't mentioned them. Ribas quickly explained who the two women were and when they had arrived in Lida.

"They have information that I think will help us," he said. Even that took more effort to say than it should have.

Valda rose to the occasion. No Tavin, most likely, had ever encountered such guests, but she greeted the two women courteously and gave them her formal protection during their time in Namora. Ribas translated the greeting into Lasska, but it was clear Tama and Khari had both gotten the gist.

Valda said, "Please come upstairs. We have a meal set out."

The meal was in Valda's sitting room. They sat around a small table by a warm hearth. Valda had kept the elegance of the room, but it was more comfortable than lavish. Ribas would have liked to have appreciated it, but he could barely touch the food, much less make easy conversation about the trip back from Lida. Everything in him tried to brace for what he would have to say.

It came soon enough. Valda said, "You said our visitors might be able to help us, Ribé. Please tell me more."

Ribas tried to ignore the cold that wrapped around him like a heavy coat. He must do this. Khari's people must win their safety. Shurik must not take out his aggression against Namora.

He explained Khari's role in her tribe and the importance of her dreams. "I know we've never seen that kind of ability," he said, "but I have every reason to believe her dreams tell the truth. They told her to find me, someone she couldn't have known existed. They showed her what I looked like, so clearly that she recognized me at once." So far, he could speak steadily enough. Then he had to say, "Her dreams also showed her the dovne kenavnis."

Valda couldn't hide her shock. "How could that be?"

Khari leaned forward. Ribas thought she might want to explain the dreams herself, but he had to get through this while he could. He said to her in Lasska, "Please, let me tell her for now."

Khari nodded and sat back. He saw concern – concern for him – in her face. She shouldn't worry for him when she carried such a weight of her own.

He told Valda, "The Vaia believe that their goddess, the Moon Woman, sends the dreams. At least I think you could call her a goddess. Lamp-Carriers like Khari are recognized when they're young and trained to interpret their dreams. I don't know much about how it works, but we have to agree that if the dovne kenavnis is possible, Lamp-Carriers are possible too."

Valda agreed with this. "And her dreams showed her something that can help us?"

Ribas made himself lay the words out, one at a time. "She showed me that we have to use the dovne kenavnis."

Maryut turned to him. When Ribas saw her fear, darkness and grief welled up in him again, as hard and fast as dammed water bursting free. He must hold them back, whatever it took.

He couldn't look at her or Valda now. Instead he stared down at the table and forced himself to describe Khari's dream as clearly as he could. The part about Kenavi, or the girl who would become Kenavi, got gasps from Valda and Maryut both. But when he described the bear, and the net around it, and then how the net was cut, there was total silence.

"We weren't sure what the bear was," he said, "but I thought about it and my best guess is that somehow it means the country. All of Lassar." He felt vaguely surprised at how calm he sounded. "It's mired in fear and anger, which explains why Shurik wants to do this thing to Khari's people. If the net is cut, things will change." He added, "I don't know how to find the net, not yet. That part is like nothing I've ever done. But I believe Khari's dream says there's a way."

When he finished, the silence filled the room like a dense fog. Then Valda said, "Cut the net...around a country?"

"Yes," Ribas said. He still couldn't look up. He heard Tama say in Lasska to Khari, "What are they saying? What does he have to do?" Ribas knew he should explain it to them too – Khari had not heard the Lassar idea – but he didn't know how he could stand to say it again. The grief rose around him, wave after wave crashing against him. He couldn't catch his breath.

Maryut's hand closed around his. As if they had been alone, she said, "Ribé. Look at me."

He made himself do it. Had he ever done anything harder? Her face. So much fear in it.

She said, "You know what using the gift can do to you." She spoke quietly, but her mouth trembled.

Ribas nodded. He didn't trust himself to speak. She went on, "If you tried to do something like this. Something this size, that would take so much strength...what do you think would happen?"

Her eyes told him that she already knew. *Forgive me. Oh, my love, forgive me.*

He didn't have to answer. She was shaking her head. "No." The word was very quiet, but her fingers tightened painfully around his. "No."

He must try, if he could find the words, to show her, so she would understand. She must see that he didn't want to do it. Everything in him wanted to stay with her for as many years as the Goddess granted them, but they had no choice now.

To his shame, he couldn't say anything. The strength he had held onto so tightly so many times, that he had clung to as his only defense against fear, that he was never, ever supposed to lose...under the pressure of the load he could no longer carry, that strength gave way and collapsed around him. The grief rose up to swallow him whole.

So much shame. Somehow he drew his fingers out of his wife's; somehow he hid his face in his hands. He was never supposed to give in like this. *I have to be brave. Forgive me, Goddess. I can't.*

Maryut had her arms around him, holding him as if she could shield him from the world. From somewhere else, he heard her telling

Valda what price the gift would demand if he tried to use it this way. She was crying too, her voice taut with anger and grief. Again Tama asked what was going on, and on the very edge of hearing, Ribas heard Khari telling the Lasska woman about the end of her dream. "It showed me he would die." Her voice sounded light and distant and sorrowing.

Ribas knew he had to speak up, tell them all that there was no other way, but pain of a kind he hadn't experienced since childhood gripped him in its jaws and shook him like a rag doll. He had not cried like this since he was six years old.

Da fell and hit his head and never woke up. He fell because I was there. I didn't go to bed when Mama said to. My fault.

Mama said it was an accident. But I know he died because of me...

Someone put a hand on his arm. A firm, clear voice said, "Sventin Ribas."

Valda. Ribas must pull himself together, must catch his breath. But it was so hard.

"Sventin Ribas. Listen to me."

Her voice made a sliver of light through the shadows. Ribas forced air into his lungs. One breath. Another. Somehow he lowered his hands. Maryut still held him tight, but she let go as he made himself raise his head.

Valda's steady eyes met his. She let go of his arm. "Sventin. I am your Tavin, and I am telling you that if we cannot find a way to bring you through this safely, you will not do it. Do you understand?"

She was not only Valda now, the girl from the viduris, the woman who had shown him so much of her heart only a little while ago. She was, yes, his Tavin: Namora's ruler, with all the authority of hundreds of years of the Tavinate behind her.

But he was Tavo Balsa, and everyone called him stubborn. "Valda." He had to reach for each word. "There's no other way. I can't let..." *I can't let anyone else get hurt because of me.*

"You will not do it, Ribé."

I have to help. He found he could pull the shreds of his self-control around him. "If I can do anything to solve this, I have to try. I'm afraid you're too partial, not wanting me to risk myself."

Her expression didn't change. "This has nothing to do with my personal feelings, sventin. They are immaterial in any case."

She had admitted out loud that she was still in love with him. Without a pause, she went on, "We can't afford to lose you. Too many people need you."

Ribas saw her look at Maryut then. Maryut reached for his hand again and twined her fingers around it.

Valda said, "I see two problems for us to solve. The first, as you said, is to see how you can find the net around Lassar. The second is to ensure you have enough strength to cut it safely."

Ribas held his wife's hand tight. "Valda, I'll never have enough strength." Saying it aloud made it more bearable. "Even if I were healthy, I wouldn't have enough. I don't think any one person could do it." Again he thought of the girl-Kenavi. How many minds had she reached into, that day on the guarding wall? It had cost her everything.

Khari leaned forward. In Lasska, she said, "Ribas, please tell Tama and me what you're saying."

At least he could do that now. He explained his theory about the bear, what it would mean to cut the net – which they already knew – and what Valda had said about the problems they had to solve. He finished by telling Khari and Tama that he couldn't see how any one person could have enough strength to use the gift this way.

Tama spoke first. "Then it seems to me that you can't do it alone. Other people have to help you."

How could anyone do that? Ribas knew no one else in Namora had the gift. If they did, the Council would certainly know about it, and that person would be in Sostavi now too.

Valda said, "Tavo Balsa, I think one of your duties is going to be to teach me Lasska, and probably the rest of the Council too. It's ridiculous that we're so backward. For now, tell me what she said."

When he translated, she said at once, "She's right. If you need strength, you have to borrow ours."

"But how?"

"I don't know." Startlingly, in this time of shadows, Valda smiled. "Another problem to solve. But you're welcome to mine, to start with."

"And mine," Maryut said. "Obviously."

How could Ribas borrow it? The gift didn't work that way for him, or at least it never had. Khari's dream seemed to say he would be able to do something he had never done before. Maybe the gift could do things he had never thought of. But Khari's dream had also said he couldn't survive this.

As if she heard that, Khari leaned forward. "Ribas. Vatiri's dream said there was no hope for my people, but my dream was different. I don't want this to hurt you."

She looked like a girl again, young and earnest. "Khari," he said, "your people deserve to be safe."

"Yes. We do. But your people also deserve to have you with them."

Valda said, "I need to tell the Council about all of this. I'll call a meeting at once, but you, Tavo Balsa, you go and rest. You look exhausted."

He couldn't tell her he wasn't. "You don't need me there to explain?"

"Don't worry about that. They'll take it on my authority, or they'll wish they had. And they'll give their sanction to make you Tavo Balsa officially, whether you're there or not."

Ribas and Maryut went back to the House of the Sventine. Tama and Khari went out for a look at Sostavi, with two servants from the House of the Tavin with them to make Valda's protection clear. As tired as Ribas was, he didn't know how he would be able to rest with his mind working over everything they had talked about. Finding the net. Borrowing strength. He didn't know where to begin.

Maryut ordered him to lie down anyhow, on the soft bed with its smooth thick quilts. She lay beside him and put her arm across his chest. "I know why you didn't tell me sooner," she said. "But you do realize what kind of trouble you're in."

She could make him smile even now. He had no idea what he had done to deserve her. "Fair enough," he said. "I'll take my punishment."

"It's coming, believe me. As soon as we know you can get through this."

The room smelled of wood smoke and lavender. Light from the glass lamp on the bedside table made radiant arcs on the walls. Ribas closed his eyes and tried to find some peace.

How can I get through this?

That evening, Ribas served as Tavo Balsa in the service at the Great House. He and Maryut arrived early, before the congregants had started to come in, but not before most of the Council had already gathered.

Ribas wore the white robes that Luvo Azulaikas had made for him in Lida. Attending on Luvo's wife in childbirth seemed to have happened to Ribas in another life, but at least these robes came from home, not some fine Sostavi weaver's, and at least he had worn them at services in his own House. He had asked for no ornamentation of any kind on them. The plain white homespun stood out from the elaborate robes the other Council members wore.

The Council closed in around him as soon as he came up to the dais. A few hours earlier, Valda had told them everything he had shared with her. Now the sventine demanded to hear more about Khari, and the details about her dream, and why Ribas thought they could trust a Vaia heathen, and whether he actually thought he could do what the dream said, and what would happen if he did. Everyone talked at once until the House echoed with the noise.

Ribas hadn't known how it would feel to join the Council with his new rank, out of place and undeserved as it felt, draped over him. As it happened, in spite of the grandeur of the huge Great House and the wrongness of the white robes, it felt no different than standing on the dais in his own House: except that in his House, this kind of chaos wouldn't have happened.

"Sventine," he said.

He didn't raise his voice, but they heard him and quieted. *Tavo Balsa*. He was only a zhinin from a little village, made into something bigger by a trick, the way the right angle of light could make a mouse's shadow look like a giant's.

He said, "I can only tell you that I do trust Khari. She has given me every reason to do so."

Some of the Council exchanged looks and mutters. Sventin Lesvin, in particular, looked doubtful to the point of mutinous. Ribas said, "I still need to consider what to do next. I promise the Council that as soon as I find an answer, you will hear it."

Lesvin cut in. "We cannot afford to risk a priest with the dovne kenavnis. You are much too valuable to lose. I personally will oppose any and every plan that involves you endangering yourself trying to help these outcasts."

That started another storm of argument about Namora's responsibilities, the Vaia's rights, and Ribas's value. Ribas looked at Lesvin. *You are better than this*, he thought. *One day you'll realize it.*

He held up a hand. It didn't hurt, maybe, that the homespun robes did set him apart, or that he stood taller than almost all the other sventine, with the exceptions of white-haired Sventin Eldin and Lesvin himself.

He said, "We are in the Goddess's House. We must prepare to honor Her. I don't feel this is the time or place for debate."

No backwater zhinin ought to give Namora's highest dagira that kind of reminder, but they listened. Sventin Galvo said, "The Tavo Balsa is correct. No doubt we will have plenty of time for debate" – he caught Ribas's eye and smiled faintly – "very soon."

Ribas had noticed Galvo watching him closely from the minute he arrived in the House. Now, as the other Council members either went to their places on the dais or took seats on the benches, Galvo came up to him.

"I know you are much occupied, Tavo Balsa," Galvo said. "If it isn't too troublesome, I wonder if I could beg a few moments of your time after the service."

He looked tired, Ribas thought, as if he had fought against something and lost. Almost as tired as Ribas felt himself. He didn't particularly welcome talk with Galvo tonight, but he said, "Certainly, sventin."

Congregants began to arrive. The carved wooden benches filled gradually but steadily. Ribas saw Maryut with Khari and Tama near the middle of the House, on the side aisle. The news about Shurik evidently hadn't spread yet to Sostavi's people. Ribas had no sense of panic or worry in the House: it felt like any Ashdina evening. Tomorrow, the first Pirdina service in Akena, the Sacrifice observances would begin.

The Tavo Balsa's place was on the dais to the left of the great hearth. It felt surpassingly strange to Ribas to stand there, exactly as Danya stood in the House in Lida, with no role to play in the service except to follow the Tavin's lead. With less to do, in fact, than his own mosevine had.

Valda came onto the dais when the House was full. The noises of talk and laughter and footsteps that had echoed in the space died instantly when she appeared. As she went forward to the table at the front of the dais, she caught Ribas's eye with a look that told him, again, how glad she was for his presence.

If we cannot find a way to bring you through this safely, you will not do it.

What way could there be, for him or anyone else to do such a thing "safely?" As the service began, Ribas listened to the customary readings and prayers and reached out for Kenavi in his own mind. *Goddess, You know my confusion. I no longer know what to believe.*

If Khari's dream was right, and Ribas could not doubt her, then the Sacrifice of Kenavi had not happened for the reasons the stories and old texts said. Stories changed over time, and changed according to the voices of the people who told them. Ribas knew that very well. The Lasska were supposed to be a strange and brutal people, nothing like Namorans, but their own stories made them not so different at all. Tama Leben and Bereg Orlon proved that point.

So if Khari's dream was right, and Kenavi had given Her life not for the land, but for a people who were not her own, what did that mean?

You told us to care for one another. The Lamp-Carrier's dream says that all people are Your people.

The stories said that Kenavi had lived in a place somewhere near where the Great House stood now. Early Namorans had built Sostavi, the City of the Goddess, on this spot to honor Her. If She was here tonight, listening; if She had her hand on this place as Her own, and if She was calling on Her servants to do what they must, what right did Ribas have to be afraid?

He couldn't shake it completely. *Goddess, forgive me. I'm afraid of what will happen to me, but I will serve You in this, too, if You will help me find the courage.*

Please show me how to use Your gift on Lassar itself. Show me how to find the net I can work on.

By the end of the service, and the ritual of the prayer stones, Ribas felt as if he had already said everything he could say to the Goddess. He chose a stone from the elegant box and went to the nearest window with his mind open and empty.

When his turn came, he stepped up to the window with the stone, small and round and vividly blue, in his palm. For a moment he remembered the girl on the guarding wall. Khari had said she had blue eyes. Just before he released the stone into the basket, he closed his own eyes.

Lida. Home. The square, the House, the farm: he saw it all, the way it always looked, but now a wave rose up from the land, silent and beautiful, curling and gleaming, harming nothing but climbing up into the sky and glittering in sunlight. All around, across the land, he saw more waves, and more, and they came together into a single great unstoppable power and rose up high...

...and there was a voice, or a thought, or words or the shape of words forming out of silence and the pure blue of the water...

Ribas's eyes snapped open. His fingers moved automatically, letting the prayer stone go. It clacked into the basket as he stepped aside to let the next person in line take his place by the window. His heart hammered in his ears, but there was no pain.

He had never experienced anything like it. He couldn't have begun to say what the voice sounded like, or whether it was a voice at all, but he could still hear its message in his mind, as clear and strong as the breeze off the ocean.

Go. I will show you.

After the service, people crowded around the dais. Everyone felt they had the right to meet and talk to the new Tavo Balsa. Everyone knew about the gift by now. Ribas greeted face after face while the last moments of the service echoed in his mind.

I will show you.

In all his years of serving the Goddess, he had never had such a clear and strong message. It must mean that She would show him how to cut the net that bound Lassar. He didn't think he had the right to ask questions anymore, but one question refused to quiet.

What will happen to me?

Maryut cut through the crowd to tell him she and Khari and Tama were going back to the House of the Sventine. She didn't want to leave him there, but he told her not to worry. "I'll finish here as soon as I can. Don't wait up for me, love."

"I didn't hear you," she said. "And if I did, I'm not listening."

When the crowd in the House thinned out, Galvo came up to

Ribas. "I wonder if we could step into the Council's meeting room, Tavo Balsa."

Valda was still on the dais, speaking with a couple of the attendant dagira about tomorrow morning's service. Ribas followed Galvo out through the door at the back of the House.

A low fire still burned on the meeting room hearth. Ribas sat in the chair he would have to occupy as a member of the Council. Galvo sat opposite him. The firelight and the single lit lamp on the wall filled the room with flickering shadows. In that fitful light, Ribas thought Galvo looked older than he had seemed before.

Galvo said, "I wish to speak to you about something else, Sventin Ribas, but first I must say I was most interested to hear about the Vaia girl's dream. Some people will argue that we can't trust such a thing. I consider that such guidance must be possible, given that your gift exists."

Exactly what Ribas had thought. Galvo said, "Do you think this 'cutting the net of Lassar' can work?"

If it hadn't been for those final moments of the service, Ribas would have put the sventin off with some polite comment and asked why exactly he was here. Now he said, "Yes. And I believe it needs to happen as soon as possible."

Galvo looked at him closely. "You think you can do it, then."

The sventin did look as if he hadn't had a decent sleep possibly in weeks. Ribas had a feeling, watching Galvo's intent eyes, that the sventin's exhaustion had to do with more than fears about Shurik and Lassar. Galvo needed, or wanted, something from this conversation that might have nothing to do with the outside world.

He answered Galvo's question with the exact truth. "I think the Goddess will make sure I can do it." He couldn't help saying, "I wish I knew what will happen afterward."

"What will happen to you?"

"Yes."

"The Tavin would like to know too," Galvo said. "As would all of us on the Council. Tavin Valdena said the biggest concern is that it would demand too much strength from you."

"From anyone," Ribas said. "My heart trouble doesn't help, of course."

Galvo steepled his fingers. "The Tavin said we must find a way for you to borrow strength. I wonder. Would your gift allow you to use the *will* of another person?"

"What do you mean?"

"As I understand it, the dovne kenavnis lets you reach into another person's mind and touch what you find there. Yes?"

"Yes."

"Suppose you could, so to speak, harness another person's will. Their desire, perhaps? And suppose their desire for something matched your own. Might that let you borrow their strength, link it to yours, to achieve what you want?"

Ribas had never considered such a thing. Galvo laid it out quickly, confidently, as if he had been turning it over in his mind for years. He seemed to see Ribas's confusion. "You might say I'm thinking like a Capture player." He smiled. "Considering strategy."

"I've never been very good at that," Ribas managed. Could the idea work? The gift did show him desire. Sometimes he could cut it, or sometimes he could turn it away from its object, if the source mind needed that. But harness it?

Galvo leaned forward. "I must admit I mention this not only because of our trouble with Lassar. It brings me to the real reason why I wanted to talk to you."

Ribas made himself pay attention. "Please tell me."

The sventin's face changed with that "Tell me." Something like an echo of pain flickered over it and was gone. He said, "Can your gift erase a memory?"

If Ribas had expected anything, it hadn't been that. What memory? Why would anyone want such a thing?

He wouldn't pry. Galvo would say more if he wanted to. "I've never used the gift that way," he said. "It might be possible." Right

now, he would hesitate to say anything was impossible. "If it is, I don't
how to do it."

"Suppose you could harness my own desire to forget something.
To take something out of my mind as fully as if it had never been
there. Could you use my desire to do that?"

Ribas didn't understand what Galvo could want to forget so
completely. "If I saw your desire, I could direct it," he said carefully.
"But I've never tried to turn it back on a mind." Desire, like anger,
could be potent and dangerous. "I don't know if I could control it. To
speak honestly, I wouldn't want to try that."

For an instant Galvo's face showed the most profound disappointment Ribas had ever seen. The sventin recollected himself in an
instant, but that was already too late.

"Sventin Galvo," Ribas said, "what do you want to forget?"

His animosity toward Galvo had gone. The sventin was a person
who badly needed something. Ribas found himself wishing he could
give it.

Galvo gave him a long look. Then he sat back in his chair, folding
his hands on the table in front of him.

"Since you left Sostavi before," he said, "I knew I would speak to
you again. I've tried to decide how much to tell you."

As Ribas listened, he gave into the curiosity he had felt before
with Galvo. Gently, counting on the idea that Galvo was too focused
on what he was saying to notice, he let himself look into the sventin's
mind. Grief, in lines of dark green and hazy green-blue. And Ribas
did see desire: a line of pure white light, strong and sharp enough to
burn.

Could he harness the desire of others? He remembered another
piece of Khari's dream. *A flash of white light. The net disappeared.* He
remembered, too, the folk tale every Namoran child knew: how a
woman got her house built, long ago. Klaya, the rebellious girl with
the bright blue eyes. Ribas's attention drifted as he thought of the girl
on the guarding wall again, the girl-Kenavi with her eyes, too, like
pieces of sky. Klaya and Kenavi had always seemed, to him, as if they

could have been two halves of one whole. Stories did change over time. Was it possible…?

Then Galvo's words brought him sharply back to himself. "To be frank, Tavo Balsa, I wish to erase my memory of your father."

Ribas tried to hide his shock. "I beg your pardon?"

Galvo leaned forward again. His sharp attention made Ribas think of a hunting animal. "Tell me, Tavo Balsa. Have you ever wished you could forget him yourself?"

That is not yours to ask. Ribas bit back the words. Yes, he did wish he could forget everything that had happened, but he had reasons not to. Especially now, with Gedrin. "I would forget some things, if I could. I don't think that's the right answer."

"Do you remember knowing he loved you?"

"I don't believe he ever did."

This time, Ribas heard his own anger. Mama would have said that wasn't true. Mama had told him, more than once, that Silvas had been happy for a while, that he had loved the wife and child he'd never expected to have. Apparently he had even told Mama he wouldn't have traded his life in Lida for anything, certainly not what he'd left behind in Sostavi.

But the man Ribas remembered had not been that kind of father. That man hadn't known what love was. Ribas tried to tell himself that he knew better, that Silvas must have hurt and struggled the same way Gedrin did now, that he must have loved his family and wanted to make things right. That compassion frayed and slipped away.

Galvo was watching him. Ribas didn't care what the sventin saw in his face.

"I understand," Galvo said. "That's a different kind of grief." He went on as calmly as if the two of them had been talking about the weather. "My trouble comes from the fact that your father and I were like brothers once. I remember that. And then he left here, and I have reason to think he always hated me afterward."

Ribas made himself pay attention again. "Why would he have

hated you?" Strangely, it helped to hear that someone else, especially this urbane lifelong politician, might also have come in for a share of Silvas's anger.

Galvo said, "That's one of the things I couldn't decide to admit to you, Tavo Balsa. It seems I might have to. Because, you see, if you can't erase my memory, I wish you could give me something else."

His face looked open and vulnerable. Ribas's anger ebbed away. "What is that?"

"Forgiveness."

"But I have nothing to forgive you for, sventin."

"Your father did. As I can't ask him for his pardon, I wonder if you might stand in his place."

Ribas wouldn't choose to stand in Silvas's place for any reason. If Galvo needed help, though, he must give it. "I will if I can."

Galvo said, "I must tell you as simply as possible. I beg the favor that you will not repeat this to anyone else. It's too long ago to matter, but I would rather that no one else knows my shame."

Automatically, Ribas held out his hand. Galvo seemed to hesitate before he accepted the ritual, but he did it. Their palms touched and Ribas closed his fingers, creating the contact. "Tell me," he said, and let go.

Galvo spoke steadily, as if he had planned out what to say. His eyes stayed on Ribas's face. "Your father and I served as zhinine here together, in the Great House. After some time, we were both promoted. You must understand that we had different personalities. We were very close friends – very close," he said, after a short pause. "But I was eager to advance as high as I could in the dagira, and your father was satisfied serving the House and the Goddess in whatever rank came to him. Both of us, I think, had the same idea – to do as much as we could with our knowledge and training – but we had different views about how to achieve that."

Ribas had always assumed that his father had a hefty share of restless ambition that made Lida not good enough for him. What Galvo said put a different cast on things. Galvo went on, "We both served as kunine for perhaps a year. Then one of the older members of the Council passed away, and a Council seat opened up. Silvas and I were both, if I say it, exceptionally talented young kunine, but Silvas had no particular interest in the seat. I did. Unfortunately for me, an older kunin, Azulin Getraikas, rightfully stood first in line for it."

Ribas tried to form a picture of his father as a kunin, serving the Great House with dedication and, perhaps, humility. *I wish I had known,* he found himself thinking. *I wish he had told me.*

Galvo said, "I didn't want to wait for the next chance at promotion. As a Great House kunin, if you wanted to join the Council, you effectively had to wait for someone to die." His smile mocked himself. "At the time, many of the Council members were fairly young and reasonably healthy. I thought if I missed my chance, I might never get another. So I took it upon myself to ruin Kunin Azulin's chances."

Ribas tried not to let his face show his reaction. Such things no doubt did happen in Sostavi, given the kind of people who served here, but he hadn't expected to hear it stated so baldly. Galvo said, "Azulin was a skilled kunin and a good man, but I knew – because I made it my business to know – that he had a weakness which had actually cost him promotion to the Council once before. When he drank, he couldn't moderate himself or control his behavior. He had abstained for years for exactly that reason."

Ribas listened with increasing distaste he knew he must not show. Galvo said, with no noticeable emotion, "One evening, Kunin Azulin was supposed to help officiate in an evening service in the Great House. By that point it was an accepted fact that he would be promoted, but the Council hadn't formally approved the decision yet. I went to the kunin before the service. I invited him to share a glass of wine to celebrate his new future."

Ribas kept his voice level. "And he agreed?"

"He did. You may imagine, Tavo Balsa, that though he resisted, one glass quickly became many. By the time the service began, he was in no fit state to be part of it. I stepped in, kindly, as it was believed, to relieve Azulin of his responsibilities, when it became clear he should not be standing on the dais in front of all the people there. The damage to him was done. The Council were disappointed and disgusted with his behavior. I was promoted instead."

Ribas felt disgusted himself. Such a petty thing for this man, an intelligent and skilled priest, to have done.

Galvo paused for such a long time that Ribas finally had to speak. "My father knew what you did?"

"Yes. You see, Azulin himself told the Council that I had invited him to drink that evening. He pleaded for another chance. The Council decided, despite my involvement, that they could not approve a member who showed so little ability to control himself. Silvas was furious. Injustice of that kind..." His calm veneer slipped. "I need not speak of your father's temper, Tavo Balsa. Perhaps you can guess how he spoke to me."

Ribas could, perfectly well. Galvo said, "Sventin Ribas, your father was an honorable man. He couldn't accept that I was not."

So much grief in Galvo's voice. Ribas couldn't feel any indignation or anger now. Galvo went on, "After I was approved for promotion, Silvas left Sostavi and the dagira. I never heard from him again. I have no doubt he carried his anger at me for the rest of his life, and perhaps anger at the Goddess too, that She saw my actions and did nothing."

Silvas hadn't needed to leave the dagira for good. He could have chosen to serve in another House somewhere else, but Ribas found himself understanding why his father had abandoned that life entirely. Betrayed by the Goddess Herself? How angry would that make a person feel?

I wish I had known. If his father could have seen Ribas now, in Sostavi, or if his father could have seen him in Lida, serving that House, doing all he could for the people who came to him, might that have helped heal Silvas's mind?

Galvo said, "I betrayed Azulin, but I betrayed Silvas too, you understand. I'd shown myself to be the kind of man who did not deserve his friendship or the closeness we'd shared. I never asked him to forgive me. Now that you know all my shame, Tavo Balsa, I would like to ask for your forgiveness instead."

The sventin's face showed nothing but exhaustion. Ribas had already forgotten his disgust. Galvo had gotten to his own position of power by wronging another man, and his actions had driven another priest out of the dagira entirely, but he had waited so long to ask for this one thing.

Ribas said gently, "This is why you wanted me to come to Sostavi, fifteen years ago?"

"Yes. I wanted to meet Silvas's son, because I hadn't known he had a family. And I thought your gift could serve the Council well. But I did think you might be able to help me."

"I forgive you, sventin. On my behalf and my father's."

He thought he heard the old sventin sigh. "Thank you, Tavo Balsa."

Ribas knew he should go back to the House of the Sventine. He had so much to think about, especially whether Galvo might have solved the problem of borrowing strength. For a little longer, he sat with his father's old friend in a silence that neither asked nor expected anything.

Finally Galvo said again, "Thank you." He stood up and Ribas stood too. "I will see you tomorrow at the service. But may I ask you one more thing?"

"Certainly."

"Have you ever forgiven your father?"

That should have felt like a blow to the gut. Ribas still couldn't find any anger. "No," he said. "I might, if I could forgive myself."

Galvo couldn't know what that meant, not knowing the truth about Silvas's death. He didn't ask. "I hope you will, Tavo Balsa." He bowed. "Good night."

"Good night, sventin."

Ribas went out through the Great House into the clear, chilly night. Part of his mind turned over the white line of desire he'd seen in Galvo. *Suppose you could channel that. Suppose you could gather more desire together. Think how strong it would be.*

A solution, maybe. But as he walked across the square, Ribas wasn't trying to think how to make it work. Instead he heard Galvo's words.

Your father was an honorable man.

Ribas woke up the next morning with a plan fully formed in his head. He hadn't gone to sleep thinking about the question of cutting the net, but the answer had arrived and sat waiting for him as soon as he opened his eyes.

He told Maryut about it before they went to breakfast. She didn't like it. "But you aren't sure, Ribé. You can't be sure it will work."

She was right. He would never put her through this unless he was certain they had no other choice. "I'm as sure as I can be," he said. They were waiting for Khari and Tama to join them before they went down to the dining hall. "There's a risk, Marya, but you know there's a risk every time I use the gift. This is the right thing to do."

She reached up. Her hands lay lightly on his shoulders. "I can't lose you."

He wouldn't consider the idea of his soul out in the world without her. Surely, if it found itself so alone, it would find a way back. "I can't lose you either, love."

When Khari and Tama arrived, Ribas laid the plan out briefly for them. Neither of them particularly liked it either, but Ribas knew Khari, in particular, felt the same way he did. It was their best hope. They had no way to know what Shurik was doing right now, or whether Khari's tribe was still safe, but every day – every hour – increased the danger her people faced. They couldn't afford to wait.

Tama looked more doubtful. "I would like this better if you were doing something about Shurik himself. Without him, there would be no danger to the Vaia or your own country."

Ribas couldn't agree with that. Another ruler could step into Shurik's place, he pointed out, even if he had any way to act directly on the Lasska impera. Khari's dream hadn't said he should try that. He felt certain he was taking the only path open to them.

"All right," Tama said. "You can borrow anything you need from me. I'm strong."

At breakfast, Ribas sought out Galvo. The sventin still looked tired, but his face had a peace in it that Ribas hadn't seen before. "Sventin," Ribas said, "I think you gave me an answer last night. I would like to tell the rest of the Council now."

Galvo had no trouble gathering the rest of the Council. Agreement and disagreement with the plan fell along the usual lines. Sventin Lesvin said he wanted nothing to do with it. Ribas said, "If it has any chance of working, I need everyone here to help. If you want to keep the dovne kenavnis in Namora" – this was an open shot at Lesvin – "I must have your agreement." *You must help me survive this.*

That brought the Council into reluctant line. Lesvin said, "But how can you be sure you can do this, even with our help?"

Ribas didn't risk looking at his wife or the other two women, who were listening tensely. "I can't," he said. That truth ought to frighten him far more than it did. The certainty that had begun to bloom in him at last evening's service seemed to strengthen every moment. "But I have a far greater chance of success with your help. If I tried it alone, I'd have no chance at all."

Lesvin said, "Then do you need more people? We could bring the rest of the Great House dagira in. There are many of us."

On the edge of hearing, Ribas heard Galvo murmur, "Too many of us."

He was right. Ribas had also thought about bringing more people in, but that would mean more questioning and arguing and debate. They didn't have time. And Ribas had never tried this before. He thought he could harness what the Council could give him, but he didn't know if he could control any more than that.

"No," he said, with as much confidence as he could summon. "The Council will be enough."

Valda was the last to hear the plan. Ribas told her about it before the morning service, in the Great House's library, where she was putting together the day's readings. At first, she looked at him the same way Maryut had. "Tavo Balsa, I will not let you risk yourself."

"Forgive me, Tavin, but we don't have a better chance."

She set the books she had gathered down on the library table. "Tell me exactly what you think this will do."

He couldn't be certain, exactly, having never done anything like it before. He told her what he guessed. "It'll make a change that Shurik will feel. I think he'll see things differently. It may not be permanent, but it might be enough to help Khari's people for some time. We can do it without force or confrontation with Shurik himself or his army. Don't you think that's worth the risk?"

She weighed what he said. The fire crackled in the library hearth. Finally she said, "If anything happens to you, you know I won't forgive you."

She had said her personal feelings didn't matter, but she laid them out baldly, not asking for sympathy. "You and Marya both," he said.

"You're lucky that you wouldn't be around, then."

"Yes."

She smiled. He saw the tears in her eyes, but she lifted her chin. "Very well, Tavo Balsa. You will have your chance this afternoon."

In the afternoon, after the first Pirdina service of Akena to honor the Goddess's Sacrifice, the Council convened in the meeting room. Maryut and Tama and Khari joined them. Ribas sat at Valda's right hand.

He ought to have felt afraid. Maryut certainly was, as proudly as she carried herself and as firmly as she controlled her face and voice.

Her hand gripped his so tightly his fingers ached, but somehow, Ribas didn't share her fear. In his mind, he saw the girl on the guarding wall, lifting her face to the sky and then collapsing into the water far below. *The Sacrifice.* But here and now, there was strength in this room. He couldn't see it yet, but it waited, as quiet and intangible and real as light.

In a few words, Valda reminded the Council that their Tavo Balsa had shown them their best hope and they must trust his guidance. She turned to Ribas. "Tell us what you need from us."

Ribas looked into one face after another. "As I told you all this morning, what I need most is your strength of will. You must focus your minds on Lassar. You must wish to see change there, of the kind we've discussed."

He knew that the others, who had never seen or used the gift, could not guess what it showed him. He said, "We will try to create a break in the fear and hostility surrounding that nation. To help me, you must desire this."

Sventin Lesvin looked skeptical. He wasn't the only one. Ribas said, "I realize it sounds as if you're doing very little. As the Tavin said, I must ask you to trust me. I know how the dovne kenavnis works, and I believe I can channel your desire to create the change we want."

Galvo nodded. Valda's face showed iron determination. So did Tama's. Ribas said, "I can use the gift to see and harness that desire, but to do so, it must be there."

Valda spoke then. "Whatever you may think of Lassar and the Pala Vaia, Council, realize that we are also trying to ensure the safety of our Tavo Balsa. Accordingly, we must do what he asks."

There was no need to wait longer. Ribas said, "I would ask you to do this now."

Now. Kenavi, Goddess, I trust Your guidance. Please show me the way.

He waited for a time he didn't measure, a few moments or a handful of heartbeats. Maryut's fingers held his tightly, anchoring him. Then Ribas closed his eyes and looked into the minds around the table.

Lines of white light. All with direction, all pointing toward the power in the east. Some were strong and bright, others thin and uncertain, but everyone in this room had done as he asked.

He had no words for what he did next. Gently, reaching out, he drew those lines together, gathering them like stalks of wheat at the harvest. He had never done such a thing before, but the gift itself seemed to guide him. As he did it, he knew he had been right. He could control this sheaf of wills, but more would have been too hot and bright for him to contain. They would have burned away at his strength too soon.

When he had collected them all, the wave came for him.

It rose around and within him, lifting him far away from his own imperfect body with all its frailness. Even as he rode its pure exhilaration, he knew he would never feel this kind of power again.

It carried him into a place he had never seen, away from the room and Namora and perhaps outside the world itself. In this new, strange darkness, it showed him a shape. It was land – plains and mountains and cities and people – but at the same time, it was the shape of a great bear: shaggy fur, vast teeth and claws, eyes that filled the world.

A net bound it in lines of red and orange and the blue-purple of a bruise. They were brighter than fire, thicker than the trunks of trees, and they burned.

Ribas held the white light in hands he could neither see nor feel. The lines of it came together to make a single shape as solid and strong as the blade of a sword.

He had never felt power like this before, never would again, but as he reached out with his mind, directing the light toward the lines of the net, he wondered if some of this might stay with him, a shadow or lesson to let him see what he never had before.

The white light swung through the darkness, as unstoppable as a rushing wave. It drove into the net and flared brighter than any sun, a flash of pure and absolute brilliance. Even as it blinded him, it showed Ribas the lines of the net parting and falling away.

Then the strength left him, draining from him faster than any tide. The dark closed in.

~

"Ribé."

There was darkness. It hurt to breathe. Pain covered him like a heavy blanket.

"Ribé, my love."

He couldn't tell whether his eyes were open or shut. He couldn't tell where his body was, except for the pain.

Someone's voice reached him from a great distance. Someone was crying.

"You have to come back."

Marya.

He wanted to reach out, comfort her, but she was so far away. Everything was so far away, except for the dark all around him.

"You can't go, love. I won't let you."

A dream from a long time ago. Arms holding him. A voice saying, *You'll stay here with me. I won't let you go.*

He thought he felt a touch, the warmth of a hand against his face, the strength of fingers around his own. So far away.

"I won't let you go."

23

VALDENA

To any outsider, Valda thought, it would have looked bizarre. The Tavin, the Council, Maryut, the Vaia girl, the Lasska soldier, all sitting around the meeting table, doing nothing but closing their eyes and concentrating. International diplomacy didn't look like this. In a situation of such great complexity, involving such stakes and the kind of power Lassar had, it seemed impossible that these few minutes of quiet could do anything at all.

Ribas had explained what he was going to do. Valda wished she could see inside her own mind to make sure she gave him what he needed. If she did not give enough, if she and the others failed at what he asked, she could not face the consequences of what might happen to him and all of them.

She didn't know what she would see or feel. She had no idea how they would know if what Ribas did had worked. She sat with her eyes closed, thinking as clearly as she could that he must come through this safely. Her desire for that made a beacon in her.

For a long time – an impossibly long time, it seemed – nothing happened. Valda listened to her own breathing and heartbeat, heard someone's chair creak as they shifted their weight, felt the hard meeting room table under her folded hands. How would they know when Ribas had done whatever he was doing? Would he say something? Could she hope he would come through it that easily? She didn't dare open her eyes, didn't dare stop concentrating for a moment, but she couldn't shut out the wondering.

And then she felt it.

A surge of power like a wave. It seemed to sweep her up and hurl her into the air. For a moment, in the dark behind her closed eyes, she saw a flash of such brilliant white light that she wondered if she would ever see again. And then, as suddenly as it had come, the wave fell away. She was rushing back toward the ground, knowing she would crash into it, it would batter the breath out of her. Then, just before the ground rose up to meet her, the vision vanished.

Her eyes flew open. She was sitting in the Council meeting room, confronting a circle of faces as baffled as her own.

What just happened?

No one said it. The question hung in the air, solid enough to touch. Valda saw that the Lasska soldier, Tama Leben, looked more stunned than anyone else. The soldier lifted her hand to her head, distracted, as if she thought it might have changed shape or disappeared entirely.

The silence lasted for one or two endless heartbeats. Then Valda heard a sound beside her, nothing more than an exhalation. She turned her head in time to see Ribas slump forward in his chair, his eyes closed, his body as limp as a dropped rag.

No!

The scream echoed in Valda's head, though it hadn't left her mouth. Nor Maryut's either. Maryut looked so pale Valda thought she could have fainted, but she set her lips in a firm line, got out of her chair, and leaned down to her husband. She gripped his shoulder to draw him upright and peered into his face.

A murmur and buzz of questioning started. "What was that?" "What happened to him?" Valda couldn't listen. She got up too, thought her body felt so stiff and heavy she could barely move.

Maryut held Ribas up with her arm around his shoulders. Valda saw his face, the dead white of a fish's belly, except for the ugly bruised circles under his closed eyes. She couldn't tell if he was breathing.

The talking-noise in the room got louder. Valda couldn't make sense out of any words. Maryut was calling to Ribas, fumbling with her free hand for the buttons of his shirt. *Ribé. My love.* Valda knelt on the other side of his chair and helped her undo his collar and the two buttons below it. She drew the fabric away from his chest with fingers so cold she had to force them to work. Maryut felt for his heartbeat. Her eyes met Valda's. The agony in them went through Valda's body like a spear.

Maryut said, "He's alive. But his heart..."

He's alive. Light and motion rushed back in. Valda found she could stand up, found she still had a voice.

"Quiet!"

Silence crashed down on the room. All the faces turned to her. "We need Tayo Bodin," she said. "Someone go and get him."

Sventin Galvo and Sventin Lesvin, both already on their feet, left the room together. Valda said, "The rest of you, leave us. The Tavo Balsa will need rest and care. If you wish to help, pray for him."

She sounded as if she were scolding children. The Council members, confused and shaken, obeyed.

Tama Leben and the Vaia girl, Khari, didn't leave. The Lasska soldier sat motionless in her chair. She looked dazed, as if someone had hit her with a heavy weight. Khari came quickly around the table and knelt beside Maryut. In halting Namoran, she said, "What can I do?"

Maryut said, "I don't know." The words could have been tears.

Valda said gently, "Marya, Tayo Bodin is the best healer we have. He can help."

Again, the woman's dark eyes raked Valda. "I don't know if anyone can help. When he..." She swallowed. The curve of her throat looked pale and fragile. "When he gets sick, no one can do much. We just have to wait."

Had he ever been this sick before? Valda couldn't bring herself to ask. If only she had the right to hold Ribas's hand, to press it to her lips as Maryut did now.

They waited for the healer. The only sound in the room was Maryut's quiet voice, trying to reach her husband. Valda joined her own thoughts to the words she couldn't say aloud.

Ribé. My love.

The tayo had Ribas moved back to the House of the Sventine. He agreed with what Maryut had said. "He's exhausted. Too much strain on a bad heart." Valda wished Bodin would give them a comforting word or two, but the healer believed in strict honesty. "I don't like his pulse," he said, "but his breathing could be worse. I won't try to bring him around. His best chance is to rest. We'll keep him comfortable and quiet, and we'll wait."

Valda wanted to shake the man. *Will he wake up? Can you promise me that?* He couldn't promise, and she could do no such thing. The hours she and the tayo had spent by Tavin Ardinas's bedside stood out stark and cold in her memory. *That will not happen this time. I will not watch him die.*

Maryut didn't leave the bedside. Valda would have kept the same vigil, but the duties of the Great House went on. By now, too, the rumor had flown from the Council through the dagira and out into the city.

The Tavo Balsa performed a miracle.

Everyone wanted to hear about it. Everyone wanted to know exactly what Ribas had done. Crowds gathered outside the House of the Sventine. Valda stationed a guard of servants on the outer doors and a second guard on Ribas and Maryut's chambers. "He is not to be disturbed for any reason. Is that clear?" The guard kept everyone out, but the whispers and rumors flew.

The truth was incredible enough. Tama Leben and Khari came

to see Valda soon after Ribas had been moved back to his chambers. Both of them were visibly distraught about him, but the Lasska soldier wanted Valda to hear what had happened to her after Ribas used the gift.

Valda couldn't stop thinking that the only person who would have understood everything Tama said might never open his eyes again. She clung to her patience and tried to follow as Khari, with the help of some heavily accented Namoran words and some hand gestures, did her best to translate.

"She felt that her head" – the Vaia girl touched her own head to be sure it was clear – "did this." She folded her hands tightly together and opened them like a flower.

Valda thought she must mean that the Lasska had experienced new thoughts or ideas. She tried to communicate that to Khari, but the girl shook her head firmly. "She felt," Khari said, "that she was..." Again the flower-opening gesture, but this time, she separated her hands completely from one another. "And then she was..." Khari put her hands back together, but this time in a different shape, with only the fingertips and heels of the palms touching each other. "Not the same," she said.

Broken and put back together? Valda did her best to ask whether Tama thought this was a good thing or not. Khari and the soldier spoke back and forth quickly in Lasska. Then Khari said, "It was good. Hard." She grimaced as if showing that something had hurt. "But good."

Valda asked Khari, speaking slowly and carefully, "Did you feel that way too?"

The girl shook her head. "I am not Lasska. But I felt..." She moved her hands again, like leaves blowing on the wind. "I felt life."

Life for her people? Hope? Again, Valda knew Ribas would have understood. She tried to ask one more question. "Does she" – she pointed at Tama – "think all Lasska felt..." She imitated the opening gesture.

More back and forth in Lasska. Tama said something quick and emphatic. Khari thought for a few moments, her face still and serious. Valda knew she was piecing words together.

"Tama is not real Lasska," she said. "She says, real Lasska feel it more."

More? Valda wondered what that would be like. And how was the soldier not a real Lasska? But there wasn't time for more questions. The sickroom drew on Valda. She couldn't stand to be away from it any longer than it took to discharge the duties she could not ignore.

She and Maryut waited through four endless days. The hours stretched so long in the sickroom, one minute dragging after another, that Valda thought they should have measured the time in weeks or months. Ribas was still alive. Valda clung to that hope, every minute of every hour, while she sent up prayer after silent prayer for his safety. *Goddess. I beg You to heal him. We need him so much.* The formal words traditionally invoked over the sick and suffering had no place here.

Maryut was wearing herself out. She didn't sleep, and she only seemed to take something to eat or drink when the tayo made her. Every time Valda came back to the sickroom, everything looked exactly the same except for the other woman's face, which got paler and more set all the time.

Tayo Bodin told her she had to rest. "You'll do him no good if you collapse." But Maryut seemed to feel that by sitting beside the bed, keeping Ribas's hand in hers, stroking his hair and talking softly to him, she could tether him to life. Valda would have done the same.

On the fourth night, after the tayo had left, Maryut said abruptly to Valda, "I was angry with you."

Valda, startled out of another prayer, looked across at her. In the sickroom, Maryut sat on the far side of the bed. Valda stayed near the hearth and never made any move to come closer to Ribas. She knew she didn't have the right.

Maryut had bruised-looking circles under her own eyes, but her face was calm. "When your letter came, in Vienela," she said, "I was angry. I thought about when you both were at the viduris. When you and he..."

She stopped. Valda didn't need to hear more. "He was never meant for me," she said. She realized how tired she felt. She hadn't had time to be tired for the past four days, but now she could have collapsed right here. "I wished he could be. I won't deny it. But he was always yours."

Maryut held Ribas's hand between both of hers. Valda looked at the other woman's strong fingers and wished, not for the first time, that she could at least touch his other hand where it lay on the quilt. No, she would never deny that she had wished that what she and Ribas had so briefly shared could have snared him as completely as it did her.

Out loud, Valda said, "He told me he should have known himself better. He said he should have known his heart better, because you were the only girl he could share his life with."

Again Valda remembered, like a picture in her mind from a different life, Ribas standing before Lida village in his new blue robes, with his arms around the girl who had run to him. She, Valda, ought to have let go of what she couldn't have, right then.

Maryut said quietly, "It must have been hard, when he told you that."

"It was."

For a while, they sat in silence. Maryut held her husband's hand and looked into his face as if she could will his eyes to open. Valda watched the faint but steady motion of the quilt over Ribas's chest, up and down, up and down.

When she had raised him to sventin rank, she had hoped he would change his mind about wanting to leave Sostavi. Now she must let go of that hope. His village and his people needed him. After so many years, she must finally let go of what she could never have.

She said, "Once he's better, I know you'll want to go home as soon as you can."

She spoke firmly, as if his recovery were a certainty. Maryut raised her head. Valda saw the glimmer of a tear on her cheek. Valda herself felt as empty as an abandoned house.

"Yes," Maryut said. "We will."

"I'll need him to stay a little while longer, until we know what's happening in Lassar. I'd also like him to teach me and the Council at least some Lasska." Valda laid this out as she might have explained how to make a pot of tea, as if it were that simple. "But I promise you that you'll be free to go as soon as possible." She would not think of how it would feel to lose him again.

"Thank you," Maryut said. A fragile smile touched her face. She said, "I can't help thinking you'd rather sit closer to him."

The quiet words fell across Valda's heart like a lash. Didn't Maryut understand? "I would," she said. "But..."

She didn't trust herself to finish. Maryut said gently, "If he knew you were here, I think it could only help."

Valda stood up and moved her chair closer to the bed. She sat back down and took Ribas's free hand in her own. She and Maryut stayed there together in the firelight, holding onto the man they loved.

The next evening, as soon as Valda finished the service in the Great House, a servant came up to the dais. "Tavin Valdena," he said. "Maryut Ribenis asks you to come to the House of the Sventine right away."

Valda left everything on the dais as it was and went straight out the back of the House. The guard on Ribas and Maryut's chambers let her in.

Maryut sat beside the bed as before. The tayo stood on the other side. And Ribas...Valda hardly dared to believe it...Ribas was sitting up, and when Valda came in the room, he looked around at her and smiled. His face still looked much too pale, and he still had those terrible bruised circles under his eyes, but that smile felt like a sunrise.

Oh, Goddess. Your name be praised.

The tayo was saying that Ribas wouldn't be able to get up for a while yet, that he had to take regular doses of pain medication, and must be careful of what he ate, and must not overtax himself when he did get up. Valda had trouble paying attention. She met Maryut's eyes across the bed and saw her own joy reflected back to her.

The tayo went out to order broth and see about the medicine. Ribas said, "I apologize, Tavin. I'm afraid I've caused some trouble lately."

Valda wanted to laugh, and cry, and she wanted to catch his hand up and cling to it, or better still, throw her arms around him. She made herself sit down in her usual chair. "It's true," she said. "You did give us some excitement."

Maryut made a sound like a laugh mixed with a sob. Ribas touched her face. "You need to rest, love," he said.

"Don't you order me around, sventin." She took his hand, pressed her lips to it, and held it against her cheek, closing her eyes as if she wanted to shut out everything but the warmth of his palm against her skin. Valda looked away at the tapestry on the far wall. The old ache curled and snagged in her chest, but somewhere, it had lost its power over her.

When Maryut let Ribas's hand go, he turned to Valda. "So I'm told it worked," he said. "Or we think it did."

"You certainly did something," Valda said. "Tama Leben will have to tell you about it. She and Khari tried to tell me, but you can imagine I wasn't much use."

"I've never felt anything like it before," Ribas said. The memory seemed to daze him. "It was astonishing. I wish I had better words."

Maryut said, "If I have my way, you'll never feel anything like it again. I'm not going through this another time."

Ribas laughed. It sounded too tired, but it was the laugh that Valda knew so well. "Don't worry," he said. "I think it could only happen once."

Valda said, "I told Marya, Ribé, and now I'll tell you too. Once you're able, I'll still need your help for a little while. We'll see what kind of communication we can get from Cheremay and confirm what Shurik is doing now, and I do want you to teach us as much Lasska as you can. But after that, say in a few weeks, you'll be free to go home."

She tried not to show how she felt at that thought. He was still too quick, even as worn out as he was. "We won't be in any real rush," he said, holding out his hand to her.

She took it and let herself hold it between both of her own. She knew she could let him go, as she should have many years before, but she still knew how empty the city would seem when he was gone.

He seemed to hear that. "Valda, you know you won't get rid of us so easily. We won't lose touch with our friend again, even if she is the Tavin."

Maryut said, "We certainly won't. And, you know, you gave him a taste for traveling again." She touched her husband's hair. "That probably means he'll make me come back to Sostavi once in a while."

Valda couldn't help laughing at that. "I hope you will."

"We will," Ribas said. "I wonder, too, if the Tavin might find time to visit one of the smaller villages under her authority."

"I'm sure it's good for a ruler to show she cares about the little places," Maryut agreed. She smiled at Valda. "We don't have a grand house like yours, but you're always welcome."

Valda let herself imagine visiting Lida. She had only been there the once, for Ribas's installation, but she remembered the peace of the village, its pleasant little square, the quiet beauty of the surrounding farmland. She had understood what Ribas saw in it.

Did the Tavin have that much freedom? Could she leave Sostavi for that long? Valda no longer had any thought of casting her authority away if she could. She hadn't chosen it, but it belonged to her now.

"I'll have to see what I can do," she said. "I would love to see Lida again."

The chamber door opened. Tayo Bodin came in with a tray that held a bowl of broth and a cup of what Valda guessed was the pain medication. "You'll take this now," he told Ribas, "and then you'll go back to sleep. As for you," he said to Maryut, "one of the servants is bringing you a meal, and then I want to see you get a decent rest too."

The authority of the Tavo Balsa and the Tavin mattered not at all next to the healer. Valda got to her feet. "Rest well," she told Ribas and Maryut, and she went out, closing the door quietly behind her.

Outside, the sky looked like velvet. It was much colder tonight than it had been on the night when she'd had her last talk with Tavin Ardinas, but the square was as quiet, and the stars shone as clearly as they had then. Valda lifted her face to the sky and closed her eyes.

For this moment, she was not the Tavin. She was only a woman, tired with all that had happened, aching a little for what was to come, but grateful – oh, how grateful – to imagine a future.

Kenavi, Goddess. Thank You for all that is.

24

BEREG

Bereg resented being left behind in Lida while Khari and Tama went on to Sostavi. After the surgery, when the old Namoran healer cut open Bereg's knee, found whatever was torn, and sewed it back together, Bereg couldn't try to get on his feet at all. He had to spend his days on his back in the bed that Ribas's mother Pelayut had given over to him. It was a comfortable bed, with a feather mattress and feather pillows and hand-stitched quilts, and the room itself smelled pleasantly of wood smoke and chamomile soap, but Bereg would have given a lot to leave it. He couldn't make himself useful to his Namoran hosts. He couldn't do anything but think and worry about what was happening in Lassar and what might happen in the Namoran capital city.

The surgery itself had gone more easily than Bereg had expected. The healer had given him some kind of herbal compound that made his wits fuzzy and dulled all his senses. He'd still felt pain at first, but Ribas had taken that away with the strange "gift" that Bereg didn't understand. He'd been reluctant to let the priest do anything to meddle with his head. That sounded like dangerous magic that a mortal person shouldn't touch. But Bereg had to admit that he would have felt much worse during the surgery, and no doubt afterward too, without Ribas's help.

And Bereg also had to admit that Tayo Nevas knew his business. Bereg wouldn't have been surprised to come out of this cutting and stitching with a knee that looked like something had gnawed on it, but the healer had made neat cuts and sewn them back together with tiny precise stitches. The repaired knee would only have two thin scars on it, like roads running parallel. Bereg didn't know if a Lasska doctor could have done as well or would have tried. In Lassar, they might simply have consigned him to one-legged hobbling for his last years.

But Bereg hated having to watch the business of the farm without taking any part. Radavan and the others didn't like being left behind any more than Bereg did, but at least they could earn their board by helping Pelayut and her son Gedrin with chores. Bereg would have been glad to haul buckets of water from the well for Pelayut's washing or chop firewood with Gedrin to feed the house's various hearths. He might not have a young man's stamina anymore, but he still knew how to swing an axe.

Gedrin's children, especially the little boy Raulin, were fascinated with the Vaia. Raulin had struck up an unlikely friendship with Handan, who genuinely liked the boy and was teaching him to use a bow and arrow. Bereg got the idea that neither Pelayut nor Gedrin's wife Virta liked that particularly, but Handan was careful, and Gedrin himself also often joined in the bow-and-arrow lessons. During those times, Bereg saw the anger and tension around Gedrin fade for a while. Meanwhile, the little girl Asira tagged around after Rahul, who explored the farmlands and surrounding countryside every chance he got. The two of them traded Namoran and Vaia words for the things they saw.

And Bereg himself was useless. Pelayut and Virta had to check and change the dressing on his knee multiple times a day, and bring him food, and make sure he was comfortable. He knew what a burden he had to be on them. They certainly had no reason to care about him as Nela and Ania would have. Every time one of them came to tend to him, Bereg had to swallow the lump in his throat that started up when he imagined Nela unwrapping his knee and tsking over it, scolding him for being reckless, but rewrapping it with gentle fingers and tucking the blanket carefully back around it. He couldn't let himself wonder if she would ever get to scold him again.

He never complained to Pelayut or Virta about pain, boredom, homesickness, or anything else. He could only give them his silent cooperation, so he did.

That changed one afternoon a few days after Ribas and the others had left for Sostavi. They couldn't have gotten to the capital yet; Bereg understood the journey would take about a week. Bereg had submitted to Virta's nursing in the morning and dutifully eaten the midday meal she brought him of bread, hard sausage rounds, and cider made from those remarkable apples. She couldn't talk to him, knowing no Lasska, and she seemed shy and reluctant to talk to strangers in any case. Bereg wondered how a delicate woman like her had ended up with a man like Gedrin, all hardy strength and uncertain temper. She wouldn't have looked out of place in some of the finer neighborhoods in Cheremay.

It came as a relief, a couple of hours later, when Pelayut checked in on him instead. He and she couldn't say much to each other either, but they could talk a little, and Bereg appreciated that Pelayut was closer to his own age.

She was a great deal like her older son. Bereg and the others had all noticed that. Ribas had some of her looks, certainly, but more noticeably, he had her temper. Pelayut spoke and acted as if her steadiness needed to anchor her and everyone else during hard times. Bereg could see where the priest had gotten his calm strength.

This afternoon, though, Pelayut looked noticeably tired. She sat down in the straight-backed wooden chair she had put beside the bed for the times when she felt Bereg needed company for a while. She wore her hair, which must once have been a lighter shade of Ribas's leaf-brown, coiled in a silvering knot at the back of her head. With her fine features, those blue eyes, and the strong hands folded in the lap of her homespun dress, Bereg realized she was still quite lovely. She must have been a beautiful girl. He wondered how she, like Virta, had ended up living on a farm in a tiny village.

She smiled. Bereg liked her smile: anyone could see she meant it. "How do you feel?" she said.

"Very well. But do I wish I could get up." He wouldn't have told Virta as much.

"No, we can't have that. The tayo says you have to wait."

Bereg had every reason to trust Tayo Nevas, and he would do as the healer said, but he had no idea yet how long he would "have to wait." Pelayut said, "You must not worry. We are glad to have you here."

Her Lasska got better every day. Bereg said, "That's very kind." Looking closely at her face again, he wondered if she might have been crying. No doubt, if she did, she never let anyone else see it. "Forgive me," he said, "but are you all right?"

She did look tired. Exhausted, in fact. "I am quite well," she said, but he noticed how her hands closed more tightly around each other. She added, "I did not sleep much last night."

"I didn't either," Bereg admitted. "It's hard to want to sleep when you get so much rest all the time." He motioned at the dead weight of his leg, propped up on a pillow on the quilt. "And when you think too much."

"You must miss your family."

The sympathy in her voice loosened his tongue. "Very much. And I worry about them." He should not talk about this, even with her. The words came out of the long lonely hours and pushed themselves past the new lump in his throat. "I wonder what will happen to them, if I can't..."

Can't go home. He couldn't say it. Pelayut reached over and pressed his hand briefly. "I understand worry." Her Lasska had the same formal inflection Ribas's did.

Bereg said, "I'm sure you do. You must worry too." He had no doubt she did, for both of her sons: Ribas going into unknown dangers, and Gedrin, who plainly had troubles of his own.

"Yes."

He thought she might not say anything else, but after a brief pause, she continued. "Last night, I did not sleep because I thought about Sostavi. I thought how I can do nothing for my boys." She lifted a hand to wave away what she'd just said, both the statement and the pain that went with it. "No. I can care for them, and pray for them. But that is..." She scanned the opposite wall as if she would find the word she needed there. "That feels small."

Yes, prayer did feel terribly small. "I know."

"I should not think that way, when Ribé is a priest. But I do."

"I've never been much for praying," Bereg said. "I never thought Mesha would pay attention to someone like me." Thinking about the mysterious city where the others had gone, wishing he could at least picture it, he said, "Have you ever been to Sostavi?"

"No. I have always been in Lida."

"Were you born here?" That possibility hadn't occurred to him.

"Yes. Here, in fact." She motioned at the walls. "This was my father's farm."

So she hadn't ended up here at all. She had simply never left. Bereg said, "Did you ever want to live anywhere else?"

Her smile came back. "Oh, no. This is home."

He understood that too. He said, "I don't think many people would want to live where I come from, but if I had a choice, I wouldn't live anywhere else."

That afternoon marked their first real talk. Bereg knew they both felt the benefit of it. Over the next days, Pelayut took over most of his care. When they sat together, she let herself tell him a little about what she thought and felt. Never too much, as if she thought it might overtax him, or as if she simply couldn't give in so much to her feelings, but he saw how it eased her mind to talk about where Ribas was right now and what he might be doing, or share her concerns about restless, unhappy Gedrin. Bereg was more than glad to listen to anything she wanted to say. As he listened, he learned more about the village, this family, and the religion of the goddess Kenavi. He had to admit that he liked the sound of this goddess, who offered her people her love and protection. He wondered what made Mesha so different.

On the day the Namorans called Ashdina, Eighth Day, a week after the travelers had left, Pelayut said they had probably reached Sostavi. "I'm sure they will send us word when they can." By then, Bereg recognized the proud set of her shoulders and back when she wrapped her courage around herself. "No doubt we will have news of them soon," she said. If she did have any doubts, she didn't plan to share them.

Gedrin did have doubts. Bereg could see that. The younger man's tension and surliness had deepened with each passing day, except when he practiced target shooting outside with Handan and the little boy. Part of Bereg wanted to shake Gedrin and tell him to be a man, stop worrying his mother with bad temper when she already had so much on her mind. Part of him couldn't blame Gedrin. Winter was a quiet time on the farm. Snow fell almost every day. Without enough hard physical work to keep him busy, an active man like Gedrin probably felt like a tethered bear. Bereg, old bear though he was, felt much the same.

The next day, which the Namorans called Pirdina, the family went to the morning service at their Circle House and stayed for the meal afterward. Pelayut had offered to stay home with Bereg, but he had insisted on her going with the others. He wouldn't let her miss the Namorans' most important weekly ritual for his sake.

Rahul and Radavan stood outside the bedroom window and talked with him. Bereg had persuaded Pelayut to leave it open on purpose, because the Vaia still preferred not to come into the house unless they had to. None of the three of them had any useful ideas about what might be happening in Sostavi, but it helped to trade worries on the chilly draft. They all agreed Tama could take care of herself. They agreed, too, that nobody with sense would give Khari any trouble either, she was tough and a good fighter – but though none of them said it, Bereg knew how much all of them would have given for a line from her. The Vaia had a written language, rarely used by any except their Lodestones and Lamp-Carriers, but Radavan and Rahul also knew it and Khari had promised to send word when she could. Rahul, in particular, looked as if he'd had about as many sleepless nights as Bereg himself.

When the family came home in the early afternoon, Tayo Nevas was with them. He and Pelayut came into the bedroom. "The tayo will take a look at your leg," Pelayut said, "and then I will bring your meal. There's food from the Circle House."

She had put a plate together for him. Bereg could see her choosing from the spread of dishes on offer, taking portions of her own favorites and anything she thought he might especially like, and wrapping it all up carefully to bring home. Exactly what Nela would have done.

The tayo undid the bandage around Bereg's knee and peered at it. He grunted with what sounded like satisfaction and directed a question at Pelayut.

"He says to ask you if there is any pain," she said.

Bereg had been taking some sort of bitter tonic for pain, not as fiery as Khari's pepper-and-orena tincture, but apparently just as effective. "No pain. It feels fine," he said.

Pelayut told the healer this and listened to his answer. Bereg wished he could teach himself some Namoran, but so far, he'd had no more luck with that than he'd had learning Vaia. Pelayut said, "He says it is healing well. He says in another week, you can get up, but you will need..." She mimed using crutches. "And you will not be able to stand on that foot for a while yet."

Bereg sighed. Another week in bed, and then crutches and hobbling. How long would he have to drag on Pelayut's hospitality? The tayo was telling her something else now, lifting and lowering his own leg presumably to demonstrate the exercises Bereg would have to do to get the use of the knee back. He knew he should be grateful he would get it back at all.

He was watching the tayo, trying to learn the exercises himself so Pelayut wouldn't have to do everything for him, when something impossible happened.

A flare of white light cut across his vision. It was so intense and blinding that for an instant the room, the bed, the faces of Pelayut and the healer, all disappeared. Bereg didn't think he closed his eyes, but instead of what he knew was in front of him, he saw something entirely different.

A great bear, bigger than worlds, lay curled on its side, trapped in a net of fire. It snarled, slashing out with claws the size of trees, trying to rend the orange and red and blue lines with its impossibly huge teeth, but the net held it tight and scorched its fur down to the naked skin. The bear roared in pain...and then there was light.

White light that sliced like a sword. A flash of such brilliance that Bereg thought he might never see again. The net fell to pieces, individual strands parting and falling away and winking out like the last embers of a dying fire.

The bear rose to its feet, shaking itself. It reared up and roared in triumph, stretching its paws into the infinite dark sky...

...and its shape changed. Bereg seemed to see that it was not a bear at all, but a land, with contours of mountains and curves of roads and rivers, and swathes of forest and deep golden plains that he knew well.

He saw the piece of it that meant the most to him. Dark forest, slopes covered in snow; but in the midst of the cold, a small house with brightly-lit windows and smoke curling up from the chimney...

...and then the land changed again, and he saw the shape of the bear, suspended in that infinite space. The bear's immense dark eyes looked straight into him, and he felt words, though no voice carried them.

"Today, we are free."

"Bereg?"

Bereg realized he was staring at a wall of smooth wooden boards seamlessly joined together. Yes: the bedroom. The farmhouse. He knew that the woman watching him, with concern in her face, was

Pelayut, and that the old white-haired man was Tayo Nevas. But Bereg didn't know if he could speak. Something had happened inside his head. It felt as if the walls between him and everything else, even the normal walls of body and bones and skin, had disappeared. As if a haze of light hung around him, and he were dissolving into it.

"Bereg? Are you all right?"

It didn't scare him, somehow. Not at all. If he had to name the feeling, he would call it joy.

The bear reared up for the sky…

But he must pull himself together. Pelayut was watching him as if she thought he might faint. Bereg concentrated on the feeling of the mattress supporting him, the soft quilt under his fingers.

"I'm all right," he said. He couldn't stop himself from lifting a hand to touch his head. It felt the way it always did, thin hair and warm skin over the hard shape of his skull. He had thought his fingers might pass through it, as if it actually had become no more solid than light.

"What happened?" Pelayut said.

How could he explain? She and the healer might think he was rambling, turning senile or some such. Bereg knew he wasn't. The vision had been as real as anything he had ever seen or felt. Crazy-sounding or not, he had to try to share it with her.

Today, we are free.

"I saw something," he said. "I'll try to tell you."

The words came more easily than he'd thought. The flash of light. The bear and the net. The message, if you could call it that, that he'd heard. And the fact that he had seen home, that it had been close and clear and exactly the way he remembered. As he talked, he felt the joy rising in him again. "I don't know what it was," he said, "but something did change." He couldn't help touching his head again. The change had happened there, somehow, but not just there. It was deep and potent and it went beyond himself. "Something is different."

He didn't know how much she would be able to understand, but her Lasska had gotten better. As she listened, he thought she was following him, but her expression surprised him. The more he said, the more worried she looked. When he described the net, her eyebrows came together and he saw actual fear in her face. Maybe she did think he was hallucinating or dreaming.

When he finished, she said carefully, "You saw a net, and it fell apart?"

"Yes. I know it all sounds impossible, but..."

She held up a hand to stop him. He thought he saw that hand trembling slightly. *No, please don't worry*, he thought. *I haven't lost my senses.* But then she was talking to the healer, back and forth in a flow of Namoran. Bereg caught the name "Ribé." Pelayut asked what sounded like a question. The healer nodded once, a curt gesture. His face looked grim.

Pelayut whispered three words. One of them sounded like the name *Kenavi*. Her hands came up to cover her face. To his shock, Bereg realized she was crying.

He looked helplessly at the healer. "What's wrong?" he said, though he knew Nevas couldn't answer him and probably would not understand the question. The old man ignored him completely. He put his hand on Pelayut's shoulder. The two of them stayed that way, motionless: the woman with her face hidden behind her strong fingers, the white-haired healer with his head bowed and his age-rough hand on her shoulder. If it had not been for the almost-stifled sound of Pelayut's sobs, and the faintest motion of her shoulders with each one, she and Nevas could have been statues.

Bereg had no idea what to do. Something had wrung her; something was terribly wrong. He couldn't stand the idea that he had caused it somehow. He couldn't leave the room and give her privacy; he couldn't even make himself look away, though decency should have compelled that. He watched her, longing to see something he could do to help her out of what looked like unbearable pain.

Finally the healer said something quietly. Pelayut was still weeping, but she nodded. For a little while she went completely still; she didn't even seem to breathe. Then she lowered her hands, drying her eyes with a corner of her homespun shawl. The healer let go of her shoulder.

Her face looked as calm as ever. Bereg could only imagine how much that cost her. She said, "I am sorry."

Mesha guard us, don't apologize to me! "No," Bereg said, "please don't be. Please tell me, what's wrong?"

Again she folded her hands in her lap. Bereg saw how tightly they held onto each other. "What you saw," she said, choosing words carefully. "It sounds as if Ribas used his gift."

The mental ability Bereg knew so little about. "Do you mean he used it in Sostavi, and I felt it here?" What kind of unknowable magic was this?

"I think so," Pelayut said. She nodded at Nevas. "The tayo and I both know what he can do with it." Her voice stayed so steady that Bereg wouldn't have guessed what she felt if he couldn't see her face. "The net that fell apart," she said. "Ribé has done things like that before. But this time, it sounds as if he did something much bigger." Her eyes closed, only for a moment before she opened them again. "That would be very dangerous."

"It would?" Bereg felt like a fool.

"Yes. If he tries to do something that is too hard, he can become very sick."

And he had a weak heart. Bereg understood one thing: whatever Ribas had done, Pelayut was afraid of what it might have cost him. And she was here, miles and miles away. If her son was hurt, or sick – or worse – she couldn't help.

Bereg reached out. He had never done this before, but he put his hand over both of hers, where they lay in her lap. "I'm sorry," he said.

She gently disengaged one hand to take hold of his. When she tried to smile, the look in her eyes went straight to his heart.

Mesha guard us. Bereg said, "I will pray for him." For the first time he could remember, he thought the God might hear him.

They sat quietly together. Bereg listened to the wind whispering around the old farmhouse and thought of the bear's joy in its freedom. Could Mesha care for the life of a Namoran who served a foreign goddess? Bereg thought it was worth asking the question.

Then Pelayut said gently, "Thank you." Bereg let go of her hand as she stood up. "I will get your meal," she said. "You should eat before it gets cold."

The healer went out with her. Left alone, Bereg offered a prayer. *Mesha, You who see all, take care of her son.*

A week passed. To Bereg, the days before he could try to get on his feet would have stretched out interminably in any case, but without any news from Sostavi, each hour seemed like a day in itself. Pelayut looked worn out, always, but she sat and talked with Bereg and brought him meals as usual. Gedrin rushed around the house, not actually doing much work that Bereg could see, but trying to stay active. There wasn't much laughter anywhere, even from the children.

On the following Pirdina, in the afternoon, Tayo Nevas supervised as Bereg hauled himself out of bed and propped himself up on a pair of sturdy wooden crutches the healer had brought. They fit well under his arms, the grips comfortable in his hands. Bereg could learn to flex the knee again. Meanwhile, he could drag himself out of the bedroom. He still couldn't go outside, except to the front porch, because the uneven ground would have been too much for his unsteady balance and he couldn't afford another fall. Nor could he make himself useful in any way. But he could sit on the porch and talk to Radavan and the others, and he could start to hope that one day, he would be able to stand and walk unaided.

By halfway through the second week, he had gotten used to crutching down to the farmhouse kitchen for meals, and his knee ached again with the exercises the tayo gave him. Then, one evening, a courier arrived in the middle of supper.

Asira had run to answer the knock. She came back to the kitchen with an envelope she handed to Pelayut. Bereg, sitting next to Pelayut, saw the color rise into her cheeks. She smiled, a faint, tremulous smile, as if she thought a happiness too great to be true would be snatched away from her.

Everyone at the table had stopped eating. All the eyes fixed on Pelayut as she broke the white wax seal on the back of the envelope and took out a single sheet of paper. Bereg saw it was covered with a strong, fluid handwriting, front and back. Pelayut scanned it quickly. The paper shivered like a leaf in a breeze when she turned it over and Bereg could see how much her hands shook. Then she wordlessly held it out across the table to Gedrin and ducked her head to hide her face.

Gedrin snatched the paper. He read for what felt like half a second; he didn't even turn the letter over. Then he thumped his hand down on the table and shouted something. Bereg had never seen so much joy in his face. He looked years younger.

Both children jumped up and ran to him. His wife reached eagerly for the letter. Questions and answers flew back and forth across the table. Bereg knew the news had to be what he hoped, but he still had to make sure.

He touched Pelayut's shoulder and said her name, raising his voice to make himself heard over Gedrin and Virta and the children. She turned to him. Tracks of tears gleamed on her cheeks, and she didn't bother to brush them away. Bereg had never seen her so happy.

"He is all right," she said. "Ribé is all right. He will come home."

Later, when the excited children had finally been put to bed and the house was quiet, she and Bereg sat by the fire in the front room and she told him more about what the letter had said. Ribas couldn't come home yet; he'd written that the ruler in Sostavi would need him for several more weeks. But he and his wife, and Tama and Khari, were all well. "He thinks they will come home early in Ivesta," she said. Bereg knew Ivesta was the third month of the Namoran calendar: planting season. "They will be back for spring."

Her exhaustion had lifted. Her joy brought that lump back up in Bereg's throat. "I'm so glad," he said.

"Someday soon," she said, "you will write and tell your family when you will come home. And they will be happy too."

Bereg had not dared to hope for such a thing. Right now, it didn't seem impossible.

Today, we are free.

25

KHARI

During the anxious days after Ribas used his gift in the Council meeting, while he lay sick in his chambers, Khari and Tama both felt frustrated and useless. They were on the edges, strangers in Namora with no real way to communicate with the people around them. Khari gladly would have waited in the sickroom with Ribas's wife, and she knew Tama would have done the same, but Namora's ruler, the woman called Valdena, was so often there too. Khari thought if she and Tama had tried to be part of the vigil, they would have intruded on what didn't belong to them. They could only wait, sometimes each alone, sometimes together.

On the fifth night, they sat in the hall in the House of the Sventine a little distance from Ribas and Maryut's chambers. The hallway windows had wide, deep wooden sills, big enough for the two of them to use one as a seat. They kept out of the way of the servants who guarded the chamber door and the priests and curious onlookers who drifted through the hall. Everyone in the city, it seemed, wanted news of Ribas, but the guards did their work well.

No one asked Khari or Tama any questions, or seemed to see them at all. Khari felt silly crouching there on the windowsill, like a child trying to overhear an adults' conversation. Tonight, though, it meant she and Tama both saw it when a servant went running from the chambers to the temple. They saw it a little later when Valdena arrived in breathless hurry and was let in, and then, some time after, they saw her leave.

Her face told Khari everything she needed to know. "He's going to be all right," she said to Tama. The relief left her so weak she had to lean against the window and let it prop her up.

The older woman wiped her eyes. "He'd better be."

The next afternoon, Khari insisted on going up to the guards on the door. By then, word had spread that Ribas was getting better. People crowded the hallway, wanting to see and talk to him, wanting to know exactly what he had done. The city seemed to be on fire with gossip. Khari knew she and Tama had more right to see him than anyone else the exasperated servants turned away.

Khari didn't know whether her rough Namoran did any good, or whether the two guards – both scrawny young men – simply didn't like the look of Tama, but one of them reluctantly knocked. Maryut answered the door. When she saw who it was, she stood aside and motioned them in.

Ribas was sitting up in bed. Khari thought he looked too pale and tired, but he said, "I'm very glad to see you."

Khari didn't have the words, either in Namoran or Lasska, to tell him how glad she was to see him, or how glad she was for the one great flaw in her dream. He could see into minds without the need for words. She hoped he could see into hers.

She sat down in the chair next to the bed, opposite Maryut. Tama stood at the foot. Khari had moved through the past five days with all her thoughts trained on Ribas and what might be happening in Lassar; she had barely had time to notice the finery that surrounded her on every side. Now she took in the trappings of this room and wondered why people chose to burden themselves down with so much. It was all beautiful, to be sure, but she preferred the farm back in the little village, and the quietness of the sleeping apple orchard.

Tama wasted no time telling Ribas exactly what she had felt when he used the gift. "I thought my head had come open. I've never felt anything like it. Whatever you did, I'm certain it worked."

"I think I opened a door," Ribas said. "At least, I hope I did." Khari was so glad to see him smile. "Impera Shurik will have to decide whether it stays open."

Tama looked skeptical. "I hope you did more than you think. Lassar's imperi aren't known for their flexibility. Or their intelligence."

Khari said, "Shurik is young. He might see things differently, better than his father could."

Tama raised an eyebrow. "You're young too, my girl. How much do you know about it?"

The words teased her, but in Tama's expression, Khari saw her mother-in-truth again. *Your eyes are better than mine.* She lifted her chin. "I knew enough to get us here."

Ribas said, "You deserve more credit than any of us, Khari. I would never have known what to do without your dream."

Valdena's healer, Tayo Bodin, had said Ribas wouldn't be able to get up for another week or so. The healer reminded Khari very much of the white-haired man in Lida who had opened up Bereg's knee. She wondered if all Namoran healers were chosen for their age and a certain shortness of temper.

During Ribas's recovery, Khari and Tama visited him every day. While they were there, they often spent a while talking with Maryut and Valdena too. Khari found herself picking up Namoran easily. She could get by with only occasional help from Ribas, and she liked to see how her quick command of the language impressed him. She also found herself liking the Namoran ruler. Valdena was a strong, sensible, practical woman. She didn't put on unnecessary pride, and she cut through problems efficiently without getting lost in confusion or arguments.

Valdena expected a reply from Shurik to a letter she had sent a few weeks earlier. While she waited for news from Cheremay, she sent an envoy to the Senai to see what Shurik's border guard was doing. Ribas's health got steadily better during the time it took for the Senai envoy to go and return. Once the healer decided he was fit enough to work, he got caught up in the business of the city and the group the Namorans called the Council.

Khari and Tama spent more time exploring the city. Tama couldn't wait to get rid of her Lasska soldier's uniform, but she didn't like the clothes Namoran women wore. "I haven't put on a dress since I was five," she said. Finally, with Khari's help, she got a milliner to measure her for a man's outfit. The new shirt, slacks, and vest suited her. "Much more practical," she told Khari. "These women don't know what they're missing."

Maryut sometimes came with them on their walks, but she stayed near Ribas as much as she could. "I won't have those people wearing him out," she said. "As far as I can see, he's done plenty."

Tama thought so too. "They should let him go home," she said one afternoon, while she and Khari walked down by the harbor. "He's done what they needed him for."

Khari had done her best to follow Namoran politics, and she understood Ribas's role as Valdena's second-in-command. "They will," she said. "They have to replace him first."

"I hear that priest Galvo is going to replace him," Tama said. The two of them walked down to the pier at the far end of the harbor and stood for a while, looking out at the blue-gray water. Clouds hid the sun, but the cold breeze off the water had a delicious fresh taste. Boats bobbed at anchor along the shore. Over her shoulder, Khari glanced back at Sostavi, rows and rows of white buildings climbing the side of the tall hill like a cluster of crystals. Tama said, "I don't know if I care for Galvo much."

Khari pictured Galvo. He and another, much younger member of the Council, a man called Lesvin, had visited Ribas often during his recovery. Ribas seemed to like talking with Galvo in particular. The two of them discussed Namoran stories and texts until Khari had hopelessly lost the thread of the talk, but she could hear in

Ribas's tone how much he enjoyed it. She said, "I think he's all right."

"He reminds me too much of some of the soldiers I knew," Tama said. "Always hunting for the next promotion. And he looks like a ferret."

Khari laughed. It was good to want to laugh again. "I don't think he looks that bad," she said. "And it's probably not his fault if he does." She remembered something Ribas had said, one of the times they had talked about how he would go back to Lida as soon as he could and take up his life the way it used to be. "There aren't any more promotions after this one," she said, "so he'll have to stop hunting."

The envoy to the Senai came back about a week later. Khari and Tama joined the Council meeting to hear what Valdena's people had found at the border. When the envoy reported that they had in fact seen watchtowers of the kind Khari and Tama had described, both at the pass itself and at regular distances to the north and south, and that they had seen soldiers busy along all the roads, for a sickening moment Khari thought Ribas had failed. Then the report went on.

"We saw soldiers taking down the towers," one member of the envoy, a fair-haired young woman, said. "They are keeping one at the pass itself, but that seems to be a formality and no more than a sensible precaution. All the activity we saw seemed to do with reducing the guard or, in some places, dismantling it entirely. We met no resistance or hostility at the border. In fact, everyone we saw seemed inclined to welcome us, though of course we couldn't speak with them, not having enough of the language."

Tama looked at Khari with her eyebrows raised. She, too, had picked up enough Namoran to follow what people said, though she couldn't yet speak the language very well herself.

Valdena said, "Perhaps Tama Leben can tell us more about what to interpret from this news. Tavo Balsa, if you will translate for her."

Ribas listened as Tama spoke quickly in Lasska, and then translated for the group. "She says she finds the news about the towers hopeful, but she is more impressed that Lasska soldiers acted friendly and welcoming to outsiders. This isn't usual behavior. She says if it's true, it does confirm that Shurik has changed his intentions."

Whispers and murmurs started. Galvo spoke over the noise. "In other words, Tavo Balsa, she says that the soldiers' behavior confirms that you succeeded."

Tama spoke up directly then, in a few words of firm Namoran. "Yes. He did. He must have."

The murmuring and muttering swelled. Khari couldn't catch enough of the words, but she heard joy and relief in the voices. She saw that Ribas sat absolutely still, head down, staring at the tabletop. His face looked flushed and she thought he might be fighting back tears.

When he raised his head and lifted a hand, the noise stopped. His eyes looked very bright. "We still have to wait until we hear from Impera Shurik himself," he said. "But meanwhile, colleagues, I must remind you that we couldn't have done anything without the help we've had from Khari and from Tama Leben. Please give them the credit they deserve."

He began to applaud. The other members of the Council joined in at once. The noise was a storm, filling the room and sloshing back and forth off the walls. Khari saw Tama's shocked expression, as if the Lasska had never met this kind of appreciation before.

Khari hadn't either. She had to look down, to avoid all the eyes, but just before she did, she saw Valdena smiling at her.

Vatiri, Amma, I wish you were here now.

The letter from Cheremay came a week later. During the time in between, Khari and Tama helped Ribas teach some members of the Council, including Galvo, Lesvin, and Valdena herself, how to speak some Lasska. The lessons involved complaints, especially from the older Council members, about how difficult the language was. "What do you mean, a different alphabet?" one of the white-haired priests said. "Why should I learn new letters at my time of life?" Valdena said, "Sventin, perhaps I should remind you that Impera Shurik has a good command of Namoran. Are we going to show ourselves less able than he?"

Khari remembered how she had teased Bereg and Tama about learning to speak Vaia. Now, during the sessions, she watched Tama lay into these reluctant Namorans and scold them when they didn't want to put in the effort. "I'm learning your language," Tama would say, in clumsy but decent Namoran. "You can learn mine."

Khari herself came in for a great deal of respect and attention both from the Council and from the people in Sostavi. Everyone wanted to see and talk to Ribas, but everyone wanted to know about her too. She knew most of them would probably never see another Vaia. Certainly she, in her childhood in Vatiri's tent, learning to recognize and interpret pathdreams, had never imagined traveling with Lasska soldiers, crossing the mountains, learning to speak two new languages. In talking to the Namorans who wanted to satisfy their curiosity about her, she tried to do justice to her people.

The Council gathered again when Shurik's letter arrived. Khari stood in her usual corner of the now-familiar room with Tama beside her. The older woman refused to show it, but Khari knew she was frightened. Khari was frightened too, so deeply that she had to lock her hands together to keep them from shaking. Soon, she and Tama would learn for certain what the impera intended. They would learn whether they would go home.

Valdena stood before the Council with the letter in her hand. Tight silence filled the room. Just before she began to read, Valdena's eyes rested briefly on Khari's face.

Then the words began. Valdena read slowly. Khari, listening so closely her head ached with tension, followed them one at a time.

To the Tavin of Namora, Valdena Filtraikas, respectful greetings from Impera Shurik of Lassar.

Tavin Valdena,

I have had the honor of receiving your Council's letter in response to my earlier communication regarding the people known as the Pala Vaia. In reference to this, I wish to address you directly.

Khari hadn't seen Shurik's earlier letter, but she had heard about it. Ribas had said it was distant and formal, referring to "the Impera wishes" and "the Impera intends," as though Shurik had been speaking to a servant. Here, he addressed Valdena as one leader to another. Khari saw that everyone in the room heard the difference.

She had some trouble following the next words Valdena read. Shurik used formal phrases she didn't know. Valdena paused after a few lines and looked up. "Tavo Balsa," she said, "will you please translate what I have just read for our friends from Lassar?"

Ribas took the paper. Now Khari heard every word clearly.

Upon reflection, I find it not fitting that any person, whether citizen, soldier, or Impera himself, should claim to know the precise will of the God. Lord Mesha is rightly possessive of His land and His people, but it seems only just to conclude that the Pala Vaia, as residents of His land Lassar, also belong to Him. Only He may render His judgment upon any who are rightly His.

Khari swallowed. Tama reached out and took her hand. Khari held it tightly. When Ribas finished that piece of the letter, he handed it back to Valdena.

Shurik's campaign is over. Now they knew it for certain. Khari could go home. But what about Tama and Bereg, who had made themselves traitors?

Valdena went on reading. Khari found she could follow the next part more easily. *I have learned that certain of my own people objected to the measures I intended to take against the Pala Vaia. In acting against my orders of the time, they anticipated how my will would change. With these people, I can therefore find no fault.*

Khari looked at Tama. The soldier stood rigidly at attention, staring at Valdena, still gripping Khari's hand. Khari wasn't sure Tama had understood the words until she saw the older woman rub her eyes with the back of her wrist. She herself noticed the way

Shurik had saved face: "they anticipated how my will would change." Pradesh would like that trick.

Tavin Valdena, you of course know that I have only recently come to the throne of Lassar, after the death of my esteemed father Impera Mangevar. My father and others before him had their methods of governing. I must find my own way forward.

Again Valdena paused, and again Ribas translated what she had read so far. Khari watched Tama listening closely, weighing each word, deciding whether Shurik might have something to him after all.

Valdena continued. *In particular,* Shurik wrote, *I would value closer fellowship and exchange of ideas with my nearest neighbor to the west. Too long, Namora and Lassar have remained strangers to one another.*

Khari saw Ribas shaking his head as if he had trouble believing what he heard. He had caused this. She hoped he knew what a change he had made. Valdena was reading, *To bring us closer, I would ask the Tavin's permission to send...*Here Khari stumbled over a word. She couldn't make sense of it, but the letter went on, *I would also welcome a Namoran guest in Cheremay.*

Tama saw Khari's confusion. "I think he's talking about an ambassador," she whispered. "Sending an ambassador from Cheremay to Sostavi, and asking her to send one back."

Valdena finished, *I look forward to the favor of your reply, and to our friendship in the future. Yours in the sight of the Great God Mesha, Impera Shurik of Lassar.*

Ribas translated the last piece of the letter, but Khari didn't need it. That was just as well, because the rest of the Council were talking over him before he had finished.

Tama squeezed Khari's hand and let it go. "Ribas said Shurik would have to keep the door open," she said. Her voice sounded as brusque as ever, but Khari knew that was only to hide what lay underneath. "Sounds as if he might actually do it."

"I told you," Khari said. "He's young. He can think differently."

Tama stared at her for a moment. The noise in the room had

swelled into chaos. Council members got up, wrung one another's hands, even hugged each other. Khari saw Valdena put her arms around Ribas.

Tama laughed. "You're right." For the first time Khari could remember, her face looked young and hopeful. She drew Khari into a hug.

We can go home. Khari sent up a prayer in the silence of her mind as the joyous noise in the room wove a blanket around her and Tama's arms held her tight. *Moon Woman. Your guidance has blessed us all.*

That night, Khari dreamed.

Tama had told her that afternoon that once they could go back to Lassar, she first wanted to see Bereg safely home. "He's an old man. He'll need help getting to those forests of his." After that, Tama had asked if Khari's tribe might let her stay with them awhile. "I don't have any real place of my own," she said. "Being with you and the others has felt more like home than anything else."

Khari couldn't give the tribe's permission. That would be up to Pradesh. The Lodestone might not want a Lasska soldier – even a former one – traveling with them, but Khari would use all the influence she rightfully had. Now, in the too-soft bed in her opulent chamber, with the too-slippery and too-embroidered sheets covering her, her hidden eye stayed open while she slept.

On the plains, sunlight poured down on tall summer grass. Orena bloomed purple. Yellow poppies bobbed and danced in a light breeze.

Near a stand of trees that marked a creek's edge, a herd of deer lingered to graze. Fawns scampered and chased one another. Older does lay down in the grass to let the sun warm their coats. A tall buck stood guard, watching them all.

Khari seemed to ride the breeze that moved above the herd. She saw another guard watching over them: a bear, her coat brown in the sun, her muzzle only lightly touched with gray. She paced at the edge of the grazing ground, back and forth, lifting her head now and then to sniff the peaceful air.

The deer didn't fear her. In fact, two of them went close to her: a young doe and a young buck, both small and strong-built. The buck examined insects in the grass and nosed new plants that reached for the sky.

The buck and the doe walked side by side with the bear a while. Then she went on in one direction and they turned and went the other, the two of them alone together.

26

RIBAS

The highest of holy days took on new meaning in the Great House, with all the loveliness it held up to honor the Goddess. As much as Ribas missed home, and wished he had been there to take the burden of these weeks off his mosevine, he would hold onto the memory of the Akena and Algima services in Sostavi as long as he lived.

He and Sventin Galvo, as the current and soon-to-be Tavo Balse, served as Valda's seconds together in many of the services. Valda and Galvo both had insisted that Ribas retain the Tavo Balsa rank until it actually came time for him to leave Sostavi. He and Galvo, meanwhile, found more chances to talk over the oldest texts that, as Galvo had said, showed striking similarities between the beloved heroine Klaya and the woman who became the Goddess. They agreed, with some regret, that it would be impossible ever to know for certain, but the girl on the guarding wall who had given her life to save a Pala Vaia tribe could well have been the same girl who had insisted on building a house of her own. Two halves of one whole, no matter what the stories said: even the ones that argued that Kenavi had lived hundreds of years after Klaya. "After all," Galvo said, "you and I both know how stories can change."

Ribas honored that girl during the Akena services. As he and Galvo assisted Valda with prayers, readings, and the rites of water and salt, in the deep and gracious silence of the Great House, Ribas held that girl in his memory. Perhaps they were one and the same, rebellious Klaya and gentle Kenavi, one woman who was fierce and strong and full of love for all and everything in the world around her. Such a Goddess deserved the most faithful service.

The solemn, grieving mood of Akena slipped away early that winter. As soon as the news about Shurik's letter spread through Sostavi, Algima seemed to move in. The time of renewal, the joyous celebration of Kenavi's Ascension.

Friendship between Namora and Lassar. Ambassadors going back and forth between the two countries. At first, some of the Council thought Shurik must be looking for an advantage, pretending cooperation while he planned something very different. Soon, though, the impera followed up his first letter with a second expressing his hope that Sostavi would welcome his chosen ambassador, a woman named Selia Balem, in the early spring, and hoping as well that he would soon "have the pleasure" of showing a Namoran ambassador "the finest hospitality at Cheremay's disposal." Meanwhile, the border guard stood down, and Lassar opened itself up for the first time in remembered history to visitors from the west. Shurik, it seemed, did in fact mean to govern his country in a new way.

It also seemed that everyone in Sostavi knew what had changed the Impera so much. *The Tavo Balsa worked a miracle.*

Visitors came in droves to the House of the Sventine and the Great House. They all wanted to meet and talk to the person who had *used the gift of the Goddess to change the world.* Explanations about how the gift worked, and what Ribas had actually done, didn't help. They wanted to see him as a hero.

"Well, you are," Maryut told him on the first night after Tayo Bodin had said he was strong enough to get back to work. They had finally shut the chamber door against the last visitors and stolen a few quiet minutes by the hearth. "No one else could have done what you did. Of course they all want to talk to you. But you watch yourself, love." She took his hands and scolded him the way he loved so much. "I won't let you wear yourself out. Never again."

He did his best. He couldn't turn people away, not when he knew that if Shurik had to keep the door between Namora and Lassar open, he himself could help on this side. If people wanted to see him as a hero, he could use that. But the word didn't fit him. It felt like a too-thick cloak draped over the already heavy white robes. While he talked to the faces, he conjured up the apple orchard at home and held it in his mind, and he listened to Maryut every time she told him he'd done enough for one day.

With Khari's and Tama's help, he also taught the Council some of the Lasska language. Another way to keep the door open. Khari, especially, picked up Namoran so quickly that she was practically fluent in a few weeks. Ribas wished he'd been half as quick to learn Lasska. Between the three teachers, even the oldest and most reluctant Council members got basic grounding in the language that, yes, they ought to have had when they took their seats as sventine. Valda had made it clear she would make some changes to the way dagira were taught in the viduri.

Khari herself had become an ambassador of the Vaia. With her different looks and different way of dressing, she drew attention everywhere she went. Ribas watched her talking and listening, answering questions about what life was like with the *klayine*, the wanderers, and explaining more about her gift of dreaming. "It gets tiring," she admitted to Ribas. "I miss the quiet back home." She told him, though, that she liked giving the Namorans a chance to learn about something they hadn't heard of before. Every piece of that meant change for her people too.

She and Tama, and Ribas and Maryut, took whatever quiet time they could find. One evening, as they sipped tea by the fire in Ribas and Maryut's chambers, they talked about the old language Pirlevis. It was the oldest "Namoran" language, but Khari thought it must have come from Vaia. Nothing else would explain how similar the two sounded.

"It could be the other way around," Ribas suggested. "Maybe you got it from us."

"No," Khari said. "We were the first people. First and Lost Ones, you know that."

Valda had joined them that evening. She took every chance she could to visit quietly with Ribas and Maryut especially; Ribas knew how much she dreaded their leaving Sostavi, though she always talked about it matter-of-factly. Now she said to Khari, "Why Lost?"

"Because we're always outsiders. Not wanted, wherever we are."

Ribas hoped the Vaia might find a new kind of home in Lassar now. If they knew they were safe, even welcome, might they take on a new name someday? He wondered if he would ever know.

Khari was thinking about something else. "I wonder," she said, "why my people don't know more about your Goddess. We have a few old stories about your round temples, but not much more. If Kenavi did sacrifice herself for us, don't you think we would remember her?"

Valda said, "It depends on how much your people actually knew about what Kenavi did. Maybe the story only lived with her people, not yours."

Khari said, "So to your people, she became a goddess because of what she did for my people?"

Ribas had talked about that with Galvo too. The idea that Kenavi might not, after all, have walked into the ocean to save her own people from the wrath of the old gods, but instead fallen into the water after she had used the only means she could to prevent murder: that idea upended everything the dagira taught. Galvo, for one, had been as willing to accept it as Ribas was himself. "Not everyone will agree," he said. "But when do we priests ever agree on anything?" Ribas knew how hard many dagira, including ones on the Council, would fight against the new version of the story. "It makes sense, though," he'd said. "It even makes sense that someone decided to bury it." Someone who had changed the story to keep "alien" people out of it. Ribas couldn't help thinking about how interested his father might have been in the new theories, if Silvas had actually been the kind of man Galvo remembered.

Valda said now, "If we accept what you saw as the real sacrifice, Khari, it seems that's exactly what happened. Kenavi became a goddess because of what she did for the Vaia."

Ribas agreed. "And since our people have forgotten that," he said, "I think it's time they remembered."

Valda gave him a sidelong look. "What are you planning, Tavo Balsa?"

Ribas laughed. "Some baffling readings and talks for my Circle House when I get home. They'll wonder what got into me."

Home. The time to go back couldn't come soon enough. Especially because now, finally, he thought he saw how to help Gedrin.

Valda said, "I might have to try a few baffling talks myself. Let me know how your Circle House takes it. I'll see if I can light a fire here too."

Maryut said, "We can do better than that. You can come and see for yourself how they take it."

"Next spring, maybe," Valda said. Ribas had no doubt that, this time, she did want to come to Lida, not like the only other time she had been there, when he'd seen exactly how unhappy she was. She said, "I'll see if I can leave things here with Sventin Galvo and come visit you. And by that time, Sventin Lesvin should also be back from Cheremay."

Ribas had suggested Lesvin for the first Namoran ambassador to Shurik's court. The young sventin had proved quick and apt with the Lasska language, and while he initially resisted the idea of leaving Sostavi, Ribas had mentioned to him that a Council member who might, one day, again find himself a candidate for higher office would find it well worth his time to broaden his experience. The new relationship between Lassar and Namora meant that anyone who had spent time in Cheremay would be valuable indeed. Lesvin had seen the sense in that and agreed to leave for the Lasska capital in early Ivesta. Whatever he saw and learned there, Ribas guessed, could only make him a better priest.

Maryut was saying, "Valda, you know you're welcome in Lida whenever you can come."

"I'm glad." Valda's face said more than her words did. "But Ribé, I have to ask you once more. Are you sure you won't go home a sventin?"

They had argued about this before. Ribas would give up the Tavo Balsa rank, but Valda had said there was no reason to demote him. He could serve Lida just as well as a sventin, since she could create the exception that let such a small House have a priest of that rank. Then he could install a zhinin to serve under him, to have the extra help he had to admit he needed.

It all made sense. Ribas knew his own objection didn't, but he said it anyway. "Valda, you know how I think. I don't need to be a sventin to do the work I care about."

"But you can still do your work," Valda said. "It doesn't make any difference what color robes you wear."

Ribas kept his face straight. "If it doesn't make any difference, then let me be a zhinin again."

Maryut burst out laughing. Valda gave Ribas the look he knew. *Always so stubborn.*

"Only you, Ribé," she said. "Very well. You'll have your demotion. I suppose I have to say you've earned it."

He did agree to let her put an exception in place for Lida's House, so he could install a second zhinin to serve with him in equal rank. As Maryut said, stubbornness could only go so far. And he would still have mosevine every year. "If you want them, you'll have them," Valda said. "You'll be swamped once all Namora knows what you did here."

As far as he was concerned, that news could spread as slowly as spilled honey in the winter. He did wish the weeks would move faster, but finally, early Ivesta came. The Lasska ambassador arrived in Sostavi. Sventin Lesvin was dispatched to Cheremay. It was time to go home.

Ribas's demotion came easier than his promotion had. There was no ceremony in the Great House, no need for witnesses; only a meeting with Valda in her chambers, in which she spoke the ritual words usually meant to chastise some errant member of the dagira. *I hereby remove from you the rank of...* In this case, she added the words "at your request." Her formal tone didn't quite hide the undercurrent of laughter.

Sventin Galvo was the new Tavo Balsa. He requested that Ribas help officiate at the Great House service on the last evening before Ribas, Maryut, Khari, and Tama left for Lida. Ribas put away the white sventin's robes and brought out the set of blue homespun he wore for ordinary services at home. He had brought them to Sostavi this time only because he couldn't bear to leave them behind. As he drew them on, feeling the so-familiar weight and texture of the fabric around his body, and as he adjusted the belt and collar as he had so many times, he had to close his eyes with relief and thankfulness. His reflection in the mirror in the chambers looked blurry until he blinked the mist away and recognized himself again. *Raimaté, zhinin.* His own eyes looked back at him, bright with humor. *It's about time.*

After that final service, the goodbyes in the Great House took some time. There were mutters and grumbles from Council members about losing such a valuable Tavo Balsa, though none of those happened within earshot of Sventin Galvo. Galvo himself was as sorry as anyone to see Ribas leave. "May the Goddess keep you always," he said. "Perhaps you might not mind a letter from me, now and again, as much as you did before?"

"I'd be glad to hear from you, sventin." Ribas added a formal blessing that felt exactly right. "May the Goddess grant you Her peace."

The carriage left Sostavi the next morning, the second Antdina in Ivesta, at daybreak. Ribas and Maryut had wanted to slip out before the city was awake, to avoid any more fuss. Sostavi drowsed under the first gray light of dawn. The warmer breeze that tasted of spring carried the salt tang up from the harbor.

Valda came personally to see the travelers off. In her plain dark-green dress, with a wheat-colored shawl around her shoulders and her hair neatly coiled and pinned at the back of her head, she could have been any of the city's women. She held herself proudly, smiling, as she shook hands with Tama and Khari and hugged Maryut.

She turned to Ribas last and held out her hand. "Raimaté, zhinin. Safe travels and come back whenever you can."

He and Maryut had already talked about how they would try to come back to Sostavi once a year, if they could manage it, during the fine months of late spring or early summer. With a second zhinin in the Circle House, it would be easier for Ribas to leave for a little while. And Maryut had admitted that, in spite of everything, she did find the city quite pleasant, and she would like to make a habit of seeing the ocean again.

"We'll be back," he told Valda now. "But you might make it to Lida first."

"I might do that."

He had told her how fortunate Namora was to have her as its leader. Looking at her now, her steady eyes and the determined set of her chin, he saw the girl from the viduris and the woman she had become, strong and wise and brave. And he saw all the sadness she kept back this morning, the love she carried that had never faded, but that had now changed, he thought, into something better.

He put his arms around her. "May the Goddess keep you, Tavin."

She laughed, but he heard a sob behind it. "And you, zhinin."

Then it was time to leave. The travelers got into the coach. Valda stood in the square and waved as it pulled away. In Ribas's last sight of her, she held her head high and defied sadness with her smile.

Maryut curled up against him. "Home," she said. "You know, I still can't believe it."

Ribas held her. "I know."

Khari and Tama watched the scenery. Ribas closed his eyes.

Spring was coming. He would be back in Lida in time to see it. Once he got there, one last, most important thing waited for him to do.

Nothing could compare to spring in Lida. On the day the travelers came home, the trees had put out a new mist of green leaves and the air smelled of mint and the freshness that came after rain. The Paret coach let the four of them off at the north edge of the village. As they walked up to the farm, Ribas remembered the many times he'd done this during visits home from the viduris. He used to take the overnight coach from town, so he could get to Lida at dawn and not waste a day of his time at home on the road. Mama had scolded him about it every time, because you couldn't get any rest on the coach, but she had never been able to talk him out of it.

Now evening sunlight spilled across the fields, which smelled of new grass and freshly turned earth. Maryut took a deep breath. "It smells like home."

"Always," Ribas said. He would have stopped in the road to breathe that scent, but he didn't want to lose one more moment getting to the farm. The very gravel underfoot felt familiar. His traveling bag was a comfortable weight on his shoulders. He said, "But don't you miss the ocean smell a little bit?"

Maryut tossed her head and looked up at him. "No." Then she laughed. "Don't worry, zhinin. I already told you, you were right about the ocean."

As they came up the lane to the farm, the front door opened. Ribas remembered the morning in Derla when Asira had come running to meet him and Maryut. Tonight it wasn't Asira but her father who stood framed in the doorway, and then Gedrin was coming down the path with his arms out.

"Goddess be thanked. It's about time."

He reached Ribas first. As his brother's arms wrapped around him, traveling bag and all, Ribas remembered the first time he had come home from the viduris. He'd gotten to the farm just past dawn. Gedrin had been coming back from morning chores in the barn. Ribas still remembered how the little boy – only six years old then – had stared up at him, and then how the brown eyes had filled with tears before Gedrin threw himself into his brother's arms. *I missed you, Ribé. I missed you so much.*

Now Ribas held his brother tight. "How are you doing, Gedrí?"

His brother's voice sounded muffled against his shoulder. "Better now."

Now Mama and Virta and the children had come out of the house. Bereg came with them; Ribas was delighted to see the old soldier walking easily, without crutches or cane. Radavan and the other Vaia hurried down from the orchard. Ribas saw the youngest man, Rahul, take Khari's hand.

Raulin and Asira were running around trying to welcome everyone at once. Mama came over to Ribas and Gedrin. Her face told Ribas what the past weeks had cost her, and how much this evening meant.

That first time he had come home from the viduris, she had stood in the middle of the front room with her hands on her hips. "You took the overnight coach, didn't you. Child, I told you not to do that." Her tone scolded him, or tried to anyway, but Ribas had seen the smile glimmering behind the sternness. Then she had held out her arms. "Come here."

Now, when Gedrin let him go, she held out her arms again. No words. Ribas went to her. She held him tight, her familiar chamomile scent wrapping around him. "My dove. I'm so glad to see you."

Supper was crowded and full of talk and laughter. Tomorrow Ribas would go back to the Circle House, to take up the work he had missed so much. Tonight was for the family and the people who had become part of it. Raulin bragged to his uncle about how "Uncle Handan" had taught him to use a bow and arrow. "I'll show you, Uncle Ribé. I'm good at it now." When Ribas pointed out that hunting was very different from the usual things the little boy liked –

"I thought you were working on your Capture game, Raulí" – Raulin scolded him playfully. "I can do both. And it's not so easy to hit the target. You have to be a good thinker."

During a lull in the talk, Gedrin said, "You'll have to brace yourself, Ribé. The whole village will want to see you tomorrow. Everybody's heard about what you did."

"They have? I don't remember writing to everybody."

Maryut said, "You mean the Sheaf and Barrel heard about it, Gedrí."

"Well, I may have said something to Seldo," Gedrin said. "Over a Capture game, you know. And a few other people heard. And people do talk."

Maryut sighed, but Ribas laughed. "I might have expected that."

Mama said, "You couldn't think we wouldn't say anything, my dove. Everyone was asking about you." Her pride in him was written on her face, so clearly his eyes smarted. She said, "By the way, your mosevine didn't want to bother you tonight, but you might want to see them anyway when you go down to the village. Danya came up here today. I thought she might burst if she didn't get to talk to you soon."

Ribas's mosevine had taken on so more than apprentices should have to. They deserved all the thanks he could give them. "I'll see them tonight," he said. "I need to see the House too. It's been too long."

And tomorrow, before the Lasska and Vaia travelers left for home, Ribas must do the last thing. *We'll help you, Gedrin,* he thought, watching his brother across the table. *We'll make it right.*

Danya and Jano didn't need to be asked twice to come up to the priest's house that night. Maryut aired the rooms and lit a fire in the kitchen grate while Ribas did his best to answer the flood of questions. The mosevine were overjoyed to have him back, but Ribas felt new shyness from both of them even as they wanted to hear everything about Sostavi, the Council, and most importantly, *please tell us, zhinin, how did you do it?*

He explained as well as he could how he had borrowed the strength of the Council, and how that had let him cut the great net. When he finished, both mosevine stared at him as if they had never seen him before. "But how were things here?" he asked. The two of them, Danya especially, had written to him in Sostavi to let him know the services were going well, and that the four babies born during the winter had had their ceremonies of bringing in and welcome, but the news had always been quick and to the point, as if they didn't want to take up too much of his time. He said, "Tell me about everything I missed."

Danya and Jano glanced at each other. They sat as mute as if their tongues had suddenly disappeared.

"What's the matter?" Ribas said. "Did something go wrong?"

Jano flushed at that. "No, zhinin, not at all." He spoke up with difficulty. "Everything was fine. It's just..."

His voice trailed off. Danya stepped in. Ribas saw how she had to make herself meet his eyes. "You were the Tavo Balsa," she said. "And you did so much. And we...well..." She glanced at Jano again for confirmation. "We're just apprentices."

As if they didn't have the right to talk to him now. Ribas had to put a stop to that at once. "You're *my* apprentices," he reminded them, "and you are both all I could ask for. I can't tell you how much I appreciate everything you've done."

Danya ducked her head. Ribas saw her shy smile. Jano flushed again, this time with pleasure. Ribas went on, "And I need to tell you, I'm still going to need your help. The Tavin has given me permission to install a second zhinin here. I'd like it to be one of you, if you're willing."

Both looked stunned. Danya raised her head. Her face looked as if she had been handed a dream made real. "*If?*" she said. All her shyness had disappeared. "Oh, zhinin, that would be..." Then she stopped. "But, Jano, do you want it? Because it could be either of us."

Jano shook his head slowly. "No. I'd be honored, but..." He looked at Ribas. "I'd thought about going home," he said. "Serving there. There's a space for a zhinin in our House, and I'm set to have it if I want. If that's all right."

"Of course," Ribas said. He would never argue with anyone who wanted to serve at home. "Then if you both agree, let's finish up your apprenticeship as usual. After that, Danya, I can install you here."

She was on her feet at once and around the table in two steps. She threw her arms around Ribas where he sat. "Thank you, zhinin."

After the mosevine had gone back to their quarters, Maryut said, "She won't sleep tonight."

Ribas laughed. "Maybe not. She'll do well here, though. She's come a long way."

"She has. And now *you* had better get some sleep, love. You heard what your brother said."

Gedrin had been right. The next day, visitors started arriving at the priest's house first thing in the morning. Ribas spent the day greeting the village and thanking everyone again and again for the welcome home. In the evening, the Circle House filled up for the service, standing room only even though it was an ordinary Tretdina. Ribas stood on the dais in the familiar robes and felt gladness fill him like light. Tonight, he wouldn't introduce the new ideas he had brought back from Sostavi. It was enough to be here and perform the rituals exactly the way he always had. Later, he would tell the people more about stories, and how they could change.

Afterward, he and Maryut went back up to the farm. Bereg and Khari and the others would leave tomorrow to start the trip back to Lassar. Tonight, Ribas needed their help for Gedrin.

At supper, he explained to everyone what he was going to do. Gedrin heard him out. When he finished, Gedrin said, "Brother, understand something. If there's any chance this will make you sick again, like it did in Sostavi, you're not doing it. I can get by."

"It'll be all right," Ribas said. "You know we cut a huge net then, the biggest and strongest I've ever seen. Next to that, yours is nothing." He smiled at his brother. "I need your strength, and everyone's here, because we're going to try to uproot it this time." He had never tried this before either. Sostavi had shown him the gift could do more than he had ever known. "Even then," he said, "I don't know how long it'll last. It might be like weeds in the garden."

"So you might have to do it again," Gedrin said.

"Yes. As long as I can have help, it'll be fine."

He told them he wanted to try it now. "All of you together will give me more than enough strength. Just remember, I need your will for it to work."

Gedrin closed his eyes. Ribas knew his brother was summoning all the will he had. Gedrin's will alone might do enough, but there was safety in numbers.

Ribas closed his eyes as the gift showed him the patterns. The net around Gedrin looked as clear and obvious as it always had, the lines as strong and vivid. Ribas knew he couldn't have managed it alone, but it was nothing at all compared to what had bound Lassar. And everyone here had done as he asked. The lines of white light were bright and strong, all of them directed toward Gedrin. Gedrin's own stood out like a flare.

Ribas reached out carefully. The white lines came together. Ribas needed not only a blade this time, but a strong hand to grasp and pull. Now, even without the wave of strength that had lifted him in Sostavi, he saw how to do what he had never tried.

He gathered the light and gave it shape. The net around Gedrin burned, but Ribas interposed the white light between it and himself. There was no pain this time.

As he reached out, he thought of his father. If only he, Ribas, had known how to do this, all those years ago...but he would make certain that what had happened to Silvas would never happen to his son.

He reached out. Now the shape he held in his mind connected with the net that bound his brother.

Pull.

Cut.

He felt the net give way, felt it shred into pieces, watched the pieces of it wink out like the last embers in a fire. Strength left him, but gently. Not an outrushing tide this time, only an exhalation.

He opened his eyes. The kitchen, the table, the faces around him, everything looked perfectly clear. It was as if nothing had happened. He could almost have thought nothing had, except for the look on Gedrin's face.

"How..." Gedrin said.

Ribas ought to have felt tired, dizzy. Not this time. "You know I can't tell you that," he said. "I would if I could."

"And you're all right?"

"I'm fine. I barely felt it." He teased, "You'll have to give me more trouble next time."

Gedrin reached across the table. Ribas took his hand. Neither of them needed more words for this.

Later that same evening, when everyone else had gone outside to enjoy the sweet air and talk with Khari and Radavan and the others while they got ready for their journey, Ribas spent a few minutes alone by the hearth in the front room.

This hearth. For a long time after his father died, Ribas hadn't wanted to come into this room at all. Before the accident, it had been the family's favorite place. Afterward, if he had to walk through it, he'd crept along the walls as fast as he could, like a mouse looking for cover. The sight of the hearthstone itself had made panic climb up his throat. Invisible hands had seemed to push him away from it.

He hadn't managed to sit here again until weeks into his recovery from the fever, when he had finally gotten strong enough to spend most of the day up and around. Mama had brought him in here with her. She'd had to carry him, he remembered. In the hallway, panic had overwhelmed him again and he had wanted to turn and run.

He remembered her now, lifting him up, promising him it was all right. He remembered her sitting with him in the rocking chair here by the hearth, how he had hidden his face against her shoulder. Her quiet voice had reached him through the terror. *It wasn't your fault, my dove. We mustn't be scared to be here in our home.*

It wasn't his fault? Again, he heard Galvo asking if he had ever forgiven Silvas. *I might, if I could forgive myself.*

He felt a touch on his shoulder. Mama's voice said, "Do you mind company?"

He looked around to smile at her. "Not at all."

She sat in the chair beside him. Tonight they had a fire in the hearth. Before too long, the evenings would get too mild to need the extra warmth. She said, "Rauli's talking about how he wants to go to Lassar when he gets bigger."

"I wouldn't mind seeing it myself," Ribas said. "Cheremay sounds like quite a place."

She gave him a sidelong glance. "I don't think we can spare you that long."

He knew it. He also knew that Cheremay was too far for him to travel. "Then I'll just have to hear about it. Rauli can write to me."

"I'm sure he would. I like to think of him going."

"So do I." Ribas liked to think of travelers from both countries going back and forth through the passes. Once that started, he hoped it would continue for a long time to come.

Mama reached over and put her hand on his. "Marya told me how much you thought about your da, in Sostavi."

They hadn't had time to talk about this before. Ribas said the first thing he thought. "I never knew he'd been a kunin."

"I know. He never talked about it, and I never told you."

He covered her hand with his free one. "I wouldn't have wanted you to." When he was a child, once it had been decided that he would go to the viduris, he hadn't wanted to know any more than he had to about what his father had done in the dagira. As if knowing it would force him, Ribas, to become the same kind of man. "In the Great House," he said, "I saw..."

He would have liked to tell her how easy it had been to imagine Silvas there. As the picture came back into his mind, the pain swarmed in too.

Your father was an honorable man.

Ribas drew his hand gently free of his mother's. He must stop this. He turned his face away from her. *If I could forgive myself...*

She touched his cheek. "Ribé."

So often, he'd done his best to obey her, but that night, so long ago, he hadn't. *He died because of me.* Ribas knew he was supposed to be stronger than this, smarter than this. He was supposed to have dealt with these memories a long time ago.

I'm sorry. I wish everything could have been different.

"Ribé," Mama said. "Don't shut me out."

He didn't trust himself to answer or turn to see her. She said, "You know, your brother told me he was worried about you. How you take care of everyone but yourself. I want to hear what you're thinking." Her hand reached out and reclaimed his. "Tell me."

He had to say something then. If he could make himself joke, even a little. "Mama, that only works the other way around."

"Not when I'm talking to my son." She touched his cheek again. "Come now, my dove. Look at me."

Those words, in her voice, seemed to send him back to childhood. She had held him in this room, by this hearth, and when his shivering had finally eased, she had touched his face. *Look at me, my dove.* He hadn't disobeyed her then. He couldn't do it now.

In her eyes, he saw the same love and worry from all those years ago. She said, "Tell me what you're thinking."

He had to do it. As calmly as he could, he told her about the Great House and how he had pictured Silvas standing on the dais in blue zhinin's robes. The words came more easily once he started. He told her what Galvo had said – only the parts he had the right to repeat – about Silvas's skill as a Capture player, and how the Silvas Galvo had known must have been a very different man from the one Ribas remembered. He started to tell her about his own promotion ceremony, but then, to his shame, his throat closed over again.

"I wondered…" He forced the words out. "I wondered if he would have been proud of me."

Mama's hand tightened around his. Ribas said, "And tonight, with Gedrí…I keep thinking how everything could have been different, if I had known how to help Da too." He didn't realize what he had called his father until his own voice reached him.

Mama's eyes held his. "You know you couldn't have helped him. You didn't have your gift then."

"I know. But then I thought, if I had done what you said that night, the night he died, none of it would have happened. I've always thought that."

He died because of me.

He couldn't keep going. He tried to draw his hand out of hers, but this time, she didn't let go. Instead he heard the slight scrape of her chair against the floor, and then her arms were around him, holding him as if he had been a child again, scared and in pain.

He let his head rest on her shoulder. She didn't say a word, but he felt her hand smoothing his hair. When he pulled himself together, she let go.

"We can't change what happened," she said. "He hurt me, and you tried to stop him, and none of it was your fault. You must know that." She took his hand again. "We know he was in pain too. But he's free of all that now."

Ribas knew he ought to understand that. Mama said, "And yes, he would be proud of you. He would be as proud of his boy as I am."

Ribas remembered the same sympathy in her face, that day here by the hearth, when she had drawn him out of his fear. She said, "You've done so much, my dove. You must put this to rest."

Quiet settled on the room. The fire crackled on the hearth and the warm smoke scent filled the air. Ribas felt his mother's strong fingers around his hand, anchoring him to this place. A weight he had carried for a long time seemed to loosen its hold.

Mama said, "Now, you should come outside." She let his hand go. "It's a beautiful evening, and you know soon enough, we'll just have the family here again. We need to enjoy our guests while we can."

She was right. Soon, only letters would link them to Lassar, at least until one side or the other could make another trip across the mountains.

Ribas stood up. Together, he and Mama went out of the old house and into the evening, which was soft and fragrant with the new spring.

END

ABOUT THE AUTHOR

Photo credit: Laura Walker

Kris Faatz (rhymes with skates) is a musician and award-winning writer. Her short stories have appeared in many journals and have received honors from DISQUIET International, *NELLE*, and *Tiferet Journal*, among others. Her first novel, *To Love A Stranger* (Blue Moon Publishers, 2017), links her passions for music and storytelling, and was a finalist for the 2016 Schaffner Press Music in Literature Award. *Fourteen Stones* marks the start of her immersion in fantasy and magic.

Kris lives in Baltimore with her husband and feline contingent. She and her husband are enthusiastic hikers who love to explore all green spaces. When not escaping into the world of story, Kris teaches creative writing, provides editing services, and is a performing pianist. Visit her at <u>krisfaatz.com</u>.

 facebook.com/kristinfaatz

 instagram.com/krisfaatz

 tiktok.com/@krisfaatz